ONE HEAD TOO MANY

Recent Titles by Peter Tonkin

The Master of Defence Series

THE POINT OF DEATH *

The Mariners Series

THE FIRE SHIP
THE COFFIN SHIP
POWERDOWN
THUNDER BAY *

ACTION *
THE ZERO OPTION *

* *available from Severn House*

ONE HEAD TOO MANY

Peter Tonkin

This first world edition published in Great Britain 2002 by
SEVERN HOUSE PUBLISHERS LTD of
9–15 High Street, Sutton, Surrey SM1 1DF.
This first world edition published in the USA 2002 by
SEVERN HOUSE PUBLISHERS INC of
595 Madison Avenue, New York, N.Y. 10022.

British Library Cataloguing in Publication Data

Tonkin, Peter
    One head too many. - (The master of defence ; 2)
    1.   London (England) - Social life and customs - 16th century - Fiction
    2.   Detective and mystery stories
    I.   Title
    823. 9'14 [F]

    ISBN 0-7278-5724-X

Typeset by Hewer Text Ltd.,
Edinburgh, Scotland.
Printed and bound in Great Britain by
MPG Books Ltd., Bodmin, Cornwall.

For Cham, Guy and Mark.
As always.

CHAPTER ONE

The First Head

London, 1594

The instant Tom Musgrave saw the girl he knew she had scant seconds to live. He knew this despite the fact that she was standing alone in the middle of Borough High Street looking up over the slope of the South Wark on to the festive gaiety of London Bridge, dressed in garlands and decorations in anticipation of the next day's Midsummer festival. The only sour notes struck in the holiday theme were a Puritan churchman limping out of the arch below the Great Stone Gateway and the twenty-four traitors' heads stuck on long black poles above it.

Tom strode out of the Borough Counter gaol and the girl's mortal danger struck him as he saw her. He was in action at once, heedless of the danger, running out on to the rough cobbles, his hand to the hilt of his lethal rapier. His wise eyes told him that a call would never help, even could she hear it above the gathering rumble whose portent she so clearly did not understand. She was golden-haired and white-capped. The slim length of her body was attired in a Delft-blue dress, light enough to be stirring in the zephyr of a summer breeze. Her feet were wedged in clogs so very different from the pattens favoured by the apprentices hereabouts. They and the stirring skirts above them were liberally dusted with white powder

1

peculiar to the pipe manufactories hard by, almost exclusively raised and run by Hollanders.

A young Dutch woman, then, calculated Tom, the Master of Logic – and but newly arrived from the Low Countries, if she knew no better than to stand on the South Wark at sunset on Midsummer's Eve alone and unprotected. Especially in a week which had seen yet more dangerous doggerel scrawled on nearby walls blaming the immigrants for a range of local ills and threatening the most horrible revenge.

He pounded onward, too well aware that time was running out in direct proportion to the rapid gathering of the wild and warlike roaring. The jaws of Tooley Street flashed by upon his right hand, gaping like hellmouth; then the watering trough and the hitching post where the drovers might take their ease and ready their stock before leading them over the Bridge to the morning markets. He swerved to avoid this, his eyes on the girl's shoulders now, careless of the skidding of his feet upon the treacherous ground. He raised his right hand, the left still hard on the hilt of his sword.

But even before he could catch at her arm, out of the gape of the street at his back and over his head like a black moon across the darkening sky, came the football.

The ball was made of a pig's bladder, recently cut from the pig itself, roughly rinsed and blown to the size of a big man's head, all its tubes tied tight. It was stout-sided and heavy, still caked with drying blood and as slick with stinking mud as the cobbles. His eyes remained upon it even as a hand closed on the Dutch girl's arm and the first wave of footballing apprentices boiled out of Tooley Street to come roaring up towards the Bridge like the terrible hordes of the Vandals set to desecrate Rome itself.

A glance over his shoulder even as he whirled the stunned girl against the broad cliff of his chest warned Tom that the first rank of the charging horde was well armed with clubs to boot. Narrow-eyed, he looked from right to left, searching for the tiniest doorway that he could wedge two bodies into until the fearsome flood was past. But there was nothing.

2

Crushing the slight, hot, shivering body to him, Tom looked up the slope towards the Bridge itself, but there was no hope of protection or escape up there either – only the tall black figure of the churchman topped by the black-headed spikes of the traitors' gallery. Even as Tom looked, so the Bridge Warden's men, alive to the situation and careful of their charge when so much care had been taken with the festive decorations, were swinging the doors of the Great Stone Gateway closed against the wild apprentices.

Disquietingly aware of the vital heat of her lissom form burning through the kissing tissue of their clothes, Tom swung his fair charge round and ran her straight into the jaws of hell. Ten steps back along the treacherous old cobbles down the sloping flank of the South Wark towards Borough and the unreachable safety of the Borough Counter gaol and his old friend the Bishop's Bailiff safe within. Ten steps out from under the wild-haired shadow of the stake-topped gateway. Ten steps towards the thundering madness of the howling apprentices, until her shoulders slammed into the tethering post, and she stood like a witch for the burning against the stout shaft of wood at the top of the empty watering trough. The granite-sided trough, bigger than a royal coffin, was even now cleaving the tearing swirl of apprentices, as the ancient stone-faced starlings of the Bridge itself cut the constricted welter of the River Thames when the tide was running full.

Tom glanced down at her then, and caught his breath at the simple beauty of her face, all flushed peach cheeks and wide eyes as blue as the Delft dress that seemed to be close to catching fire between them.

'*Guten abend*,' he hazarded in the execrable Dutch that Ugo Stell, his friend and gunsmith, had essayed to teach him of late.

'*Meinheer* . . .' she breathed, then anything else was crushed to silence against his breast as he wound his arms around both her and the hitching post and stood against the buffeting stampede.

3

Distantly, upslope towards the Bridge behind his back, he heard the voice of the lone, black-clad Puritan raised in some bellow of damnation as hot as Knox himself, no doubt; and, in arrogant answer, the explosion of foot against bladder, sending the thing over the disapproving preacher and like the charge from a petard against the Great Stone Gateway.

A cheer rose and, as it did so, the surge of bodies eddied. Tom had the chance to swing round, walling the girl like a nun in a cloister with his back. He was taller by a head than any around him and he saw easily up the slope to the gateway. Saw the Puritan standing against the surge of them with a stout staff raised high. Saw the big hard ball of the pig's bladder soaring high above him – high above the tight-shut doors – high above the Great Stone Gateway itself. Saw it vanish in among the grim-topped stakes.

Saw it bounce back to tumble over the Puritan's black-brimmed hat and fall into the centre of the South Wark itself. Saw it bounce low and come, skidding, rolling and tumbling back down the slope over the treacherous, filth-grimed cobbles as even the hardiest brute apprentices jumped hither and yon out of its way.

The gutter ran down the centre of the street, back into the Borough, hard by Tom's feet where he stood by the tethering post and the watering trough with the Dutch girl pressed to his back. And, in spite of the widdershins wildness of its bouncing, the gutter gathered the ball and carried it down to Tom's boot-toes.

There it stopped and there it lay, glaring up at him with wide, slightly bulbous, mortally offended eyes; mouth agape and tongue wagging silently. Mud-smeared, battered and untidy, for all the green glint of an emerald jewel in its ear – not the football after all.

Tom glanced automatically upwards to the ragged bunch of the other staked heads, outlined against the darkening sky; the picture of them, the familiar pattern, seared itself into his head. But before he could kick his brain into further motion, the

4

stunned immobility of the apprentices broke. From howling full assault upon the gateway itself, they turned into equally violent, equally dangerous full retreat. The better part of three hundred of them charged down the slope to crush Tom and his slight companion hard against the post that had held them safe so far.

Tom had an instant to glance down again and up before the first of them could come crashing into him, and in that atom of time he saw all too clearly what he was dealing with here.

No football at his feet – instead it was the severed head of a red-haired, green-eyed, hook-nosed woman. A twenty-fifth to add to the two dozen heads that should have filled the gateway; that did so now, in perfect series as they had done for months past. Yet it had come from there; never a doubt of that. One football had gone up over the gateway and one head had bounced back down whence it had come, leaving twenty-four safely, still in their places, impaled by the order of the Queen and her Council.

One head too many, in fact, Tom calculated grimly. Then he swung into action again.

CHAPTER TWO

Eureka!

R eaching behind himself, Tom took the Dutch girl by the waist and hefted her, one-handed, round over the lip of the great granite trough. He glanced down at the head on the cobbles again, but he saw all too clearly that he would never be able to get it and stand against the wild charge hurtling down the slope of the South Wark. He leaped backwards, therefore, twisting and taking care to protect the precious length of his rapier, before he fell into the trough atop the shuddering softness of the Dutch girl.

Gentleman to the last, in action if not quite by title, and satisfied as to the safety of his sword, Tom took his weight on widespread elbows. Gripping the rough sides of the trough with his knees, he raised himself a little from the panting frame beneath. With unaccustomed intimacy, he looked once more into the still deeps of her eyes. Like her fine-edged nostrils and bruised-tulip lips, the eyes were as wide as they could be. The peachy flush of her cheeks had darkened towards a passionate scarlet. Had they not been adventurers in a trough amid a riot in Borough High Street, they might have been lovers in bed at play.

The trusty trough spent a few minutes behaving like a little Thames wherry shooting the Bridge at fall of tide. As though tossed in the whirling rapids and races set up between the great stone piers and starlings that bore the spans of the Bridge across the river, it heaved, plunged and tossed. Then, finally, blessedly, it shuddered and settled. Even so, it was a long moment before Tom realized that the roaring of the apprentices was rushing away down Tooley Street whence it had come.

Lithe as a cat, he pushed his long frame lightly up on to the granite side, then swung his legs over and sat, his eyes busy on the ground. He sprang to his feet at once, widening the compass of his search, turning to scan the opening into Tooley Street even as the girl rose out of the trough like the pearl that was cast before swine in the Bible.

As Tom reached for her he saw, past her bright-blue shoulder, that the Puritan had chased the mob into Tooley Street and was lingering there now, also apparently looking around on the ground. With his eyes busy on the stooping man, Tom caught at the girl and lifted her high even as the Puritan swung round with a great shout: '*Eureka!*' he bellowed, echoing Archimedes' cry, 'I have it . . .' and rushed towards St Olave's Church.

Tom lowered the trembling girl on to her feet, his mind reeling – reeling and racing as he fought to fathom the immediate relevance of the strange man's declaration. He too had been looking for something on the ground, as Tom had. But he alone could call, 'I have it!' Surely it would be stretching credibility too far to suppose that, in the presence of a severed head rolling through the streets of Southwark in place of a pig's-bladder football, the Puritan should be declaring his satisfaction at having found anything else.

Suddenly and overwhelmingly, Tom wanted that head. It was a terrible thing, a thing of great evil – he saw that instinctively. On the battlefields of his youth, such a matter would hardly have warranted a second glance. In the European cities of his training – Siena and the rest – a slit throat or a severed head might have passed as a warning to the wise.

Even now, years later, had the thing been parboiled and tar-dipped, one of the twenty-four polls standing spiked at Her Majesty's pleasure, it might have passed without much remark.

Had not the head of Thomas More dropped into his daughter's lap as she passed beneath the old Drawbridge Gateway in the days of Harry the Eighth and been buried with her in due time? Such things were by no means unknown.

Or, had it fallen on the far side of the Great Stone Gateway, to become the business of the City Watch, then that would have mattered not at all. Had it even rolled to any other toe-caps here in Southwark, it would have remained a matter to be passed quietly to the Bishop's Bailiff, the Law south of the river, and none any the wiser.

But this head had come to Tom. It had come to him in person and it had looked him in the eye like the ghost in the hoary old play of *Hamlet*, seeking redress. It was more than a riddle. It was more than an intellectual challenge. It was a gage hurled in his face. It was personal.

Tom turned to the shivering girl. 'Go home,' he said in English, the foreignness of the language made more impenetrable to her, no doubt, by his flat northern accent, the abrupt rudeness of his action – probably far beyond her virginal understanding – aroused to something so much more complicated by the forces with which they had wrestled here. 'You'll be safe now,' he assured her as he turned away.

'*Meinheer . . .*' she called again as he wavered with unaccustomed indecision, his eyes on the hunched black figure bustling down Tooley Street. Safe as she now might be, he could not leave the shocked and frightened girl here alone. Roughly, he caught her by the arm again and pulled her back across the road to the door he had exited mere moments ago. Two mighty blows begat an answer and Tom tersely exchanged one companion for another, handing the shaken girl down into the shadows of the Borough Counter gaol and pulling up in her place the Bishop's Bailiff himself, the Law south of the river, his old companion Talbot Law.

'Whither away so fast, young Tom?' grumbled Talbot as the pair of them pounded across the cobbles and into the gape of Tooley Street.

In as few words as possible, Tom explained. Talbot knew him too well to question his account, asking instead, 'Should we not call my watch to help us go chasing heads through Southwark?'

'No, Old Law. Even your watchmen would take time to assemble and our head is making off too fast to allow the wait.'

'Our head, forsooth! And making off to boot. Has it grown legs?'

'It has borrowed some, I fear. Good stout Puritan legs, for all they seemed to limp a little . . . Ah!'

They were level with St Olave's Church now and Tom dived sideways towards it, seeing a secretive scurry of black cloth against the black shadows of the inner porch. The pair had fought in more than one battle side by side and they moved as one, diving under the shadow of St Olave's tower and tearing shoulder to shoulder into the chilly darkness within.

Against the light from the westering sun, shattered to red rainbow dazzle by stained glass, Tom saw his quarry part-way down the aisle. 'Hold!' he shouted, heedless of where he was – or to whom he was talking. Skidding on flagstones now as he had skidded on the cobbles outside, he swung himself down the nave, careful only to keep his sword from getting tangled in the pews between which his passage lay.

The Puritan froze and turned. Red light from behind him glowed around him like the very flames of hell itself. The shadows before him gathered under the brim of his hat and masked his face, except for the gleam of two eyes and the tumbling silver of a beard. And, in between . . .

'What desecration is this?' he demanded, taking a step back up the aisle towards them. His voice was strange, constricted, unearthly. There was a familiar tone to it that Tom could not quite define. The Puritan took another step towards them; the light leaped about him, revealing the dark roundness clutched weightily to his chest. Talbot bit off an oath, thinking of where they were.

'No desecration,' answered Tom, slowing to a walk and

9

crossing his right hand to the hilt of the sword at his left hip. 'But we seek what you carry.'

The Puritan looked down. 'What I carry?' His strange voice was blank with astonishment. He stopped moving and looked from side to side.

'We will not be denied,' warned Tom smoothly, forcefully.

'You must render it to me,' chimed in Talbot. 'I am the Bishop's Bailiff. Even here, I am the law.'

The Puritan stepped forward and the light from the transept fell upon his face with more than natural force. Under shaggy brows his eyes gleamed. Pocked cheeks fell hollowly into the silver of his beard and above the parted gape of his lip, over the silvery wings of his moustache, a length of twine held in place the simple silver beak of a false nose.

Tom knew him then. This was Nicholas Hazard, the curate of St Magnus' Church, which sat at the northern, City end of the Bridge as St Olave's sat here at the Southwark end. Nicholas Hazard had a great reputation as a brimstone preacher, Puritan second only to Knox himself, and author of the gruesome pamphlet 'In the Hands of the Inquisition', which explained, amongst other matters, where his nose and the ears that should have stood beside it had all gone to.

If the truth be told, Hazard was something of a hero to Tom. During his years at University in Glasgow, he had fallen under the potent spell of a particular teacher to whom the great John Knox had seemed a paradigm; and Hazard, more than a generation later, had seemed John Knox reborn. Both had been great preachers against the dangerous folly of the Catholic Church. Both had suffered for their faith, one at the hands of the Catholic French and the other at the hands of the Inquisition itself. Both had been doomed to die in the galleys but both had escaped to renew their thunder, Knox against Bloody Mary and the Queen of Scots from Geneva, Hazard against the Catholic tendencies and plots still simmering in London even now. However, Tom realized with a very new insight born of recent experiences, Hazard was more likely to be a common spy

10

than a heroic martyr after all. His work abroad, famous through his miraculous survival of the terrible Plague at Rheims in 1580, some fourteen years since, even before he had gone south to Spain and the Inquisition, all marked him as one of Sir Francis Walsingham's secret intelligencers.

Tom opened his mouth to speak again, but he was prevented. A shadow fell across Curate Hazard's strange face, and the man to whom the shadow belonged spoke instead.

'Brother Nicholas,' drawled the newcomer lazily, 'you are confronted by the minions of Caesar. Render unto them that which is Caesar's therefore. They'll give it back to us in due time, I doubt not.'

Tom swung round, squinting into the light. Behind him, he heard Talbot Law mutter a quiet oath, in spite of where they were, for they both recognized the newcomer's voice. It belonged to Robert Poley, latterly the head of Walsingham's spy network and, since Walsingham's death, the head of Lord Robert Cecil's Secret Service; a man whose toils they had but recently escaped and whom they had both most vehemently hoped never to meet again.

While they stood, tricked into gaping silence, Brother Nicholas obeyed his master's voice and dropped what he was carrying. Slowly, unpredictably, heavily, it bounced up the aisle towards them.

It was a second pig's-bladder football.

CHAPTER THREE

Poley

B etween St Olave's Church and Bridge House further east
along the street, at the end of a little alley running up
towards the river, stood St Augustine's Inn. Like many of the
more solid buildings nearby – like the Borough Counter and the
Clink Prison further west – this had once been a church; but the
building had been reassigned during the Dissolution under old
King Harry and never quite reclaimed under Bloody Mary after
him, so it was a tavern now.

In what had once been a little chapel the four men now sat.
On the table in front of them stood two leather tankards
stiffened with pitch and filled with ale; a Venetian-glass goblet,
thick and green and full of sack; a battered silver chalice full of
water, and the filthy, flaccid puddle of a disembowelled football. And a message.

The message lay before them now, wrapped in waxed paper
to keep it safe and dry, still sealed closed and secret. Tom for
one was looking at it over the top of his tankard with a great
deal of suspicion. If the football was part of a plan, then so was
the riotous game. So, perhaps was the head. Though, thought
Tom, the spy master had seemed as surprised as his clerical
secret agent to hear all about it, and neither had demurred at
sending a pot-boy to the Borough Counter to rouse Talbot's
watchmen for a search.

Tom looked up. Poley was watching him. 'Go on, my Master of Logic. Tell me about the message,' he purred. Nicholas Hazard gave a peculiar, derisory snort, and Tom's eyes flicked over to the ravaged profile that was all that God and the Inquisition had left to the man.

Without his hat, Hazard's bald pate served only to emphasize the scar-circled holes of his close-cropped ears and the black line of twine holding his false nose in place. Terribly scarred cheeks, marked with smallpox, sank into the silvery fullness of his beard. Apart from his face, only his hands lay uncovered, huge, brutal and powerful – hands that had pulled oars for years after the Inquisition condemned him to rot in the galleys, from which he had so famously escaped in Armada year. His mouth was lipless and twisted. His teeth were blackened stumps. Yet his eyes burned clear and blue with a fearsome intelligence – mingled with contemptuous disbelief now.

It was the glance more than the note that drew Tom on at last.

'The note must be one of a pair. One in each bladder. Logic dictates that the messages in each will be identical so that if one be lost the other may yet be found. As is the case now, unless we are all bound to climb up atop the Great Stone Gateway to seek this unfortunate ball's companion.'

Tom swung round, looking at Talbot with a frown. 'You and I must thither in any event, Old Law, and with some urgency if your watchmen discover my head.'

'As may be,' purred Poley. 'And in due time, perhaps. But for the nonce, Tom, we discuss my note and you continue to raise the curate's eyebrows.'

'And his belief in witchcraft,' growled Nicholas Hazard.

'The note is from one of your spies, Master Poley,' Tom proceeded. 'A young one. A cunning lad who must conceal from his companions the fact that he can write. A Cambridge man, perhaps – of the sort you have always favoured – but one who can pass himself off as a local youth if he must. Someone fit to mix with the apprentices. Lusty enough to be the man they

13

choose to blow up their footballs – or how else came the notes inside with no notice? A leader amongst them, then; or someone near to his side. And your agent, Master Poley, because the Council wishes to know the names of the troublemakers and the signwriters so active amongst these young men. They wish to know the fomenters of sedition against the Hollanders to whom we have opened our doors in this time of need as they support us in our great war against the Whore of Babylon and its strong hands in Rome, Rheims and Cadiz.'

Tom swung round to look at Hazard once again, his burning brown eyes meeting the curate's stunned blue gaze and staring it ruthlessly down. 'Which brings us to the instruments you have chosen to facilitate this little plot. One glance at that steely nose and the hardiest apprentice might waver. Such a man as the good curate here is known through all the land. He has walked by a miracle out of the plague in Rheims and out of the hands of the Inquisition and Philip of Spain's Armada galleys. One sight of him calling down damnation on the band might make any man hesitate for long enough to allow your messenger's boot to connect with your pig's bladder here, and the message to be delivered.'

'It is the plan . . .' whispered Hazard. He looked across at Poley, who answered with his most wolfish grin.

'Did I not say?' growled the spy master. 'And he has told us what the message will contain, to boot. Do you care to give us the names on the paper now, Tom? Or shall we open it first?'

'If you want to know who hates the Dutch, perhaps you should ask a Dutchman,' suggested Tom abruptly, losing patience with Poley's game.

The hawk-nosed spy master pulled at his beard and grinned. 'And you have just the Dutchman we need, do you not? Your friend and gunsmith Ugo Stell, assistant Master of Defence, who stands just behind you, just outside the door to the Guild Hall of your peculiar Science, Art and Mystery.'

'You speak in riddles,' spat Talbot.

'He speaks the truth – or part of it,' said Tom, for he could

14

see reflected in the battered silver of Hazard's water-filled chalice that Ugo was in fact coming into the chapel behind him. 'As much of it as he is ever likely to part withal . . .' He rose, turned, and went to meet his friend.

'Do you come to chide me for some student I have forgotten or some lesson missed?' Tom asked easily as he closed with Ugo out in the main part of the tavern.

Ugo gave one of his brief grins. 'Neither. You know your schedule as well as I. There are no more lessons this side of Midsummer.' The Dutchman hesitated, his gaze going over Tom's shoulder, past Talbot's approaching figure to where Robert Poley still lounged at his ease with his curate, his pig's bladder, his secret and his sack. 'Or none at the Blackfriars School. And none in the Science of Defence.'

'None here either,' said Tom, his fist tightening automatically on the hilt of the sword that was the object of his mastery and the source of his livelihood as he spoke. 'Though, truth to tell, I could have done with a lesson or two in the Dutch tongue this afternoon. For I met a girl . . .'

'Hell's teeth,' spat Talbot Law. 'The girl!'

The three of them hurried out into the humid night. This side of Southwark Street was quiet. As the three men hurried towards the gaol, therefore, they were able to exchange snatches of conversation, for Ugo had come looking for Talbot, not Tom. 'Fräulein Van Der Leyden is but newly arrived,' he was calling to the Bailiff. 'She went out at sunset . . .'

'We have her safe,' Tom interrupted his friend.

'I pray you have,' puffed Ugo, 'for—' But he got no further with his comments. The stout door of the gaol was before them. Talbot threw it open and the three of them all but tumbled in. Down four steep steps they clattered to the little Watch Room, empty now, for the watch was out. Beyond it stood a snug little parlour where the gaoler sat at his ease under a flaring flambard with a nervous girl in Delft blue beside him.

As soon as she saw Tom come stooping under the low stone

lintel, the girl sprang erect and the air between them seemed to crackle. Tom opened his mouth to demand from Ugo the most elegant and irresistible Dutch greeting, but the weight of Talbot's hand on his shoulder stopped him and turned him. Ugo was straightening to stand, gaping, as callow as any country Jack gazing upon his Jill. And, as the girl's eyes swung away from Tom to his dumbstruck companion, so something deeper, more gentle, came into them as they crinkled into a shy smile. 'Ugo,' she whispered. And Tom discovered that he already understood more than enough Dutch.

Talbot's hand smote down again and the pair of them turned back even as the door burst open again. Poley strode in alone, seeming to bring a breath of cold river air with him out of the sultry night.

'This is what you sought, I understand,' he said. He raised a sack that swung from his left hand as though a large turnip or cabbage was contained within it.

'Where was it?' asked Tom, his voice suddenly dry and broken.

'The watchman I took it from said he found it down in Gully Hole,' he said.

'That's opposite Bridge House,' mused Tom. 'Only a little way further on than we have been tonight.'

'So?' asked Poley, right eyebrow raised and sack still a-swing.

' 'Tis close enough for the thing to have been kicked there in the rush. But far enough for it to have been carried there on purpose.'

'On purpose?' demanded Talbot. 'To what end?'

'To deepen the riddle, perchance,' answered Tom almost thoughtlessly, his mind elsewhere.

'How so?' asked Talbot.

Tom was silent, so perforce he looked to Poley. 'To guide us where we must go next,' supplied the spy master. 'To the house and its keeper, the Warden of the Bridge . . .'

Tom was back with them suddenly, and he took up Poley's thought. 'For it is the Warden who can give us permission and a guide to climb the Great Stone Gateway. That is where the football went and that is whence the dead poll came.

'But first,' he said decisively, 'we must be rid of Ugo and Fräulein Van Der Leyden. For the poll has fallen into your jurisdiction, Old Law, and you and I have some questions to ask it before we stir a foot.'

CHAPTER FOUR

Poll

T hey sent the gaoler out on the heels of Ugo and his fair Fräulein Van Der Leyden to fetch a pail of water. Then, under the flambard, in the brightest spot in the Counter's cellarage, he placed Poley's sack on the table top and began to unwrap its weighty contents. Poley and Talbot Law gathered around, entranced, watching what Tom's steady fingers slowly brought to light.

Soon the head lay snugly, looking upwards, held in place by folds of the sacking. It was dirtier now, at first glance more battered – but not grossly so. The same eyes stared with outrage above the same hooked nose and gaping mouth. 'It is the same woman,' said Tom quietly.

'You doubted it would be?' demanded Poley. 'You thought there might be more heads rolling around Southwark this evening?'

'It's been a strange nightfall,' countered Tom.

'And like to get stranger,' added Talbot. 'But in the meantime, give your wits a cudgelling, Tom. What can you tell us of this poor wench?'

However, before Tom could deliver himself of his first pronouncements, the gaoler returned with water and a cloth. Tom cleaned the woman's face and then the rest of her head as best he could, returning it to the state in which he had first seen it. As his fingers worked, his mind raced.

'The first question we must ask of the lady is the last that was of any great concern to her,' he began quietly. 'To wit, how did she die?'

'You're holding her head, Tom,' said Talbot, 'a head that's been bouncing round Southwark all evening. Surely that must tell you something!'

Poley gave a grim laugh. Tom frowned and shook his head. 'Poley,' he said, 'you saw Babbington and all the rest executed, did you not? And the Queen of Scots with whom they plotted our Queen's overthrow, come to that?'

'I did,' said Poley shortly, no longer in the mood for humour, grim or not. Tom and Talbot exchanged glances. They knew well enough that Poley had been present at the executions. They knew he had gone in amongst the schemers of the Babbington plot in disguise, seduced their leader's trust – perhaps even his love. That he had unmasked the plot to his master, the late Sir Francis Walsingham, had revealed the treachery to the Council and the Queen and had joined in their questioning as well as their executions.

'Aye,' he said shortly. 'I was at Tyburn and at Fotheringay. 'Tis seven years since, and some months and days, but I mind it all clearly enough.'

'Then you alone amongst us have seen a woman's head like this,' said Tom gently. 'Did the Queen of Scots die with one stroke?'

'Of the headsman's axe? No. It took three. The first stroke missed altogether and the second wavered before the third one cut true. Her head rolled free and he held it high. The lips were still praying and the eyes looked around us all. Looked into the very soul of every man of us there, as the executioner held it high. Then the wig slipped and the thing fell. It rolled off the stage and down the Great Hall with that cur of a terrier of hers skittering and howling in its wake.'

'Two cuts, with a big axe?' persisted Tom.

'Aye. A cleaner job by all accounts than the swordsman Harry Eight brought over to see to Her Majesty's mother.'

Tom nodded. 'Did you see the head close to?'

'I held it,' answered Poley. 'It was still warm. Why the questions, Tom?'

'This poor woman's neck was never cut so cleanly,' observed the Master of Logic, turning the grisly object for him to see. 'No headsman's axe nor executioner's sword here, Master Robert. This has been sawn and hacked and torn from her shoulders.'

'Like enough,' conceded Poley shortly. ' 'Tis none so neat a job as was done on the Queen of Scots.'

'Not a job as could easily be done on any living woman,' said Tom. 'And look at her face. What see you there? Outrage. Scorn, perhaps. Surprise, certainly. But no terror. No agony. No horror. This is never the face of a woman fighting through her last seconds as her murderer saws her head off her living shoulders.'

'Done to death in a trice,' said Talbot, his voice filling with wonder.

'But no secret blow to the back of the skull, no killing strike to the nape of the neck,' continued Tom. 'There are no lumps or softnesses as might result from the wielding of cudgel or bludgeon. No. The woman was stabbed – to the heart, like as not, for her death to be so swift and unexpected.'

'Strangled?' asked Talbot.

'I think not. There are no Tyburn markings to the throat. Her eyes bulge a little but that may be just their normal position. Her tongue wags a little . . .'

'A shrew in life, I'd wager,' said Poley, 'especially with those red curls . . .'

'But no great swelling or blackening or bleeding, as strangulation brings,' said Tom. 'She was never strangled.'

'Poison?' mused Poley. He and Tom were expert in such things. Both had friends recently returned from death's door because of the application of them.

'No traces on lips or tongue,' said Tom. 'But a poisoned blade in her side might not leave a mark on her face. Still and all, I see no dilation of the eyes, such as Master Apothecary

20

Gerard warned us of when dealing with such subtleties as hemlock . . .'

'So,' said Talbot slowly, taking up the reins of the investigation, as was his duty as the Bailiff into whose jurisdiction the head had come rolling. 'She died suddenly, swiftly, unexpectedly. Stabbed more likely than poisoned and definitely not bludgeoned or throttled. Then her murderer hacked off her head and stuck it up with the traitors' gallery atop the Great Stone Gateway. Is that all we can learn?'

'By no means,' said Tom. 'She has told us a little about her death. Now I think she can tell us a little more about her life.'

He fell silent again and a thoughtful hush fell upon the Borough Counter, broken only by the animal snufflings of the two prisoners chained within the cells. Then the Master of Logic began to voice his reasoning again – beginning, as usual, not quite where the others expected. 'Tell me, old Law, what was the last woman murdered in your Liberty?'

'Long Meg Trotter, the Bull's Head whore, done to death by her whoremaster Black John Cutter for falling in with the Bull's Head's bawd Joan Curtain and refusing to turn over his percentages any longer. He was done to death soon after by persons unknown, likely employed by said Joan Curtain to protect her girls and reputation.'

'An edifying tale,' sneered Poley. 'But where does it get us with the current case?'

'Did you see the woman's body?'

'As was my duty.'

'Prithee, describe it. Leave no mark out.'

'She was filthy. He had beaten her down into the kennel in the alley hard behind the tavern itself. She was in desperate case before he came upon her – that's why she had changed her master for a new mistress. She was near to starving, poxed, lousy. In need of a bath, a comb – the shears and a wig for preference – a new dress, some pearls or jewels in her ears; and an inch or two of paint upon her face – an inch or two most patently lacking when I saw her last. A sorry sight, living or dead. A man would need to be desperate to have ventured his sixpence her way, in truth.'

'There are plenty enough, desperate or worse,' observed Tom. 'But is such a corpse unusual in the Liberty? Or are they rather the rule?'

'The rule, of course. We have poor whores aplenty but only one lady amongst a thousand. This is the stews, not the City. Where does this road of reason lead us, Tom? For this woman could hardly be more different from poor Long Meg.'

He stopped then, for he realized what Tom had made him do.

'Aye,' confirmed Poley, too impressed even to smirk at Talbot's discomfiture, 'by causing you to tell us about the sort of corpse we might expect to find down here, he has shown how unusual this one actually is. Even this fragment of one . . .'

'You see,' began Tom quietly, gently, speaking to his companions but addressing the dead woman herself: 'her hair needed no comb. It has been arranged by deft and careful fingers – or had been before it fell into the Southwark kennel. It required no powder to thin out the lice, for there are none. She needed no wig, for this red profusion is her own.'

'She could still do with some jewels to her ears,' observed Poley, pointing at the naked lobes.

Tom fell silent at that, and closed his eyes for a heartbeat, remembering. The head that had rolled to his feet beside the trough during the riot this afternoon – had it been wearing earrings then? Yes it had, he was certain. He looked more closely at the little flap of flesh beneath Poley's scornful finger. It was torn. He turned the head. So was its companion. Torn where the hooks of the earrings had been ripped free.

'But she has worn earrings, look.' His fingers showed the rents in the waxen flesh. 'Nor was she starving,' he persisted, brushing the pallid plumpness of her cheeks. There were dimples, in her chin and at the corners of her plump, pale lips. 'Her teeth are black, though she is no great age. I have a friend – a friend currently close confined and recovering from a poisoned drought . . .' Here he glanced at Poley again, whose

22

machinations he still blamed for the near-death of Constanza d'Agostino, his one-time mistress. 'A friend from beyond the water who blames such afflictions as black teeth upon our English love of sweetmeats. And many a sweetmeat, I suspect, went into the dimpling of these cheeks and the blackening of these teeth. Expensive sweetmeats, numerously supplied, over a good length of time.'

Tom sat back to sum up his latest chain of reasoning, suddenly weary of this part of the game and keen to be pushing onwards. 'Not one of your Southwark women, then, but a well-to-do of merchant's wife or daughter. To tell you more I will need to see more. Preferably a body – though that will have to wait until tomorrow, of course.'

'But what does she do down here?' asked Talbot, still confused. 'Well-to-do merchants come here in plenty, chasing our Winchester geese, our gambling hells and whatnot; but they do not bring their wives and daughters. The only well-to-do merchants who keep their families – briefly – down here are those like Van Der Leyden of Bleeke House away along Horsely Down, and he will be buying a house up in Blackfriars as soon as he's able after his daughter's adventures today!'

'The Bailiff has a point,' said Poley. 'The sort of family you speak of lives the width of the river away at the very least and would never come closer than that – save when they process through on some pilgrimage or visit.'

'No,' said Tom, 'you are both wrong. There are rich merchants and their families – pillars of their guilds and men of the Church as well as the City – living so close to this place that I could break their windows with a well-aimed slingshot.'

'What,' scoffed Poley incredulously, 'English merchants and their families? I think not. Great men of the City live in the City. Unless she is some Hollander, or French woman addicted to an English vice, she could never have lived as close to Southwark as you say!'

'One place,' said Tom, unshaken by Poley's scorn. 'One place in all the City. So close under your nose you cannot see it.'

23

'Where, then?' asked Talbot, for he, too, could not follow Tom's reasoning. 'Where do the rich folk live with their fancy wives and daughters so close to our hells and stews?'

'She lived and likely died where we must go to next,' said Tom. 'She lived in one of those great garlanded mansions up on London Bridge.'

CHAPTER FIVE

Traitors' Gateway

T he three of them hurried back along Tooley Street to Bridge House, where they battered on the door until a servant agreed to take them to the Warden. He, as might be expected on the eve of his busiest day, had neither leisure nor humour to indulge his visitors. He certainly had no intention at all of allowing them to go poking around amongst the staked heads up in the traitors' gallery. But Poley produced a general warrant from Her Majesty's Council and Court of Star Chamber, demanding that anyone granted sight of said document give aid as required to said Robert Poley Her Majesty's Good and Faithful Servant.

Then Tom produced the head.

The Bridge was an ill-contained blaze of light and colour, a scarce-controlled riot of noise and bustle. Since the ending of the football match and the setting of the sun, its gateways had been open wide, its fires, flambards and candles all alight, and its shops, taverns and ordinaries open for business; and the bustle spilt down the South Wark into Tooley Street – indeed, all the streets of Southwark teemed with coster-folk.

Fishwives, who had carried baskets of fare plucked fresh from the river that morning, had traded their wares for charms, nosegays and herbs, such as might catch the fancy at the closing of the day; but they had lost none of the raucous wit and roguish promise for which they were famed. Little stalls, laden with everything from pomanders to pamphlets, jostled for attention. Open ovens offered a range of foods from roasted nuts to boiled sturgeon – for today was a fish day – hoping to tempt the hungry before they reached the great ordinaries up above. Owners of barrels and tuns brought in from the breweries and vintners hoped to slake the thirst of the impatient before they got up to the taverns beside the ordinaries. Girls – and boys – with painted faces and belladonna eyes tried to attract the lustful before they went downhill to the Bankside stews.

Tom pushed through the importunate throng at the shoulder of the Warden's man. His mind was racing, trying even now to see ahead, to calculate what he should be looking for as he went up in the footsteps of the murderer himself. He knew little enough about the routines of the Bridge as yet, but it seemed to him that an extra head would have been noticed by the men who had dressed it today. Therefore it had been placed there since the decoration – to wit, this afternoon. Thus they were in all probability going to be the next men up after the murderer himself.

So Tom disregarded everything around him, readying his eyes to take note of anything on the route, especially that section of it where the murderer must have walked alone and no one could have disturbed matters since. But, as he often did while thinking most fiercely, Tom talked to cover his preoccupation; and, as often as not, he listened to the replies he got. This time, unable to converse with Poley, whose presence here he mistrusted, or Talbot – for fear Poley might overhear – he talked to his guide.

The Warden's man was a bluff, upright individual of middle years, thinning hair, square grey chin and solid aspect. The snatches of conversation they exchanged seemed to establish him as the sort of man able to turn his massive hands to anything from cutting a loaf to chopping a timber, from lighting a fire to laying a brick. His name was Perkin, and he had been born and bred in Southwark; the farthest abroad he had ever stirred by land was Newington Butts, a mile to the south. He had been along the river as far as the North Foreland, however, and had stood at the top of the thirty-nine steps to look out on the great North Sea.

Tom took a liking to him at once, because the steady, solid, reliable artisan reminded him of Talbot and Ugo, for all he had travelled so little. He was exactly the sort of servant a wise warden would require, for the Warden's major responsibility was the maintenance of the Bridge itself. Like as not, Perkin would know every stone and timber, pin and panel of the public sections of the Bridge, and a good bit of the private sections to boot.

Therefore, when Perkin said, 'Now that's strange,' Tom closed up behind him, his eyes busy over his companion's shoulder.

They were within the arch of the Great Stone Gateway, tucked away from the bustle right on the western side, hard behind the wing of one of the great doors that had been shut against the mob that afternoon. It was open now, and secured wide, apparently hard back against the stones of the gateway, but actually a little way in from them, allowing entrance to a small embrasure where a flight of steps led up to a little padlocked door. In a sconce just above its lintel, a blazing torch shed restless yellow light down a little chimney closed on three sides with stone and on the fourth by the back of the open door.

Perkin turned to him, key in one hand and padlock in the other. 'Padlock's been broken,' he said. 'And that's a shame, for it was new. I'll have to use the old original now.' He shrugged. 'That's been done since noon, for I locked it up around then, all safe and secure.' He turned back and pushed the little door that was no longer padlocked safe and secure. It creaked open.

'Hold!' snapped Tom. As Perkin stepped willingly backwards, Tom reached up and lifted the torch out of its sconce.

27

When he reached with his other hand to push the creaking portal wider, the head swung against it, knocking dully as though demanding entry. Or rather, thought Tom, *re*-entry. For the head, at least, had been through this door before.

Through this door and up the narrow twisting steps. It was like following the stair within a castle tower. Scarce a fortnight since, he had followed steps like these within the great keep of Elfinstone Castle away down in Kent, where he had come so close to death himself – and had sworn never to associate with Poley or his murderous spies again. An oath as short-lived as a lover's vow, he thought grimly. The steps were narrow and turning in a constant spiral like Archimedes' screw; but they were clean and well maintained. 'Perkin, is it you that oversees the cleaning of this place?' he asked.

'Aye,' came the reply. ' 'Tis cleaner than usual, mind, for the whole bridge has been dressed for the morrow during the last day or two.'

'And you came out of here last at noon?'

'Or thereabouts.'

'And no one near the door since then?'

'Oh aye, any number. The Bridge was as lively a bustle as ever I've seen it all afternoon. And then, with the football match at eventide, we had men in behind here closing the doors as though against Sir Thomas Wyatt himself and the men of Kent beside him.'

'You were here for that? For the great rebellion?' demanded Tom.

'I was, sir, as a lad you understand, for 'tis forty years since, in the days of Bloody Mary. Fired by John Knox they were. By the "First Blast of the Trumpet against the Monstrous Regiment of Women" – a terrible, powerful piece of writing.'

'Hmmm . . .' Tom's interest in Perkin's history abruptly vanished. The stair spiralled out into a little chamber with a narrow window looking up the river to the afterglow of the set sun, as red over Green Park as though the sky had a throat to cut. Tom stepped forward carefully on tiptoe, as though

28

essaying a new dance step. The stair had been made of dark stone – granite-grey; but the floor of the room was made of ancient wooden boards that creaked a little as he proceeded on to them. There was enough red light to make the torch unnecessary, but Tom carried it still, peering into every corner of the little room as he crossed from the door from the stair leading back down, to the door to the stairway leading on up. And here he found his first clue, just where the floorboards were bedded back into the strong grey stone of the upward-twisting stair. It was a kerchief, a thing of silk and lace. At first he thought it bloodstained, but then he realized that what seemed like thick colour was only the ruby light. He brought it to his face and smelled perfume – civet or musk. A woman's kerchief most likely, then. He tucked it into his black jerkin beside his suddenly thundering heart.

Because the little silken square had lain just in the threshold of the doorway, he paused and looked there with even more care than before – and discovered, just where the wooden flooring gave way to stone steps once again, a spray of splinters strewn in pale profusion across the dark stone of the stair-foot. Automatically, he looked upward, and there, on the old wooden lintel of the open doorway, stood an ashen scar.

Tom turned to Perkin. 'That's new,' he said. Perkin's eyes followed his gesture to the lintel. Talbot's and Poley's eyes did likewise.

'Done since I was here last,' confirmed the Warden's man. 'Though what it can tell us, the Lord in his mercy knows.'

'The Lord in his mercy and the Master of Logic,' said Poley, relishing the little play on words. Perkin frowned, and Tom saw him at once for the man of simple faith, careful of his Good Lord's name, and less than happy that Poley chose to play with it.

'That's as may be,' he said. 'But what these motes would tell even a mind diseased is that feet have walked this way several times since they fell. See . . .' He put the head down, crouched and lowered the torch as the others crowded into danger from its flaring flame. 'At the mid-point of the step here, where the stone has been worn to a hollow by the weight of feet over the years, the rough pattern of their falling has been stirred. They have been spurned aside by thoughtless feet – feet coming down the stair, for see, some are scattered out into the room; and feet going upward, for look, the splinters lie up on the second step. And the third, where surely they could never have fallen from the lintel.'

Tom stopped speaking and they all looked up the dark, twisting stair. 'The trick,' said Perkin slowly, with no tincture of Poley's accustomed irony, 'would be to tell us if the feet that stirred the splinters belonged to the man who lopped the head . . .'

'Must have,' said Tom, 'for how else was the mark made except with a pole to spike the head, and who else would carry that pole but the man we seek?'

'Then a further act of your familiar sorcery, Tom, and a welcome one,' said Poley – and for once his tone was as innocent as Perkin's, and as nervous, of a sudden – 'would be to tell us whether those feet stirred these tell-tale motes on their way up to the walk above, and whether they are still up there even as we speak!'

'Alas, even the Oracle at Delphi would hesitate to predict so much,' said Tom. 'But I know a sure way to find out the truth . . .' He left the head where it lay in its sack, transferred the torch to his left hand and reached for the hilt of his sword as he spoke. Perhaps only under a hand as practised and expert as his would that long silver-steel Solingen blade have whispered so easily into the shadows of the stairwell.

'Let's go and look,' he said.

CHAPTER SIX

Traitors' Gallery

N o, thought Tom suddenly. He had followed a flickering
light up a spiral stair like this, not only at Elfinstone
Castle but also at the great house of Wormwood in Jewry here
in London. Those stairs had led to a mad room, full of
medicinal chains, shackles and whips designed to secure and
cure a lunatic; and these stairs promised no more comforting
ending. Though, to be fair, the occupant of the mad room had
been no raving monster but a mysterious and beautiful woman,
now mistress of the castle and of the fortune it comprehended.
The likely occupant of the gallery above would be fitter for
Bedlam than baronetcy, if his handiwork was anything to go
by.

Tom paused and turned back, peering into the shadows
below with a question that should have been asked a while
since. 'Perkin, do these steps end in a doorway or a trap?'

'A trap.'

'Has the trap a door?'

'Aye, and like to be closed or we would have felt the draught
before now. There's no lock on it, though, nor bolt on either
side.'

Tom nodded, turning, and proceeded with more confidence.
A closed trap, unsecured, would give them a vital element of
surprise. Although he had established through observation and

31

logic that the dead woman's head had been hacked off with a knife or saw – or both – he could not clear Poley's description of the Queen of Scots' execution from his mind. Visions of a monstrous lunatic wielding an axe kept rising before his straining eyes.

As he came up under the trapdoor itself, therefore, he curled his body down while the others came up hard on his heels. The door was solid and heavy. He was able to push the forearm of his sword-arm firmly against it before he felt it stir and he was confident that no glimmer from his torch would escape through any chink or knot-hole to give them away.

Thick and heavy as the door was, it was not proof against a mumbling sound that seemed to seep down from immediately above him as he waited, a half-rhythmic gibbering, as though a mad father were rocking his rotting infant in one of Tom Kyd's tragedies. It was a sound that sorted very well with Tom's nightmare visions.

As soon as they were in position behind him, Tom straightened. Using all the massive strength of leg, back, shoulder and arm lent him by years as trainee and master swordsman, he heaved the door up and open to thunder on the stone floor like the clap of doom. As he did so, he hurled the spitting, guttering torch as high as he could and bellowed, 'Hold!'

Using the word to cover further movement, he sprang out on to the bare stone of the great square walkway, his eyes narrowly searching for his gibbering monster with the headsman's axe. He felt the others come boiling up at his back and range themselves at his shoulders, their blades like his gleaming wickedly in the torchlight.

And there, over on the far side of the gateway-top, the monster reared in answer with the most hideous of shrieks. Twisted and misshapen, it howled and capered. Torch high, Tom raced forward, swinging his deadly sword-point in a glittering arc ahead of him, as though the legendary temper of his Solingen blade was indeed enough to cut the shadows aside.

Then two hands slammed down on his shoulders – one hand on each. Talbot Law and Perkin were wise-eyed enough to see what he did not, and their laughter, like their steady grips, slowed and eventually stopped him just beside the iron stand of the sconce positioned in the midst of the gallery, designed to receive his torch. He reached up and slipped the torch into the bracket, allowing his sword-point to drop as he did so.

Into the circle of his torchlight stepped his monster, resolving itself like a modern Proteus from one wide body into two slim ones – from twisted horror to sheepish embarrassment; from mad axe-man to young lovers. A tall young gallant strode first into the light, tightening the strings to his fashionable codpiece and hoping to mask the action by reaching for his sword. The lady remained shyly in the shadow, allowing no more than her shoe points and a hem of petticoat into the light.

'What make you here?' the gallant demanded, mightily affronted. 'God's my life, you have near killed the lady with terror! I shall hear good reason for this sound and fury or I will be answered for it!'

'Why, Master Petty,' said Perkin, also stepping into the light. 'I had not thought to find you up here!'

'Perkin!' snapped the young worthy, pegging the company all alike with the Warden's servant. 'Wherefore are you and your confederates sneaking and spying up here on your betters? Be off with you or I will have the Warden cool you in the stocks tomorrow. Away with you! All of you!'

'Not so quick, young master,' said Talbot, weightily, stepping forward. ' 'Tis you must answer a question or two. You and your lady-love back there.'

The young man's temper flared at this and he wrenched out his rapier, falling into a well-tutored stance.

'Will you deal with this, Tom?' asked Talbot wearily. 'I'll kill the little popinjay, like as not.'

'Best not kill him,' said Perkin. 'His father's in the Haberdashers' Guild.'

At this casual talk of killing, the girl in the shadows gave a whimpering scream and young Master Petty frowned and looked dangerously resolute. 'Well. Come on, one of you,' he said, mistaking their conversation for hesitation. 'I demand satisfaction, or if you're not gentlemen enough, then it's the stocks or the cage for all of you!'

'Tom!' said Talbot impatiently.

However, Tom was distracted, just at that moment, for he realized abruptly that Poley had disappeared into the shadows. The logic of Poley's actions struck him at once, of course, and he could have kicked himself for underestimating the spy master's singlemindedness. Had he not himself said, in the chapel in St Augustine's Inn, that if there were two footballs, then there would be two copies of the secret message slipped within them? Poley had one – the one Curate Hazard had found in Tooley Street, calling *Eureka!* in his joy; but there was the other one to be secured – the one that had knocked the head free – and that was likely to be up here somewhere.

'Old Law,' he hissed into the deadly tension under Master Petty's blade, careful to keep the tones too low for Poley's ears, 'Poley seeks the other football. Find it first!'

'Oh is that all?' sneered the youth. 'Your toy lies in a puddle over yon behind the lady, burst with the same blade as will puncture your insolence!' And, so saying, he hurled himself into the attack.

For Tom, there was no question of coming *en garde*. This was combat *al la maccia*, scarcely better than a brawl. The boy attacked high and wild in *tierce*, and Tom was hard-put to bring his own blade up into line in time to parry the first thrust. But he tore his shoulder and whipped his blade up into the *prima gaurdia* as Maestro Capo Ferro had taught him so long ago. The boy's blade slithered, singing, along the Solingen steel. It was a good sword, and well wielded, for as Tom sought to settle things with a seizure – by grabbing his opponent's hilt – the boy disengaged and stepped back.

At the just distance, Master Petty fell into his position again for exactly a beat, then attacked in *quinte* but still in line. Tom accepted the thrust and enveloped it within the circle of his blade, judging the moment with masterly precision at which the defensive manoeuvre, turning the boy's point aside past Tom's hip, opened an avenue for a counter-thrust. 'Hey!' he shouted, and threw himself forward.

The Solingen blade, seemingly a thing of light, travelling with the speed of a silvery moonbeam, sang up through the padded shoulder of the boy's fashionable jerkin. A pin's width in any direction and it would have wounded him. A blade's width and it would have killed him. The basket on the hilt of Tom's sword slammed into the boy's shoulder with shocking force – and shocked him, as it was designed to do, out of his rage. Tom's left hand closed on the hilt of his opponent's drooping rapier, just in case.

They stood thus for a moment, just on the very razor's edge of balance, gasping in each other's breath, winded, not by exertion, but by the nearness of death. 'You have been well taught,' offered Tom, a sop to the boy's pride.

'I will seek a new master tomorrow,' snapped Petty. 'To have been bested by a ruffian, the friend of the merest servant . . . And I shall purchase a new sword, for this is spoilt . . . soiled . . .'

'A pity you did not learn manners as well as defence,' said Tom and straightened. He kept tight hold of the other hilt, plucking the weapon from the boy's hand. As he pulled his blade free, the boy hissed with pain.

The girl stepped forward then, escorted by Talbot Law, who seemed to have ventured into the shadows merely to bring her out of them. 'Mistress Alice Panne,' mourned Perkin. ' 'Tis as well your father knows nothing of this.'

'Is that Master Panne the goldsmith?' enquired Poley, suddenly surfacing.

'It is, so please your worship,' whispered Mistress Alice with a curtsey, much, much wiser than her paramour.

'Moved up to the Bridge out of Barton and Panne, Goldsmiths, of the South Wark, to set up on his own at last?'

35

'Even so, your worship. Barton was my mother's name . . .'

'With an apprentice called Matthew Terrill?'

'Indeed, your worship. A great, heavy-set lout, but quick with his hands and his mind. Fit for the mysteries of the guild, my father says. In time.'

'This same Master Panne who has a goodly knowledge of alchemy? Under investigation for using the black arts?'

'Sir! Not this year and more! Not since we moved out of Southwark, as you said, sir, and on to the Bridge, sir. He's a well-respected man, like Master Petty, sir, my Daniel's father, sir. A Master of the Guild.'

'A Master of the Guild,' purred Poley. 'Well, of course that must whiten every blot and grant absolution to every sin, must it not? Well, take your coxcomb hither. When you see your father, mention Master Poley. Tell him my eyes are wide, in Southwark or on the Bridge itself.'

Alice led her Daniel out of the lions' den, then; and he followed willingly enough, pausing only before Tom in mute supplication until Tom gave him back the sword he was proposing to throw away in any case – which he took as he had taken back his life, with no thanks but an arrogant sneer.

After the young couple had gone, Tom turned to Poley. 'Terrill,' he said. 'Is that the name of your apprentice-spy?'

'And if he were,' snapped Poley, 'would I have been so free· with his name?'

'Not knowingly so,' countered Tom cheerfully.

'But then,' added Talbot, 'if all the world were perfect, scarce a one of us would need an absolution.'

Poley paused, lost in calculation. The light of the torch up in the sconce guttered, falling weirdly across his saturnine coun- tenance, making him look, for an instant, like the Devil in the old plays. Then he was gone.

The three that remained stood in silence for a while. The wind that had made the torch gutter came again, wet and cool from the east. It was strong enough to stir the thick-tarred hair on the heads immediately above them. The relative silence up here above the bustle on the Bridge was suddenly shaken by distant thunder. The whole of the stone gateway stirred and shook. 'Tide's turned,' said Perkin. 'That's the mill wheel beginning to work beneath us; and the Dutchman's great pair of water wheels at the north end.'

Silence fell again for an instant as the stakes shook in their tight-tied lashings, and all the gull-pecked, crow-spattered, black-faced horrors of the heads seemed to be in earnest conversation.

Then Tom said to Talbot, 'Did you get the list from the football?'

'Aye.'

'We'll look it over as soon as may be.' The Master of Defence sheathed his sword and the Master of Logic stooped to pluck out of the gutter at the wall's foot a long, pale, recently fallen spear of naked wood. 'In the meantime I wonder, what sort of lover brings his mistress to a charnel place such as this, be they never so desperate for privacy.'

'Aye,' said Talbot again, 'and what sort of mistress agrees to come?'

'Questions for the morning,' said Tom.

'How so?' asked Talbot.

' 'Tis near ten. The gateways will shut and the City Watch will be stirring soon. We must north of the river to seek another master; then to bed and clear our minds with good repose.'

'To what end in particular?' asked Talbot once again.

'We have a head. It has told us much, and it may tell us more; but it cannot tell us the whole tale unaided. And we have Poley's second list. Therefore, Old Law, thee and I must be up to Saint Helen's tonight and eastward ho with the dawn.' He crossed to the east-facing wall of the gallery and looked out into the wind towards the tidal reaches of the Pool and beyond, where the restless lights of the ships burned like fairy lamps from there to Deptford. 'I'll lay my life upon it – my life and maybe more. A message for Poley means a code or a cypher; and a head on the Bridge means a body in the river. And we must search them both out and discover all their secrets with all the haste we may.'

CHAPTER SEVEN

Eastward Ho!

T he secret message from the football lay on the top of the travelling trunk at the foot of Will Shakespeare's bed, held flat by three daggers. Tom's was there, and Talbot's – and Will's, which had been there first, for Will was recently awakened and not best pleased. It was on the stroke of midnight, as the Watch was loudly calling. Will had been knocked up from an exhausted sleep earned by working on his new play. A crowd-pleaser, this, guaranteed to extend the success that had been *Romeo*. *Romeo* had opened at Philip Henslowe's Rose playhouse in Southwark less than a month ago, but what was needed now was something that would rival it at the Burbage brothers' rival Theatre playhouse without the northern walls, close by Finsbury Fields.

'I had thought the Burbage brothers my friends,' snarled the sleepy, stressed, frustrated playwright. 'And yet I find them now as ravening wolves after the fawning spaniels that were Ned Alleyn and Master Henslowe on the Bankside mere weeks since.'

'The code, Will,' said Tom gently. 'What do you make of the code?'

The paper that lay stretched between the daggers like a spy on one of Rackmaster Topcliffe's racks, bore a message composed of two letters only, and this is what it said: 'aaaabbaaaa-

39

baabbbaabaaababaaabaaaaaabaaabbaaabaaabaaaaaabaaabaaa-
baababbaababbaababaabababaabababaaaaaababaaaabaaabaabaaaa-
bbaaabbaaaaabaaaaaaababaabaaaaaabbaababaaaabbaaaa'

'Well, Will?' prompted Tom again.

Their temperamental code master pulled at his beard and crouched down over the paper, squinting in the poor light. ' 'Tis a code,' he conceded.

'And one you can unravel?'

'Perhaps you could dash me off a scene or two while I busy myself about your work,' suggested Will, bitterly.

'Gladly,' offered Tom. 'Is the play of *Thomas More* completed? Or are you set to resurrect your *Titus*, maim more ravaged virgins and eat more child-filled pastries? Ah. *Thomas* it is, I see. Perhaps I could add a scene or two between the Saint and Old Harry.'

Both Will and Talbot hissed at such dangerously seditious wit. It was death to refer to Thomas More as a saint, for his beatification was a matter for the Catholic Church. It was a good deal more dangerous to confuse the Queen's father with the Lord of Hell, even if both were called Harry on occasion.

Will Shakespeare's interest was caught, however. He reached for a sheet of paper, glanced distractedly at the scrawl of blank verse on one side, and turned it over to begin his calculations upon the back.

'Have you no wench-warmed beds awaiting you in Black-friars or Southwark?' he growled. 'This is not a task to be dashed off lightly or quickly, even by a master such as I.'

Tom looked across at Talbot. The pair of them shrugged wryly. Talbot's wife Bess was sleeping soundly, no doubt, at his all-too-distant inn hard by the walls of Winchester Cathedral. Tom's current light o'love, the tempestuous Kate Shelton, was visiting Audrey, her sister, down at Thomas Walsingham's great house of Scadbury in Kent. Thus, thought Tom wistfully, if any bed was warm in Blackfriars tonight, in the rooms beside his fencing school, it would be Ugo Stell's, warmed by the delectable Fräulein Van Der Leyden; but, in truth, he knew the wicked thought did no justice either to his solidly Protestant friend or to the no doubt well-raised damsel.

At that moment there came a sudden rapping on the shutters just beside him and Tom looked down to see his friend standing in the street with a handful of stones. 'Invite him up,' said Will wearily. 'The more brains the better.'

In fact the ever practical Ugo had not come carrying mere stones. No sooner was he through the door than he was passing out hunks of rye bread and baked capon and offering great draughts of blond Dutch beer.

'Meinheer and Frau Van Der Leyden were pleased to get their daughter safely back?' hazarded Tom.

'You saved her life, Tom. She made no secret of that,' answered his friend. 'The footballers would have trampled her. They are more grateful than they can tell – as am I.'

'She hasn't any grateful sisters, has she?' asked Tom.

'Best stick to the matter in hand, boy,' observed Talbot, paternally.

'You're right,' said Tom. 'Headless wenches and codes in footballs are still ponds and calm waters compared to the raging torrents of love.'

'Why eastward?' demanded Talbot in the dawning as the three of them hurried down Tooley Street towards St Olave's, the alley and the stairs. 'Ugo, has he explained himself to you?'

Tom's Dutch assistant, gunsmith and friend shrugged. His gesture seemed to say: 'What secrets does he ever share with me?' But the revelation of the hitherto secret Fräulein Van Der Leyden and her place in his heart seemed to Talbot to make the Hollander less than trustworthy in the matter of secrets, even now in the weary dawn after a frustrating, fruitless night.

Tom answered, seeming not to notice this byplay. As he talked, his voice seemed to gain energy, depth and decision, a virile timbre that had been missing from the discussions that had brought them down from Will's lodgings and over the stirring Bridge so far. He was happy to be back in charge after the fruitless hours poring over Poley's code with Will; back in action after the discussions about the two-letter riddle that seemed set to worry them all into Bedlam. 'Consider westward, Old Law. On the south bank lie Bankside, Lambeth, the Archbishop's Palace, the Horseferry. On the north bank, the Coldharbour, the Hay Wharf, the Steelyard, Queenshythe, Baynard's Castle, Blackfriars, Bridewell, Whitefriars, the Savoy, White Hall, West Minster. And between them, every wherry, barge and boat.

'But to the east, whither we are bound, the Beer Docks, the Pool, the marshes, Limehouse, the Isle of Dogs, Deptford and Woolwich, Thurrock, Tilbury and the great North Sea. Big boats, ships. A bustle, perhaps, but high above the water, navigating, not playing or rowing; never like the crowds to the west.'

The three of them turned north into the high-sided, narrow alley leading up to the stairs and the open riverbank. They were so early that not even the most intrepid Midsummer revellers were stirring behind them; and before them, only the earliest of the fishwives and ferrymen were up and about. 'Even had our headsman been too slow to calculate on this, Chance herself must have taken his part – for had a headless woman been swept upstream, then she could never have lain for long undiscovered and therefore thou or Ugo or I would have heard of it by now.

'But downstream – downstream to the east – matters are very different in the east.'

St Olave's Alley opened directly on to the stairs, but the stairs stepped down to a brown heave of river, this being slack water at the top of the tide. At the head of the stair, a square figure turned towards them, cut black against the dazzling dawn brightness of the water.

'Well met,' called Perkin. 'I have matters in hand, just as we agreed on parting last night. Though the Warden's business must keep me here today, I have hired you a transport.'

A tall, dark man with a lean, weatherbeaten face and a shock of dark hair looked up at them from a sizeable ferry.

Tom nodded then turned to Perkin. 'Our thanks for your help in this, Perkin. But we value your silence equally also.'

'As you wish,' said Perkin affably enough. 'But keep in mind that there were many as saw the head fall into the Borough kennel yesterday; and more that have been brushed by your exercising of logic since. This matter stands about as secret as what will play at the Rose this afternoon.'

'You're in the right of it,' said Tom ruefully. 'Particularly as I would expect Master Panne and Master Petty to be beating on your master's door before his fast is broken this day with complaints about the treatment their offspring have received at the hands of those looking for missing footballs among other things!'

'You underestimate their paternal love, Master Musgrave. Or the power of children, perhaps. They were in his parlour when I arrived home last night. I am fortunate indeed that the Warden is a reasonable man. I hope what you discovered up on the gallery was important, for it came near to costing me a day in the Bridge's stocks. And, come to that, a day in the cage for you two.'

Ugo choked with ill-concealed hilarity at the thought of the Bishop's Bailiff and a Master of the Corporation of London Masters of Defence caged in public ignominy amid the dazzling bustle of the Midsummer celebrations.

'I fear that Master Petty and Master Panne may find things run too hot for them if they go that way,' said Tom icily.

'Particularly if they extend their aim to your friend Master Poley,' agreed Perkin. 'As I said to the Warden, he'll have them dragged off as witches, like as not. 'Tis only a year since that half the goldsmiths in Southwark were under suspicion of alchemy. And the Warden knew of Master Poley too, come to that. Not a man to be lightly crossed, the Warden said.'

'We none of us are,' said Talbot. 'Tell the Warden to think on that when folks come calling for cages and stocks. He needs to lie secure in his bed and know that his mills and corn-stores are safe. Who else can guarantee he sleeps easy if he's at odds with the Bishop's Bailiff?'

'Fear not,' answered Perkin, still affably enough. 'The Warden and the Warden's men would never offend the Bishop or his Bailiff.'

Tom leaped down into the wherry and disposed himself comfortably in the stern. Ugo came next and Talbot, after he had finished his little exercise in the art of diplomacy.

'Whither away, gentles?' demanded the cheerful waterman, no whit abashed by the dreadful business they were on.

'Follow the tide down towards Deptford,' ordered Tom. 'Unless there is some volume of water lore open to you but closed to logic, then reason suggests we scour the south bank on the way down until slack water then search the north bank as we return on the flood.'

'If you have the leisure and the coin, then my river lore concurs with your logic well enough. And we search for a headless woman.'

'The body of a woman cast into the stream, most likely from the Bridge. Yesterday, perhaps, but likely earlier than that,' answered Tom, warming to the man.

'Why earlier?' asked Talbot as the wherryman eased them away from the steps and into the gathering flow of the falling tide.

'Again, Poley's words on the death of the Queen of Scots. She wore a red underdress so that it should not be soiled by the blood. What blood there must have been. What a flood of it, what a lake. But our head, it is a thing of cold and waxen flesh. Even where the earlobes were ripped, no drop. Nothing. The head at least was drained, over time and in another place. For there was no blood up on the gallery last night. No blood on the sharpened staff I brought back down with me. I can make no learned estimation, but it seems to me that the head at least must have sat for enough time to be thus drained, but not enough time to become fly-blown or rotten. Not less than one day and not more than three. Thus that is likely when the body went into the water. Not yesterday, but the day before or the day before that.'

'And early in the morning, just before dawn,' supplied the waterman prosaically. 'To catch the tide, like us.'

CHAPTER EIGHT

The Body in the Water

T hey went east into the gathering midsummer dawn, past the little creeks, smelly little cousins of the great open sewer of the Fleet river up by Bridewell. Then past the water mill, smaller brother to the huge mill that thundered in the arch beneath the Great Stone Gateway when the tides and currents were running full, and ground the Warden's corn.

Then the southern bank spread into woody relief beside the first great Beer House. Here, opposite the Tower, the river ran deep enough for big ships to anchor and there seemed a very fleet of them sitting securely across the placid water. The loading bays of the Beer House showed where the ships and barges from Germany and the Low Countries could unload their beer, wines and spirits – raw and finished. It was not unusual for vintners and stillers to live on London Bridge, finding their suppliers so convenient down here. Brewers, like weed merchants and pipe-makers, tended still to live in Southwark, though some, like Van Der Leyden, could afford sizeable houses and rolling estates such as that which belonged to Bleeke House, next along the shore west of Van Der Leyden's Beer Dock. Even so, there were as yet no great City guilds to establish their social standing. Like actors and playwrights, they needed to use their earnings to purchase coats of arms and titles if they wished to rise above their common fellows.

But Tom, for instance – Tom was a coming man: a member of an important guild. He was a Master – and like to become one of the Four Ancient Masters in time. Not many Lord Mayors of London had come from the Corporation of London Masters of Defence, but all of them had come from one guild or another, from Dick Whittington on down; and, like his friend Will Shakespeare, Tom was also a coming man at court. Scarcely a lordling worthy of the title but he came to Blackfriars to learn either Sharpes or Blunts with him. Daniel Petty had been well taught – but by one of the lesser masters. He would never have had the money or the standing to afford Tom's mastery, unless his father's guild had asked Tom's guild for a favour – as was by no means unknown.

These thoughts occupied Tom's mind, excluding even the nagging distraction of Poley's surface-simple code still, no doubt, spread-eagled on Will's travelling trunk. As they did so, the wherry eased into the Pool of London, swinging south of the lazily nodding fleets tethered there below the southward thrust of Wapping on the north bank.

As the sun burned through the midsummer mists, Tom's mind began to focus on immediacy, like the sun's rays coming through a glass. They searched the southern shore from Bermondsey to Rotherhithe, following the tideline as near as they dared. Easing past gull-thick mudflats, in and out of otter-loud creeks. Poking amongst the detritus floating there awash with scummy bubbles with long hooked poles like the pikes, partisans and halberds beloved of Talbot's watchmen.

'Everything out of the City seems to collect here, to bob and rot,' said Tom. 'Faugh! The stench is enough to start a plague. If the silent woman awaits us anywhere, Old Law, it must be here!'

'The water lies still,' concurred Talbot.

'*Over there*,' said Tom.

The waterman twisted to see what Tom was talking about, for Tom was pointing dead ahead, exactly at the boatman's back; but when the waterman turned he saw swiftly enough.

There, perhaps half a mile ahead, at the back of the bay, beyond a weary stretch of grey and green scum-set flotsam, a busy column of gulls joined the still water and the misty sky. Even at this distance, their calls echoed distantly but ecstatically, like the song of Sirens intermingled with the howling of Harpies.

'Oh yes,' said the waterman grimly. 'In matters such as this, the birds rarely lead us astray. Is any of you handy with an oar?'

As chance would have it, a childhood spent in the watery wildness of the northern Borders – what would one day be known as the Lake District – had tutored Tom in the ways of small boats well enough; and he was quicker than Ugo – raised near the Zuyder Zee – to own to the skill.

With Talbot and Ugo in the little prow, armed with their staves to push rubbish away and – in time – pull the birds' meal close, therefore, Tom and the waterman eased them slowly but powerfully straight ahead. It was the work of near an hour – had any of them the means to measure it – to shove the boat through the heaving mess. Even with Talbot and Ugo clear-eyed and active, rubbish of all sorts still captured the blades of the oars. Even with Tom and the waterman pulling at their most manful, still the simple stinking thickness of the element through which they were moving slowed them further.

' 'Tis as though all the phlegm and rheum in all the world had been poured into this one place,' grunted Tom. There was likely to be little more than phlegm and rheum left in his own body, given the speed he was sweating out his lighter elements, he thought. He had not perspired like this since the first onset of the Tercian ague he contracted five years ago in Siena.

The waterman grunted grim agreement.

'Nearly there,' called Ugo at last, over the cacophony of the birds. 'Two fathom; scarcely more.'

'What can you see?' called Tom.

'It looks like a dress, sure enough,' called Talbot. 'I'd not like to say what's within it!'

'You'll likely have to do more than say, in a few minutes' time,' warned Tom. 'You'll likely have to lift it all aboard.'

As it chanced, Talbot Law and Ugo Stell were not men to whom it was easy to delegate the nasty jobs. In a few minutes' time, therefore, the waterman used all his expertise with two long oars to hold his wherry steady while Tom joined his confederates at the side, spending a little while scaring the birds off before they got the chance to look down properly.

It was immediately obvious to Tom that boat hooks would be useless. Pulling the sack of rags and scraps with which they seemed to be dealing with iron hooks would damage it too badly. They used the staves of the handle-ends, therefore, to manoeuvre their object until it was hard against the right side. In face of the others' hesitation, it was Tom who reached down. At first hesitantly, and then more confidently, he started feeling for purchase on whatever was contained within the dress afloat on the sickening surface of the Thames' stillest backwater.

The water was warm – pleasantly so. The material that brushed his fingers was surprisingly abrasive. The naked arm that he recognized at once as an arm, was firm, solid, lacking the slimy softness the stench had led him to expect. He felt its muscles and bones almost as though it belonged to a living woman bathing in the tepid river. He came to a shoulder and felt the back of his hand brush against a telling swell of breast. He swiftly calculated that she was face-up and spread like a crucifix with its head to the gunwale and took firm grasp. 'One of you,' he ordered without further thought, 'get a grip and help me pull her in.'

Both of them sprang to obey – and only the waterman's skill, coupled with the settled breadth of the steady craft, stopped them all from joining their deceased naiad; but in she came, one arm in Tom's grip and the other in Ugo's with Talbot taking the handle offered by the skirts over her belly.

Had she still possessed a head, of course, thought Tom distantly, the thing would never have been accomplished half so easily. But as her shoulders stretched innocently from arm to arm, without even a ruff to spoil the smoothness, they had no trouble heaving her into the bottom of the wherry. Here she lay quite decorously, almost as though sleeping, while the effluent around her ran down into the thurrock of the little boat.

This time it was Ugo who joined the waterman on the oars as Tom and Talbot knelt on either side of what they had found. Tom looked down at the despoiled dress. His mind raced, thinking of the head lying in the Borough Counter, carefully under lock and key. What would the clothing tell him of the woman whose head that was? Nothing – nothing to begin with, at any rate. It was the flesh of the head that had revealed so much to him. The hair, the waxen earlobes, the full cheeks, dimples, lips and teeth.

In the gathering heat of that golden noon, with the creaking of the oars as the waterman and Ugo powered them back into the river's main flow and Talbot sitting in silent thought beside him, Tom, the Master of Logic, began to question the flesh. Lacking the space to strip his subject, and the leisure to be courteous or kind, he simply folded back the sopping clothes and studied what his rough actions laid bare.

He looked at shoulders and breast, then pulled up her skirts and looked at her intimacies. The most cursory examination sufficed. It was a pale face that he raised to the others, and an unsettled voice that spoke to them.

'This woman has been whipped at the post or the cart's tail. She is a branded whore – marked on the shoulder and, like as not, on the cheek.'

Talbot Law knew what he was going to say even before he said it, though neither of them fully understood the dreadful import of the words so casually tossed into the noontide of Midsummer's Day on the river hard by Wapping.

'For all that her hair is almost as red as the hair on the head in the Borough Counter, this body does not belong to it at all. The cheeks of the head in the Counter gaol have never seen iron or brand,' said Tom with grim, unarguable decision. "We must seek another body. And, certes, another head. *At least* one other head.'

CHAPTER NINE

St Thomas's

Tom stood between two tables that almost filled a small room in the ancient Hospital of St Thomas. In the larger room next door two attendants were trying to splint the leg of a local girl, snapped by a wagon in Tooley Street less than an hour since. Her master the local innkeeper was scraping together enough money to pay a surgeon in the vain hope of keeping the lass off crutches. A vain hope, because the Master and the doctors of St Thomas's only rarely dealt with broken bones. Fallen women and bouts of the pox were more their stock in trade.

The promise of a headless woman such as Tom was bringing proved even more of a rarity, however; the Master offered her house-room merely to repay an obscure debt to Talbot Law.

Tom had taken one look as Talbot and he had carried the shrouded, dripping body past the little group round the screaming girl twenty minutes since and he knew the hope was likely to be vain. By the look of things, the poor girl was a crutched beggar for sure, if she survived the afternoon; and would be lucky to end up a halfway successful whore like the headless woman in his arms.

Now her screams echoed past Tom's preoccupied ears and swept hauntingly out through Gully Hole into Tooley Street, where they simply added to happier screams of the Midsummer revels. As they did so, they followed Talbot out while he went to report what they had found and discover what authorities he was like to hear from, and when.

On the table by Tom's left hand lay the body from the river. Her form reclined as innocent of clothing as her shoulders were bereft of head, her modesty preserved by Tom's better instincts and a napkin or two until such time as the Master of Logic should turn his full attention on to her. Except for the matter of her head, she was not so different from the women who had been treated in this place – to much local disapproval – for the better part of four centuries.

On the table by Tom's right hand – over which he was turning to pore even as the broken tavern girl sobbed into blessed unconsciousness next door – reposed her clothing, arranged as though she was lying in it still. Only one shoe, of red leather, well cut and expensively made; the other taken as tribute, perhaps, by Poseidon himself, or by Gog, lord of legendary London. And yet, thought Tom, looking at the long laces that had clutched the stockinged ankle as tightly as the stocks after which the hose were darkly named, the river would have needed a knife as sharp as his own to cut its tribute free. The stocking that had dressed the leg beneath the sopping shoe was stained with the lace's dye but the other was not. The whole of the stocking foot, in fact, looked as though it had stepped in blood ankle-deep; but the other was white. He turned to the other table and found that, as it was with stockings, so it was with her feet themselves. 'What may we make of that?' asked Tom of the Master of Logic. But reply came there none as yet.

The door opened and Talbot bustled back with Ugo close behind, fresh from paying off the wherryman and reporting via Perkin to the Warden of the Bridge. 'Well, Old Law?' asked Tom, as though the question to his friend was part of the conversation he had been having with himself like one of Will Shakespeare's characters soliloquizing.

'Crowner's quest,' said Talbot. 'There's never a doubt. The Queen is at Greenwich and we found the body well within the verge. We'll have to entertain Sir William Danby at the outset at least.

'That's certain,' said Tom. As he spoke, he turned again to the clothing and followed the pale ghost of the stocking up to the apron of the dress. Both, he noticed, were expensive – and the dress not a little gaudy: cherry velvet picked with a pattern of golden thread. Not of the current fashion, though – not if Mistress Kate's attire was anything to judge such matters by; and it most certainly was. 'Unless Queen's Coroner Danby hands the case over to you local men. London Bridge seems to lie at the heart of this and Greenwich Palace is never thirteen miles from the Bridge, even following the river's course.'

'But on the other hand, the same can be said for the whole of London,' Ugo observed. 'And Danby doesn't poke his nose into every crime committed here.'

'He will if there's anything questionable about the matter,' said Tom grimly. 'Look at how swiftly he became involved in the murder of Kit Marlowe down in Deptford.' Beneath the red-and-gold-patterned dress he had placed the shift – also fine and clean, like the stockings, for all it lay as flat as a pressed flower in a shallow puddle on the plain deal boards. He examined it now, scrutinizing the intricate lacework with a gathering frown.

'True enough,' agreed Talbot. 'But that was a crime committed by one of My Lord Essex's men, one of Thomas Walsingham's men, and the leader of Lord Burghley's spy network, giving one of their own a swift quietus.'

'Skeres, Frizer and Poley, aye,' growled Tom, frowning more deeply still – frowning, not at the oft-rehearsed crime and cover-up of little more than a year's age, but at the way in which the dress above the waist was so much more red than the skirts below; dark red, like the lees of old claret. Even after the river's work, the heavy cloth was still saturated with blood. He was put in mind once more of Poley's description of the death of the Queen of Scots. He must ask, when next they stumbled across each other, whether Scottish Mary's red underdress had been so saturated. There had been blood enough by all accounts – it had actually screamed out of the vessels in her lopped neck – but how much on the dress itself? And he must enquire whether she had worn a bodice pinned to her bosom or a ruff around her neck on that final morning at Fotheringay, he thought.

This woman wore neither now. Could they, like the shoe, have been purloined by the grasping river? Certainly a ruff would have slipped off more easily than a tight-laced shoe, all things considered.

'None of them are like to be involved in this, surely,' said Ugo. 'Certainly not Master Poley.'

'Perhaps not,' conceded Tom. 'Not directly, at least. Old Law, speaking as the Bishop's Bailiff, can you describe for me how you might expect to find the most expensive bawd in Bankside dressed?'

'In cast-off finery. Cloth that has fallen from a gentlewoman to her servant, from the servant to the market, from the market to the stews. In faded feathers long since plucked, like Will's actors up at the Theatre.'

'And how plump would you expect your goose to prove, once plucked of her faded finery?'

'Thinking back to the last one I saw stripped – that poor wretch slaughtered by her pimp that I told you of last night – I would say there's not one in a hundred of them more than skin and bone. Geese they may be, but there's not a capon amongst them.'

'The bawds and the pimps are fatter, like as not,' said Tom.

'Fatter, perhaps. But not fat. 'Tis a lean trade in a lean year, Tom. You've seen the folk come starving in from the countryside, bad harvest after bad harvest. Fresh country girls are plentiful and only a few of them are poxed – for the first few months at least.'

Tom stood, nodding, through Talbot's speech, his hands on the table beside the woman's body. Even with the napkins still in place, there was enough of the woman on display to make clear the reason for Tom's questions. The legs, slightly swollen from their sojourn in the water – swelling attested by the marks of the red lace – were never those of a desperate, starving girl. The hips were matronly and wide, the waist by no means lissome and nowhere near lean. Beneath the shift that lay beneath the blood-boltered bodice, there lay the ruins of the corset Tom had cut free with the knife he had needed to loosen the one red shoe.

Talbot's eye followed Tom's speaking gaze.

'A fair-fleshed woman. Well fed and well lined,' said Tom.

'And yet a whore,' persisted Ugo. 'Carted and branded, you said?'

By way of answer, Tom rolled the woman over so that her right shoulder came uppermost and the right half of her back was on display; and there indeed on the round flesh where the arm joined the body was the black-burned W above which was another mark, as clear in her flesh as an assay mark in gold. Below and behind it, from shoulder blade to buttock cleft, were the tell-tale scars of at least one brutal whipping.

Then Ugo's eyes followed Talbot's down to the pale ridges on the soft white flesh of her back, where Tom's frowning gaze already rested.

'Roll up your sleeve, Old Law,' said Tom. 'Your right sleeve, to the shoulder.'

As though in a trance, as though Tom had been Dr Dee or Kelly the Necromancer, Talbot Law obeyed; and there, on the firm white flesh of his upper arm stood the scar of a wound he had received at Nijmagen seven years since. And it had the same silvery sheen as the marks on the woman's back.

'Old scars and an ancient brand, you see,' said Tom. 'A trull for certain, then; but a trull reformed, long since come up in the world.'

'*A trull come up and gone down,*' thundered a strange new voice. '*Down to the flames of perdition.*'

'What make you here, Master Hazard?' asked Tom without looking up, his voice dull with all the sorrow of a man who finds his hero stands upon feet of clay. 'There are no footballs here. Nor no spies or secret messages.'

Both Ugo and Talbot spun round to find the strange, silver-bearded, pewter-nosed curate crowding into the door with a slighter, ferrety companion at his shoulder.

'I come with Brother Viner,' said Hazard. 'He is a doctor as well as an ancient friend, to the Hospital as to me. And he has been called to poor Sister Judith out there. She is of my congregation, and like to need the services of a divine more than a physician.'

'But Master Viner will try his skill first, like as not,' said Talbot with sudden loathing in his voice. 'He is of the Guild of Barber Surgeons and will not like to leave without his fee. First the poignard, then the prayers.'

'*Primum angeli, tum angeli,*' suggested Tom, drily. 'First the angel coins and then the angel choir. But hold; if Viner is a friend to the hospital, then his expertise is in the pox and its treatments in any case. His reputation, surely, is as a mercury man, a master of the stew . . .'

But neither Dr Viner nor the Reverend Hazard was paying attention. They were both seemingly entranced by the body on the table. The headless woman lay on her side, her napkins both on the floor. Tom raised his eyes and rolled her back until she was at her ease once more. Talbot pulled his sleeve down and something about the action seemed to claim Tom's attention.

'Old Law,' he said, as he stooped to return the napkins to the woman's privities. 'Do you remember how you got that scar?'

'I'm never likely to forget. A fragment from a culverin shell shattered it until the bone came sticking out. It was a blessing Bess knew what to do and had you there to help.'

'Indeed,' said Tom, much struck. 'Come through.'

The two old soldiers pushed past Viner and Hazard, then Talbot followed Tom across to Sister Judith's pallet. Without the slightest ceremony, Tom whipped the coverings back and pulled up the girl's skirt. Between the ill-tied splints, the livid swelling of the thigh lay at a strange angle. Tom eased a slat aside to reveal a dagger of bone sticking out. He looked up at

Talbot, his eyes seeming to shine in the gloom. 'Do you remember?' he said urgently. 'You must do my part and I will do Bess's.'

Talbot nodded, pale to the lips. At Tom's sign, he stooped and caught the girl's ankle.

'Stop!' shouted Viner. 'How dare you . . . ?'

Tom gestured once again. Talbot Law pulled with all his solid strength while Tom's hands closed like Ugo's strongest vice around the top of the young woman's leg. She stirred, unconscious though she was, and whimpered.

'What is it that you do . . . ?' bellowed Hazard, his strange voice loud enough to call the attendants into the room.

'Stop them!' shouted Viner.

But he was too late. Tom felt the bone grate into movement, saw the dagger of bone slide back into the poor girl's thigh. In a trice, as Bess had done to Talbot's arm on the battlefield of Nijmagen, he tightened the bindings on the splints until the bone was held safely and together.

'Bess herself could not have bettered that, I think,' said Tom. He looked up at the attendants, cudgelling his brain to remember what Talbot's wise wife had done next. 'You must wash the leg with water boiled with salt and sage then cooled,' he said. 'That will dissipate the fiery humours. Doctor Viner here will supply leeches to thin the blood. An operation worthy of Galen himself, I think,' he said to Talbot with some satisfaction as he rose.

'Of who?' demanded Viner, shrilly. 'We know no foreign tricks and witchery here, sirrah. This is England, where your Gay Lem has no name nor reputation.'

Tom gave a half-smile at the pompous little doctor's ignorance. It was Galen's drawings, drafted in the gladiatorial circuses and on the battlefields of antiquity, and hardly rivalled until Da Vinci, that had been a good part of his study with Maestro Capo Ferro in Siena. For the grand old sword-master had always maintained that the true Master of Defence must know where all the bones are, if he is to avoid them as he runs his blade through his opponent's body for the cleanest and swiftest kill.

'But as I said, sir, surely your expertise is in the pox; of which my ancient master Galen stood in blessed ignorance, I think.' Tom's words were civil and placatory. Their effect was explosive.

'In God's truth,' spat the venomous Viner, 'and as this place stands testament, it is the French disease that needs the knowledge of the best, sirrah, and such a one am I. Have I not scoured the stars in all the houses of the Zodiac for the origins and endings of the thing? Have I not made decoctions for the common baths without the Hospital? Have I not advised the private stews in matters of mercury and gumma and toadstone? Was it not I who discovered that force of water immediately after congress is like to clear the dangerous humours?' He leaned forward, his little ferret eyes almost mad with justifiable outrage. 'Was it not I that discovered that the wood guaiac, which proceeds from the Indies where the disease took origin, will also cure it? That the Good Lord, who taketh health, will give also the means to restore it?' He glanced over his shoulder as though demanding support on this theological point from his companion; but Hazard had turned away.

'Was it not I who first proved the pox to be the sovereign remedy for the plague?' hissed the outraged man. 'Have we not seen how the body cannot hold the two infections together? Do we not now know how the apparent curse of the Almighty may well be a blessing close disguised? And you mock at me with your Gay Lem of antiquities!' So saying, the little Master of the Guild of Barber Surgeons stormed out after his great friend Curate Hazard. And Tom turned back to the matter in hand.

It was his memories of Galen that Tom took back into the little room with its two tables, however, and that made all the difference. For, as he thought of those drawings and the bones that they revealed, so his eye fell where it had scarcely glanced before: upon the neck itself; and he saw at once how different the wound was here from the wound on the head in the Counter

58

down the road. There, the head had been hacked and sawn free. Here it was severed cleanly, at a stroke.

Between the one killing and the other, their self-appointed headsman had found himself an axe.

CHAPTER TEN

Young Love

A nd yet . . .
  That change came over Tom when his faculties sharpened almost without his conscious will, and he became the Master of Logic. Lithe as a hunting cat, all eyes, he paced around the two tables, silently at first. The other two had seen him like this and knew better than to interrupt. Their eyes followed his glance and saw all that he saw, no doubt; but they understood little of what he understood and Talbot felt the shiver creep down his back, which combined the stirring of excitement with a suspicion of witchcraft.

As ever, when he started to speak, Tom began mid-sentence, mid-thought, away in some abstruse Bermuda of logic far removed from anything they were expecting.

'. . . but this is not the Queen of Scots, nor our own Queen's mother Ann. For all she has been beheaded, this is murder and not execution.'

'True enough,' answered Talbot after a minim beat of silence. 'Yet I can conceive of a mind deranged that might suppose it is an execution.'

'True, Old Law. But it is not the murderer's mind I am thinking of – it is the woman's. The Queen of Scots and Ann Boleyn laid their heads on the block to welcome sword or axe. I cannot conceive of this woman doing so.'

'And you proved by logic that the other woman, the first, was like to have been dead before her head came off,' acknowledged Ugo. 'But I see no killing wound upon this body here.'

'Nor I,' agreed Talbot.

After a while Tom continued, turning to the sopping dress, 'The bodice is gone, if there was one – and a catch or two in the velvet together with a bent pin wedged here makes me believe there was. Even so, the front of the garment is thick with blood, even after its holiday in the Thames. And, if we look at the shift beneath, we see, if anything, even more blood.' Suiting his words with action, he held the garment up as though a ghost were sitting in it; and both his companions could see the truth of his words.

'But,' he persisted quietly, 'if we look at the back, we find both garments clean. It is like the stockings: one red and one white. Blood on the bib but none on the fastenings. She lay face down in a pool of blood, then. And for some time too, I would judge, for even the most indifferent washerwoman knows that cold water cleans fresh bloodstains better than anything else.'

Tom laid the dress down again and crossed to the victim's corpse. 'But there is more. Talbot, Ugo, you are old soldiers, as am I. Were we out together on a night patrol and needed to silence an enemy guard swiftly, surely and silently, how would we go about it?'

'With our sharpest blade,' suggested Ugo at once.

'Indeed,' agreed Tom. 'But where to place it, that's the question. In the back? Between the ribs? Through the heart?'

'Not if we wanted to be swift, silent and sure,' said Talbot. 'For those things it must be the throat . . .'

He stopped, the wind knocked out of him, for Tom's fingers were pointing to the terrible wound in the woman's neck, and the two apprentices in logic saw briefly with their master's eyes – saw, as he did, how one great axe blow had chopped the bones of the neck apart as cleanly as could be; but how that one swift slice seemed to have wavered at the throat, for the flesh was more torn here. More than one cut must have been made.

'Her throat was slit,' said Tom, his voice as low as if this were a holy place. 'She died face down and lay there in a great pool of her own blood. Then, later, he brought an axe and took her head. After a while, in the dark before dawn, if our waterman is to be believed, he moved her. He dropped her in the river and went on his way.'

'As she went on hers,' breathed Talbot. 'But in God's name who is she? Where did she come from? Why did he choose her?'

Tom raised the lower napkin for an instant. 'One thing unites the two women we have found,' he said, glancing down at her privates: 'red hair.

'As for who she is and where she comes from, I think we may exercise some more logic to good effect. She was a whore but is fair of flesh now – a whore no longer, then. She is well dressed in velvet picked with gold. A wife, perhaps; a mistress more likely. To a well-to-do widower, perhaps. A merchant or a smith. I favour a goldsmith. Possibly one that lives up on the Bridge. Possibly one such as Master Poley was investigating in the matter of alchemy and witchcraft.'

'You cannot know all this!' sputtered Talbot. ' 'Tis impossible!'

'The dress is not in the first flight of fashion and yet it has not been through the market. It has been handed on only once. But it is not such a dress as a woman would willingly hand on, for see, the golden threads make a pattern or design here, and here, and here. It is the badge of a guild, I believe. Of one of the lodges of the Goldsmiths, I think. And look: the undergarments are fine, with the lace here woven into a pattern of letters. "P" is plain. And "R"? These have been woven for a particular woman.'

'Perhaps for this woman,' countered Talbot. 'Why should she not be Mistress Patience Rowe and have the letters picked on her shift.'

'Indeed, Old Law; it is possible. I did not rush to dismiss the thought. And here, on the dress itself, below the Goldsmith's badge there are the letters "P" and "R" again. But then I thought, what is more likely? That a whore rise to be the wife of a goldsmith, fit to be decked for the Guild Hall and the Lord Mayor's table? Or that such a woman die of a sudden and her grieving husband find solace in the arms of a reformed trull and deck her in his dead wife's finery?'

'Then slit her throat, lop her head and drop her in the Thames?' concluded Ugo grimly. 'Gone Bedlam-mad with guilt and grief?'

'Perhaps,' said Tom accommodatingly. 'Perhaps. Guilt is apt enough, in a goldsmith.'

He swept the dress up off the table. 'But the truth of the matter lies up there on London Bridge, I'd lay my life on it. Of all the days and times of the year to find it out, this is the worst,' he said cheerfully. 'But we have the dress and we have the will. All we lack is the doing of the deed.'

He slung the sopping garment over his shoulder and strode out through the door with the others at his heels. The doctor and the curate had gone, but the two attendants were still there, their number made up to three by a strapping young giant in his straining holiday best.

The newcomer rose from the girl's bedside as Tom swung into the room and stepped forward to block his way. Tom stopped, resting his hand negligently on his sword hilt. He glanced down at the girl and saw her eyes wide enough almost to be aglow in the shadows. He glanced up at her massive companion. 'Brother or lover?' he enquired easily.

Thrown, the young man hesitated, as though searching for an answer.

'Lover, I'd hazard. There's no family resemblance obvious. A true heart, I hope, for she'll stand in need of you.'

Tom's eyes met the giant's, the brown eyes quizzical, the blue beneath a shock of straw-bright hair, at once oddly guarded and defenceless. The young man thrust out a hand the size of a ham. 'Terrill,' he said. 'Mark Antony Terrill. This is mistress Judith Yeomans. I am told we are beholden to you, sir, in the matter of Judith's leg.'

'Your family is down in the country, Mistress Judith?' enquired Tom courteously. 'I had supposed so when I heard it was the tapster at The Tun who was paying the good Doctor Viner for your treatment.'

'I will repay him,' said Terrill at once. 'And I will meet the bills for any further treatment.'

'You are well placed, then,' said Tom easily. 'There are not many apprentices who could promise so much – even apprenticed goldsmiths. Perhaps there is some truth in these rumours of alchemy, eh?' The lightness of his tone and the sparkle in his eyes robbed the words of much of their offence, but young Terrill frowned again and some more of the open candour of his gaze clouded.

'Your hands,' said Tom at once, in answer to the unspoken question. 'Even recently washed for the holiday, they are blackened and cracked as only a smith's hands get. And yet they preserve a delicacy soon lost in wielding the cold hammer and shoeing horses. God knows, you are big enough to be an apprentice to a blacksmith, but I see beneath your nails a range of colours that bespeak alchemical work, and there, in the deepest crack of your knuckle, I see just the tiniest glimmer of golden light.'

For a moment, the blue gaze seemed to Tom to grow hot and dangerous, as though his simple cleverness had uncovered some terrible secret unawares; but then the gaze in question cooled once more and shifted from Tom's bright brown eyes to his hunched and dripping shoulder. 'What are you doing with my mistress's dress?' demanded Terrill.

'Your mistress's? Has she been dead for long?' asked Tom, his tone still easy, for all that his mind was racing now.

'Since the Feast of St Nicholas last.' At least young Master Terrill didn't stop every second to stutter *But how did you know . . . ?* as some of Tom's acquaintance were prone to do; and that in itself bespoke a suspiciously sharp brain.

'Six months since and a pair of weeks. A good time, in all faith. And how did she die?'

'The river took her.'

'And how was that?' The ease had gone from Tom's voice, for now it was his turn to be more than somewhat shocked.

'The river was frozen from the close of November well past St Lucy's Day, when the storms came and broke it all up. Mistress Panne went down upon the ice on St Nicholas' Day for sport – she loved to play on the ice. Nor was she alone in that. But there was some flaw in the stuff below where she stood and the ice cracked open and the river gulped her down.'

'Did anyone see it happen?'

'Several men nearby. One of them knew her by sight. Nicholas Hazard, curate of our church and a frequent visitor in those days. He was the closest to her but even he could not reach her in time. So he told the Watch and the Watch told the Justice and so it came home to us. It had all happened within sight of our house on the Bridge, but no one there saw anything, though the young mistress her daughter was there. The master and I were at the smithy here in Southwark. We had not moved out of the old shop then. We were still at the sign of Barton and Panne, as she had always wished. We'd be there still, were she still alive. It was Master Barton, her father, that founded the business, you see . . .'

'But she was not wearing this dress then,' said Tom, his quiet voice tense as he pulled the apprentice's wandering thoughts back to the matter in hand.

'No. She wore another dress the day she died. That one was her dress for visits to the Guild Hall with the master. I say again, how did you get it?'

'Also from the river. Was the body of your mistress ever found?'

'I cannot say for certain. Some weeks after the accident, in the spring when the Thames came back to life, a couple of men came by with things that might have been hers: scraps of clothing; jewellery and the like, found in the river. But Master Panne and Mistress Alice – they said it was nothing to do with her.'

'Could this be she?' Tom turned and led the young man back into the little room. He filled the door frame and used it to steady himself, for the sudden sight of the headless corpse seemingly made his knees go weak.

'No,' he said. 'That's never her. How could that be Mistress Panne six months dead?'

'No,' said Tom decidedly. 'I knew it was not her, but I hoped . . .'

'Mind,' continued Terrill thoughtlessly, 'I know who it does remind me of.'

'Ah,' said Tom.

CHAPTER ELEVEN

The Frighted Silversmith

T he ceremonial part of Midsummer's Day on London
Bridge was long since over. The Lord Mayor had come,
attended by the leading guildsmen of London. He had read his
speech between his fanfares, asked God to preserve his Queen
and departed. Now it was the time of the revellers and those
that preyed on them. From the Great Stone Gateway overlooking the South Wark to Saint Magnus' Church on the
northern shore, the length and the breadth of it were heaving.

His head full of Terrill's directions, Tom ran into the crowd,
using his shoulders – one damp and one dry – to get his way
clear. Behind him the body still lay on one table with its
clothing returned to the other. Ugo was helping the young
giant move his lady-love back to her garret in The Tun while
Talbot went to the Watch records to seek information on the
name the goldsmith's apprentice had given them.

Tom himself, of course, was going after the lady. Up the
slope of the South Wark he rushed and on to the level roadway
of the Bridge itself. Beneath his feet, between the first two
arches of the Bridge below, the great wheels rumbled, making
the ground seem to quake, using the eastward pressure of the
falling tide to grind the Warden's corn.

Hardly registering the relentless shuddering, Tom shoved his
way under the arch of the Great Stone Gateway with never a

glance upward at the two dozen traitors' heads. Immediately behind the gateway was the first square open to the afternoon sky. Here the near forty-foot width of the Bridge was allowed to stand under the brightness of the summer sky, walled only with palings to keep the unwary safe. The roadway plunged onwards, however, a mere fifteen feet wide, under the arch of the first great set of houses. Five storeys sheer they rose in front of him, joined above the second storey in a great tunnel fifteen feet high and wide. Or it would have been fifteen feet wide had not all the shops been open with their shutters wide and their stall-fronts down.

Nothing daunted by the thousands thronging there, Tom pushed into the heaving shadows, acutely aware that he had been in rooms wider than the crowded space between the bright, demanding, shop-fronts. His head rang with a cacophony of cries, his stomach heaving from the stenches of so much trapped and unwashed humanity. Then, with his eyes watering from the sudden passage from shade to sunlight, he was out on to the open drawbridge section with the mullioned windows of Nonesuch House glittering like diamonds before him. Five storeys high to its smoking chimneys, three great double windows wide on either side of its central arch, the place stood as gaudy testament to the Dutch builders who had fashioned it twenty years ago in Antwerp and shipped it here in barges.

Tom gasped in a great breath and strode forward once again. 'Twelve pence a peck, oysters,' sang out a fishwife close at hand. The odour of her wares swept over him, warning him that the oysters on offer had been out in the sun too long. A sideways glance told him much the same about the hopeful woman offering them. A country girl pushed out in front of him with a basket held at her breast. 'Care to try my cherries, my love?' she asked. 'Or my noranges? Fresh from Seville, they are, and soft and juicy.' She raised her basket higher, offering more than the colourful fruit.

Tom slipped past both of them and into the arch under Nonesuch. If young Terrill was right, the body was Mistress

Margery Midmore, a widow come up from the country, with a woollen drapery in this great block of houses stretching across the very heart of the bridge between Nonesuch and St Thomas's Chapel. Master Panne's gold shop was immediately across the great square beyond the chapel – but not so far as to make a liaison difficult, if a man had a mind to it.

Tom had no difficulty in finding Mistress Midmore's drapery next door to the long-closed chapel. Like the chapel itself, closed since King Henry had split away from Rome, Mistress Midmore's shop was shuttered and barred. Opposite, less than ten feet distant, there blazed a silversmith's. Roughly, Tom pushed his way through the throng until he could attract the attention of the thin, pallid apprentice standing wearily, warily, behind the counter.

'Trinket for your lady?' the young man enquired.

Tom leaned forward, as though selecting from the wares gleaming beneath the flames of the cheap candles in the little shop-front. 'I had hoped to buy a jerkin,' he said, fingering a thumb-ring of unusual filigree.

'Oh yeah?' responded the boy. He glanced over Tom's shoulder at the shuttered shop. Something unpleasant stirred in the depths of his eyes, but when he looked down at Tom again they were shallow, closed.

'I had heard that Mistress Margery opposite had some fine woollen ones.'

'Mayhap. I never saw none.' Was there a catch in the flat voice to match the quiver of his thin lips and the tremble of his pointed chin?

'Have you seen Mistress Margery herself lately?'

'No. I ain't seen her since Friday last.'

Tom replaced the ring and took up a cheaper-looking buckle. He glanced up at the boy, wondering if a bribe would elicit any further information. The boy met his gaze with stony eyes. Something about him made Tom pause.

'What is it, lad?' he asked without thought.

The apprentice jumped, then looked over his shoulder into

the bright depths of the shop. Shadows moved there but no one was visible. A kind of desperation came into his expression. 'I got to get home,' he said. 'I got people dahnriver . . . out in Gravesend. All I need is the fare.' The hoarse young voice contained more poignant need than Tom ever remembered having heard before.

With thoughtless generosity, Tom reached into his purse and pulled out an angel. Gold among the silver, he placed it on the counter.

It was there for a twinkling – literally – and then it was gone into the boy's pale fist. 'Place is haunted,' said the 'prentice, matter-of-factly.

'How so?' Of all the answers possible, this was the last that Tom was expecting; but he never doubted the truth of it.

The boy gave a dry laugh. 'Wiv a ghost.'

Tom allowed the full weight of the Master of Logic's insight to rest on the apprentice. He was terrified – there was no doubt of that. How could he have missed it? – mistaken it for shallow indifference? 'Only Mistress Midmore's shop, or the whole building?' he asked quietly. 'Or the Bridge?'

'The shop and the chapel perhaps.' The boy's face gathered a little more life. He was unused to having people believing him, thought Tom.

'You sleep up in the garret hard by both?' It was hardly a question. Where else would the apprentice sleep? Up in the roof space where the walls were thin. Little more than lath and plaster kept all the tight-packed dwellings here apart. 'And you have heard strange noises.'

'Smelt strange stenches. Seen strange things.' The boy nodded fiercely.

'An instance of either?'

The boy paused for an instant, going absolutely still, his face as blank as a statue's. 'There's the flies,' he said.

'Flies?'

'You never seen so many flies,' said the boy. 'They come and go out over the river. But they live in there.' He pointed across the roadway with his trembling chin. 'I can hear them of a night. Rustling and buzzing.'

'Anything else?'

'The sobbing.' In the face of Tom's raised eyebrow the boy plunged on. 'Like as of someone crying. It goes on for hours. All night some nights.'

'But what is it you have seen?'

'Nothing, thank the Lord. Nothing clear, at any rate, or I wouldn't be telling you of this, would I?'

'Nothing clear. What unclear, then? Lights? Shadows?'

'More than that. I'm river born and bred. Such things are like to make me think . . .'

'Of smugglers, not ghosts – I understand. But there was nothing more?'

The boy shrugged. Frowned. His eyes grew trapped; hunted. Darting desperately like cornered rats. 'I seen a glimpse. Just a glimpse, mind . . .'

'Of what?'

'Something.'

'Something human?'

'Something that looked human. But it didn't have a . . .'

'Didn't have a head?' whispered Tom, a tremble in his own steady voice.

'A face. It didn't have a face . . .'

Tom stood for a moment, his mind racing. In spite of the jostling bustle all around them, he and the terrified boy might well have been alone. 'Have you told anyone else about this?'

'If I told the master I'd only get a whipping . . .'

The master in question came into the shop then, his mean little eyes sweeping over his apprentice and fastening greedily on the customer. Tom leaned forward at once and picked up a solid-looking clasp. 'This,' he said.

As Tom turned from the shop, with the clasp he didn't want and the information he didn't trust and could not bring himself to believe, he heard a familiar, utterly unexpected hail.

'Tom! Is that pretty gaud for me, my love?'

He turned, his heart seeming to take wings. There, in front of Mistress Midmore's sinister, shuttered shop, stood two women and a man. Even under the shadows of the tunnel-mouth, the women's hair flamed red. Strange, he thought, crossing to them with his broadest smile, he had never noticed how red was the hair of the Shelton sisters.

It was Kate who had called to him, the younger, more beautiful, more dazzling of the pair. His mistress.

''Tis yours!' he called at once, sweeping her into his arms. 'But what make you here? I had thought you down in Scadbury.'

The man stepped forward at that, and took Audrey under his arm. 'I brought them both up with me,' said Thomas Walsingham quietly. 'Nothing would do them but London at Midsummer and I have business here.'

Thomas Walsingham's business was likely to overlap more than somewhat with whatever Robert Poley was up to, thought Tom, broadening his grin. For he still had ambitions to snatch his late uncle's secret service from under the noses of Lord Burghley, his son Robert Cecil and the Earl of Essex. But Thomas had continued speaking gaily, unaware of the dreadful reputation of the shuttered shop against which he was leaning.

'I have opened some rooms I acquired a year or two since down in Nonesuch itself. Come to dinner, Tom; I brought the staff from Scadbury up with best of the venison from the park.'

'And I,' said Kate irresistibly, 'have brought up something hot and sweet for you as well.'

CHAPTER TWELVE

Nonesuch

T homas Walsingham was up to something and Tom knew
it.

The Master of Logic twitched as he slyly watched his host
and observed his host secretly watching him. It had the smell of
spycraft about it, whatever it was, for it had already put that
poison in Tom's cup which made him wary and guarded even
here, amongst his friends. Why should Thomas Walsingham
leave one of the most beautiful houses in the country to come
up to London and open these rooms, closed since the death of
his uncle, mentor and adoptive father, spy master Sir Francis?
Why should he leave the very real country pleasures of the
Midsummer to drag his household and their Midsummer feast
into this strange and haunted place? Haunted. The word gave
him pause. Perhaps there were ways that a body might pass – a
body corporeal or spiritual, with or without a face – from St
Thomas's Chapel down the block to Nonesuch, through the
very fabric of the Bridge.

'I made him do it,' answered Kate as though she could read
his mind like the red witch she so temptingly resembled. 'I could
live apart from my beloved master no longer. I needed more
tutoring in the Classics.'

That sally came close to bringing a blush to Tom's pale
cheek, for he was prone to using the words of the ancients to

prolong his strength at love-play – or rather, to put off the crisis, at least. But when his eyes met hers, he found that her twinkling green gaze slid away from his steady brown scrutiny, for all her flirting; and he knew Kate was the excuse in this, not the *primum mobile*. So he turned his gaze to Thomas once again, over the rim of his Venetian goblet.

'You sought me out, Thomas. Therefore you want something from me. Your blade is near the equal of my own and you wield it near as well as I, so you do not seek the Master of Defence. The Master of Logic, then. And you sought me; you did not summon me, so it is something I am already engaged in that interests you, not a matter of your own that you wish me to examine.'

Tom paused to savour the wine and it was truly excellent. Thomas Walsingham watched him: still; attentive. Both Kate and Audrey had been spies from girlhood and knew better than to interrupt this duel – even to add to the fictions of their cover stories. They sipped their sack silently instead. Out along the river the gulls wheeled and screamed amongst the masts of the restless ships. The westering sun spilt blood across the floor. There were hardly any walls on the shell of the place – just windows filled with thick Dutch glass.

'But to bring you up from Scadbury at this season with your whole household bespeaks urgency if not desperation. You must have almost as many well-packed carriages at your back as Will Shakespeare's actors take on their journeys around the country. Is it the matter of Robert Poley's coded messages and strange apprentices? Is it the matter of the heads upon the Bridge?'

At the earliest opportunity, Thomas caught his chamberlain's eye and caused the great windows facing westward to be opened, for the room was sweltering. Cool sweet air blew in from the river, now that the falling tide had scoured the floating sewage far downstream. The cries of the gulls were joined by the calls of watermen, the tapping of cordage, the flapping of sailcloth and the restless heave of the river itself.

Over his own gleaming goblet, Thomas raised his face and his voice to answer Tom: 'I have come to offer you an invitation and to urge you to accept another one.'

Tom shrugged. 'Make your offer, by all means.'

'We stay here for a week or two. I have business at Westminster and Whitehall. I know the Queen is at Greenwich but there are enough of her officers here to suit my purposes; and I wish to test this residence. If I like it, I shall keep it. If I do not, I am assured there is a ready market.'

Tom glanced across at Kate. Perhaps the thickening light – disturbingly like congealing blood – had made her eyes seem wider. They were two still green pools now, dark enough and deep enough to drown him in. 'In the meantime I would be pleased if you would stay here with us,' concluded Thomas.

'I see. And which of you requires protection?' asked Tom gently, his voice at its most drily cynical.

'You do,' answered Thomas, after a heartbeat of silence; and there was absolute truth ringing in his tone, like the chime of one of his priceless goblets.

'I do,' answered Tom, more gently still. 'And from whom?'

'I had hoped you would know the answer to that,' said Thomas, frankly. 'I had the message from Ingram Frizer, who came down to his house on the estate yesterday. There are certain sections of the city a-buzz – sections that Frizer commonly frequents – with the news that your life has been bought and sold within the last day.'

'Frizer works with Poley.'

'He has done so. Which of us has not? He has worked with Nick Skeres, who is My Lord of Essex's man to boot. But Poley works for the Cecils, *Père et fils*. Have you upset them – or might you be just about to do so?'

Tom shrugged and shook his head, eyes narrow, mind racing.

Thomas Walsingham continued, 'Well, then. Not My Lord Burghley nor his son the Lord Robert. But remember neither Poley nor Essex has any call to love you. Have you upset either of them of late?'

'Poley, perhaps,' said Tom, wondering whether Will Shakespeare could have told Poley of the second message in code. Will also, of course, had worked for Poley in his time. So had Kit Marlowe and Tom Watson . . . The list went on and on.

'And I have no doubt,' added Kate slyly, 'that in my absence you will have added other contenders to the list. Virgins outraged, coxcombs challenged, mothers insulted, fathers angered . . . The count, no doubt, is endless.'

'Curates crossed, guildsmen aggrieved, apprentices affronted, watermen wrangled, wardens worried and doctors demolished,' admitted Tom. 'It's been a busy few days.'

'On this level you need fear nothing from watermen or apprentices . . .' mused Thomas, taking the list more seriously than Tom had intended.

'So long as I keep clear of Tooley Street . . .' admitted Tom, realizing with growing surprise that the list was indeed quite serious. As, perhaps, the danger was.

'But if you are serious about the curate . . .' prompted Thomas.

'Nicholas Hazard of Saint Magnus . . .'

'Late of the galleys and the Inquisition dungeons. Not a good man to cross,' observed Audrey. Kate said nothing but sat wide-eyed.

'The guildsman?'

'Two. Masters Petty and Panne; haberdasher and goldsmith.'

'God save us,' said Thomas. 'Two real powers in the City. Subjects – both of them – to investigation by Sir Francis in their time. And Panne since, I think. By Poley. Ruthless men in their business and not likely to be less so in life. The doctor?'

'Viner.'

'As bad a man to cross as the Earl of Essex himself, by all accounts,' supplied Audrey again. 'You choose your enemies as well as you choose your blades. They are as sharp and as dangerous. As likely to cut both ways.'

Tom pushed his glass away, feeling the need to keep his wits sharp.

Thomas Walsingham smiled with ready sympathy. 'And this enmity has all arisen within the last few days?'

'Much of it within the last twenty-four hours,' admitted Tom. 'This time yesterday, without a care in the world, I stepped out of the Borough Counter and it started raining footballs and heads . . .'

'Ah yes. The heads. Tell us about the heads,' insinuated Thomas.

'Not until you have told me of the second invitation – the one I must accept.'

'Ah yes. I had forgot . . .'

Tom's eyebrows rose. Thomas Walsingham forgot nothing – forgave little; forgot nothing.

'There is a merchant seeking a Master of Defence to tutor his son. It is a man whose favour might be of use to me. To us.'

Tom gave a bark of laughter. A man such as Thomas busying himself about such petty business – as though the Lord Mayor himself had turned costermonger.

'Tell him to send the boy to my school in Blackfriars.'

'You do not understand, Tom. He wishes you to visit him. To teach the boy in his own home.'

'The last man who asked that was Lord Outremer, who called me down to his great castle at Elfinstone; Lord Outremer, the Earl of Southampton and the Earl of Essex, all three of them called me down – three men but a little step behind the Queen in standing, wealth and power.'

'I know. And I know what came of it.' Thomas glanced across at Kate, who had been there and who, like Tom himself, had been lucky indeed to survive.

'And you would rank a merchant with men such as these to have me at his beck and call?'

'This man I would. I called on him today about some other business and heard nothing from him but your praises.'

'Who is it?'

'His name is Julius Van Der Leyden.'

CHAPTER THIRTEEN

The Shuttered Shop

'**B**elgiae!' gasped Tom.

'Very good!' giggled Kate, wantonly astride him, her upright body a thing of silver and shadow in the light of the waning summer moon, which found itself breathtakingly mimicked – and doubled – above Tom's dazzled gaze. She moved the hips that rose out of the tumble of bedding like a mermaid gambolling in the surf. The twin moons swayed distractingly.

Tom gasped again, sucked in a shuddering breath and focused his mind with all his will: upon the campaigns of Caesar's Gallic Wars. 'Helvetiae!' His great hands clasped the delicate curves of her ribs and the curved bones flexed beneath them like the bows of Caesar's saggitarians. He tried not to consider the state of his warmly embedded *pilum.* 'Nervii,' he grated.

'How many tribes did Caesar destroy before he returned to Italy?' asked Kate, calculating no doubt how much longer her pleasure had to last.

'Six. Then he crossed the River Rubicon and invaded Italy itself. No turning back after the Rubicon.'

'Hmmmm. But this is working better even than the sayings of the Stoic philosophers.'

'Love and death are closer bedfellows than love and philosophy. Teutones!'

Their conversation stilled – unlike their bodies. The old bed creaked and Tom hoped that the walls in Nonesuch were thicker than those in the garrets down by St Thomas. Particularly as it was dead water now; the tide would not return until after moon-set. The gulls were asleep and the wind had fallen so that all the ships, their cloth and cordage seemed but a painting between the gathering banks. In all the mighty heart of the City it seemed the only sounds were the creaking of their bed, the gasping of their breath and his sudden call of, 'Cimbri!'

A night-wind whispered through the open window: a harbinger of dawn. Strong enough to stir the tumbled perfumed strands of Kate's hair; cool enough to make her shiver.

And, 'Suebii!' he called – too late. For he had crossed his own personal Rubicon.

With the first grey finger of the dawn, Tom's eyes flickered. Opened. Gently, silently, he rolled away from Kate, then piled the bedding round her slumbering form as he reached for his clothing.

Ten minutes later he was picking his way down through the shadowed stairwells of the sleeping house. It was too early for even the lowliest of Scadbury's uprooted establishment to be up and looking to the grates, too early for the junior under-cook to be scurrying out to the markets at Smithfield, Billingsgate and the Cheap after meat, fish, bread and milk.

It was even too early, Tom discovered, as he stepped out of the side door between two shop-fronts into the deserted tunnel below Nonesuch, for the Bridge itself to be astir. Nothing sounded except the morning chorus of breakfasting gulls. Nothing moved except the web-grey mist sucked up from the still waters by the distant stirring of the sun and set a-dancing by the elder brother of the chilly zephyr that had finished things for Kate and him last night.

But that was just how Tom had calculated matters: so that there would be enough light for him to search Mistress Midmore's haunted shop, but no eyes – except those of an escaping apprentice, Gravesend bound, perhaps – to watch him as he did so. Even so, he did not swagger about his business. He tiptoed swiftly and silently through the gathering grey, his hand to the hilt of his sword and his eyes everywhere.

The door into Margery Midmore's woollen drapery was on the northern side of the shop, where the shop itself joined St Thomas's Church. It was secured by a practical-looking padlock that would have stopped many a man. Tom, however, had spent some time with two worthies who gloried in the names of Nick o' Darkmans and Kit Callot. Locks held few secrets for him nowadays. This one yielded as swiftly as a bankside virgin, and Tom stepped into the haunted place.

With the door closed behind him, Tom stood in near-total darkness. His eyes adjusted swiftly, however, and his memory of the simple layout revealed by the flash of light from the street through which he had stepped in, soon served to guide him forward. Dead ahead was a stair, leading up towards gloomy brightness. To his right hand a doorway – no doubt into the confines of the shop itself. Behind the shop, if the design reflected the silversmith's opposite, another room or two. A parlour perhaps. Some kind of kitchen.

But the sobbing, the buzzing and the haunting came from the garrets, according to the frightened boy. So, using the pause as his vision cleared to whisper his sword out of its sheath, onward and upward went Tom.

The first room he came to was a store-room. Immediately above the shop it served, it was piled high with the kinds of clothing, stock and wares to be expected in a woollen drapers. It was well ordered, well placed. It bespoke a careful, organized mind. A woman possessing a good head for business and organization then – while she had still possessed it, at any rate, he thought grimly.

Behind the store-room was situated a little sitting room that looked down the river over the ships whose stirring had echoed through his dreams last night. The windows were tight against the swirling mist. Out beyond them stood a little balcony, wide enough to accept a couple of stools and a table, but in here there was a settle obviously more favoured – more worn, at least. Beside the settle stood a little table with a birdcage on it. In the birdcage lay a pair of white turtle doves, dead on the floor. No one had fed or watered them, perhaps since Friday, and they had simply died unheard, alone.

The stairwell led upward once again. Right up to the garret this time. At its head there stood a little landing leading right and left, with the slope of the roof ahead. Hunching under the eaves, Tom turned right. A crazy doorway led through to a pleasant bedchamber high enough at the back to accommodate a modest four-poster bed. Opposite the bed foot, the roof rose into a last westward-facing window high enough to be looking out above the river mist into a bright and glorious summer's morning. The cheerful promise of the rising sun should have brightened Tom's spirits as easily as it gilded the cloth-of-gold bedspread and the silken robe woven with the pattern 'RP' that lay tidily across it; but it did nothing of the sort. And when a seagull suddenly flew against the thick glass of the window, Tom shouted aloud with shock.

For there, just below the level of clear hearing, like the rumble of a far-distant battle or a gathering tempest away beyond the horizon, more felt than heard, there was the buzzing.

Tom turned and crossed to the crazy door again. Out on to the odd little landing he went, hunching like King Richard Crouchback in the old chronicles under the slope of the roof; with his sword-blade whispering across the sloping plaster, he crossed to the other door. Just for a moment, he paused with the handle in his left hand, steadying his jangled nerves and waiting for his heart to stop pounding.

Long before it did so, he ran out of patience and threw the portal wide. He stood in the doorway, frozen with horror and disgust. He did not step in at that point, but the picture of what he saw seared itself into his mind so that even after he slammed the door shut once more to stand shuddering outside safe from the slithering susurrating buzzing of it, he could see every detail as though he were still inside – could smell the overwhelming stench as though it were an infection now rooted in his nose; Could almost taste the metallic alchemy of the terrible, tainted air.

Slowly, as though suddenly much advanced in years, he slid down the slope of the roof until he was seated on the top step with his sword resting flat across his lap and his eyes closed. Behind their lids he saw what he had seen behind the door.

It was a chapel. Against the west wall, beneath a sister to the window that the gull had battered in the bedroom, there was a little altar. Lying on this, toppled on its side, lay a golden cross perhaps a foot high, crusted with jewels. The altar cloth, like the bedspread, was cloth-of-gold. Before it stood a little altar rail, smashed to kindling now. And behind the altar rail, upon the floor of the room, the flies: across the floor, upon the walls, over the sloping ceiling; over the gilt-framed picture of the Virgin, even; everywhere the blood had spattered, pumped, slithered and gathered, there were great flies feasting on it. Tom could hear them buzzing and battering against the closed door now, beating with the terrible numbers of their bodies like an overwhelming army of pygmies fighting to get out at him. And he shared with poignant vividness the feelings of the boy from Gravesend whose bedroom was only a lath wall distant from the horror.

An almost silent stirring made his eyes leap wide with shock. Even so he had to blink twice, fiercely, before he could clear the sight from his eyes and see that Kate was standing in the shadows of the stairwell immediately in front of him, her head exactly level with his own.

'I knew,' he said, his voice grating like a creaky hinge.

She smiled; but the tone of his voice and the expression on his face made her own expression uncertain. Her eyes clouded, for she had never seen him like this; and she in turn seemed uncertain, hesitant. But the Master of Logic had seen enough in the little chapel and had little time to fathom what Kate was up to.

'What did you know?' she demanded.

'That you would follow. I should have stayed to stop you.'

'You could never have stopped me. And anyway—'

'I wish I had.' He cut her short with unaccustomed rudeness.

There was a little silence. He wondered that she did not ask about the overpowering sound of the buzzing; but then he began to understand that much of it was inside his head.

'What have you found?' she asked.

'Where Mistress Midmore died.'

'And is that so terrible?'

'Yes.'

He had told them as little as possible about the heads last night. Certainly, he had signally failed to pass on to either sister the full horror of what he had become involved in here. But then, up until now, he had hardly understood it himself.

'It's a chapel,' he began, then found he couldn't quite bring himself to proceed. 'Why did you come?' he asked.

The question was rhetorical. It was a cry of frustration and concern. He had not expected an answer; but he got one.

'I am a messenger,' she answered.

'What?' He actually shook his head as though he could clear it of the sights, the sounds, the confusion.

'As soon as you left, the message arrived and I came after you, because I knew where you were bound for.'

'Message? What message?'

'From Talbot Law. They have another.'

'Another what?'

She shrugged. 'They said you would know. That you would come at once. To the Great Stone Gateway.'

He knew then – though there had been precious little doubt – and he suspected that Kate knew well enough too.

'Let us pray it is Mistress Margery,' he said.

He reached forward and cupped her cheek in his right hand. Distantly he observed that it was shaking just a little. Her hair spilt across his wrist like blood. He took a great hank of it and shook her lovingly and gently. 'This is what he takes. This is what he chops and takes.'

'Red hair?' she asked, her voice a little awed, but still not really understanding.

'No,' he said. 'Red heads.'

CHAPTER FOURTEEN

Danby

M istress Margery Midmore looked disdainfully down upon Sir William Danby and Tom looked up at them both with narrow eyes. Mistress Midmore's head remained where the Warden's men had found it at dawn, where the sleepy and grumpy silversmith, hauled from his bed in his apprentice's absence, had identified it. He had identified it, but Tom had recognized it the instant he had seen it. The red hair matched that of the body in St Thomas's. The scar on one cheek told of the brand burned out by the steady hand of a proud and desperate woman willing to go to any lengths to hide her shameful past. Even so, even in death, she was prettier than Tom had expected – comelier and younger.

Tom had decreed – with Talbot happy to enforce the decree, though through negotiation rather than by right of jurisdiction – that it should remain on the pole where they had found it. There it remained, therefore, with the three of them and Perkin to guard it until matters should begin to resolve themselves more clearly, like the grey mist dissipating beneath the sun and within the wind.

Up on a second pole she stood, in the midst of the sun-filled, stinking gallery above the Great Stone Gateway with the rest of the traitors' heads; and this time, at least, it was plain to Tom, if to no one else, that the new head deserved to be in the old company, for the blood-boltered chapel where she had died was plainly Catholic. Probably Jesuit. Designed to undermine and eventually overthrow Her Majesty, her Church of England and her Protestant governance of France, England and Ireland, whose faith she still defended in the thirty-sixth year of her reign. Its simple existence was a capital act of treachery and anyone found to be knowingly associated with it would swiftly follow the Queen of Scots, Babbington and the rest.

The Warden had summoned the City Watch immediately on discovering the head. He knew nothing as yet about Jesuit infiltration of his Bridge, for Tom was holding his peace and awaiting events, while Kate at his side, her red hair stirring more brightly and vividly than Mistress Margery's, knew better than to open her mouth for the moment.

The City Watch had summoned a justice and he had sent hot-foot to Greenwich. Sir William himself had answered the call, arriving well before noon and striding up on to the Great Stone Gateway followed by his usual retinue of doctors, lawyers and soldiers. One doctor, Theodore something, had trained in Geneva and was almost impenetrable in English. In Latin, however, his tones would have graced even Cicero in the Senate. A brace of lawyers, seniors at the bar, men of gravitas and worth – neither introduced, but one faintly familiar to Tom; from the City, perhaps, or the Court – and half a dozen soldiers, beautifully turned out and clearly fresh from Court as well.

'This is the second, you say, Master Curberry?'

The Officer of the City Watch huffed and puffed. 'So I have been told, Sir William – though the first head fell outside my jurisdiction into the Borough.'

'We have it here, Sir William,' said Tom easily. 'And the stake upon which it stood.'

Sir William's piercing gaze fell upon the two tall men and the striking woman between them. 'Mistress Shelton and Master Musgrave are known to me . . .'

'This is Talbot Law, Sir William, Bailiff to the Bishop of Winchester. The law in the Liberty and in Southwark beside.'

'Ah. I had not realized. The Bishop's Bailiff is well known to me by reputation; and that reputation, coupled with the presence of Master Musgrave, must mean that there is already a quest under way in Southwark if not in the City.'

'We have much that might inform your further actions,' said Tom shortly.

'Then let us take the head down to a convenient resting place. Perkin, is it? Indeed. Perkin. Bring the thing, staff and all, and guide us to the Warden's house.'

Danby turned to Curberry with a rueful smile. 'We must into the Bailiff's jurisdiction again, Master Curberry. But I am sure there will remain much for you and your officers to do.'

Tom paced up and down the big, cool cellar room beside the grain stores that the Warden had turned over to them. The water mill beneath the Great Stone Gateway rumbled unvaryingly, adding to his disquiet, for its dreamlike persistence reminded some deep part of him of the relentless buzzing of flies. The soldiers stood outside the door. The two lawyers sat with Danby at the long trestle table on which Mistress Margery now lay entire, if piecemeal, covered by decorous napkins, with her clothing piled beside her whither it had been carried over from St Thomas's. The first head lay beside her, bodiless and as yet nameless. Dr Theodore was leaning over the corpse, speaking slowly and beautifully in classically modulated Latin. Tom could hear Kate whispering a translation to Talbot, whose education had been more in arms than academe.

'Dress it up however you will,' rumbled Talbot in reply, 'he tells us nothing more than Tom told us yesterday.'

Tom was learning, through observation and the exercise of logic if through nothing more. Sir William was the Queen's personal representative. He was her 'Crowner', literally. He stood for the Crown. His quest here was to assess whether there was anything of danger to Her Majesty's state or person. That was the point of the Verge – a circle thirteen miles from Her Majesty's person, in which all law gave way to that overriding imperative; where all officers gave way to the Crowner and all investigations became subsumed in his quest.

From what Tom understood of the way Danby usually worked, he would arrive on his quest himself – with enough force to see him safe – and then assemble what expertise he needed; but here it was already, and brought in from as far afield as Greenwich, the Temple and Geneva. Two possibilities sprang at once to mind. Either there was already some disquiet at Court, something afoot for which Sir William had felt he should stand prepared; or this place – Southwark and the Bridge – was a focus of such concern that anything out of the ordinary here might call forth such a reaction. Or, Tom suddenly realized, a combination of both.

For here already was Robert Poley about some secret investigations – at the behest, no doubt, of men close to Her Majesty, such as Lord Burghley and his son Sir Robert Cecil. Here also was Thomas Walsingham, apparently called up from delicious rustication by the uncontrollable love of his mistress's little sister and understandable concern at an all-too-convenient threat to the life of her lover – to whit, himself. Here was a corpse of Catholic taint close linked to one of the powers of the City Guilds – a man already investigated for alchemy in his goldsmithing; whose business, by the sound of things, had come as dowry with his wife, since deceased. Here was a coil indeed. A Gordian knot somehow growing tighter and tighter around them all.

Dr Theodore stood back, shut up and sat down.

Sir William said, 'Thus far medicine, then. What says the law? Master Bacon?'

The vaguely familiar lawyer rose in his turn. Tom knew him now: Francis Bacon, MP, lawyer and courtier – Essex's man, they said, soon to be Solicitor General or some such, if My Lord got his way from the Queen; and man of huge intellect, if rumour spoke true. As high in intelligence as low in moral fibre, so they said. Certainly, his quiet summation of the legal aspects of the case so far was a paradigm. All it lacked was the elements the young lawyer was ignorant of. Tom looked across at Kate and found her watching him. He was walking on thin ice now, like Master Panne's unfortunate wife last winter. He should interrupt Bacon now and add the vital information to the unfolding quest. Failure to do so could lead to Rackmaster Topcliffe's racks, manacles and red-hot irons, to Tyburn and to hell. And yet Tom still held his peace. For there was something here he still could not quite fathom, some element of the puzzle waiting, instant after instant, to fall into place – that would fall into place if only he dared wait for long enough.

'. . . Thus the law of the land clearly allows without emendation to current statute,' Bacon was concluding, 'that the City Watch co-operate with the other watches north and south of the river, out of Southwark and into the shires, that the banks of the river be searched for the body with all despatch. That the lightermen, wherrymen and watermen of all sorts, fishwives, oyster girls and the like be ordered to search in their work. That even the crews of foreign shipping come into English waters upriver of Foulness and the Cant assist us in this search.'

'Thank you, Master Bacon. Before you sit I must ask your opinion. Does the law allow the alerting of the Lords Lieutenant? Should the standing troops be set to the task?'

'There is provision at law, Sir William, should Her Majesty or her Council or even her Parliament decide that the national interest stands threatened here in any degree.'

'It does, Master Bacon,' said Tom, breaking his silence at last. 'Sir William, you must know that Mistress Midmore here died in a secret chapel. She was a Catholic . . .'

Sir William and Francis Bacon both insisted on coming along with Dr Theodore, a fact that added to Tom's increasingly feverish speculation; and, for a wonder, neither of them seemed particularly surprised at Tom's revelation. The soldiers escorted them to the woollen draper's and stood guard outside. Then the three courtiers followed Tom up the stairs.

Tom opened the door into the foetid little room and stood

back, reaching into the breast of his doublet for his scented kerchief. Dr Theodore stepped in without hesitation and Bacon followed him, coldly indifferent to the stench and the flies. Tom went next, feeling a strange possessiveness as the original discoverer of the place, and Danby stood in the doorway, pulling his own kerchief across his face below his wrinkled, stench-offended nose.

The three men in the room immediately started exchanging observations and ideas in Latin, muffled only by the fact that they were all, now, conversing through their kerchiefs. Tom felt, strangely, that the Master of Logic was almost under attack on two fronts. Theodore saw with minute precision and speculated with meticulous care; but Bacon was really a wonder. Tom had only ever felt awed in the company of Will Shakespeare when the playwright began to unravel his beloved cyphers; but now here stood a man that was very near his equal.

'She knelt here, praying to the altar,' said Tom, gesturing. His companions nodded. Bacon swept the hem of his robe across the floor, disturbing a cloud of flies and revealing great pale marks among the dark stains on which they feasted.

'He stood behind her,' observed the lawyer through obviously slitted lips.

'A trusted friend, therefore,' observed Tom. 'Unless he can pass through walls.'

'Or her priest,' said Bacon. 'A strange mass, but needfully so. The room is too small to have it otherwise.'

'The priest must be a trusted friend in any case, must he not?' observed Tom. 'They hold each other's lives in their hands.'

Bacon gave a grim laugh. 'One more so than the other.'

'He pushed the knife in from this side, on her right,' said Theodore. 'See how the blood bursts forth?' His own right hand gestured up the wall beside the door.

'A thin blade, sharp as death,' said Tom, sliding his Solingen dagger, companion to the matched pair of his rapiers, out into the buzzing light. The other two looked at it and nodded, glancing across at Sir William in the doorway.

'She fell forward then, her throat cut neatly enough, as though by a razor,' said Theodore, gesturing at the downward spray, the thicker the blood the thicker the flies.

'And he battened upon her, holding her down,' said Tom, 'for see how the altar rail is splintered. Even her death throes could not have done so much.'

'A heavy man?' surmised Bacon.

'Not necessarily,' answered Tom. 'I'd judge that a slight man would be strong enough to hold her still as she kicked and choked her last. Two slight weights and a deal of writhing would wreak this destruction. And there is the matter of her dress: the bodice is gone but the back has no great marks upon it. No. A great man being gentle or a slight man working harder.'

'This is so,' concurred Theodore. 'But you must not underestimate the power of even a slight frame in its death throes.'

'He left her dead,' concluded Bacon. 'Though there is blood elsewhere in the room, I can see no way to link it with the woman's corpse. There she lay and there she stayed while the murderer went away and then returned.'

'Could he not have stayed?' asked Danby from the door. 'Done his throat-cutting, waited and then gone about his beheading just a little later?'

'No,' said Tom Musgrave and Francis Bacon both at the same time. They exchanged a look, then the Lawyer and MP took precedence even over the Master of Logic. 'He stood here as the blood flowed – ' he gestured at the foot marks – 'then he stepped out and away, scraping the blood from his shoes at the doorstep there and walking cleanly down the stairs.'

'Returning later,' Tom took up the story. 'There was time for the turtle doves below to sob themselves to death, so if the throat was cut on Friday last, after which Mistress Margery was not seen again, he could have waited several days. But two nights since, he returned with the axe he could never have concealed about his person – even beneath priest's robes, did he dare wear them out and about. He let himself in through the lock below with a key. He climbed the stair, stepped in through the doorway and paused. He stood there, where the blood had not yet gathered. Perhaps he was surprised by the flies, the stench, the fact that the stuff had not set hard in the interim.

'Howsoever, he reached over and raised the axe. You see the mark on the ceiling here above the most clearly damaged section of the altar rail?' He paused to a square grey-marked indentation in the white of the sloping plaster. 'Then he struck down with all his might.' He glanced across at Bacon, who was watching him with narrow, burning eyes. 'A big man after all, perhaps. For see, the blade drove through her neck and into the floor down here. He leaned on the axe to steady himself, I would guess, and tore the head free. That is where the blood behind you comes from, Master Bacon, that last spray across the Madonna and Child just there.'

Bacon stepped forward and looked back, nodding.

'Then he rocked the axe from side to side and lifted it free. The axe in one hand and the head in the other. Then both of them into a sack, I would judge. There is no mark or sign of them anywhere I can discover. This was the evening before last, I believe. And through the night, as the flies buzzed increasingly madly and the heat and stench grew, he knelt here and prayed. Wept and prayed. The boy in the room next door, apprentice to the silversmith, heard it and was terrified.

'At some part of the night, he moved the head and the axe out to safety and placed the first head – the head he had readied earlier – up on the Great Stone Gateway. Then he returned. He took up the body and carried it downstairs under the brightness of the moon, westering like the sun towards moon-set, near sunrise, and shining through the casements here bright as day. Past the dead birds he carried the dead mistress and through the windows, opened earlier for the purpose, and out on to the balcony. Over she went into the falling tide to be swept down-river in the dawn.

'Back he came the last time to find her bodice – and perhaps

92

her ruff set in the blood and needing to be torn free. Then off he went about his Bedlam business.'

'Impressive,' said Bacon. 'You have covered all the aspects of the incident that I can think of.'

Sir William Danby nodded, as did Dr Theodore.

'And all that I can think of except for two,' said Tom.

'And what are those?' enquired Danby civilly.

'When and why he took her shoe. And how and why the apprentice silversmith, alerted by the sobbing, spied on the place, saw him and thought he had no face. But time will answer these details, I am sure – time and your quest, Sir William.'

'Quest there must be,' said Sir William heavily. 'That much is clear – was clear ere I set out from Greenwich. But the quest will not be mine. I have other duties that call upon me too urgently for that.'

As he spoke, the three came out of the room on to the little landing beside him. 'Who then?' asked Tom, glancing across at Bacon.

But Francis Bacon also shrugged. 'I am in like case to Sir William. I may be consulted – called upon, even. But my time is not my own. And I have neither the experience nor yet the standing to conduct such a quest.'

'Then who?' asked Tom. 'Who is it will follow the quest into this matter if not the Crowner Sir William Danby?'

A voice echoed upwards from the foot of the stairwell in light, almost mocking answer to the question; and the next piece of the puzzle, that piece he had been awaiting in the Warden's cellar just before he told them about the chapel, fell snugly into place.

'That would be me,' said Thomas Walsingham. 'I have been deputed to pursue the quest for the Crowner and the Queen.'

CHAPTER FIFTEEN

Crowner's Quest

After Danby left, Tom went back to Nonesuch House with Thomas Walsingham and, for reasons of his own, Francis Bacon tagged along. Audrey and Kate were out, with several members of the Scadbury staff. These latter, Tom surmised with grim amusement, were to escort, protect and act as beasts of burden for them.

The body and the two heads, the two staves and the clothing had all been moved into the cellarage here. Thomas led the two men down a narrow spiral stair into a large, damp and chilly room obviously part of the almost timeless fabric of the stonework of the bridge. Here, under the flaring brightness of several flambards augmented by the steadier, stellar illumination of several candles and lamps, everything so far discovered lay arranged on trestles. As Thomas and Bacon pored over effects and body parts that had already felt the weight of his attention, Tom found himself drawn into exploring the place. Apparently without thought or particular motive, he took one of the flaring torches and wandered away across the damp and dusty floor, his eyes on his feet.

There was an eerie atmosphere of age here. It was something Tom had felt in some churches and cathedrals – both here and abroad – that had stood since time immemorial. It was something he had felt standing in the Coliseum at Rome, and in the overgrown ruins hard by his beloved Siena; but there had been a sense of grandeur in those places, a sense of public space. This was different. It was small-scale, personal, disturbingly intense. Walking into the shadows at the edges of the great dark cellar reminded him intensely of childhood experiences exploring the timeless forests up on the Borders that still stretched in places from Scotland to Sherwood and away on to the south: becoming lost in brakes and thickets amongst great trees that had been ancient before even Caesar was born; listening for the sound of the grey wolf and the brown bear, and the great man-killing boar – and, most terrifying of all, the huge spectral Barguest, the giant dog that roamed free in his father's ghost stories and perhaps through the fells, fens and forests also, to freeze the blood of anyone that saw it.

How old was this place? Tom knew that the Romans had built a bridge here. Perhaps Caesar himself had ordered it as he had ordered the foundation of the Tower of London. Was that the same bridge as the one named in the Chronicles, standing against Viking marauders a thousand years later? And was this the same again, built up and up on the ancient foundations? It seemed so strange and haunting. If the age of the world was, as the Bible scholars claimed, a little over six thousand years, the Bridge must have stood for a third of that time. And here stood Tom now in the very bowels of the place, looking at a grille of rotten, rusted iron that closed off a black-throated passageway leading away, further and deeper into the passages of stone-walled time.

Tom raised his torch a little, looking fixedly at the ground. Then he knelt, his fingers busy on the dank flag. He lifted them, examined them with his eyes, his nose. He raised his head and scented the air like a hunting hound. 'When was this place opened?' he called.

'When I came up from Scadbury, two days since,' came Thomas Walsingham's answer.

'And this dungeon?'

'This day, for this purpose.'

Tom leaned forward and thrust his torch against the metal. In the edges of the sudden light, an army of rats scurried back towards their cloak of darkness. Then he took the metal grille and shook it, his eyes busy at its left side, where two hinges were cemented to the wall. At top and bottom, amid the red rust they gleamed with a thread of steely light. He leaned across and looked at the old lock that secured the grille, seeking for the same signs of more recent usage on its face and by its keyhole.

'Who would have the key for this?' he asked.

'There are keys above. It may be amongst them. Otherwise, the Warden.'

'And, therefore, Perkin,' said Tom to himself, frowning as he began to turn the implications over in his mind and think of actions that might arise from them. 'Perkin, who is like to have access to any number of keys to the Bridge. And *ergo* to any number of places upon it, be they never so secret.' He raised his voice and spoke aloud once more. 'You must ask him when you see him. And that you must do soon, of course.'

He straightened and followed the faint footmarks back across the dungeon to the tables with their ghastly burden.

'For a particular purpose?' asked Thomas with that Poley-cunning of phrasing that would allow him to claim that he had already fathomed out anything that Tom disclosed to him.

'To search the Bridge. This is where the Crowner's quest must start and, likely, end.'

'Search for what?' asked Francis Bacon quietly. 'We have the heads and one body plucked from the river. It is likely, therefore, that the second body is in the same place and Master Danby is calling for the banks to be searched in consequence. What remains here that must be found out?'

'The second room. Or the first, if we order them in time.'

'The room? What room?' Again it was Bacon who asked. Thomas frowned, his eyes moving from one man to the other, his mind obviously racing also.

'The other murder room,' answered Tom quietly. 'Some-where on the Bridge there is another room filled with flies and blood. Where the first murder was done. Where the first head was taken.'

Thomas Walsingham opened his mouth to frame some reply to this; but the words he was preparing were never spoken. In stead Scadbury's chamberlain appeared by the cellar door.

'The ladies are returned, sir. They crave your immediate presence – and that of Master Musgrave.'

They had brought great armfuls of vegetables, sackfuls of bread and flour, sides of meat and gallons of ale and wine. They had brought provisions for an army for a month in food and drink and dress and ease; and they had brought Will Shakespeare, who carried the better part of a bushel of paper and the expression of an exhausted but victorious man. Will had not come alone: he had with him a tall, secretive-looking friend some forty years of age.

'This is Anthony Munday,' he said to Tom as the introductions were made. 'He's at work with me on the play of *Thomas More*.'

It struck Tom immediately that he was the only one in the room who had not already made the acquaintance of Master Munday and he began at once to rack his brain, for the only thing that bound all of these people together was the secret world of Robert Poley. Time for speculation was short, however. Will and Munday were big with more than waste paper.

'We began with one hundred and sixty-five letters,' Will began, spreading the paper across the table at which Tom and the others had supped last night. This time, in spite of the heat, Thomas signalled his chamberlain to close the windows, for the breeze threatened to disturb the sheets and the lecture; and, though no one was churlish enough to say so, it was speed they wanted here, not erudition.

'One hundred and sixty-five letters. Forty-nine of them the letter "b" and one hundred and sixteen of them the letter "a". My first question, therefore: what was the significance of having near fifty "b"s? A false trail, as it proved, but a good starting place.'

'The next step was more productive,' said Munday, 'and it was mine. How many "a"s and "b"s to a letter?'

'Three or five,' said Bacon.

'Five,' said Tom. 'Three's too few.'

'Well well,' said Will tartly. 'Clearly we should have left all the work to your wise heads and saved ourselves a deal of worry and lost sleep.'

'And a deal of play-acting to poor Dick Burbage,' added Munday, lightening the mood. He put on Burbage's booming voice: '*Why Will, what is the point of this code?*'

He became Will to the life: '*Why, Master Burbage, sweet Diccon, dost not know Sir Thomas wrote to his sweet daughter in the most cunningest of codes? Let me transliterate: "AAAAA" is, "My sweetest Meg, how dost thou?"*'

'"Aaaaa",' said Will severely, 'we first essayed as "A".'

'A logical place to start,' agreed Tom.

'And a fortunate,' added Munday smoothly. 'For it allowed us to try for a pattern and so work our way towards the truth.'

'If "aaaaa" represents "A", then what is "B"?' asked Will. The question was rhetorical, but Bacon was an MP, unused to holding his peace.

'"B" would be "baaaa",' he suggested at once.

'A fine, logical suggestion, Master Bacon. And so we thought at first,' said Munday to cover Will's growing exasperation. 'And our thinking then suggested "C" would be "abaaa", "D" would be "aabaa", and so forth.'

'Thus your first four letters look like "F, B, P, X", or some such,' observed Tom.

'Or some such,' agreed Will, and his tone told Tom he was at least pleased to see the others all running down the same blind alley that he and Munday had already explored. But there was still a gathering sense of tension in the room as the temperature soared and they all began to sweat over the matter in earnest.

'But that was clearly wrong,' said Tom, placatingly, 'and we waste both your time and your good nature, Will. You are the Master of Cyphers, old friend. Tell us what you have done and let us marvel, then.'

'Grammercy. Well then, let us return to our home port and set sail with a different compass. What if the progression is reversed so that "aaaaa" remains "A" but "B" is "aaaab"? That would make "C" read as "aaaba" and "D" as "aaabb".'

Digging amongst the papers as they gathered round, increasingly entranced by his mellifluous actor's voice and his fierce logician's intelligence, Will pulled out a handwritten list showing how the letters would be arranged according to the pattern he had just described. 'And here indeed is our America, our new-found land. For the code works without our further testing it. We have no need of searching for what might represent such common letters as "E" or "S". Once we had the map, we were like Drake, like Hawkins on the main. No galleon of code could stand against us. Thus the letters reduce to thirty-three. And they are these:

brutecassc
ascmetttre
bcinncalid
ebr

'What does the Master of Logic make of this? We have broken the code and discovered you a new country of meaning. But can you speak the language, Tom?'

Tom looked down at the list of letters Will spread out upon the table. Then he glanced up at his old friend, suspecting some play-acting here – a kind of drama. There was a sharp sense of frustration that all the lecturing and sweating should have brought them merely to this impasse. 'Do you know the answer, Will? Have you broken this second riddle?'

' 'Tis all Greek to me, Tom,' answered Will shortly.

'And to you, Master Munday?'

'I have my suspicion in the matter and Will here knows my mind. But we test my theory in the simplest way . . .'

'By seeing if a like mind can discover a like answer,' said Tom, letting his eyes fall again.

'I see "brute",' said Kate. 'What is this brute? A warning of some violence?'

Thomas looked worried at that. 'A warning to do with the headsman and the heads?' he ventured.

Audrey said, 'The second line says: "a, s, c, m, e"; could that say: "Ask me"? Is that possible?'

'If so,' said Bacon, adding his thoughts to hers, 'we are bid to ask about three trees are we not? What trees are these? Tyburn trees, where traitors are taken to be hanged?'

'And beheaded,' said Audrey, still thinking of the heads in the cellarage.

'And the third line,' added Kate with a shudder. 'What can be this "b, c, i, n, n"? Is it asking us to be sinful?'

'You need no special bidding to that, madam,' said Kate's elder sister tartly.

'Seek not the mote in my eye, sister dear,' Kate quoted, biblically but bitterly, 'till thou hast married the beam in thine own.'

This exchange offended or upset almost everyone in the room, and the simmering tension was just threatening to explode when Tom spoke.

'*Eureka*. I have it. 'Tis a list – a list of names. Each is made of four letters except the first. But if you begin at the end, the pattern emerges. Thus: DEBR, CALI, CINN, TREB, METT, CASC, CASS, BRUTE.'

He looked across at Munday, who nodded grimly, as did Will at his side; then over at Bacon and up at Thomas Walsingham.

'What names?' demanded Kate. 'What list?'

'Brutus, Cassius, Casca, Metellus Cimber, Trebonius, Cinna, Caius Ligarius, and Decius Brutus,' he answered her. 'The men who murdered Julius Caesar on the ides of March more than a thousand years since.'

'So your secret message tells us,' said Kate, 'that there is a conspiracy of at least eight people, all plotting some kind of attack sometime soon.'

'I would have thought before March,' said Bacon, 'unless this is a slow-growing, deep-laid plot indeed.'

'And before any ides,' said Tom forcefully. 'That would be near a month in any case. We are just past the ides of June. The ides of July are on the fifteenth. Logic dictates that the crisis must be nearer, for there was much urgency and great risk in getting this message to Master Poley.'

'And yet,' said Thomas Walsingham, leaning forward, 'there can be little doubt that Master Shakespeare and Master Munday have cracked this code like an egg; nor that Tom has expounded their findings correctly to us. Therefore we stand as well warned as Robert Poley. There is a plot afoot that may be dangerous or even fatal. And three main questions must immediately arise from this. Firstly, who are these people really, for they cannot be the ghosts of famous citizens risen from tombs as ancient as the foundations of this bridge?'

'And secondly,' added Bacon coolly, 'when is their ides of March, that date on which they must take their dreadful action?'

'But most importantly of all,' said Tom quietly, 'who is their Julius Caesar that must die for the good of Rome?'

CHAPTER SIXTEEN

At Hazard

T om strode out of Nonesuch with his fastest, most purpo-
seful tread. In the breast of his doublet he carried Poley's
code, Will's translation and his own list. He had a clear mission:
to find the one man that might have the answers to the three
questions just posed – and to get those answers. Or, he thought
practically, pushing into the throng on the Bridge, if not the
answers, at least an assurance that they would never overlap
with the quest that Thomas Walsingham and he were under-
taking in the matter of the heads.

He had no sense at all of being at risk, no idea how close
he was to sharing the murderous fate of the man at whom
the actual conspiracy figured in the list had been aimed. For
once the Master of Logic's eyes were turned inward. Tom
pushed northwards through the crowds on the bridge, seeing
and hearing nothing more than he needed to hasten his
progress.

It was nearing four, according to the sundials on Nonesuch.
The others had gone long since – Will and Munday to their
afternoon performance up at Burbage's Theatre, Bacon to his
offices, Audrey and Kate to make friends with each other again
in the fashionable goldsmiths' shops near Cheapside markets
and Thomas Walsingham about his quest. Tom himself had
stayed merely to go through Will's calculations and his own

extension of them once again, and then had sallied forth, full of his mission, after the one man that might answer it.

Of course, Tom had no real idea where Robert Poley might be found of an afternoon in midsummer. He knew little of the man's haunts. He knew Poley lived in Hog Lane, that he was sometimes to be found in the gilded reception rooms of White Hall Palace and that he often visited the filthiest depths of London's fourteen prisons – as well as its innumerable taverns and ordinaries between these two extremes – forever seeking information for those powers at Court to whom he owed his dangerous and variable allegiance. Therefore, on this particular afternoon, Tom had no idea at all where betwixt White Hall Palace and White Lion Gaol Robert Poley might be.

But he knew a man who did.

At four o'clock on any afternoon the curate of St Magnus' would be about evensong, and as the hour approached the evening, so the man would approach the church, if he were not already within it. Tom hurried out into the square, therefore, with his attention firmly fixed on the distant church. Out of the tunnel under the Chapel of St Thomas's, into the brightness of the last uncovered full-width section he strode, and the last thing he clearly remembered was looking up at the lovely frontage of the next fully built section. Again it stood five storeys high, joined from the third, but with overhanging turrets topped with flags and weathervanes. It dazzled Tom, both his mind with its beauty and his eyes with its west-facing windows. He hesitated for an instant, shaking his head and blinking.

And that was the moment they hit him.

They tore themselves out of the crowd and attacked from two sides at once. No warning. No threats. No conversation at all. The first one went for his right arm with a club. The rough wood connected well enough, but the crush around them shortened his swing and the blow bruised its target instead of breaking its bones.

Jarred breathless with the force and the shock of the blow,

Tom threw himself to his left, crashing bodily into the second assailant and creating enough room to pull his sword free. The first assailant knew his business, however. He too used the space to widen his swing, doubling its power. This time when it connected with Tom's elbow, the sword master felt his right arm go numb. His newly liberated sword-point dropped as he lost the use of his right hand almost completely. Knowing that it would be death to hesitate, however, he gritted his teeth and forced his shocked body to continue its violent action.

Spinning to shield his damaged arm with his back and ribs while searching narrow-eyed for his second assailant, Tom just managed to swap the drooping rapier into his left hand. The club came into his ribs, sending him staggering forward, his mouth suddenly full of blood. The second assailant was there, a thickset, brutish man with a club in one hand and a long dagger in the other. He was watching Tom's apparent demolition with a grin, utterly unaware that the master was as dextrous with his left hand as with his right. Tom disabused him and near disembowelled him at once with a thrust that would have gladdened Capo Ferro's warlike heart.

The first man's club struck again instantly, higher this time, aimed for the back of the skull with deadly force, but glancing off Tom's crown because he had angled his body and dropped his head for the first thrust. There was enough force in the glancing impact, however, to make him see stars and to blow the blood out of his mouth; and to bring a great deep thundering into his ears.

Disregarding the second opponent, who was falling slowly to his knees, Tom whirled, seeing the club coming in for his head again, and threw himself forward once more. The long Solingen blade of his rapier skewered the bully's inner thigh, down by his knee, as Tom nearly measured his length and slammed one knee into the dust of the roadway. He grunted with pain as he felt his damaged arm automatically try to take some of the weight. Then he was up once more, spitting blood, red eyes raking the scattering crowd for more assailants. There were none immediately obvious.

All too aware of his right arm flapping uselessly at his side, Tom whirled on the second attacker, who was kneeling, shocked, in the gutter, trying to hold a nasty gash in his belly closed. His dagger and club lay in the dust between his knees. 'Who set you on to this?' rasped Tom.

The man looked up, his face white with shock. His mouth worked wordlessly, as though he were transmuted into a fish. His eyes glinted, glancing past Tom's shoulder in mute answer to his question.

Tom whirled back to see the other man making off as best he could, leaving a bright-red trail behind him as he hopped wildly towards the dissipating crowd.

Tom's sword whipped back towards the codfish which was all that was left to him. The razor point came to rest immediately above the upper lip in the little valley just below his nose. 'Who?' he snarled, his voice and aspect given extra force by the sudden onset of the most excruciating pain from his damaged arm. His hand trembled. The point of his sword grated on his assailant's teeth. 'Cully,' gasped the codfish. 'It was Cully!' And he gestured towards his fleeing confederate, careful to keep hold of his belly and to keep his near-spitted head from moving.

Without another thought, Tom went after Master Cully, the organizer of the attack. As is ever the case, the fleeing Cully seemed surrounded by some poisonous miasma, as though he carried the plague, and the crowds melted away before him. The eastern side of the square lay open as far as the palings except for one or two individuals braver, more inquisitive, slower or stupider than the rest; and there amongst them, a familiar black-clad figure with a Puritan hat and a pewter nose. No time for that little conversation now, thought Tom; and then it occurred to him that perhaps it was Hazard who had hired friend Cully after all.

That thought was the last Tom had before he hit his quarry. Had Cully not been half-crippled and clearly terrified of doing himself even more damage, the would-be murderer would easily have got clean away; but as it was, Tom caught him before he reached the safety of the next tunnel beside where Hazard stood. Tom did not call or threaten; he simply continued his wild charge, taking the hopping assailant and running him with all his might straight into the wooden wall. The two bodies hit the flimsy fence like the bomb from a mortar. Such was the creaking and cracking of the impact that Tom thought he must have broken every bone in Cully's body – and a good few more in his own, to boot.

It was only when they rolled together along the paling wall that Tom realized what he had done. It was not bones that were breaking, but battens. The wood was falling away. All that stood between Cully and a long drop into the wild water of the falling tide was a flimsy, waist-high rail. Cully himself saw this as well as Tom and threw himself forward. Tom fell back with the weight of the big assailant threatening to overwhelm him. His right hand was useless. His left still held the priceless sword he was loth to cast away, even to protect his life. There was no way he could sheathe it at his left side with his left hand. He stepped back again, seeking space to fall into the rudest *garde*, but Cully was no fool and crowded in towards him. So they staggered back two steps from the rail and then Cully returned Tom's compliment by throwing his arms around the sword master and trying to bear him down.

Tom smashed his assailant on the shoulders and head with the pommel of his sword and drove back fiercely. Cully's grip broke and once again the pair went staggering back against the creaking rail; but the would-be assassin remained quick-thinking. Face to face he grappled Tom again, filling Tom's face with the stench of rotting teeth and recent onion even as Tom filled his with a spray of blood. Round they swung as though at some clumsy, rustic dance until it was Tom's turn to feel the unsteady little rail across the small of his back.

The first shot came then – or rather, the first bullet, for Tom never heard the shot. Tom never doubted that it was aimed at him, but the wildness of the wrestling threw the marksman off target. The bullet took Cully in the neck, exploding through to howl past Tom's ear. The force of the impact spun Cully round again, but it was clear that his body was no longer moving under its own control. The heavy bullet had damaged the big man's neck and he spun into some kind of spasm or seizure, seeming to hurl himself with all his force down on to the roadway at Tom's feet. Instinctively, Tom reached for him, but the battered right arm was too slow. Cully fell twisting, his back arching and his heels drumming.

Tom straightened, looking for his new assailant – straightened and shouted with shock. Nicholas Hazard slammed against him, charging in like Cully had done. The curate's hat was long gone. His bald pate glinted in the evening sun – ridiculously, thought Tom – seeming to drive into his face. His arms wrapped round the curate willy-nilly. His left arm, hand still trapped within the basket of his rapier's hilt, felt the strange solidity of the man. His nose twitched with an odour worse than teeth and onions. He saw, distantly, that the twine holding the pewter nose was knotted tightly in a fold behind Hazard's neck – and that even that fold was marked with the craters of smallpox.

He raised his sword to strike at his new, utterly unexpected assailant; but as he did so, the second shot rang out. This time he heard it clearly and looked instinctively across the square to the gape of the tunnel under St Thomas's Chapel. Even as he registered the slim outline of a stylish, modern pistol and a puff of smoke issuing from the otherwise featureless arch, so Hazard seemed to slam against him with renewed force. The curate's shoulder seemed to explode, throwing a great gout of blood up into his face as he was driven backwards with much more than human force.

The rail behind him shattered. He felt it go and threw himself sideways to his right. Down he rattled, feeling the cross-piece and uprights battering against his head and shoulders; and away over the top of him lurched Nicholas Hazard, curate of St Magnus'.

Tom's shoulders hit the roadway and he rolled with the speed of a striking snake, bidding his right arm to catch the falling man. But the right arm was too badly damaged to obey. Instead, Tom found himself rolling up on his left side, rapier trapped dangerously beneath his body, looking down into Hazard's face as the curate hung briefly from an out-thrusting beam. The curate's mouth opened, revealing black stumps of teeth, then blood boiled out of it to flood the fine, filigreed silver of his beard. Tom reached over, using his arm as though it had been a length of wood. But he was too late. Hazard's grip on the beam broke before Tom could reach him and he fell into the boiling torrent of the water below.

Tom rolled back instantly, rolling right over and pulling his sword out from under his body, coiling himself to come erect again and go for the gun in the archway by St Thomas's. But a stout pair of legs prevented him and, as though in a dream, he looked up to see one of the constables of the City Watch who had accompanied Master Curberry to the gateway that morning.

'Curate Hazard's dead,' he said distinctly, and pitched forward on to his face in the dust beside the writhing Cully.

CHAPTER SEVENTEEN

Doubting Thomas

'Gently. Ah! Gently.' Tom lay spread upon Kate's great bed in Nonesuch while she ministered unto him in the matter of his toilet. As ever with things concerning Mistress Kate, this was a process by no means bereft of hazard. A lesser man than Tom might have surrendered in all sorts of ways long since. But, true as his Solingen steel, and near as stiff, he held on to the last.

It was the early afternoon of the fourth day after the assault and Tom was still a creature of almost Ethiopian darkness above the waist – and as supple as an ebony statue. Dr Theodore had been treating him for three days now, and that was a blessed relief. All the way back along the Bridge in the mourning procession that had carried his apparently dying body, his only word, whispered with mad insistence had been, 'Not Viner! Never call Viner!'

The good Dr Theodore had prescribed an infusion of belladonna for the pain and an application of leeches to ease the fiery humours clearly burning him almost African black before being whisked away by Thomas Walsingham about some other, deep-laid plan.

Ugo, meanwhile, an occasional visitor, had nevertheless taken over the lessons in the Art and Science of Defence up at Blackfriars, passing out sad word of his friend's failing condition amongst the disappointed clientele. He had also asked Will to visit the wardens of Tom's church to explain why he was missing services a'Sunday – and like to miss more. At least in this way Tom escaped public naming and the threat of a whipping for illegal non-attendance; but both at the school and in the parish, there was much dark speculation. South of the river, too, as Talbot's watchmen searched Southwark for the wounded bully and the secret assassin who had both run southward, word began to spread that this was no longer a matter of assault – but of murder.

So it was that, as the searches continued along the riverbanks for yet another body – that of Curate Hazard – so word began to filter through that Tom himself had succumbed to the bullets and the beatings.

This, Thomas Walsingham had explained intensely – seated on the edge of the bed last evening after Dr Theodore had gone, bearing his leeches with him – was no bad thing. For the warning that had brought the entire Walsingham household up from Scadbury was clearly well founded. There was an assassin out there whose aim – both literally and figuratively – was Tom's life. If he thought his murderous job well done, then that life might be expected to remain safe – for the time being at least.

In reality the apparently dead Tom lay throughout those first three days, bruised, drugged and leech-covered in the great bed in Nonesuch; and it was Mistress Kate who found the stubborn spark of life within him, and all manner of ways to fan it. Which was indeed no bad thing, as chance would have it. For, the distractions of his hot-blooded nurse aside, the unnatural and unaccustomed inactivity gave Tom a chance to think; and what else should he think about but the deep and deadly events at whose dark heart he had found himself – seemingly by the merest of chances?

Tom was that unusual type of spirit whose merest thoughts engender actions, and if his own body, for the time being – and as part of a deeper stratagem – could not be up and about, nevertheless there were hale limbs and hearty souls enough to do his bidding. Thus it was that, in the continued absence of a name and a corpse belonging to the first head, Mistress Kate was despatched to St Paul's churchyard, from whence she brought a draughtsman's apprentice employed by Richard Field the publisher. The reserved but steady youngster was led down into the dungeons below Nonesuch and left there with his pens and his papers – and the nameless head. Two days later, even as Kate was washing Tom to the uttermost point of ecstasy, posters adorned with a likeness of the dead face were being pulled from the bed of Master Field's press – vacated of the quarto proof of Will's new play of *Romeo* for the task. Tomorrow they were destined to adorn every wall and public noticeboard between St Magnus' and St Saviour's along all the length of the bustling Bridge. And this was but the beginning.

Never one to leave a keen tool unused – be it never so battered – Thomas checked each step of his quest against Tom's dagger-sharp acuity. And Tom in recompense received information – information, in truth, that he found more invigorating even than Kate's ministrations. Dark men in the darkness had secretly visited the woollen draper's, removing from thence everything Thomas might use as clue or proof. Keen eyes remained on the place, secretly set. They had reported nothing so far, other than a sad miscalculation by the silversmith's unfortunate apprentice. The boy had been sought after all. And found. And returned to his garret with well-boxed ears and well-whipped back for his pains.

Tom, made brutally pragmatic by his own recent experiences, perhaps, was secretly glad of the fact. He had now in place a pair of eyes likely to be worth a round dozen of Thomas's secret agents, as well as a tongue whose story he had not yet heard told to the very end.

It was at this point in his thoughts that Kate put her tongue where her wash-cloth had so recently been and broke his concentration entirely by tickling his chest. 'This little heart

111

is lucky still to be hopping,' she observed, and not for the first time.

'Tush,' he croaked manfully. 'The merest scratch. The leeches did me more harm. I lost more blood to them, for certain.'

'Hum,' she said.

Before their conversation could proceed any further or deeper, it was interrupted. Thomas Walsingham tapped on the door and entered. 'Poley's men have found a body hard by Baynard's Castle,' he said without preamble. 'They say it is Curate Hazard.' He crossed to the west-facing window and stood framed, his face masked by shadow.

'He's not so hard to identify,' observed Tom, adjusting the pile of bedding athwart his loins. 'No hair, no ears, no nose . . .'

'No teeth to speak of, come to that,' agreed Thomas. 'But it looks, so I am told, as though he was swept upriver through one of the Dutch pump wheels that stand in the last arches hard against the north shore as the mill wheels stand hard against the Southwark side. The head may not be so well preserved as to feature heavily in the matters of hair or ears or noses . . .'

'Or teeth,' concluded Tom. 'I understand.' Then he proceeded without even pausing to take breath. 'Poley's men? You did say *Poley*'s men?'

Thomas shifted a little from foot to foot, as though he was embarrassed to have been caught in a thoughtless indiscretion. His shadow danced across the bedding. His teeth gleamed as he licked his lips. 'Poley offered. Hazard was one of his own, after all.'

'And any one of Poley's men,' purred Tom, 'is like to be worth ten of Curberry's City watchmen – in all but honesty.'

'They answer to their master,' snapped Thomas.

'True enough,' agreed Tom. 'But who does their master answer to?'

'In this matter he answers to me!' grated Thomas Walsingham, his voice hoarse and dangerous.

'So he does, Thomas. So he does,' soothed Tom. He was silent for a heartbeat. Then he opened his mouth to add a thought . . .

'Then Curate Hazard is dead and there's an end,' observed Kate.

And Tom thought better of his afterthought. 'Indeed,' he acquiesced, 'and there's an end. The only question remaining seems to be, was he trying to keep me safe or kill me for certain when he died?'

'Shot by his own confederate?' asked Kate, with whom Tom had discussed these events at some length. 'Or martyred in the cause of humanity?'

'Stranger things have been known,' said Thomas, turning in from the window against which he had been framed since his entrance.

'Stranger than which?' teased Kate, dangerously, given her host's mood.

'Than either,' he rebuked.

'Or both,' supplied Tom obscurely. 'Have we at least secured Master Cully, whose capture was all but accomplished before the curate's divine intervention?'

Thomas Walsingham had the grace to blush. 'We had,' he admitted. 'Or rather, the City Watch had him.'

'And he is 'scaped? Must we now search Damnation Alley for him?'

'He is gone well beyond that. Beyond the alley, at least, if not beyond damnation.'

'How?' asked Tom, already fearing the answer.

'He was sore wounded, as you are bound to know . . .'

'Indeed . . .'

'So they carried him to the nearest hospital . . .'

'St Thomas's, by my calculation . . .'

'And summoned the nearest doctor . . .'

'Doctor Viner,' calculated Tom; and at Thomas's nod he continued, 'They might as well have called the Devil from the old plays to carry him straight to hell. Well, Cully's cured of the pox then, for all the rest of eternity. Mind – ' he stretched warily – 'if they have the plague in hell, he's maybe in trouble . . .'

'So,' continued Kate with a shudder, 'we are no nearer our mysterious assassin, or the man who hired him.'

'Nor the reason he was hired in the first place,' added Thomas.

'Logic,' said Tom dreamily, 'would seem to suggest that, as no one was ready to kill me last week, it is a matter I have become involved in since that has caused circumstances to come to such a pass.'

'Well?' said Kate, intrigued.

'Then it is the matter either of the message or of the heads.'

'I see that,' purred Thomas, also baited.

'But the matter of the message already involves Poley and his people. And if Poley wished me dead, then this, it seems to me, would be the last way he would go about it.'

'Why do you think that?' demanded Kate.

'Because I am still alive,' said Tom darkly. 'Therefore it is the matter of the heads. And in that matter I hold some knowledge or pose some threat beyond those held and posed by Thomas here or Talbot Law, for neither of you has been attacked.'

'True,' said Thomas. 'But a chilling thought. I am like to start seeing an assassin with a pistol or a bully with a club in every alley for a while.'

'But there were two bullies,' said Tom. 'No news of the other?'

'Vanished,' admitted Thomas. 'Not even Talbot Law can lay hands on him.'

'Ask Poley, then,' suggested Tom. 'If there is anything like truth to be got from him in this, then he will at least close off one alley in our maze. For as Hazard was his man, if Hazard was confederate with the murder attempt, then Poley would know the two bullies with the clubs and daggers also – and perhaps the third man with the pistol.'

'If and if . . .' agreed Thomas.

'And *if* . . .' added Kate, bringing them round in a little circle, 'if he was minded to tell us the truth.'

'Have we nothing with which we might buy the truth from

him?' asked Thomas, as though this was a new and unconsidered thought.

'Certainly,' said Tom, easily. 'We have his secret message: his
list of names; and that might be worth the offering, for it could
further our other matters – of the heads and the assassins.
Especially if those two matters are, in fact, one matter.'

'The men who murdered Caesar!' said Thomas. 'The code
that Will and Anthony Munday laid open for us when Master
Bacon was here. But what good can such a thing do us when we
have no knowledge of its meaning?'

'Especially,' added Kate darkly, 'as Munday and Bacon –
aye, and Will, for all I know – will have been swift to tell Master
Poley of what we know.'

'A little,' countered Tom. 'For we have some knowledge that
none of the others knows that we possess.'

'And what,' said Thomas Walsingham, 'is that?'

'They know we have the names of Brutus, Cassius and Casca
and the rest – though it is we have not yet unmasked their true
identities . . .'

'So then?' asked Thomas, frowning.

'They do not know we also hold two other cards – that finish
the hand, like gamblers at table all set to steal the pot.'

'What cards?' asked Kate, looking across at the frowning
Thomas.

'What names do we hold, Tom?' he asked.

'Why, we know both Antony and Caesar,' explained Tom
slowly. 'Antony, who is in all probability Poley's spy; and
Caesar, who is like to be the victim of the plot. If they stick
to their Plutarch – and why should they not, good Cambridge
men all, as they are?'

'Who?' demanded Kate.

'Aye,' echoed Thomas. 'Who?'

'Young Mark Antony Terrill, for one,' said Tom. 'Apprentice to Master Goldsmith Panne, late the subject of Poley's
investigations in the matter of alchemy, recently moved out of
Southwark and on to the Bridge, out of his wife's family shop

into his own good premises – aye and into some power at Goldsmiths' Hall. Recently widowed under strange circumstances and lover to Mistress Margery Midmore, whipped and branded whore turned successful woollen draper, the Catholic corpse in the cellar – father, by the way, to the daughter we discovered on top of the Great Stone Gateway, hard below the heads.'

'And the other?' demanded Kate, much struck – by his ability to string together such a sentence in his condition, if by nothing else.

'The man who is marked as Caesar?' Thomas completed her thought.

'Why, the greatest and richest of all the foreign interlopers who are the object of the dissident, dangerous threats in the first place. The man whose daughter started all this by lingering at the Gateway on Midsummer's Eve. Whose daughter was already, by the greatest of coincidences, the sweetheart of my friend and bosom companion, sharer of my rooms and secrets, Ugo Stell.

'The man, Thomas, into whose household you would still have me go, as Master of Defence – and Master of Logic, like as not.

'Meinheer Julius Van Der Leyden.'

CHAPTER EIGHTEEN

Caesar

A s though the agile mind of the Master of Logic lent the battered body of the Master of Defence a new lease of life, Tom began to mend rapidly after his exercise in the art of logical reasoning. On the other hand, his dogged determination to quit his bed and rebuild his catlike strength and sureness with all possible speed may also have been a way of escaping his all-too-active nurse. Fortunately for all concerned, however, his improvement through that afternoon and into the fifth day was generally credited to Dr Theodore and his ministrations.

The morning of the sixth day after the attack saw Tom trussed tightly in his courtly best, a Ferrara-hilted rapier at each hip, stepping carefully down from Thomas Walsingham's carriage outside the great door of Julius Van Der Leyden's residence at Bleeke House in the parish of St Olave's, Southwark. At one shoulder Thomas Walsingham descended behind him, as did Lady Kate Shelton at the other – the first to present him to the influential alien merchant and the second to stare at his riches like some country Jill come to gawp and goggle at London Town.

Or so it seemed.

Walsingham's best carriage was a good-sized vehicle, fortunately, for out behind the three of them, blushing with simple pleasure at the prospect of entering the familiar mansion and seeing at least one of its fair occupants, came Ugo. Even so, it was dwarfed by the carriage marked with the letters 𝕍𝔻𝕃 beside which it drew to a stand.

In a clatter of clogs and a chatter of welcome, the Dutch housekeeper and senior servants came out to greet the distinguished guests and escort them into the reception rooms where Meinheer the master and his family were waiting.

Tom's stiffness owed much to his lingering pain, but it suited perfectly with the courtly formality of the occasion. Van Der Leyden awaited them on a dais at the end of a long gallery, seated on a gilded armchair that was almost a throne. Wide windows framed him and over his shoulders the prospect of his rolling property fell away across green fields to the distant river and the docks where his ships sat nodding on the tide.

On Van Der Leyden's left hand sat his nodding, smiling Frau, a well-fleshed woman with pale skin powdered as white as porcelain and luxuriant curls piled in the latest courtly style, tinted fashionably red to match the Queen herself. Her dress was of the style favoured that year at court and her plump pale fingers burned with jewels. Behind her stood the two daughters of the house, like a pair of golden lilies, one in bud and the other in blossom. Both smiled and curtseyed now, their eyes everywhere.

On Van Der Leyden's right hand sat his son and heir, a likely lad of some sixteen summers, slim and tall, whom his father proudly introduced as Guillem. Guillem shared with his sisters the Dutch colouring of hair and Delft-blue eyes; and he shared with his father a look of keen intelligence every bit as sharp as Tom's rapiers – the rapiers that were the business in hand, in fact.

After the formal introductions had been completed, the women departed, taking Kate. The men fell to talking in variously accented Latin, which sat upon their tongues as easily as their native languages, for they were all educated men. Even unlaced, as it were, there remained a formality – almost a stateliness – that set Tom's subtler instincts quivering, however;

118

and it required a very conscious effort of will to set aside the Master of Logic and let the Master of Defence do the business for which they had been summoned here.

'I do not fear these scurrilous threats myself, you understand,' said Julius Van Der Leyden. 'Fear of such a common thing is far beneath such men as I. But I fear the possibility that the outcomes may threaten the comfort of my children. It was you, Master Musgrave, who stood protector to my daughter on the South Wark of the Bridge at Midsummer. The good Lord, therefore, has put you in our way. You are to us a tool of His providence, and it would seem little short of sacrilege not to make further use of your God-given talents in the further defence of our house.'

'A patrician such as yourself,' said Tom, calculatedly, his eyes glinting across to Thomas Walsingham, 'could hardly have arrived at your years or standing without a well-tutored sword arm at the very least.'

'Indeed, Master Musgrave. I fear I stand in little need of your services for myself.'

'But Meinheer, your son . . .'

'Indeed. As you observe. Meinefrau Van Der Leyden and I would rest more easily in our beds were we certain that our Guillem had the skill to stand against *the unexpected*, shall we say . . . ?'

'Meinheer Stell has no doubt supplied him with a dag or a pistol guaranteed to do precisely that,' insinuated Tom, the Master of Logic still exploring exactly what was going on here.

'Indeed. But one is forcefully minded how unreliable gunpowder can be, compared with steel. Especially when the fates dictate its instant use under great pressures of time and circumstance. But of course everything lies in the hand of the Lord.'

'Man proposes, but God disposes,' agreed Tom, only to find himself the subject of a cold and outraged look. He was quoting Thomas à Kempis, he realized; and if Julius Van Der Leyden wished to indulge in the imitation of Christ, it would never be in the way proposed by the Catholic philosopher. Of Luther, rather; or of Calvin. Or John Knox, who went to sojourn with him in Geneva while railing against the 'Monstrous Regiment'. 'However,' he continued smoothly, 'we must do whatever we can to ensure young Guillem's safety; and in the service of such an object I am entirely at your disposal, Meinheer.'

'Then to work,' said Van Der Leyden. 'To work at once.'

Even as he spoke, he led them through into the room next to this. It was another reception chamber, but down the centre of this a rough *piste* had been set and a range of sticks and swords, sharps and blunts, had been readied. Van Der Leyden swept Thomas over to another low dais. Tom loosened his jerkin and stripped it off, then unbuckled his sword belt and laid the rapiers aside. He glanced across at Guillem with a grin. 'These are for a different type of instruction,' he said.

Guillem grinned back, a shy flash of white teeth, as he unfastened his own doublet and revealed the snowy whiteness of his linen. Tom straightened slowly, stretching. 'You will have to be gentle with me and move to the slowest of beats, I fear. I have about me all the suppleness of an ancient oak.' Oakenly, he fell into the first position as Ugo began to count his beats as though leading a funeral. Guillem fell into the mood of the thing, performing the simple dance of the first exercise as though it were the stateliest pavane. Stick whispered against stick, bodies leaned and recoiled, thrust and parried. But so elegant was the performance that both Thomas and Van Der Leyden applauded the first set, and even Ugo smiled.

After the first session, the men retired to the private butts at the back of the house, looking down across the sheep-dotted home farm reaching down to the water meadows and the river, in parallel with the great herb garden close by the house. Here the ladies joined them and the air of courtly formality began to loosen as all of them displayed their varying abilities with the longbow and the crossbow. After half an hour or so, Ugo produced the wares for which he was famous. The men demonstrated their marksmanship with ball and bullet while the women made a game of shrieking at the reports of dag and pistol, and wrinkling up their noses at the saltpetre stench of powder. Then the morning ended with a glass of light blond beer for which the Dutch were becoming increasingly famous, and a restorative Dutch pipe of Dutch tobacco.

Conversation was easy now, Tom and the others accepted as friends – almost as equals – even though they came as instructors rather than guests. Conversation ranged across all the warlike activities they had enjoyed this morning. Amongst the ladies it wavered into mazes of fashion, perfumery and shopping, but inevitably, among the men, kept returning to the matters of defence. The boy had received some basic training – as what well-to-do youth of his age had not? But Tom had seen at once that there was much work to do here if the doting parents' fears were ever to be laid to rest. That, he calculated, going through the motions, would establish him as a constant visitor to Bleeke House this many and many a day; even as Thomas, for his own inscrutable reasons, had hoped.

'Van Der Leyden,' said Tom on the way back. 'Did not Maurice of Nassau, son of the assassinated William of Orange, Statholder of Zealand, the Nether Land and ruler of much else besides, study at the University of Leyden?'

'So I understand,' said Thomas, guardedly. 'Why do you ask?'

'The double coincidence struck me at once. Especially as, by the greatest of coincidences, Ugo and I had met another of the leading characters within it.'

'Double coincidence?' purred Tom.

'Met? Who have you met?' added Kate. 'Not Julius Caesar, surely.'

'That this Julius might be the target of assassination like that ancient Julius, Julius Caesar,' Tom answered Thomas, disdaining to rise to Kate for the moment at least.

'Indeed . . .'

'But that a much more modern re-enactment of the tragedy

took place ten years ago – ten years ago in two weeks' time, upon the tenth of July, when the Catholic-paid assassin and traitor Gerard shot the Protestant King and General William of Orange at Delft. Then Prince Maurice was called away from his studies at Leyden to succeed his father as Statholder of Holland and Defender of the Protestant faith in Europe; and just as Julius was succeeded by his equal – some say his better – Octavius Caesar, later named Augustus, so was William succeeded by the greatest general since Roman times, Maurice of Nassau. To whom, in company of the Earl of Leicester, Ugo, Will Shakespeare and I rendered some small service at the Battle of Nijmagen seven years since. And by whom on land, as our own Queen is doing by sea, King Philip of Spain is being whipped and racked until he will beg anyone that will listen to take up the assassin's pistol and strike and strike again.'

'You were there?' Kate asked Ugo, who nodded and kept nodding, his eyes fixed on Tom. 'At Nijmagen with Prince Maurice of Nassau and Earl Robin of Leicester?'

'Chatting to them as we are chatting now. As was another who stands tightly wrapped in the coils of this coincidence,' said Tom quietly. 'One *Robert Poley* by name.'

'Then it is no coincidence at all,' said Kate roundly.

'But what is it, then?' asked Tom; and his keen eyes were riveted to Thomas Walsingham.

'My quest,' said Thomas at last, scarcely louder than a whisper. 'Alchemists and Catholics, heads and horror. Apprentices and riots, codes and threats, coincidences and all – it is my quest to find it out.'

Tom sat back in his seat at that, apparently satisfied; but all the way back to Nonesuch, his eyes remained riveted on Thomas and his broad brow stood furrowed by a frown.

' 'Tis too dangerous, Tom,' said Kate in the thickening darkness later that evening. The slightest suggestion of it, cast in among the battles of Caesar's Civil War had been enough to bring their love-play to an abrupt halt.

She curled against him, hot as a newborn phoenix, whispering earnestly into his ear. 'Yesterday, when all the world supposed you dead, it would have been dangerous enough. Now that Van Der Leyden knows the truth it would be madness, for who knows whom he might tell?'

Tom sat silent for a moment as a cart or carriage rumbled busily through the archway beside Nonesuch. It was early – not yet ten – and the Bridge was still busy. The day had exhausted his still convalescent body and stilled his appetites – all except one, at least. 'Early to bed and early to rise,' Kate had joked, as he had refused dinner and whisked her off; but her tinkling laughter had rung as false as a counterfeit coin, and here was the reason for her worry. Tom had a plan to further his investigation in the teeth of Thomas Walsingham and Robert Poley both.

'There are things Thomas is not telling me,' he said as the sinister rumbling died away. 'Thomas and Poley know something that neither of them dares share. Let us hope it is the same secret, too. Two such secrets – each one different – held by two such men, must spell doom and danger beyond calculation.'

'Even so. The danger . . .'

'But it must all come back to the heads. What are they? What do they mean? Find out that and we'll find out the secret, I doubt not. And when we have the secret, like as not we'll have the man – with or without his axe.'

'But you cannot begin to plan it without some help. Thomas at least must help, or you stand no chance of success and little enough of surviving.'

'I do not agree. It is with the plan as it is with evil, they say. All it takes for success is for good men to do nothing.'

This is as far as Tom had got in his dark logic when Perkin the Bridge Warden's man started hammering on the door of Nonesuch House and calling for Thomas Walsingham.

And everything was suddenly standing on its head.

CHAPTER NINETEEN

Caesar's Wife

T he first thing Tom noticed about Perkin was the blood, and he knew the instant he saw it what the Warden's man had come to tell them; but he did not begin to suspect the full horror of it, nor the full impact, as yet. The next thing Tom noticed was the crowd at Perkin's shoulder, silent and shocked, looking like their leader for some help from the Queen's acting Crowner here.

Such was the urgency that Tom scarce had time to pull on doublet and hose before they were off, with Kate in little more than a shift and a smile at his side. Such eyes as were likely to be wandering over the crowd were far more likely to light upon her than the tall black-clad figure passing from shadow to shadow beside her. Without his blades, out on the edge of such a bustle, Tom was all but invisible, and content for the moment to remain so.

At the fringe of the gathering bustle, therefore, Tom followed as Thomas Walsingham was led along the Bridge. The flambards and occasional fires outside the shops, taverns and ordinaries were still alight, but many in the crowd had brought torches too and so the whole procession of them proceeded in a great golden glow down towards the Great Stone Gateway.

Tom began to work his way as best he could in secret up towards the front: he wished to be unremarkably on hand when

Thomas found himself presented with whatever Perkin was discussing so earnestly. But, as he whispered to Kate in a snatch of conversation in the depth of the last lingering shadow, secrecy was all.

Therefore, when a broad masculine hand closed upon his shoulder just as the great gateway itself was achieved, Tom jumped and flinched as though this were the axe-man himself. But no: it was Will Shakespeare.

'What's afoot?' whispered the playwright as though he had been privy to the conversation with Kate.

Tom shrugged and pointed with his chin. Then, seeing what his chin was pointing at, the pair of them pressed forward once again with Kate hard on their heels for all the world like a white-fluttering ghost.

Wedged across the narrow of the gateway itself, a big coach stood crazily, one wheel down in the sloping kennel that had carried the first head to Tom's feet more than a week since. The long shaft separating the two pairs of horses that pulled the coach had run hard against the brick of the eastern, outer, Southwark side. It was a tall carriage as well as a wide one. At each corner, reaching up over the inlaid roof that was pointing away from them down towards the Borough, stood a flambard in a bracket. Had the lights brought by the crowd failed to illuminate the proceedings, these would easily have done so, for the angle of the vehicle caused their flames to burn almost out of control, casting great leaping torrents of light and darkness down towards the Counter Gaol.

By the time Perkin and Thomas were up at the side of the wrecked carriage, Tom was in a pool of shadow between Will and Kate at his back.

'I had the driver and the footman loose the horses for the nonce,' Perkin was saying. 'They were crazed and like to add to the destruction. They bolted when it happened and would have run back home out of control had the whole thing not crashed into the gateway.'

'When what happened?' muttered Kate.

'The Warden has been summoned, of course,' Perkin was saying. 'But he is up at White Hall, and due to visit the Guild Hall into the bargain this evening.'

'A busy night,' condoled Thomas.

'The worst night possible for such a tragedy . . .'

They were up at the coach itself now and Perkin swung round. 'Keep back,' he bellowed, his voice echoing hugely under the stone arch of the gateway. Something in his voice made the mass of the crowd obey and into the moat of darkness their retreat opened up around the officials in the case Tom and his companions slipped like three dark pike. As the stench of the pitch drew away down the wind, so another stench took its place, washing over the three of them as they gathered silently, unsuspected behind Thomas.

'I have summoned you here,' Perkin was continuing, 'but would like to consider calling back Sir William Danby, if you will grant permission.'

'We'll wait for the Warden at least,' said Thomas, and the grating in the voice that uttered the courteous phrase told Tom how little the Crowner's deputy wanted the Crowner back.

'Watch your feet, sir,' warned Perkin by way of answer. He gestured at the ground and the weird light from the angled flambards showed an oozing darkness that had flowed out under the carriage door and washed back here before following the laws of God's creation and running away into the kennel and the Borough.

'I know this carriage,' breathed Tom. He gestured at the door panel where stood emblazoned in gilded lettering *VDL*.

'God's death, it is Van Der Leyden's!' hissed Kate. 'We are too late! The deed is done and Caesar has fallen!'

'What are you talking about?' demanded Will, though with the blessed good sense to use an undertone.

'Your code . . .' snapped Kate, and would have gone a good deal further had not Perkin reached across and opened the door. The Warden's assistant had muttered a warning to Thomas, no doubt, but none of the three spies heard it.

126

Kate looked eagerly across, therefore, gave a choking little gasp, opened her mouth as though to scream and fainted dead away. As she was talking to Will, he was looking down at her. It was he, therefore, and not her preoccupied lover, who caught her and lowered her on to the cobbles of the Bridge's roadway.

Tom, on the other hand, stepped forward, his gaze chained immovably to the carnage in the coach. Inside was all red velvet of so ruby a hue that it was not at first clear what was the original colour and what was blood. And the occupant wore red of the same fashionable shade, and so it was equally difficult to assess exactly where fashion ended and blood began. At about the neck, reasoned Tom grimly enough, rising like Leviathan from the depths of the shadow at Thomas's heaving shoulder.

The victim knelt in the well of the coach between the opposing benches of the seats. The corpse was angled forward in such a way as to bring to mind most vividly Poley's tales of beheadings of yore. The upper body was disposed across the opposite seat to the one it had occupied when still alive. There was a disturbing suggestion that the corpse was kneeling at prayer. Perhaps even, came the wild suggestion to Tom's reeling mind, there was a fold in the cushions against which the shoulders were so firmly thrust that might after all have accommodated the missing head.

But no. As the door of the carriage slammed back wide, so the corpse seemed to stir, sliding back to fold itself into the sloping little valley of the well, a blood-red figure in a blood-red river all flowing down into Talbot's jurisdiction. And on the shoulders there was no head. Hardly the stump of a neck. No head at all.

'Is it Caesar?' demanded Will, rising from depositing Kate in something akin to safety.'

'No,' said Tom sadly, as he recognized the porcelain-pale, jewel-encrusted fingers dead on the floor before him. 'It is Caesar's wife.'

*   *   *

They stood around the carriage as the carriage stood in the Warden's granary warehouse in the small hours. Only Tom dared climb aboard, the Master of Logic liberated from the shadows by the absolute security of the place and the utter reliability of those that stood within it. Thomas was there, recently returned, having ridden in person down to Bleeke House with the dreadful tidings. Kate was there, as though indeed a man's heart beat in her woman's breast such as the Queen said beat in hers. Will was there, his eyes as busy as Tom's but his lips silent. Perkin and his master the Warden were there. And so was Julius Van Der Leyden.

'Coming back from court, you say?' asked Tom of the latter.

'From White Hall, yes. She had been conducting business on my behalf.'

'Business that has nothing to do with the matter in hand?' Tom probed gently.

'Business known to the Warden and Crowner Walsingham here, as it is to Queen's Crowner Danby himself. If they feel it is fit you should know it, let one of them tell you. I am sworn to silence.'

'Even so,' said Tom quietly.

A little silence ensued. Even the Warden, who had almost certainly been at the same meeting as the dead woman at White Hall Palace tonight, said nothing. Even Thomas Walsingham, deputed as Crowner by Sir William Danby, whom Tom counted in the number of his friends, said nothing.

Then the Master of Logic continued: 'The coachman and the footman both sat on the box in the front, so they say. I have questioned them both at length and they have told me all they know. And I have no reason to doubt them, for this is not like to be the handiwork of either.

'The coach itself was shuttered and secured by latch though not by lock. It had returned from White Hall past Charing Cross and in through the Strand, past the Temple and over the Fleet Bridge and so through the City to the Bridge itself. Apparently the lady stopped the carriage hard by St Magnus' to make certain of the time. The hour was advancing and she was nervous of becoming trapped by the closing of the City gates at ten. But whoever she talked to there assured her that the Watch would not be out until she was well past the Great Stone Gateway.' As he talked, the Master of Logic worked through the interior of the coach as well as he could, given its semi-liquid state.

'And so, down on to the Bridge. On the Bridge, the coach moved but slowly at first, making less than a walking pace against the north-running tide of revellers city-bound from the Bridge and Southwark beyond. But nearing the mid-point, as it came into the wider reaches of the square, so it picked up speed and the coachman was able to whip the horses up into a trot, though he says he slowed again as he came under St Thomas's Chapel.'

'Why there?' demanded Van Der Leyden of a sudden, erect, his eyes narrow but burning in the pasty grey of his face.

'I know not,' said Tom easily. 'Perhaps the horses sensed something. There has been much that is untoward, in Midmore's the woollen draper's hard by there if nowhere else. The 'prentice boy at the silversmith's opposite swears the place is haunted. Perhaps the horses felt that too.

'Be that as it may, the footman swears the carriage swayed strangely as they came under the chapel. There was a knocking, one strike, such as a fist might make banging on the carriage roof. There was another, muffled sound that he cannot quite describe. The sound was repeated, but the knocking was not. Then at once a screaming, but not of a voice, nor yet of metal – an unearthly sound, rather, as of steam pulsing out from under the lid of a pot on the fire. The carriage swayed again and both he and the coachman turned to look back. It was then that the horses bolted, and they saw or sensed nothing further until the carriage crashed and they dismounted to look to the welfare of their mistress. And this blood-boltered charnel house is what they found.'

'And that is all?' whispered Van Der Leyden, looking across

at the gaudy spectacle of the coach under the flaring torchlight. At least the body of his wife was gone, to lie below with the others.

'Not all, no,' answered Tom. 'But the rest is no fit hearing for the ears of a widowed husband whose wife's blood is not yet cold. Meinheer, you might prefer . . .'

'Let me prevent you, Master Musgrave. These agonies might chill the blood of ordinary men, but that they will never touch me let me show in this: I am constant, sir – constant as the Northern Star. I will never fail or falter. Tell me what you know.'

'Very well, then. What I know is this: the man that killed your wife opened the carriage door upon the left side, here, hard by Mistress Midmore's woollen drapery and he stepped up into the carriage. He carried with him his headsman's axe and had it ready to use, so he was well cloaked, or concealed by some other means. The cloak is unlikely because it would have hampered sudden movements – and his movements were as sudden as they could be. Your wife was surprised, taken at once by the back of the head – his fingers tore loose some hairs that you may see scattered here like copper wires. He pulled her over with prodigious strength and pushed her face into the cushion of the seat opposite. See here where its velvet is marked by her tears, her nose, her teeth. He swung the axe up at once. The back of it smote once, hard upon the roof of the coach itself. He drove it down with unerring, uncanny accuracy. He must have missed his own hand by the breadth of a hair, for see the mark on the cushion here where it cut through; and here again, within the gape of the first wound in the cushion, a second blow. He had the head already. He straightened, kicked the right door open – you see the catch is shattered – and stepped down into the street, head and axe and all. Then he disappeared – vanished, as the horses, alarmed by the sound and the smell, bolted, as he must have known that they would.'

'Vanished!' whispered the widower, the Warden, Kate and Will all together.

'Whither?' demanded Thomas. 'And how?'

'I do not know,' said Tom steadily. 'But I know how I may go about to discover the truth of it. If you will help me. And if you will share with me this secret known to Crowners and to Wardens and to Dutchmen but not to your surest hope of bringing this all to an end.'

Thomas Walsingham looked at the other two. And frowned. And shrugged. And acquiesced.

'In twelve days – eleven and some hours, given the time – there will be a great procession coming across the Bridge. It will stop at St Magnus' for a blessing. It will stop at St Thomas's Chapel where the great and the good will be entertained by Meinheer Van Der Leyden on behalf of the new-formed Dutch East India Company. The Court and City – White Hall and Guild Hall – have agreed that the old chapel building may be used by Meinheer Van Der Leyden and his Company as a warehouse for tobacco and other herbs and spices. Then the procession will proceed to Bleeke House, where the entertainment will continue, as Meinheer Van Der Leyden dons his other hats as Founder of the Merchant Bank of Amsterdam, and representative, as you so acutely reasoned, of his cousin Prince Maurice of Nassau, as an act of solidarity on the anniversary of his father's assassination. As you can readily imagine, such an event has not been easily or quickly arranged. Fortunes and reputations – aye, amongst the highest in the land – are resting all upon its success.'

'But – ' said Tom, awed, 'but such a festival would only do the things you say and say the things you suggest – would only – were the Queen herself to lead it . . . Dear God, are you telling us that the Queen is soon to cross the Bridge?'

'Aye, lad, there's the thing,' said Thomas Walsingham. 'The thing I too have sworn never to reveal. But you have guessed the truth of it for yourself and now you must swear in turn. Swear all, never to reveal it.

'For the only time in all her life, so they say, the Queen herself will cross the Bridge – must cross the Bridge, come what may . . .'

131

'To give her greatest marks of favour to the men the apprentices would rise in revolt to kill, according to Poley's spy . . .' whispered Kate, her eyes wide and her face white to the lips.

'And pass beneath the blade of this mad axe-man who lops and displays red heads,' said Tom.

'Red heads!' he repeated, as though to himself; and for once his face was almost as white as that of his red-headed mistress who followed the court fashions as Frau Van Der Leyden had done, mimicking Her Majesty exactly in arsenic-powdered pallor of cheeks and red-gold colouring of hair.

CHAPTER TWENTY

Marley's Ghost

S o it was that, as June gave way to July and the third month
of 1594 got under way – cold upon the very midnight that
it did so, in fact – the lease of Mistress Margery Midmore,
woollen draper, recently deceased in mysterious circumstances,
passed to Master Apollo Marley, goldsmith.

Upon that midnight hour, a stained and battered travelling
coach was given special dispensation by the Warden himself to
deposit three travellers, their bags and baggage at the doorway
opposite the shuttered silversmith's. All was achieved with as
close to quiet as was possible, but it was a characteristic of the
Bridge that little was ever done in secret, and nothing at all in
private.

Thus the new Bridge-dwellers soon revealed themselves and
were established in the knowledge of their neighbours well
before the next midnight struck. Master Marley emerged as
a tall, clean-shaven man of middle years, lean-shanked, of
obviously Puritan aspect, attire and hairstyle. He hailed from
Carlisle and had learned his trade, and his Knox-coloured
habits, in Scotland, but was recently returned from Amsterdam, and was clearly in a goodly way of business.

Master Marley brought with him into the haunted but
exclusive little domicile beside St Thomas's Chapel a pair of
'prentice boys, whose number alone bespoke good business.

One was a plump and forward, red-headed lad, born and raised close to the City, who knew Cheapside as though he had lived there all his life. The other was a reserved young man of dazzling blond hair and mourning aspect, not much given to conversation – and that in Latin rather than impenetrably broken English. The second 'prentice hailed from Amsterdam, which explained not only his colouring and accent but also his acquaintance with one Ugo Stell, the assistant to the Master of Defence Tom Musgrave of Blackfriars, like Mistress Midmore recently deceased in mysterious circumstances.

Again the second night, after the Watch was set and the Bridge closed to all other traffic, another carriage arrived at Marley's the goldsmith's and unloaded twenty crates of various weights and sizes. The coach itself was stained with chalky mud as distinctive to the Dover Road as the markings on the crates, which revealed their origins to be Dutch.

The rest of that night was disturbed for Master Marley's neighbours by the sounds of feverish industry. It was of little surprise, therefore, that the origin of all this restlessness should present himself at the first stirring of business next morning at the door of Master Valentine Beale, the silversmith, to offer his apologies.

The silversmith's apprentice opened at his first knock and stood, frowning on the doorstep. 'Step outside with me, if you please,' demanded the goldsmith in flat northern tones. 'It will make a little profit for you.'

The boy obeyed, closing the door against the frowning gazes of the housekeeper and her girl. The goldsmith continued talking in that oddly familiar voice: 'I am sorry to see you returned from Gravesend and whipped no doubt for your pains, but I swear it is still a part of my plan to win your liberty, lad, if I can trust in your help myself.'

Kate for one had warned Tom against going straight to the silversmith's boy. Will had thought it unwise as well, but for different reasons.

'You can't trust an urchin like that,' she had said with a fierceness more to do with the loss of her hair than with her worry at Tom's plan. 'Hell's teeth, Will, must you take so much? I am to be an apprentice boy, not a monk!'

'To play the part you must look the part, my lady. Though I must admit I am more used to beautifying boys than boyifying girls. Now sit still, or the goldsmith's apprentice is like to be lacking an ear. I will have Burbage's wig-maker make good use of what you are losing. It will advantage you in years to come, believe me. Tom, remember, you are to play a part here. Take care how you step in and out of yourself or you will gull no one.'

'I understand what you are telling me, Will,' allowed Tom, scraping his razor-edged dagger across the pale, broad square of his chin. 'But the lad is sharp-eyed and likely to see through a clean shave and a Puritan cut in any case. We will have him well to friend if I can secure the key that will unlock his allegiance, which I believe I can – as we will young Mark Antony Terrill, if I can seduce him away from Master Poley's wiles.'

'As easy to seduce Faustus from Mephistopheles,' suggested Will, darkly; and it occurred to Tom that one day, when matters were more conducive, he should discuss with Will how much of Master Poley the late Christopher Marlowe, whose last known alias he was about to borrow, had put into the demon Mephistopheles when he was at public work on his greatest play, and at secret work for the man himself. Or Thomas might know, come to that – Marlowe and he had been lovers then, after all.

'Do you think that Poley will pose much of a problem?' asked Kate, more soberly.

'Who knows?' shrugged Tom. 'Who knows if he'll even rise to our bait?' Then he hissed at once as he nicked his naked jaw.

'I would never have known you,' said the silversmith's apprentice.

'You would,' said Tom. 'I cannot conceive of a disguise that is likely to be proof against you. But in any case, it is not you I am set to deceive.'

'Silversmith Beale, my master?'

'Perhaps, a little.'

'Good. Who else?' The boy's easy acceptance of the stratagem was at once a relief and – with Kate's warning still in mind – a nagging worry.

'In plain blunt truth, the man you fear the most. Which is why I have come to call on your help.'

'I fear none but my master! And Mistress Beale his wife, sometimes. When she takes the whipping stick in hand.'

'One other. One other only, from the sound of things.'

'Who, then?'

'The man who brought the flies. The faceless man.'

'The ghost!' The boy's eyes were suddenly huge, and dark as night in the pallor of his face.

'You're in the right of it, lad. I am come disguised to catch your ghost.'

'But why? Wherefore?'

And Tom, ever truthful – even when living a lie – told him.

'Even if you take the silvermith's apprentice like a bull by the horns,' Kate had said, a little mollified as she saw that Will had done well by her boyish haircut, 'you will never go and thrust yourself into the notice of Master Panne the Goldsmith himself.'

'Time is short. Of course I must. I must seek to learn his secrets, if he has any, and to contact Apprentice Terrill.'

'Poley's man will report you to Poley at once,' warned Will, who was, no doubt, speaking from personal experience. 'You cannot expect otherwise.'

'Let him do so. I wish to speak with Poley, do I not? And in this case if no other, a boy may serve two masters.'

'Three,' observed Will. 'Poley, Panne and yourself. It cannot be done.'

'No, Will,' said Tom, rinsing the soap and the blood off his face. 'When he started serving Poley he stopped serving Panne; and whatever his reason for supping with the devil, I have done him true favour in the past. It may be that the lover will be more simply thankful than the spy could ever have been. In any case, Poley will hear of Master Marley the Goldsmith as swiftly as rumour can fly. Do you not think that he too will come sniffing around like all the others? And with more reason, as Marley the Goldsmith was Kit Marlowe's last alias when he went apparently coining in Holland just before Poley was forced to murder him.'

''Tis another risk in a risky game,' warned Will dolefully.

'You will be well out of it up at the Theatre with Munday and your play of Thomas More. I was on my way to see Poley when I was attacked, remember, and I have not seen him since nor had word of him.'

'Nor I,' said Will defensively.

'Nor Thomas nor any of us,' added Kate. 'Will, must I bind my breast so tightly?'

'Then if I cannot find my man, I have found a way to make my man find me. As I have said, if Marley the Goldsmith does not bait him, nothing will.'

'You have baited a good hook, Tom,' Will acquiesced at last. 'And yes, Kate, you must bind as flat as may be. He is setting up a goldsmith's, not a bawdy house. Your curves are all too obvious where we cannot bind them; let us tie down whatever we can.'

Valentine Beale, Silversmith, was a pompous little man who seemed blissfully unaware of his overbearing, shrewish wife. The pair of them extended a vaguely patronizing welcome to Master Apollo Marley, Goldsmith, on behalf of the better sort of guildsmen on the Bridge.

'But of course we need no more goldsmiths on the Bridge, you know,' said Beale. 'We are well enough served in the matter by my friend and associate Master Panne.'

137

'The fame of Master Panne has not, alas, quite reached Amsterdam as yet,' said Marley in his quiet way. 'Is this a man of standing and probity to whom I should present myself and my letters?'

'Indeed he is. A master of his trade, honoured at the Goldsmiths' Hall and Warden of our Church of St Magnus. He is a man that must claim your immediate attention upon every front, young sir.'

'Except in the matters of raising daughters and keeping wives,' added Mistress Beale.

'Indeed, my dear. Have you decided to which parish you will add your name? St Olave's to the south or St Magnus' to the north?'

'Among the guildsmen or the whores,' said the forthright Mrs Beale, clearly drawing but little distinction between them.

'Indeed, my dove. You might even go down to St Saviour's, I suppose. St Mary Overie as was.'

'But I observe a chapel hard by. Opposite here, in fact, and beside my own poor shop . . .'

Beale was tutting at such ignorance. ' 'Twas a Catholic church – curtailed by Good King Harry and then defaced and shuttered by Edward, the saintly boy, bless his name, along with the last of the monasteries and other Papish excrescences.'

' 'Tis empty now. Though not like to stay so for long,' added Mistress Beale. 'There's money to be had in letting out such a vast space near upon the central span. And where there's money to be made, folks is not slow to act.'

'Just so, my dove. Just so.'

Master Apollo Marley next progressed in his slow, thoughtful, Puritan way as Master and Mistress Beale had variously directed him: to the shop and smithy of that master of his craft, officer of his guild, warden of his church, father of a loose daughter, master to an apprentice spy, husband to a drowned wife and sometime lover to a decapitated Catholic ex-prostitute mistress – Ralph Panne.

If knocking upon this door did not send echoes clear through the whole of this mystery, thought Tom grimly, then nothing would.

His knock was answered by a servant girl, who showed him into the private chambers behind the still-shuttered shop, above the ringing smithy in the cellarage. Here he was entertained by the young mistress of the house, who accepted his explanation of himself and his business with ill-concealed impatience, informed him that her father was away in the City about some guild business and granted permission for a brief interview with Terrill the apprentice. Terrill was summoned, and appeared through a solid-looking portal Tom had failed to notice earlier, for it was concealed behind a curtain. Now that he thought of it, there had been another such curtain in Master Beale's parlour; and another heavy door, no doubt, securely locked behind it.

No sooner was Terrill in and the door once again secured behind him than the lady herself left the two men to their conversation. Tom took post by the window as they talked, and part-way through his discussions with the grateful apprentice he saw young Mistress Panne emerge on to the Bridge. There, a young man detached himself from the bustle and crossed to her side. They spoke and he looked up. It was, of course, the coxcomb from the gallery atop the Great Stone Gateway: the sneering, swordfighting Daniel Petty.

'I would hardly have recognized you, sir,' said Terrill as soon as she was gone.

'She did not at least,' said Tom, gesturing to the closed parlour door with his naked chin. 'Though the occasion of our meeting is one she would rather forget, so there's little wonder she has forgotten me.'

'That is not true of our first meeting, sir.'

'If you talk of St Thomas's, that was our second meeting. Our first was when you kicked your secret messenger, by which I mean your football, up on to the Great Stone Gateway.'

Terrill's eyes went narrow. 'You were there? I did not see you. Were you in disguise then too?'

'No. I was in the horse trough. Disguise had not yet become necessary to me.'

Terrill grinned and lowered his gaze as though embarrassed to be laughing at his betters. A shock of unruly hair fell forward over his face and Tom saw how effectively this particular disguise hid the acuity in those sky-blue Cambridge eyes.

'But you saw through my disguise at once, as I would expect any one of Robert Poley's men to do.'

The gaze came up again at that, with all its intelligence rekindled and a good deal of steel in it besides.

'It is not a disguise I can maintain for long without some help from you in any case. I pretend to be a goldsmith new returned from Amsterdam . . .'

'Ah. You are that, Master Marley. Of course . . .'

'But I know little enough about goldworking. In conversation with a man such as Master Panne I should betray myself for certain . . .'

'Do not be too sure. He got the business with his wife. The original smithy down in Southwark was Barton's – only Barton and Panne's after the wedding. It became known as Panne's once her father died, though the name in the old place never changed. That was when the raids began – the rumours of alchemy, necromancy and such.'

'Necromancy. Have you seen many dead bodies in the smithy, then?'

'None, sir. Nor any alchemists, come to that. But it was after the raids that Master Poley put me in place – down in Southwark at first. Then, when we moved up in the world, he did change the name of the business to Panne's, much against the mistress's wishes; and kept it so when she died. Kept it and old Jeremiah, who does the real work. I am the third apprentice and I work with Jeremiah, as have we all. Jeremiah was trained by

Master Barton the mistress's father and he learned well – which is more than Master Panne did, by all accounts. It is Jeremiah who is the business, with whatever apprentice he is training up at the time. The master takes the profit and the credit and the high seat in his Guild Hall. But we do the work down there and it doesn't really interest him.'

'Show me,' asked Tom, and Mark Antony Terrill was glad enough to do so, allowing Tom through the great oaken door and inside his guard at once, before even the question of his Judith and her fast-mending leg was raised.

The instant Tom met Jeremiah everything became clear. The man was old and frail; his eyesight and his hearing were all but gone. He communicated mostly through Terrill, who was thus able to introduce Apollo Marley lately from Amsterdam in a way that established him as a true master in the old man's mind.

Before the old man on the table lay a pile of scraps and threads – *findings* Terrill called them – an important source to the London trade, which had not supplies like Master Marley had, of ingots from Amsterdam. Findings came from anywhere and everywhere – from the gutters to the riverbank. There were men down the river – aye and out along the Bankside as far as King's Field near Lambeth Palace – who made their living from sorting through the piles of rubbish and other sundries lost or cast away. Scavengers, they were called – hard men about hard labour, for the most part. And, suggested Terrill darkly, had he not got other work to do for Master Poley, then he might himself have some tales to carry to the City Watch about his master's dealings there. Here, in support of his words, he caught up a piece that Jeremiah was working on solely by sense of touch. It was the bodice of a dress: a solid bib of green velvet laced with the thickest pattern of golden threads, half-picked free to lie like an angel's curls piled before the blind old man.

'This came in a week since, brought up from downriver, washed down to the Pool. But what of the woman that wore it?

What of her, Master Marley?' The manner in which Terrill
asked that shuddering question gave Tom a little further insight
as to why the young man was being so frank with him. Terrill
really seemed to fear there was something evil afoot here –
something that was really worrying the callow spy; something
beyond the intelligence he was gathering for Poley; something
to which, therefore, Poley would never deign to listen. Like the
silversmith's apprentice of his fearsome faceless man, Terrill
was nervous; and out of that nervousness came confidences he
would otherwise never part withal.

Then, leaving Jeremiah to his slow and painful work, the
young apprentice left his dark speculations to guide Tom
through the rudiments of the craft.

An hour or so later, Master Marley was back out on the
Bridge's main thoroughfare, his head awash with salamanders,
skittles, crucibles, furnaces and scorifiers; with findings and
sundries, placer and banket; with refining, grading, alloying,
assaying; casting, moulding and working; soldering, engraving
and chasing. It was no wonder at all to him that Master Poley
was convinced there was alchemy afoot down there. And, if his
gathering suspicions were right, a little necromancy into the
bargain.

Speaking of magic . . .

Abruptly, the Master of Logic remembered his description of
Frau Van Der Leyden's death: how the murderer had stepped
into the coach, taken her head like a boy plucking an apple, and
stepped out again; and disappeared, blood-boltered – dripping,
smoking, no doubt, in the cool night air – laden with an axe in
one hand and a head in the other.

Disappeared.

Perhaps the silversmith's boy was right: perhaps it was a
ghost after all.

Across the roadway from his own new shop, shuttered still,
but distinguished now with a bright new sign and a printed
notice promising business within the next few days, Master
Marley walked his slow, Puritan walk. His hands were clasped

behind his back, his elbows tucked in as though holding a Bible against his ribs and the eyes beneath the straw-coloured fringe and deep-black hat-brim busy about the cobbled roadway and the gaudy shop-fronts.

But there was nothing to be seen except the feet, skirt-hems and cloak-tails of passers-by – nothing to be seen, that was, until he had walked the length of this whole covered section down almost as far as Nonesuch. Then and there the housing stopped and the pavements drew back into a broad square, open to the sky, brother to the one where he had been attacked. Here, in place of houses there were wide walkways reaching back to the wooden palings that walled the drop into the river; and here, in place of a section of cobbled pathway, lay a grating a good yard square, where the gutter drained through the fabric of the Bridge itself, down into the Thames.

'So, what have you learned from your first visits to these smithies?' demanded Kate, the woman in her emerging un-settlingly from within the tight-bound and girdled apprentice boy.

'The first thing – the most important thing – that we must look to is security,' said Tom. 'Both shops have heavy, well-set doors at the back that would prove a considerable barrier to anyone with robbery in mind. These doors are locked at all times, and are hidden from casual inspection. We have, with your father's help, Guillem, set up our shop and smithy well, but the gold he has lent us to further our deception and our investigation will stand at some little risk unless . . .' He crossed to the door at the side of the parlour where they sat looking out across the balcony to the ships at anchor in the Pool and rattled the handle of the door there. 'Light and easy to break through,' he observed. 'Who but a Kentish invader would want to steal wool?' He laughed. Then his face went sober again, and thoughtful. 'And, talking of Kentish invaders, I must this afternoon make contact with the third Bridge-dweller who must be confederate to our plans. Thus from tonight everything will be laid and ready – with scant days left to find the truth and settle the matter before Her Majesty comes over the Bridge, and under the shadow of the axe.'

CHAPTER TWENTY-ONE

The Goldsmith's Assay

'**A**pollo Marley, Master Goldsmith?'
'As recognized by the Worshipful Company of Gold-smiths of Holland. Banker to the Dutch East India Company. As supported and financed by the Merchant Bank of Amsterdam, under the auspices of Julius Van Der Leyden, cousin to Prince Maurice himself.' Tom displayed the bright warrants, safe in the ornate impenetrability of the antique Dutch lettering.

Perkin grinned with impressed delight. 'The Warden did not tell me,' he said, glancing at the documents and grinning again.

'The Warden remains in politic ignorance. No one must know, other than we few. As far as the Warden is concerned, he is doing a series of trifling favours for the Court and the City – and the Crowners, of course, the Queen's and his deputy. For the root of the matter remains the three deaths on the bridge.'

'I see.' Perkin's smile faded in the face of the recent tragic events and the continued anonymity of the woman whose face stood posted on every coign between St Magnus' and St Olave's. 'Well, what does Master Goldsmith Marley require of me?'

'To begin with, a door . . .'

The conversation, which had begun in Perkin's room beside the Warden's warehouse behind St Olave's on the South Bank, continued a little later in the parlour of Master Marley's shop and smithy. Perkin himself – as was one of his duties after all – came to measure up for the replacement door and oversee even such a trifling change to the fabric of his beloved Bridge.

One look around the establishment – especially after an introduction to Master Marley's two apprentices – led the Warden's man to suggest that Master Marley should busy himself in domestic matters as well as in those of security. The place stood in need of a couple of decent servants as well as of a good stout door, he observed.

Tom was amused that Perkin should have understood so much so swiftly, even without seeing the remains of yesterday's cold meat, bread and cheese, which had coldly furnished breakfast today and still lay strewn about the chilly kitchen below.

In fact, matters were well in hand without Perkin's good offices, for the Van Der Leyden household, though stunned by the tragic death of its mistress, was still active in the comfort of its son and heir. The woodman's cart that brought the makings of the door later that afternoon perforce gave way to the arrival of Van Der Leyden's second coach. This carried with it Meinheer himself, together with yet more supplies and two solid Dutch domestics from Bleeke House. These were man and wife – though it would have been hard to tell which was which but for their dress, observed the Master of Logic, keen-eyed as ever. They spoke no English and could clearly be relied upon to serve their young master to the end of life and beyond.

They set to work at once to bring the creature comforts young Master Guillem and his eccentric English friends might require, beginning with almond cakes and *schnapps*, much favoured by their master.

Tom and Julius Van Der Leyden sat out on the balcony looking down upon the Pool with a little table between them carrying the biscuits and the glasses. Van Der Leyden sipped his drink. 'A welcome restorative,' he observed, loudly, over the sound of hammering from within. 'This is the place it happened?'

Tom did not need to exercise the Master of Logic further to guess what 'it' was. 'Very near, Meinheer.' He also took a glass and sipped. The liquor burned his throat, much as Scottish whisky had in his undergraduate days in Glasgow. 'Very near in both the cases that we know. Your wife died in her coach on the street outside. Mistress Midmore died in her little chapel upstairs.'

Van Der Leyden seemed not to hear the final sentence. 'It was a marriage of convenience, of course. She was a Hooge-weegen. In English that would be a Haywain, I believe. The name is apt, for her family are brewers and distillers and deal in grain of all sorts. She brought with her beer. And this.' He lifted the glass. 'And a fortune in golden guilders. She was her own woman. Cold. Quick-witted and hard-headed. There was duty but no love.'

'I had supposed her to be unusual, even for Dutch society. She represented you at Court?'

'That is why she went to White Hall alone on the night she died. She was her own woman. She made her own decisions. Wielded her own power. Ran her own businesses . . .'

The phrase chimed with something in Tom's mind, but he could not quite recall what it was. He sipped his *schnapps*.

His guest went on talking, not really talking to Tom at all; merely completing a thought. 'Like your own Queen, in fact. And that was an amusing coincidence, for her name also was Lisbet . . .'

Van Der Leyden lapsed into silence and Tom sat quiet also. They watched the sun declining over the busy panorama as though they shared not a trouble in all the world.

Then: 'And the boy, Guillem. You are well set to continue his education in the vital arts and guarantee his protection here?'

'Indeed. Especially now that I have your two servants to aid me in my work.'

'A happy thought, was it not? They have served him since childhood and have stood against one or two trifling dangers. Is he comfortable here?'

'With them to tend him this place will be a home from home. You wish to see where I have housed him? He has the best room in the house. I have myself secured what was the chapel.'

'And the other boy? The carrot-top?'

'The carrot-top is well served, believe me,' laughed Tom.

'But you fear no special danger here?' demanded Van Der Leyden, over the sound of the door being further strengthened.

'Not to the apprentices, no. And the door is being erected to protect your good red gold. There may be some trifling risk to my own person, but that is the price of the knowledge I seek. Remember, the only people hurt in the matter so far have been women. Two boys should be safe enough. And even if you have anything to fear from the apprentices that threaten foreigners, remember, the Bridge is secured against them at night. Even were they an invading army, they would not pass the Great Stone Gateway. Once that door is closed, we lie safer up here than you do down in Bleeke House.'

'You state a strong case; and these are the reasons I am happy for him to remain here with you. And that you continue to teach him sword-play, which he could get from you no other way, now that your school in Blackfriars is shut up.'

'As it would be, of course,' murmured Tom. 'On the occasion of my unfortunate death.'

'Indeed. And that he is safely out of Bleeke House, which is but a mournful place at the moment. Mournful – is this the correct word?'

'Full of mourning. Yes, *Meinheer*. It is the right word.'

Just as the woodman and the carpenter were succeeded by the locksmith, so at the very moment Tom was showing Julius Van Der Leyden to his carriage, another, smaller one arrived. This one bore Master Goldsmith Panne, returning Tom's visit of the morning; and he did not come alone.

Thus Master Marley retired with yet more guests to the balcony overlooking the Pool of London – and discovered that one of the great benefits of *schnapps* is that it can be swapped for water and no one else any the wiser.

'These confections are fine,' observed Panne, as he passed them to his equally solid companion Master Petty, the Haberdasher. Panne's rich tone, his vast bulk and his black teeth all testified to his expertise in the matter of confections; and so did Petty's, almost to the same extent. Having both of them seated out here made Tom fearful for the timbers of his house – indeed, for the balance of the Bridge itself.

If Panne was at all discomfited to be in the house where his late mistress had met such a grisly end, he was able to disguise that better than his simple, lip-licking greed. Yet there was a steady familiarity in the way he strolled across the little balcony to lean out over the railing and sip his *schnapps* while considering the Pool and its reaches – and none of the hesitation to be expected of such a deadweight placing itself on such an apparently flimsy balustrade above such a restless river for the first time.

The chair, however, made a strange grating creak as he returned to the side of the already seated Petty and disposed himself at ease within it as he took another little sweetmeat.

'They are Dutch. I had them from Amsterdam. And the *schnapps*?'

'Nectar. I am sorry I was from home this morning when you honoured me with a visit. The responsibilities of office weigh heavy even in the Guild.'

His eyes, thought Tom, peered over his cheeks like wolves over snowbanks: cold, grey and hungry. Petty's were scarcely better. These were men about something darker than mere civility, thought Tom.

'Your daughter the Lady Alice was kind enough to entertain me and I passed a little time with your apprentice. My own establishment is still in the process of being set up, so I will be offering for sale only the trinkets I brought over from Amsterdam to begin with. Soon I hope to have the smithy working and then I can change some of my Dutch bullion into items worthy of your attention.'

'Perhaps I can view a little of your stock. I have an eye for chattels that sell well in London. It would be a pleasure to advise you – at the outset, at least. Before we become bitter business rivals!'

'You honour me, Master Panne; and I fear you amuse yourself at my expense. Neither my stock nor my poor talents could ever prove a threat to a man of such standing as yourself. But if you would be so kind . . .'

Tom rose and called through, 'Guillem!'

The boy came quickly – far more so than Kate would have done, even in her best disguise – and Tom explained in a few words what he wanted.

Before the last sip of *schnapps* could be supped or the last biscuit crumb licked, the boy was back bearing a laden tray covered with a red velvet cloth. Tom moved the glasses and the little silver-gilt dish that had held the biscuits. The boy whispered his thanks to his master and set his burden down. Modestly, as though aware of presenting mere inferiority, Tom removed the cloth.

Panne leaned forward until every seam, lace, hook and fastening about him groaned in protest, and the joints of the chair echoed them most mournfully. 'Why this is . . . Some of this is . . .' The grey wolf eyes glanced across to Master Petty, straining at his side. And back again to Tom. '. . . quite good.'

His fat fingers sorted through the careful arrangement of jewellery, haberdashery and weaponry that Tom had called for. 'The larger items are in the workroom still,' said Tom. 'These gewgaws merely demonstrate some of what I have brought with me. That dudgeon, for instance – a fancy of mine to have it wrought thus as a griffin's leg. You see how it is set to receive the hilt and blade of the dagger? And that fastening – for a cloak, of course. It is in the fashion of a Roman seal, you will observe. All the fashion in Amsterdam . . .'

'But not so well suited for our fashions here, I fear. You agree, Master Petty? Cloak fastenings are as much your province as they are mine . . . You agree. Just so. This mark,

Master Marley. It is the Dutch hallmark they use in Amsterdam, is it?'

'Your eyes deceive you, sir, for I am sure your knowledge can never be at fault. It is the thistle of Glasgow, sir, where I learned my trade.'

The two grey wolves leaped up to look Tom coldly in the face. 'Ah,' said Master Panne. 'Even so.'

'But how are you to be supplied?' asked Petty suddenly. 'You have no guild as yet – no place to hold you and your interests safe. You have no source for findings, nothing . . .'

'I have the Bank of Amsterdam,' answered Tom. 'As you will be aware, sir, London – England, in truth – is a rich investment for the men of the Low Countries; and I am but another humble pipe through which plain gold can flow in their Amsterdam ingots – then flow back again in guilders and guineas, multiplied by my industry like the corn in the parable that gave forth tenfold. Twentyfold . . .'

Thus Apollo Marley passed the goldsmiths' simple tests; and Tom Musgrave, Master of Logic, wondered why Ralph Panne and Samuel Petty should have wanted to test their new neighbour in the first place, like a piece of gleaming trash that wanted a proper assay.

But in that he had proved good metal, he struck back immediately. Following them to his door he said, as though the thought had but come into his head at that very moment, 'But you are wardens of St Magnus', are you not?'

'Indeed we are,' said Panne.

'Then may I beg of you a favour and honour: that you introduce me to the vicar there that I may join your congregation.'

'We are not of that high Puritan stamp. No Calvinists or Knoxians we!' warned Petty; and indeed, their frames, style and costumes could hardly have been more different from the simple black and white that Master Marley favoured. But he stayed with them, right to the doorway of their carriage that pointed north, towards St Magnus'. And he lingered.

Somewhere a bell began to strike the hour of four.

'Oh very well,' said Panne. 'We are bound to church for evensong. We will take you and make such introductions as we may. But do not expect too much; ours is a church and congregation in mourning.'

'Master Hazard, the curate . . .' supplied Petty; and went on with a lengthy explanation that was utterly redundant but served to take them to the door.

What Petty's explanation had failed to make clear to Tom was that Hazard was there in the church. He was lying on a trestle table in a chapel hard by the altar itself. It was covered with a rough blanket but the feet stuck out of the end nearest the aisle. One shoe was missing and the man's great toe stuck out through a tear in his white stocking.

'He lies there awaiting burial,' said Petty as Panne went about his portion of the duties that they shared. 'The quest on him was completed yesternight soon after he was hauled from the water. There are some in the locality who have come to pray over the body. He was a well-thought-of man, for all his strange ways – well-thought-of by some, at any rate,' he added with unexpected bitterness.

Not much of an epitaph, thought Tom, for a man that had walked through the very heart of the plague itself unscathed; who had preached the word of his belief in the teeth of the Inquisition itself; who had spied for Poley and Burghley and Walsingham – Sir Francis, not Thomas – in Rheims and Rome, and in Cadiz itself over the matter of the Armada; who had suffered the full weight of their tortures and still had the strength to row in their galleys until God had sent him his deliverance, like his great inspiration John Knox.

These thoughts carried Tom across into the chapel and to the bulk of the cloaked corpse. They had laid him beneath the wall plaque bearing the names of the Curates – and there he was written up, thought Tom: 'Nicholas Hazard, 1577 – blank'. It was like a tombstone already. Thoughtlessly, remembering all too well that shoulder in his chest, the wild look in the eyes, the knotted twine in the back of his neck that held the pewter nose in place, Tom rested his hand on the bulking body's breast. There was a wealth of prayer in Tom's mind as he thought of the assassin's bullet meant for him exploding into Hazard instead; the sight of the gun in the archway succeeded by the look of the hanging man's face while Tom fought to reach down to him, his arm too slow and useless.

Dear God, he thought . . .

The sight of the black blood bubbling out over the silver beard and the silently screaming face falling away into the roiling waters below. Slowly, as though a great weight were clamping down upon his shoulders, Tom arched forward, hands clasped on the height of Hazard's shrouded breast, until his forehead rested on his fists. And he prayed for the man that had saved his life.

But as he did so, like a vision from the devil himself, the picture of the gun kept returning: a flintlock pistol with a long, silver-chased steel barrel; of Dutch manufacture, rich and rare. Rich, perhaps: rare, certainly.

There was room for the new servants downstairs and they were content to settle for the night as soon as they finished clearing away the banquet of sausages and cabbage they had prepared for supper. Guillem retired with a volume of Capo Ferro's fencing lore to the big bedroom that Mistress Midmore had used, while Tom and Kate went to the garret that had been her secret chapel. Much of the work of last night had been to turn this little room into a bedchamber – a feat that had required as much to do with lime and whitewash as it was to do with bed-frames, mattresses and linen. It was a cheerful little chamber now, if redolent of paint; and had either Tom or his mistress been minded to think on such matters as damnation, axe-men and ghosts, the simple process of liberating Kate's considerable femininity from its bandaged, boyish confines would have distracted them at once.

Tom paused in his unwrapping to make a swift calculation.

Had he time to complete their inevitable sport here before stepping out to see what might lie beneath the storm drain opposite Nonesuch? Now that he had made contact with all the men he needed to see except for Poley and the murderer himself, the next order of business had to be to follow the axe-man's escape route from Mistress Van Der Leyden's carriage; but he would need peace and quiet to do such a thing unsuspected, and must therefore await the midnight hour and the passing of the watch.

That, he calculated cheerfully – and providentially – gave him plenty of time for sport, while allowing him, he hoped, to exhaust the indefatigable Kate so that he might be sure she would not follow him tonight.

He fell to unwrapping with renewed vigour, therefore, and began to try to call to mind the battles in the Punic Wars, deserting Caesar briefly for Scipio Africanus, and Rome for Carthage.

However, as matters turned out, Hannibal only had his elephants halfway up the Alps when Guillem started scratching at the door, whispering urgently in Latin.

'What is he saying?' demanded Kate, whose ears were buried in the pillow.

'Something that sounds like *observare*. Hell's teeth!'

'What?' She started to wriggle out from under him.

'*Observatus sum*! We are being watched!' But Tom had no sooner established that fact than the urgent cry changed to *Oppugnatus sum*!

'Now what?' demanded the distracted naiad in the wreckage of the bedding, her curves being silvered by the moon as she fought to disentangle herself from toils of fabric and fumes of passion alike.

'We're being attacked!' hissed her erstwhile lover as he tore his rapier out and ran, stark naked, to the door.

'Tom!' she shrieked, and threw herself across the room with a section of sheet to wrap around his loins.

'Apollo,' he reminded her as she worked.

'Zeus,' she countered wantonly, 'and still playing the bull to my Europa.' Then she was finished.

Thus rudely kilted, he stepped out on to the crazy little landing and followed Guillem, wide-eyed, alert and armed with one of Ugo's pistols, down the shadowed stair.

CHAPTER TWENTY-TWO

Death's Door

T hey were under attack indeed; and, apparently, by pirates.
Shoulder to shoulder, Tom and Guillem stood in the
parlour door, lost in the moon-shadow and invisible to the
interlopers, watching narrow-eyed as black shapes came
swarming up on to the balcony from the river below. In the
moonlight, bright hooks glinted, dangling ropes from the
balustrade; bright daggers and cutlasses gleamed.

Even as the pair of them hesitated momentarily here, the
foremost black figure stooped and slid something into the lock
on the stout glass-paned doors. Tom's mind whirled. Better to
blast them off the balcony now – at the cost of those self-same
doors – hoping that surprise and noise would panic them into
fleeing before they realized they faced only a man and a boy? Or
better to let them in, summoning more help as they did so? Van
Der Leyden's servants suddenly seemed a very wise investment
in the continued security of all of them.

He turned to Guillem, switching into his rugged Latin: 'Fetch
the servants,' he ordered. 'And . . .' It was then he realized, for
the first time and at the worst possible moment, that there was
no Latin word for 'guns'. But a whisper of motion – and the
click of the lock yielding answered his momentary hesitation.

Tom stepped back and sideways, shielding himself in the
shadows behind the doorjamb as the first of the pirates crept in,

156

preceded by a breath of river air, which clutched like a dead hand at his chilled skin.

A whisper of conversation as a second man followed the first: 'Yer a master o' the black art, Jem.'

'A king among charms,' said the lock-picker. 'With the best set of gilks in Chapman's. Best in Romeville nah that Cully's gone.'

Tom's eyes pricked up at that and his breath caught in his throat. Suddenly it seemed a wonder that they could not hear his heart. Had he been Zeus the bull a few moments earlier, now he was a very veal calf.

'Cut benely!' spat a third, coming in on silent feet, limping painfully. Tom abruptly realized they were all wearing felt boots and black cypress. Only the whispering and the moonlight gave them away. A thoroughly professional crew, then: well prepared and knowing what they were about in every way, as at least two, perhaps three of them had been when they last attacked Tom himself.

This time, of course, they were dealing with a different kettle of fish – not the Master of Defence Tom Musgrave but the Puritan Goldsmith Apollo Marley; but like as not the same paymaster had employed them in both matters, and they had selected a completely unexpected method of attack here to-night.

Because they knew they could trust the balcony with such numbers – a fourth was heaving up behind the late Cully's limping, bitter-tongued associate – Tom could not get it out of his mind that it had been Panne this afternoon who had spied out the land for them, and tested the strength of their port of entry.

A fifth figure entered, more warily than the other four – perhaps because he had the empty balcony at his back. 'Aught stirrin'?' he whispered.

'Stow you!' hissed the third, Cully's mate, the near-gutted codfish limping still from his wounds – the leader, clearly, nevertheless, signing his own death warrant with his ill temper.

The second turned and shrugged, having also felt the weight of his leader's ill humour. The first was crouching at the new door, his skeleton keys, or gilks, busy.

Now was the time, decided Tom. While they were in the room but not yet through to the gold. On the very thought he threw himself through the doorway and across the room, two steps on feet as silent as theirs. A thing of shadow and silver – hardly human at all. He was lying on thin air, his body almost parallel to the floor, his rapier extended in the fullest thrust he could manage, its point tearing into the whirling shape of the irritable leader, when Guillem fired Ugo's pistol over his shoulder.

Tom's target jerked back and spun away screaming. Tom crashed on to the floor and rolled. The fourth and fifth men sprang back out of the light, shielding themselves with shadows. The codfish was down and screaming while the charm and his mate were crouching beside the great oak portal that barred them from the gold rooms still. Thus they allowed Tom through to the glass doors, which still stood open; and through the doors, on to the balcony.

It had been clear to Tom during his near-death shooting and beating on the square that Cully and the codfish could never be the originators nor the leaders of the attack. Thus the arrival of the third man – the shooter – had hardly been a surprise; and the lingering thought that Hazard had been a confederate of theirs had died only with the man himself.

If the codfish were the leader of the men beside the strongroom door, however, then the codfish's leader was likely close at hand; and that would likely be the shooter. Since his prayers that afternoon over Hazard's corpse in St Magnus', Tom had in mind a very clear idea what the shooter's pistol looked like. Find the weapon, he reckoned, find the man. Because in Cully's absence it was the shooter who would best be able to answer a number of questions.

His Solingen blade pressed against his chest from nave to chops and beyond, Tom rolled again, his back gathering splinters from the balcony floor and his kidney collecting a bruise from the balustrade. He looked down over the edge, gasping, as close to silent as he could come in the midst of the commotion.

The tide was surprisingly high. The big wherry secured upon its seething back immediately below the balcony was shockingly close at hand. So high did the black boat sit, in fact, that it seemed the tall figure in the stern could have leaped up on to Tom's shoulders with a single bound. Like the others, it was dressed in the dull black cloth called cypress. It was also swathed in a hooded cloak that made it impossible to hope for any kind of identification – especially as the moon suddenly turned rebel to their cause and dived behind a cloud.

A second shot rang out then, a huge bellow that bespoke the arrival of Van Der Leyden's servants armed, at the least, with one of Ugo's great Dutch *dunderbus* thunderguns. Tom had seen what these weapons could do and he knew that the remaining pirates would be out through the door behind him at any moment. He reached up with hardly any further calculation and knocked their grappling hooks free. Then, wrenching his body into convulsive movement, he reached across and grabbed the solid little table on which Guillem had displayed the all-too-tempting wares this afternoon. No sooner had his left fist closed on a table-leg than he was up on his knees, with the heavy little missile above his shoulder. So swiftly had he gone to work that the hooks were still falling when, with all of his considerable strength, he hurled it down on to the dark form so seemingly close beneath.

No sooner had Tom let the missile fly – before he even saw what effect it had on his target – than he rolled over the balustrade and tumbled into the boat below. Above him as he fell, the doors exploded out into the night, the rough ironmongery with which the second *dunderbus* was clearly loaded bringing splinters, shards and probably entrails along with it.

Tom landed well, his feet spread in the gently curving bilge of the wide-bottomed boat. The grappling hooks had all fallen behind him, pulled back by the weight of their stout, black lines. The black-swathed figure was slumped before him, struggling to rise from beneath the table. His sword was out in his right hand and if his kilt had failed to survive the adventure so far, then that was nothing to worry him now.

With all his mind focused on balance, as though the keel of the boat had been an unusual *piste*, Tom ran forward. He had, he knew, only seconds to complete his work here. Any surviving pirates would be out through the blasted windows soon. The shooter would have risen from under his crude weapon at the same time. If things were not secure down here by then, he would find himself alone aboard a vessel filled with deadly, vengeful enemies, off down the river out of all hope for help or escape.

Ruthlessly, therefore, Tom caught the shooter and pulled him erect. Down on the crown of that hooded head he drove the pommel of his sword – a solid lump of metal the size of a crab apple. As the figure slumped again, Tom caught up the long-barrelled pistol that lay on the stern thwart beside it and turned, his whole being flooding with a sense of victory. It was the weapon that had shot at him and killed Hazard, never a doubt of that. He had his assassin now and it would be a matter of very short time indeed before he began to get the information that he needed next.

Two figures erupted out of the gaping doorway above. They were cypress-clad, silent-footed and screaming invective. He did not suppose them to be either Guillem or Kate. He glanced down at his priming pan and pulled back his hammer. He took careful aim. The weapon was a joy to use, its balance so delicate, its aim so true. He must show it to Ugo. Ugo would be able to tell him more about it, he was certain. He fired. The report was unexpectedly loud, as the recoil was unexpectedly powerful. The gun jerked up, having clouded the shadowed air with a great nimbus of smoke. His deafened ears rang with the sound of a distant shriek and a great commotion in the water. The little boat heaved and spray rained, colder than the chill night air. A pair of heads, heaving like pearl-backed porpoises, swept past him in the dim moonlight, hurling away downriver in the cold grasp of the falling tide.

He turned to the cloaked figure of the assassin. Grasping it roughly, he hauled it down the heaving boat until he could catch at one of the fallen hooks. Even as Guillem came carefully out on to the balcony above, Tom had lashed the unconscious figure into one of the ropes and slung the hook upwards. Together with the solid servants, Guillem hauled the body on to the balcony while Tom slung up a second hook and pulled himself up at its side.

As the four of them dragged the cloak-clad bundle into the room, so Kate arrived with a lamp lit and her modesty intact – the fiction of her gender now at last revealed almost as starkly as Tom's. The unsteady light showed grimly what a charnel the place had become. Three men lay horribly dead before them, and much of the furniture and woodwork nearby had been reduced to scraps and slivers too. It was fortunate for the servants that the outer third of the room, like the balcony that extended it, was built out over the river, and that the boards that floored it were none-too-tightly joined at their seams. What could have been a horrific mess, thought Tom, mindful of the lake of blood one corpse had left upstairs, seemed simply to be draining directly down into the Thames.

None of them was dressed, save for the shooter, who lay bundled on what was left of the settle that had faced the doors and the balcony. Kate was the best one to send for the Watch – and, after them, for Thomas Walsingham. But she would take a while to prepare for those eyes that needed to suppose her a boy. Guillem was the next most likely messenger, save that he was also the most likely at risk. Van Der Leyden would never forgive the man who sent his son out on to the Bridge alone and defenceless so short a time after his wife had died. The servants spoke no English. It was out of the question that either of them should go, could they be made to understand and then convinced it was safe to leave the boy; and Tom himself could scarce leave the whole parcel of them with three corpses and a desperate murderer, even could he manage to get his clothes on and his disguise straight in time.

Tom's racing thoughts occupied only the briefest instant; and then, as they tended to with him, events overtook deliberation and thought was replaced by action. The figure on the settle groaned and stirred. Tom moved at once, crossing to stand beside the last of the pirates, his sword ready and his pistol cocked. Still empty, for he had had no leisure to reload it, but threateningly cocked nevertheless. The pile of cypress fustian stirred and parted. A long face was revealed, pale and resolute, dark-eyed and heavy-jawed.

Tom stepped forward, more threateningly still, heedless of his feet on the shattered glass, his face gathering into a thunderous frown. The shooter was younger than he had supposed – a callow youth to be the captain of such an ugly crew.

The dark eyes caught sight of what was left of that crew and widened. The jaw squared and the gaze swung round to Tom himself; saw the pistol cocked and ready by his left hip; followed the length of his rapier up to the steady fist at his right hip. Widened. Refocused somewhere in between. Widened further still. The figure sprang erect and the cloak fell back to gather above the rope still lashed securely round its waist. Parted to reveal exactly the sort of curves Kate was at such pains to conceal under her disguise.

'I might have known it,' called the lady from the door. 'Send Tom Musgrave out to capture a pirate Jack and he returns with a rumpscuttle Jill instead! And a pretty girl into the bargain.'

'Kate,' said Tom, tricked out of his disguise by her forthright words as much as by the pirate girl's frank gaze – just as Will had warned him he would be, if he didn't take care.

Which was exactly how matters stood when Robert Poley's men kicked the front door wide and charged into the house.

CHAPTER TWENTY-THREE

Treason and Equivocation

O f all the twenty or so prisons, counters and gaols in London, Tom liked the Bridewell least – after the Tower itself, perhaps. The old palace rambled above ground and below, damp and stinking, set as it was upon the soggy confluence of the Fleet river and the Thames. It was where the bawds and trulls were brought to be whipped in and whipped out – from where Tom had rescued Kate, stripped and secured to the whipping block itself, on the occasion of their first meeting. It was where the final hopeless half-forgotten wretches captured off the Armada six years since rotted away their last of life. It was the occasional visiting place of Topcliffe, rackmaster to the Queen and archbishop's pursuivant, whose job and joy was all to tear and torture the truth out of reluctant throats.

And it was where Robert Poley had set up shop for the latest of his secret adventures.

'A perfect place for us to do our business, young Master Marley,' he said, with ill-concealed glee, some pair of hours later. 'For your two trulls are well bedded amongst the others till the morning's whipping-in; and your Hollanders may sojourn down below with those others of the foreign stamp. We may discuss, may we not, how you have chosen to thrust yourself into my notice, and what the cost in years and tears is like to be for all of you, now that you have attracted my full attention.'

Tom sat silent, calculating. Poley's threats did not frighten him, though the little cell they occupied was hardly designed to put anyone at his ease. The walls were hung with red-rusted fetters. The runnels at the edges of the dank stone floor were filled with stagnant scum and lumps of matter that might have been brought here from the wreckage of Tom's parlour. Distantly a single voice screamed unvaryingly in some wordless, hopeless, endless agony of body or spirit; and, of course, Poley was a man of almost infinite power in places such as this. Likely as not, he had in his heavy, warm-looking cloak a warrant from the Council or the Court of Star Chamber ordering anyone anywhere in the kingdom to do his bidding. Not even Thomas Walsingham had been able to protect Kit Marlowe from the man, though they had been lovers.

But, Tom thought, Walsingham, Van Der Leyden and the Queen's Crowner, coming all together after him, would be likely to pluck him free – and, probably, all in one piece.

No. What filled Tom's racing mind was how to get Poley to tell him what he wanted to know – the information that had almost cost him his life already; had cost Nicholas Hazard his life, in fact; the need for which had prompted this whole disguise and choice of name; for which all of this was but the bait.

That had now secured Poley the ravening shark – Poley, who must be played most carefully, or he would tear them all to shreds before he revealed a thing; but Tom knew Poley as though of old. In the mere month of their acquaintance it seemed to the Master of Logic that he had learned to read Poley more deeply even than he could sometimes read himself.

The man was an equivocator. As Topcliffe loved racking, so Poley loved lying. It was what he lived for. It was the very key to his soul. Hour upon hour – day, week, month, year – Poley wandered from prison to prison, tavern to tavern, mansion to mansion, tempting traitorous, damned and helpless souls to trust him – and lying to them. There was no lie for which he could not be forgiven, because he was lying on behalf of the

Queen – lying for her Church and State; lying, in fact, for God.

He had told Babbington he loved him and Babbington had told him of the plot to free Mary Queen of Scots and restore England to Rome; and poor Babbington had loved him to the end, refusing to believe his sweet Robert was a spy, supposing that the truth the rackmasters told him was just another form of their torture.

He had told Kit Marlowe he would be safe down in Deptford, in Eleanor Bull's big welcoming house on the Strand – safe to wait there until a ship could take him away to safety, out of the Star Chamber's reach; and he had lied and murdered him instead.

Asking a question of Robert Poley was merely begging for deceit.

Create a kind of truth and hurl it straight at him, however, and you might learn from his reactions more than his tongue would ever tell. Even the most ravening of sharks, after all, might be choked with the right flesh, if one could find enough of it and force it into the gaping jaws.

Tom leaned forward, therefore, his brown eyes level and narrow beneath his square-cut Puritan fringe. The gesture was so forthright, so unexpected, that Poley flinched, then covered the weakness by leaning back.

'It was the Earl of Essex, was it not?' said Tom. 'Only Essex could have talked her into it. He is desperate for money – as always. He was setting up another of his forays against the Spaniards three weeks ago when I last crossed swords with him and he has grown a good deal poorer in prospect since that time; but if Essex can bring the Queen safely into the harbour of Van Der Leyden's bank and load her with the hope of the Dutch tobacco trade, why his fortunes would be mended. And the hated Raleigh would be served a painful turn into the bargain, for his vaunted Virginia tobacco would be bettered and bested. How much a year does Essex garner simply from his monopoly of the sweet wine trade? Add to that the monopoly on Dutch tobacco imports and the man will be a Croesus. Nay, a Midas all of gold! But only if the Queen comes across the Bridge for the tobacco and goes down to Bleeke House for the gold.'

Now it was Poley's turn to sit narrow-eyed and silent.

'But of course it would not do for your master Lord Burghley nor your puppet-master Sir Robert Cecil to see the hated Essex thus gilded,' Tom persisted ruthlessly. 'None of the senior councillors at court wishes the upstart Robert Devereux any more powerful than he is at present – when he commands the Queen's rich whim, leaving them to appeal like beggars to her lean good sense!

'At first it seemed to me that your wild apprentices and your mad axe-wielder must be the very figments of all of your imaginations – aye and the Court of Star Chamber to boot – plucked out of one of Will's wild plays and set up like goblins in the night to frighten your monarch as though she were a girl. Easy enough to arrange. A list of threats in a football magically transmuted into a wild mob of apprentices apparently set to storm at her like the men of Kent marching north with Wyatt and shaking her sister Mary forty years since – shaking Mary, but slaughtering all the foreigners along the way. How many did those lusty Kentish men behead? What count of men, women and children? One hundred? Two hundred? Will we ever know the number? And yet the good people of London dipped their kerchiefs in Wyatt's blood at Tyburn when he died, keeping the tincture as though he were a saint, as 'tis said they did of the slaughtered Caesar himself. So now these dangerous rebels are to be reborn. A kind of political necromancy, perhaps?

'And at the same time, were that not enough, the very spectre of her nightmares, the creature that took her mother Queen Ann and her cousin Mary of Scots at your and the Council's prompting but at her hand and forever on her conscience.

'Even could she stomach the threat of a riotous welcome in Southwark, with Dutchmen hacked all along her way, she would never get across the Bridge for fear of the wild headsman lopping red heads there.'

Poley was white. Even under the golden light of the hanging lamp, his cheeks looked as though they had been dusted with the white arsenic so popular amongst the fashionable at court.

'And so is My Lord of Essex's new armada of hope to be destroyed,' Tom persisted ruthlessly. 'If she comes into a riot in Southwark, he is lost. If one Dutch hair on one Dutch head is harmed, he is lost. If she will not even dare to cross the Bridge, then he is lost and lost and lost.'

'But she will come,' grated Poley at last. 'He has turned her head and fired her heart. For him she will come and there will be no stopping her. Even if she were not coming for him, she would risk so little a journey, for look at what she might gain from it herself. Does she not look for tax duties levied on good Dutch imports? Does she not hope for a good Dutch guilder or twain? For Essex and for her own good self, she will come. Prince William will be remembered and the Dutch banker will be honoured. She has said it. It will be done.'

'Why, man, it is not even the right day!' snarled Tom. 'You know as well as I that the Low Countries count their time on a different calendar from us. Prince William of Orange never died on the day she has set down for this.'

'It is to be an English gesture by an English queen. She will do it on the English date. And she *will* do it.' Poley flung himself back into his chair, desperate; defeated.

'So. In spite of all, she will come,' said Tom. 'But in the meantime, another, darker sort of alchemy has happened, has it not, Poley? An alchemy so dangerous that simply because I brushed by chance against it you have set my life at nought and sought to stamp me out like a pettish boy killing a fly!'

Poley's lips parted, the expression on his livid face clearly bespeaking a denial. But Tom had neither the time nor the inclination to listen to more equivocation.

'And what is this horror I suspect? It is this: young Mark Antony Terrill has discovered that there really is a plot afoot to bring down your Julius: Van Der Leyden himself. The coded names on his list are real, Cassius and Brutus and the rest are sharpening their daggers and the ides of March are nigh.'

Poley's eyes were like rats now, darting from shadow to shadow and Tom, scarce able to believe where his fleet mind was taking him without the looked-for laughter of derision, ran on into the dark.

'And your headsman has come to life as well. Did you really let him take a head? The first head, that of the nameless woman who came to my feet in the Southwark gutter. Were you all that mad?

'No. I see not. And thank God for it. But he really is out there, is he not? Somewhere on the Bridge, beyond your reach and out of your control and preparing himself for the day. He knows it is coming and he knows what you plan, but you do not know him.

'And you do not know . . . *Ha!* '

'What?' asked Poley, lurching with shock at Tom's final cry.

'I had almost said you do not know who he is and you do not know his plans; but of course you do know what his plans are! Have you told Her Majesty?'

Poley's eyes slid away again. His white lips folded shut. His big hands on the deal boards closed into solid fists.

'So the tables are turned,' whispered Tom. 'Now it is the Council and the Star Chamber who are afraid. Now none of you dares warn the Queen that the petty fears she waved away have grown and become too real.

'Now the threat of an apprentice riot in Southwark and the loss of Dutch lives and property will close the bank to Her Majesty as well as Essex besides. And will make it look as though her Council cannot control her realm as is their duty.

'The matter on the Bridge is no longer a matter for Queen's Crowner Danby and those same men to whom he reports, for again it smacks too strongly of civil unrest and control slipping away from hands too old to be strong and heads too ancient to be wise . . .'

'You speak black treason,' said Poley.

'Bad words in a good cause,' said Tom soberly. 'And words that need to be said. For it seems to me, Master Robert, that it is only thou and I that stand in the way of all this madness. That no one will stop it if we cannot. And where will it all end then?'

Poley flung himself across the table until his nose was all but touching Tom's. His eyes burned into Tom's eyes and the veins on his face stood out as though he was screaming fit to burst his lungs. 'I tell you where it will all end then,' he whispered with the ghost of a voice so quiet that not even the rats beneath the table could have heard it. 'It will end with the Earl of Essex on the throne of England. With the crowning of King Robert the First is where it will end.'

CHAPTER TWENTY-FOUR

The Scavenger's Daughter

T om allowed matters to come this far only because the
situation was so desperate. But should they go any further
at all, he was certain to intervene.

The girl he had snatched from the pirates' boat stood now,
still, pale and silent, clad only in an ancient shift that did little
except emphasize her vulnerability. The chamber that she
shared with him at the moment was occupied also by Poley
and a tall, spare man in a brown, stained jerkin and a black
leather hood designed to cover all his face except his hot little
eyes. It was not Rackmaster Topcliffe but one of his lesser
acolytes and clearly a man ready, willing and able to follow in
the rackmaster's ways at Master Poley's lightest order.

But Poley had asked nothing; had threatened nothing – since
the girl had been brought here, moving from exhaustion to
terror in the first instant that she looked around; then from
terror to a kind of resolution. He was simply, as the masters of
the Inquisition were said to do – and were described as having
done in the late Nicholas Hazard's account of his experiences at
their hands – explaining how the engines in the crowded little
room worked.

'This is the thumbscrew,' he was saying gently, holding the
skeletal iron device up before her steady gaze. 'We call it the
thumbscrew because the screw sits here, at the top, above the

thumb. But when it is tightened, these clamps here press on all the fingers together. It is a kind of little vice, you see? Here. Let me put it on you and I will be able to explain it more clearly . . .'

The girl, white and shaking, backed away until the hooded executioner caught her. She whimpered.

'Here,' said Tom. 'Put it on me. Then she will understand.'

'Gladly, Master Marley,' said Poley, at his most grimly jocular. 'But I fear that if we demonstrate all our engines upon you before we use them on this little bawdy basket here, the night will be unnecessarily long and painful for us all.'

'I knows how the thumbscrew works,' said the girl, suddenly.

'There!' said Poley, impressed. 'And they say we do not educate our women! Let us proceed, therefore. This is the boot . . .'

'Like the thumbscrew, only for feet. It crushes off yer toes, startin' wiv yer great toe.'

'Amazing! And this?'

'The rack!'

'And that device up there?'

'The strappado.'

'Extraordinary. And it works by . . . ?'

'Pullin' yer arms out their sockets.'

'No, my little Minerva. By pulling *your* arms out of their sockets. Time after time; every time, in fact, that I think you are hesitating in telling me everything I want to know from you.'

'Who's Minerva?' demanded the girl suddenly, clearly hoping to avert the fearful threat.

'You disappoint me, child. She is the goddess of wisdom. Your knowledge seemed to demand her name for you. But I see it has its limitations. To the matter in hand, then. Do you know what this is, Minerva?'

'Me name's Portia. No I never seen one o' them afore.'

'It is new – newly invented by the Master of the Tower himself. It's called the Scavenger's Daughter . . .'

Portia choked on a sudden, hysterical laugh.

Poley straightened, his face suddenly furious.

171

Tom, who had been leaning back against the wall, straightened. 'What is it that amuses you, Mistress Portia?'

'That's what I am! That thing and me both! Who'd ha' thought it? I'm a scavenger's daughter meself!'

'Would you like to see how your amusing namesake works?' hissed Poley. 'Would you like to *feel* how it works . . . ?'

The tiny golden bubble of hilarity that had showed for an instant on the back of the darkness flooding over them burst and vanished. The room was suddenly full of the most deadly, intractable threat.

Portia could feel it grinding down on her like a thumbscrew tightening on the whole of her body and mind; and Tom could see that Portia could feel it.

He stepped forward. 'Tell us about tonight,' he said. 'All the men you awaited in your father's boat are dead. You are the last of their confederacy except for the scavenger your father.' His eyes held hers. He could see the sadness behind the resolution there. But no great shock at his words. She had known, then. Minerva or not, she had known they were all dead. Dead or downriver. They were her father's friends, clearly; not hers.

'Your father,' he continued gently, 'who ekes out his existence, I know, not only with a little boatwork but with a little assassination on the side.' He held up the pistol that Poley had returned to him now that they were working together. Or, rather, supping with the same devils.

He saw the shock of recognition and defeat in her wide eyes at last. 'Tell us everything there is to know about all of them and the men who set them on to what they did tonight.'

'Miss out no jot or tittle,' Poley added, his voice chiming like the very bell of truth, 'or you will truly feel the scavenger's daughter. And the strappado, the rack, the boot and the screw.'

'Waste not want not,' whispered Poley grimly to Tom in the prow as the apparently broken scavenger's daughter guided her father's boat down the slackening river. Out from under Tom's

172

house she steered them and towards the Pool below. Down here, among the hovels of the northern shore, lived Portia's father, a man she loved little enough to hand over to Robert Poley at the mere threat of his terrible machines. Her father was one Augustus Shaddow, named either for the man or the month, and much taken with his Roman heritage in his town of Romeville, as he called London. Shaddow was apparently the self-styled captain of a gang of scavengers, cut-throats and sometime pirates, now sadly depleted. It was he, so Portia said, who had masterminded tonight's attempt on the callow new goldsmith lately moved to the Bridge. But he had been unable to lead the enterprise himself, having important business up by Newmans in the heart of Romeville himself; and, lacking a son to take the tiller, in spite of more than a dozen various attempts, had despatched his daughter Portia to stand santar for the gang.

The boat was even more crowded sliding downriver than it had been coming up. The two leaders crouched at the very point of the vessel. Six stout constables under Poley's command filled the waist, the two most boat-wise with the oars in hand. Along the keel between them lay so many swords, pikes and guns that another ounce of shot or powder was like to have swamped them all. The last of the night sat darkly over them as the first of sunrise threatened palely over the hills ashore. The dawn wind stirred the gulls to breakfast so that they moved invisibly in the misty shadows and silently under the bedlam.

They slid past Traitor's Gate, and cleared the Tower midstream, closing with the northern shore as they swept past St Katherine's Stairs and in towards the bank itself.

Tom straightened, peering through the darkness, trying to match what he could see to his memories of the place. Here the shore rose in a series of little grey-mud cliffs above the tidal flats. Atop the cliffs sat the hovels where the families that scavenged here were housed. Through the cliff faces, one after another, came the stinking little streams to spew out across the flats; easier to smell than to see at the moment. All the hovels crouched in darkness, featureless, apparently ruined, against the gathering pallor of the sky beyond. Here and there a thread of smoke wavered up to join the mist, at the root of each some spark of fire: light and warmth that could never reach down here, where even this midsummer morn was threatening to dawn with an unseasonable chill.

'Here,' said Portia, her voice so low that Tom had to strain to catch it. She guided them hard to the left and the little boat slid into the stinking outwash of one of the little rivulet sewers. 'On the left as soon as we run aground,' she said. 'It's a bit of a scramble and the slope's none too dry nor sweet-smelling I warn you. Still, keep your heads up and you'll make it all right.'

Something in her tone struck Tom. At that very moment, however, the little craft hissed on to the mud. The constables downed oars and grabbed their weapons. Poley leaped ashore and only Tom, uncharacteristically, hesitated.

'Catchpoles!' screamed Portia, suddenly more akin to Stentor than Minerva, her voice as powerful as the greatest of bellowing messengers. 'Ware catchpoles and queer-cuffins!'

She bent to catch up an oar – thus luckily avoiding the aim of Poley's pistol as he would have shot her dead where she stood. She pushed the boat back into the stream, still shouting. But Tom was still in the bow. He reached across and hauled Poley back aboard, then steadied the vessel as the eager watch constables retreated. Three long steps brought him up beside the intrepid girl and he knocked the oar out of her hand with one fist while tearing out his rapier with the other.

Thus, when Captain Shaddow breasted the slippery rise against which many an unfortunate had slithered to his doom, he found no hopeless band of officers trapped and waiting to die but rather a well-armed band of men in a strong defensive position: in the midst of his creek, aboard his boat, armed to the teeth and holding his daughter with a rapier across her throat and his own good pistol against her temple.

The men in the boat were in little better case, however, for

Shaddow brought behind him twenty well-armed neighbours, the kinds of men who were like to eat the Watch for breakfast.

Poley, of course, opened his mouth to threaten, but Tom hissed, 'Hold your peace, man!' and Poley for once obeyed.

'Mornin', Portia,' said Captain Shaddow, deadpan. 'Wot you brought me here then?'

'Catchpoles and queer-cuffins,' she repeated. 'Fresh from the Bridewell.'

'Jem and the others?'

'Mutton,' she said roundly. 'All the lot of them.'

'Heard as much meself. These cullies' doin's?'

'His work. The one with the blade at me weasand pipe. Supposed to be a Brownist Goldsmith. Or a Puritan Familist or some such. If he is, then I'm maudlin fresh from Bedlam. He fights like the King of Rufflers, speaks like a gentry-cove and thinks like an intelligencer. There's dark work here. Tyburn work. Racks and thumbscrews for the lot of us.'

'You all right though, gel?'

'Scared witless but no scars.'

'Good thing.'

'Close thing. They was like to have racked me.'

'Was they? Like to have racked a daughter o' mine?' Shaddow's voice rose in anger and Portia saw what she had come near to doing – as did Tom and Poley well enough.

'We didn't, though,' said Tom quietly. 'We showed you the rack and we left you alone. Did you no harm but frightened you.'

'They done me no harm, though. They frighted me and then treated me well enough. Hold your temper, Dad. Don't do nothin' rash.'

'Do? What am I likely to do now in any case? They got you, but I got them.'

'And we have an army to back us up,' answered Tom, his voice gentle but carrying clearly. 'Not the City Watch but the Crowner's men and the Bailiff's men from the Liberty. We have men that'll never stop should you harm one hair of us.'

'An army that don't know where you've come to nor don't know where you've gone to neither!'

'An army that know the name of Captain Shaddow; that know who murdered the Master of Defence Tom Musgrave, friend to the Lord Chamberlain himself; and who shot Nicholas Hazard, curate of St Magnus' and hero to the nation. And who does your cloak of secrecy depend on? Who will protect you from their anger should they discover who you were drinking with, not at Newmans at all, but on the Bridge last night, when your men was dying at your business in my house – and go knocking on Master Panne the Goldsmith's door?'

There was a stunned silence so absolute that it seemed to echo over the Pool of London.

'Told you,' said Portia, her voice shrill and clear. 'Mind like an intelligencer. Nigh on witchcraft it is. I've never saw the like of it.'

CHAPTER TWENTY-FIVE

The Ring and the Rapier

F rom the top of the rise Tom could see over the shanty town to Smith's Field and the walls of the Tower itself. Although the river aspect of the place was grim enough – especially in the grey dawn – on the City side there was marshy grass and a few low trees sloping gently away to the ancient fortification. Between the low-roofed dwellings there was room enough for a few sheep and cattle; for dogs and brats to run wild; even for a horse or two, down by the crossed keys and crossed sprats of the Fishmongers' Arms tavern.

'As pretty a view as any,' said Captain Shaddow at his side. 'My kingdom. Up to Smithfield an dahn as far as the Tower, at any rate. 'Er Majesty takes over there, God save 'er. Now come into my palace an' take your ease, Master Marley.'

Tom needed no second bidding. His business here would need to be quickly completed before Poley's patience ran out and he pistolled the wench on the boat. Or Shaddow's confederates' patience ran out and they blew the spy and his constables out of the water to boot. Tom suspected that the only thing keeping them alive at the moment was the fact that young Portia was a popular item in this godforsaken little village, while Cully, Jem and all the rest of Captain Shaddow's little band of bullies were not – unless they had families close by that might be looking for revenge. But however that matter stood, they had been popular with their leader, as like as not, so Tom was careful not to let his guard slip for an instant.

'That's a fine blade for a goldsmith to be carrying, Master Marley,' observed the ruffian, waving Tom past him towards the nearest hovel.

'Is it?' asked Tom in his most Puritan voice. 'I purchased it in Amsterdam. It is from a place called Solingen, I believe. I know little of such matters except what my master taught me.'

'Your master?'

'My Master of Defence, the late Tom Musgrave. Beaten to death and shot, by yourself I believe, just across the Bridge from my own front door.'

'You want to be careful with your accusations, brother, unless you want to join your Master Musgrave. But let us in and see what we can see.' As he spoke, he pushed open the door of the hovel to reveal a surprisingly roomy and comfortable domicile.

Three steps took them down into a large room tall enough even for Tom to stand erect under a roof well supported by white-limed bricks upon a floor scrubbed of solid wood. Over at one side, a driftwood fire blazed in a brick hearth beside a solid brick oven beneath a wide brick chimney. The red-brick breast even boasted a pewter platter – snatched no doubt from the bounty of the river, but kept polished, nevertheless.

There was enough space to allow a table and two chairs for the pair to take their ease. Enough to allow a section or two to be curtained off as simple bedchambers. As the two men sat, so a woman emerged from one of these and crossed to the fire, where she began to tend a pot.

'Where's the kids, Calpurnia?' asked the Captain.

'Aht. Dahn the Fishmonger's after ale fer yer breakfast.'

Tom watched the woman idly. Like the Captain she was dressed in cast-offs, but these were by no means rags – only a step or two below the costumes Will would use on stage, Tom calculated. And there were pins at her breast, something that looked like gold around her throat, and a ring or two upon her fingers.

'I have come simply to offer you gold in exchange for information,' he said.

'You think your gold will buy the truth off of me?'

'It might. If I offer enough, and the truth do little harm to you and yours.'

'Likely. And how will you know it when you hear it? You cannot assay words. Melt 'em and fine 'em and stamp 'em like gold.'

'As your daughter Portia observed, I have an intelligencer's mind. I know more than you think I know and I will be able to see through any lies you tell me. Also I am not here to take you or your friends. Master Poley may be, but that is for you and he to settle after we are done here.

'But as we are dealing in truth here, I advise you to have a care in that. I was the one that stopped him racking Portia last night and he will kill her now if you go wrong.'

The woman at the fire gasped and looked up at the Captain. Calpurnia Shaddow seemed too young to be Portia's mother. And yet there was a strong similarity between them, and no doubting this one's relationship with the Captain . . .

She saw Tom's gaze resting on her and reached up to pull a heavy strand of hair behind her ear. Then she saw that the Captain was looking also and went back to her pot work with a pout.

'So I think I can buy some truth,' said Tom, 'and know it when I hear it. For all the good we did at Bridewell last night, I know the alternative approach does not work well with your flesh and blood.'

'Ha!' laughed the Captain, not without paternal pride. 'What do you want to know?'

'Who paid you to kill Master Musgrave?'

'Soft now . . . Who told you that . . . ?'

'Cully's mate. Cully was one of your command. He died under the surgeon's knife; but his mate did not. He escaped even the Bishop's Bailiff – at your side, I suspect. Then he came into my house last night in charge of Jem and the rest; and left this morning with a shot from your pistol in his brain. If a pair of your men attacked Master Musgrave, and beat Master Musgrave – and killed him – then who other than you, their captain, would be the one with the pistol to make sure of their work?'

'But the shooter was never seen. I talked to Lem – the one with the shot in his brain was Lem – and he said that the shooter was never seen.'

'Perhaps,' whispered Tom. 'But the pistol was seen. *This* pistol was seen. And it is your pistol, Captain, or else how did your daughter come by it? So who supplied it to you and then paid you to use it on Master Musgrave?'

Captain Augustus Shaddow looked at Tom then – full on for the first time, his eyes glinting and his chin working slowly as he chewed at the inside of his cheek. 'It was Master Panne,' he said.

'Panne,' echoed Tom, his voice dead.

'Aye. I have said.' The Captain shifted in his chair, his eyes as dark and slippery as the eels they fed on here.

'But I had given you Panne at the riverside,' whispered Tom, probing still for what was not quite right in the matter yet. 'Not *Petty*?'

'Hell's . . .'

'You deal with them both do you not? Scraps of gold to one and trifles of fashion to the other? Some plucked at their bidding by your gang and robbed out of houses at their command, as should have happened to my house last night; some washed down on to the mudflats like the corpse of Mistress Panne last winter, I would guess – and like the headless body a week since. The woman's body dressed in green?'

'Witchcraft!' yelled the Captain, springing to his feet. 'The little trull was right and you're a witch. You could not know of that! Of either, else . . .'

Then he stopped talking, for the very point of Tom's blade was bringing a drop of ruby from the scraggy skin on his weasand pipe just above the collar of his jerkin where the greasy leather stood wide.

'I can see it clear as a scryer looking into his magic glass. You found her washed up on the mudflats last week and you stripped her; weighted the body with rocks, like as not, and dumped it deep. Even down here, a headless corpse would bring investigation. The dress was fine, expensive; with lace and filigree, like as not. There would have been gilded pins – big ones. They held a heavy bodice woven with golden wire. I know, for I have seen it. Bangles, buckles, fastenings; rings, mayhap. All of it up to Petty and Panne, for cutting up and melting down as usual.

'All except that emerald ring there on the third finger of your Calpurnia's left hand. The ring that is a perfect match for the earrings in the ears upon the head you never saw.'

Shaddow leaped back, away from Tom's point and, as he did so, the woman by the fire sprang erect. Out from under her skirts she brought a nasty-looking carving knife. 'Sword?' yelled Shaddow.

'Bed's foot!' she answered, and flung herself forward, chopping at the air where Tom's Puritan haircut had been. But Tom, like Shaddow, could move with speed when he chose.

Tom was amused more than anything. He stood with his back to the door and watched as she ran in again. Then he upset the table and trapped her foot beneath it. She stopped at once and swore in pain. Behind her the curtain tore wide and Shaddow pushed back into the fray.

Tom had expected Shaddow to be armed with an old hanger, its blade almost as heavy as a cutlass, the sort of thing that in the pirate's hands might be able to deliver a crippling blow – a killing one, given time and opportunity, but against a brand-new Solingen rapier in the hands of a man like Tom, an old-fashioned weapon likely to be fighting badly out of its class.

But no.

The Captain came back into battle armed with something

181

every bit as modern as his Dutch flintlock pistol: a rapier almost as up to date as Tom's own, and every inch a man-killer.

His smile a little smaller, perhaps, but still curling the lip where his moustaches normally curled in turn, Tom fell into his guard, his eyes busy – upon his opponent and beyond. The room was square to the curtains – and looked to be six feet longer behind them. By no means a perfect *piste*; but there was room for both men to work. He had to be aware of the door with three steps below it at his back, and the hopping, knife-wielding harridan at his left.

With unusual lack of gallantry, he threw his first attack at the Captain who was freeing his feet from the curtain hem and, as the rapiers sang together along a line past Shaddow's right hip, he lashed out with his left arm and punched the woman full between the eyes. Her head slammed back and the rear of it demonstrated with a crisp clear *crack!* just how solid were the lime-washed bricks of the place.

The lack of balance made his recovery a little clumsy, but by the time he fell into his second guard, she was seated at the foot of the wall, unconscious. Then he was forced to disregard her as the Captain closed with him.

Shaddow was of the artless school of *Kill-em-quick*, but no mean blade for all that. His attacks were ill-formed, scarce considered – but energetic and all but overpowering. He had no idea of defence at all – his work was all stab and thrust and lunge. No sooner had Tom enveloped his point in one parry, falling back just enough to secure his ground, than the sword flashed at him again, pushing and pushing. His confident sneer said, *Even in my sleep I outmatch a Puritan frog like you – and even were it not so, you dare not hurt me, or my men will slaughter your friends.* His technique, in any case, such as it was, seemed based on his assumption of immortality.

Thus, almost at once, Tom was forced to decide: *was* he prepared to kill the man? If not, then he was like to die himself. There was no room for play here, no matter how skilful, nor likely to be any chance for a disarm. Even a crippling stroke – a lunge to face, shoulder or leg – would be lucky to stop him. Tom had one question to ask himself – and on the answer everything else depended: had Captain Shaddow anything more to tell him?

The answer to that was *Yes!* – which posed a problem.

Tom felt the bottom step brush against the heel of his left boot.

Shaddow threw himself forward again, his blade driving for Tom's heart. The master swordsman parried, sending Shaddow's point up towards the outside of Tom's shoulder while his own point flashed over it in an *imbroccata* that transformed into a *stromacione* attack on the Captain's unguarded face. Shaddow turned his face aside, his attack faltering and his sword slipping further to Tom's right.

Tom's heel went up on to the bottom step, its leading edge across his instep, his boot-heel anchored firm. And he fell. Hurled himself down and forward. Into the *passatto sotto*, under the Captain's guard, tearing his blade down the air across the length of Shaddow's torso as his left hand, still smarting from punching the woman, hit the white-scrubbed floorboards and his right hand extended the whole of his body in one great flying lunge.

The very blade itself seemed to know where it was bound: past the arrogant bulge of codpiece and the knitted wool of his tights; through the lowest part of the Captain's belly; past the protective arch of his pubic bone. Under the great joint where the thighbone joined his hip; out through the great gluteus at the back, slicing through tendons, muscles, viscera, reproductive organs. And side by side in the midst of all, the femoral vein and femoral artery – there, but safe and untouched by the merciful blade.

Shaddow screamed and twisted.

Tom's knees crashed to the floor but he disregarded the pain, his mind focused entirely and exclusively on recovering his sword without doing the man more damage still. Out it came, as sharp and true as the day it was forged.

Shaddow staggered back, his arms spread as though for crucifixion, the deadly sword spinning away to clatter against the chimney breast.

Tom pulled himself up as though at prayer, watching as the wounded man fell backwards on to his bed. Blood bubbled out of his clothing like water from a spring, black, thick and hot enough to be smoking on the air. There was a pool of it on the floor already and a stain that would never scrub clean.

'You!' snarled Captain Shaddow. 'You . . .' he snarled again.

But Tom rested the bloody blade across his lips then, like a finger demanding silence. 'No,' he said. 'Captain Shaddow. You decide whether you will live or die and you do it here and now. Do what I say and answer what I ask and I will save you. Fail me in one jot or tittle and you and yours will surely die . . .'

Five minutes later there came a crisp *crack!* as though someone had been struck behind the ear with the pommel of a rapier. Calpurnia Shaddow stirred and whimpered, even as Tom crossed to her from the ruin of the Captain's bed and stooped to take the ring. He opened his purse, to put it in with his Dutch guilders, but hesitated and slipped it in the pocket of his Puritan coat instead. Then he went back to the table and paid her no further heed, his fingers still exploring the length of that all too expensive, all too familiar sword, his mind clearly far, far away.

The door behind them burst open then and Tom glanced over into the polished pewter plate on the chimney breast that showed him who was there.

'Poley,' he said with some satisfaction. 'I thought you would not be long. I hope the girl is still alive, for I've taken a liking to her.'

'You were right,' said Poley quietly. 'It was well to warn Thomas Walsingham whither we were bound. I have a score and more of his constables to add to my own; and we can cleanse this nest of gannets whenever we choose. The sooner the better for me. And yes,' he added grudgingly, 'the girl is still alive. Unlike her father, I see.' Poley wrinkled his nose as he looked down at the bloody mess around the corpse-still figure on the bed.

'Good. Then restore her to the arms of her *materfamilias* and, I hope, second cousin here and the bosom of her unfortunately complicated and depleted family, if she wishes to come, and let us proceed. There is no one left to arrest here, unless you want the guts on the bed there, the women and the neighbours.'

'What have you found out?' demanded Poley as the pair of them emerged into the silence of the constable-guarded slum. Poley gestured to the watchmen who had accompanied them here.

They turned and followed them back as Tom answered, 'More than I had hoped for, and at less cost to my purse, if more to my soul and conscience. And my time – for there will be a lengthy quest into this night's work and I will have long hours of evidence to give. Hush.'

Poley, lips parted to reply, nevertheless did as he was bid. The cry of Captain Shaddow's widow echoed across the place. Calpurnia had seen what was lying on her bed. Tom prayed that the Captain would remain stiff and unconscious for a little while longer yet.

'Well, what?' persisted Poley.

By way of answer, Tom held up the sword he had taken from the Captain. ''Tis a familiar thing,' he said, 'and one I have come across before. As have you, I think.'

'I would not know it from any other . . .'

'But then, you have never felt it blade to blade against your own. It has a song, a style, that is all its own; and it belongs with the pistol. And both went to Shaddow to be used on Musgrave.'

'So? I do not understand.'

'Who were the people that wanted Musgrave dead, Poley?'

'Panne. You said Master Panne the Goldsmith, for one . . .'

'And so I thought at first. But no. It was never the fathers that I had to fear and this sword tells me so. For it belonged to the man that hired Shaddow. I will ask Ugo and he will tell me,

185

I am certain, it was never to the father, Panne or Petty that he sold this good Dutch pistol of his.'

'But if not to Panne or Petty . . .'

'To each of them in truth, Poley. But not to the fathers. To Mistress Alice and Master Daniel. It is the children that would see Tom Musgrave dead.'

'But how would a stripling and a lass of good family come across rufflers and rakehells like Captain Shaddow?' demanded Poley.

'The way they might come across salamanders, skittles and findings: at their fathers' place of work. Would you be surprised if a gunsmith's children could make use of powder and shot?' Or that Captain Shaddow's daughter can steer a boat and cut a purse?'

They came up over the rise then and looked down upon the stinking little creek well filled now with official boats and constables. Had it not been so early in the day, thought Tom, Walsingham himself might have come to see the fun.

'Is 'e dead then?' demanded a familiar voice.

'As mutton,' said Tom, watching her through narrow eyes. He risked the ghost of a wink.

There was a pause as she frowned with thought. Then: 'Weren't much of a father anyhow,' said Portia forthrightly. 'We'll be better off without him.'

She lingered for an instant by Tom, willow-straight and almost as tall as his shoulder. A cold hand peeped out from the black cypress cloak. When it returned it held his purse – and if he felt it go he never said a thing. But, he wondered, now that his purse was lighter after all, would his conscience be lighter too? Or would he have felt more virtuous if he had roundly rid the world of an arrant, murderous rogue after all?

Then she was gone and Poley turned to him.

'Children nowadays . . .' Poley said.

CHAPTER TWENTY-SIX

Hell

W hile Poley went to get a justice to sign the warrant, Tom went after the murderous Master Petty. The case against him was complete even though Captain Shaddow and his strange family were likely to be well out of reach now. But what they could not prove against him they would rack out of him, thought Tom bitterly, still in the grip of the black mood born of his sore conscience.

Tom himself hammered on the door of Petty's house and haberdashery up on the northern, St Magnus', end of the Bridge. It was still early. Shops were only just beginning to open their shutters. Tom listened idly to the bustle behind the door while the echoes of his knocking died. It needed no great Master of Logic to work out that Petty's apprentice was moving about in the shop, preparing to open up, and his servants were lighting fires, warming water and preparing breakfast. The family were still abed, no doubt, and hardly like to stir for a while yet. Well, Tom was just the man to put that right. He pounded on the door again.

It was the housekeeper who opened to Tom's imperious knock and she froze halfway through her perfunctory curtsey when she saw the Crowner's men behind him.

'The master's still abed, sir,' she warned as she showed them into the snug parlour that looked away up towards Baynard's Castle and West Minster.

'The young master?' snapped Tom. 'Master Daniel?'

'Never up 'fore noon, sir. Out gaming of an evening, sir. Or at them theatres,' she confided, clearly thinking that a greater sin.

'Well, rouse him out and down to me, or I will do it.'

'I will rouse the master, sir, begging your pardon. You should talk to him if you have any affair with young Master Daniel.'

Tom was not used to being gainsaid, even when disguised as a peaceful Puritan, and his brow gathered into a most unChristian frown when the master haberdasher himself arrived.

As befitted a man in his particular trade, his dressing robe was of the finest, and the fastenings that strained to hold it closed across his girth were of the best that his friends Beale the Silversmith and Panne the Goldsmith could supply. As befitted a man of his social standing whose routine has been disarrayed by importunate officialdom, he swept into majestic attack, much like the Spanish Armada seeking to brush Hawkins, Drake and Howard out of the Channel.

Five minutes after his first broadside, he was seated, shaking, in his strongest chair. His face was pasty white and his hands were writhing madly in his lap as though he no longer had bones in his fingers.

'. . . Thus much for yourself and Beale and Panne and Captain Shaddow,' Tom was saying. 'Now let us come on to the matter in hand. Where is your son? It is with him that I have my business today.' But before the shattered haberdasher could summon even the wits to ask why Apollo Marley wanted to talk to his son, there came another hammering at the door.

'That will be my warrant, like as not,' said Tom with grim satisfaction, but for once he was wrong.

The dazed housekeeper showed Mark Antony Terrill into the crowded parlour. The young apprentice turned to Petty and, seeing the state of him, also made a false assumption. 'Ah, sir,' he said sadly, 'I see you already know.'

'He may indeed, though I doubt it; but I certainly do not,' said Tom quietly. 'What is your news?'

'Why, that Master Daniel and Mistress Alice are fled away together and vanished. Alice has taken with her some hundreds of golden guineas from Master Panne's strongroom and I dare say Master Daniel will not be travelling with a light purse either.'

Master Haberdasher Petty was in the very act of swinging his white moon-face – eyes a-start and mouth a-drool like the veriest Bedlamite – round to confront this new catastrophe when the shrieking of his goodwife above confirmed at the very least that her darling Daniel was no longer at home.

So that when Poley did arrive with the warrant, he found himself sadly behind the times.

Tom walked back through the early throng with Terrill. 'No hint or clue that this was coming?' he asked, more out of habit than anything. His mind was on other matters.

'Not that I saw,' admitted Poley's agent. 'But then I was watching for deeper, darker matters than a pair of young lovers taking flight.'

'And reducing their parents to beggary along the way . . .'

'They were set fair to do that, did they stay or go,' said Terrill, grimly.

'And you see no connection between their disappearance and anything else going forward here?' Again, Tom had nothing specific in mind; he was simply thinking aloud – wondering.

'Other than the coincidence that they vanished on the night your house was attacked and on the eve of your attempt to arrest them.'

'To arrest Daniel. It was he who . . .'

'He never did anything without her prompting . . .'

'What do you mean?'

'Aye,' asked a familiar voice. 'And who are you talking about?' Will Shakespeare fell in beside them as they walked towards the goldsmith's shop.

'Alice Panne and Daniel Petty . . .' Tom swiftly explained the conversation so far and the coil of events that had prompted it.

'They are a pair together,' persisted Terrill, 'that do more than either would ever do alone. Daniel does nothing without Alice's knowledge and prompting; and, through her, he does much more than he would ever do alone. She drives him. But, again, he gives her the strength to do it. Do I make any sense at all?'

'Whither?' asked Will, intrigued. 'When he gives her the strength to drive him, then where does she drive him to?'

'To heaven or hell,' said Terrill roundly. 'Or, more likely, to both.'

'I wonder whither she drives him now,' asked Tom more thoughtfully. 'For it sounds as though it is Alice who planned my death, if you are right, even though it was Daniel I bested in our little duel on the gateway.'

'And I wonder whither my master drives now in such haste,' added Terrill, gesturing.

There indeed was the goldsmith's coach pulling away from the front of his shuttered shop. Though the banging of impatient fists within and the whipping and calling of the coachman did indeed hint at haste, the clumsy vehicle made slow progress against the tide of shoppers and sightseers streaming southwards out of the City.

So that it was easy for Tom – and Will, whose interest was also strangely piqued – to follow along unobserved and unsuspected, close behind. The coach pulled off the Bridge and into the warren of streets around Fish Street on the north bank. The vehicle picked up some pace as it turned left into Thames Street, but it was still easy for the two old friends to keep up with it, walking side by side locked deep in earnest conversation.

'Perhaps he suspects where they are and goes after his daughter . . .' ventured Will.

'After his gold, more like. From what Terrill says, she is not the sort of child I would want to take back. Let young Daniel

190

the rakehell have her and welcome. But for the matter of the gold . . .'

'Or mayhap he is off to his guild hall to warn his brother goldsmiths to keep careful watch in case the guineas start turning up. As they will.'

'If he dare risk the damage to his reputation . . .'

'A man who you say dealt with the scavenger and pirate Captain Shaddow, and yet still fearful for his reputation?'

'Indeed, Will, for he dealt with Shaddow in secret. Therefore he had best make sure no one looks too close beneath that precious reputation.'

'He had an active double life then, did he not? For as well as Captain Shaddow hid beneath his gilded front, he had Mistress Margery the Catholic mistress to keep from the world as well.'

'Perhaps the easiest way to do that was to cut her throat for her. There's none so silent nor so secret as the dead, after all.'

'Then, when he went back to hide the body, he decided to take her head and put it up on the gateway instead? Why do that, Tom?'

'As a warning.'

'Well enough. But to warn whom?'

'His daughter for one. It was Mistress Alice we found up there in illegal congress with Master Daniel, was it not?'

'A desperate way to warn your daughter to stay chaste, is it not, Tom? Whatever happened to a good old-fashioned whipping?'

'Perhaps he dared not do it. She knew much about his business. I'll wager it was she who knew of Captain Shaddow, if what was said of her is true. Consider: her mother falls through the ice and dies. An accident and nothing more. But the body is found and identified. I have seen the woman's clothing that he gave to his mistress later, and it has her name embroidered all over it. But who finds it? Who returns it?'

'Shaddow! And thus the link is made.'

'With both father and daughter. And the association grows, for the one with the quickness of spirit sees all too clearly how a man like Shaddow can bring a business like Panne's along.'

191

'So the dead woman makes her husband's fortune through the wit of her daughter,' breathed Will, 'and the widower mounts his mistress, the Catholic and whore – which, again, the daughter knows about.'

'Lay one stroke of the rod across those fair shoulders and his reputation's gone.'

'And his business and all.'

'Aye, Will. Aye. And would that knowledge be enough to drive a man to take up the axe after he has wielded the dagger? To chop the head off after he has cut the throat? That is the question, is it not?'

'Not a sane man, no,' said Will. 'And I see no great marks of madness in him, I'm afraid. Besides, what warning was there in the death of the first woman – or in the slaughter of Mistress Van Der Leyden? What had those to do with Panne or Mistress Alice?'

'Aye, there's the rub,' acknowledged Tom.

And the two old friends walked on through the busy London morning in such companionable silence that no one would ever have suspected how deep and dark was the business they were engaged upon nor how black and dangerous their thoughts.

At St Mary Somerset Church the coach turned north on to Old Fish Street Hill, crossed Knightrider Street and deposited its occupant within the heaving precinct of St Paul's.

Tom and Will continued their silence with more purpose now, for they had to concentrate on following their quarry. Dressed in plain dark broadcloth, wearing the most unremark-able of hats, he could vanish all too easily into the crowd, and so it required all their concentration to keep him under their eyes.

Into the cathedral itself he went, following a herd of sheep being driven through to market. In the north precinct he turned left and headed off up towards Ludgate Hill. One on each side of the street they followed him as he went up the hill, through the gate past the prison, over the Fleet Bridge and to the Temple Bar.

Perhaps he was going to seek some legal advice, Tom thought then, remembering how Francis Bacon had reduced the headless corpse to a series of legal positions for Crowner Danby – and had likely been asked to do the same for the much more tricky matter of Mistress Van Der Leyden.

But no. Master Panne suddenly turned aside off the Strand and vanished into the one place Tom had not thought of. It was a house standing alone at the end of the lane. Outside it were benches full of men who sat as though frozen by agony and fatigue. Above its door hung the sign of a great steaming pot. Out from under its eaves and up through its roof and chimneys rose smoke and steam in great abundance. But this was no eating house or ordinary; nor was it even a bath house or brothel: it was a stew.

Tom froze, in the grip of a kind of revelation so engrossing that he jumped with shock when Will's shoulder collided gently with his. 'Your man has the pox,' whispered the playwright.

Together they went past the place, looking for a spy-hole of one kind or another. And in truth a spy-hole was not that hard to find, for the place needed to let the fumes of its various treatments come and go; so there were windows, vents and flues aplenty in the stout back wall. They soon found a window that gave a kind of panorama of the inside of the place. It was a kind of communal treatment room set out in stages where those arriving were welcomed and helped out of their clothing on the far side, at the door out towards the Strand, then, by degrees, through application and fumigation to steaming and stewing. The great stew tubs were beneath the window where they watched, and most of them were full.

No one paid them much attention. Those being treated were so overcome by the pain, nausea and lethargy resulting from their treatment – let alone their condition – that they had no energy even to raise their eyes. The men at work were taking so much care with what they did – for almost everything they handled could be deadly dangerous – that they too paid scant attention to the onlookers; and those outside, recovering from their treatment, were as close to death as it is possible to get while still having the power to suffer pain.

Nor did Tom or Will have any real desire to linger looking down into that infernal little pit. They knew well enough what was going on in this place, advised no doubt by Viner or some other like him. Save that they wanted to make doubly sure of Panne, they would have left the place at once and with great alacrity.

The distant Master Goldsmith stepped out of his unremarkable broadcloth disguise and stood in his shirt. But no; Tom saw at once that the man was swathed – as Kate had been to hide her sex when disguised. Panne was still a big man, to be sure, but the girth of his legs in particular was expanded considerably by swathes of spotted bandages. At once a helper led him to a bench beside a table. Under the light of a roof-vent the unfortunate patient sat, stretching out his legs for unwrapping, followed by the beginning of his treatment. From ankle to shirt-tail the flesh of them was revealed, pitted with crusted sores. The helper took a wooden spatula and dug it into a silvery-coloured ointment – mostly mercury, if Viner could be believed. This poisonous concoction he spread over the suffering goldsmith's legs, filling in the sores one by one and continuing up on to the man's privities, belly and chest before asking him to stand and turn so that his back could be tended as well.

Aghast, Tom and Will watched as Panne, almost sleepwalking with shock, agony and reaction to the poison flooding into him, was led through to the first smoking room. Here, blankets were piled upon him and hot bricks pushed under them. Even from here they could see that his white face was bathed in slimy perspiration, his eyes and nose were running, and his gaping mouth beginning to flood with drool as the heat and poison combined medicinally to kill the vapours within him that gave rise to the terrible pox.

A glance across the hellish place assured them that all he had to look forward to was more smoking – in the dreadful fumes of

194

guaiac wood, no doubt – to the point where his ears and eyes and gums began to bleed, if the current sufferers were anything to go by. Then poaching – almost boiling – for an hour or so in the great mercury baths below until his flesh was white, soft, sagging and blistered – in far worse condition than the flesh of Margery Midmore when Tom had pulled her headless body from the river almost a week ago.

After the treatment was finished Panne would be left for a couple more hours to recover his terribly depleted strength before being rebandaged, helped back into his clothes and sent to sit with the others outside who were trying to summon strength enough to stand – perhaps to walk. Unless he had made some arrangement for the coach to meet him, then he was here for the night at least, thought Tom grimly. He would never have the strength to get back to the Bridge on foot.

It was the baths that gave the place its name – the stews – and, by association, gave its name to the places where such diseases could be caught most easily in the first place.

'Why yes,' said Dr Theodore several hours later, 'Mistress Midmore has the pox. That is quite amazing, for look . . .'

He began a lengthy explanation of why Mistress Midmore's increasingly distressed-looking corpse was not as obviously afflicted as the body of her ex-lover. Tom's mind drifted in and out of the good doctor's mellifluous Latin as his mind tried to fit the new fact into the greater puzzle. It looked to him as though Panne had caught the disease from his mistress. But why had she not warned him that she had it?

'Has she had the disease for long?' he asked, breaking into one of the less penetrable sections of the doctor's disquisition.

'Why yes. These lesions are tiny but of great age, as is attested by the age of the scar tissue. And the illness does not seem to have progressed. This is unprecedented. The two stages of the disease are well known, and a third is whispered of, though I have never met any that have survived to see it: complete madness, so I am told; general paralysis of the insane.

195

'The first stage can be slowed by mercury bath and by the application, they say, of a particular type of wood called guaiac. But eventually it will progress and consume the body with pain and disease. Oh how I wish she were alive, that I might ask her how this miracle was done!'

'Miracle?' Tom's nerves twitched of a sudden.

'Verily. The disease was contracted long ago. It has not progressed. It has somehow, it seems, been arrested in its first stage.'

He looked across at Tom. Tom frowned and glanced across at Thomas Walsingham, who had summoned the doctor at his friend's request some hours ago – before Will had departed for the Theatre; before Kate and Guillem had arrived and started a lengthy feast stretching between late luncheon and early supper up in the dining chamber, while Master Marley's shuttered shop was tidied and restored to a businesslike condition under the watchful eye of the ubiquitous Perkin.

'To arrest a disease like this,' continued Theodore with heavy jocularity, as though instructing a very slow student, 'is what we doctors like to call a *cure*.'

'But there is no cure for the pox,' whispered Tom.

'Precisely. There is only a range of treatments such as your unfortunate friend the goldsmith is suffering now. There is no known cure. And yet, by a miracle, Mistress Midmore is cured. That is why I would very much like to talk to this poor woman. Even if, as seems likely from what you tell me, she passed it on to her lover unsuspected . . .' He paused and frowned. His wise old eyes found Tom's and held them, seeming to glow a little in the gloom of the windowless cellar.

'If only there were a way,' he whispered, 'that we could talk to the dead, and that they could answer us!'

Tom, looking across the dungeon at the two sheet-covered bodies where Mistress Van Der Leyden lay beside Mistress Midmore – though her head as yet did not – and the two staring, mismatched, faces beside them, wondered whether he agreed or not. For the idea suddenly sent a shiver of something akin to terror through the long hard muscles of his body – along the long dark corridors of his mind. Perhaps it was the forcefulness with which the stew and the doomed unfortunates within it reminded him of a gaping hell itself, but just for a moment it seemed to him that, in this place – at this time – perhaps the watching, listening dead were nearer than Dr Theodore suspected.

However – why ever – that was, the sensation prompted Tom to consider the next step he must take; the step he had planned on taking last night before being prevented by the pirate raid.

It was time to follow in the axe-man's footsteps.

Following them up the Great Stone Gateway had pushed matters forward a week ago in no uncertain terms. Now it was time to follow, not up but down.

But he would be as mad as his wild, weird quarry to even consider going alone.

CHAPTER TWENTY-SEVEN

The Damned

D r Theodore's words were still with Tom three hours afterwards when, precisely twenty-four hours later than planned, exactly twenty-four hours nearer to the arrival of the Queen, he eased up the grating down which the axe-man had taken Frau Van Der Leyden's head two nights since.

Kate and Guillem were sated, safe and still at Nonesuch, for Perkin had been forced to report defeat. His men would return to finish restoring Master Marley's parlour tomorrow. They had rendered it impregnable, but not yet habitable. In the meantime he had left a well-armed guard, stolid, reliable and but little given to superstition, and sent the rest home.

To Nonesuch via the shuttered goldsmith's had also come Will Shakespeare, his ear as ever close to the ground – as a sometime colleague of Robert Poley's – seeking details of his friend's most recent adventures and of the clearly theatrical Captain Shaddow.

Tom took him under his wing at once and made him confederate to what he was planning now. Will, for reasons of his own, was happy enough to fall in with Tom's directions, though he began by reminding his increasingly overpowering friend that he was still a goldsmith called Marley, as far as the Bridge and the world were concerned.

'The last of our play-acting will take place during the next

198

couple of days at the most, if my suspicions are accurate,'
countered Tom cheerfully. 'For within that time the apprentices
will have attacked Bleeke House, if they are going to do so; the
Queen will have crossed the Bridge, if she is going to do so.'

'And the axe-man will have performed his final execution,'
added the playwright grimly.

'One way or the other,' confirmed Tom more soberly.

Tom and Will had passed a very active couple of hours, in
fact. Not only had they settled his apprentices and talked to
Perkin; they had ridden out to Bleeke House. Here they had
found a strange atmosphere, half formal mourning for Frau
Van Der Leyden, half festive preparation for the Queen's visit
in two days' time and entirely a kind of fortress defence like a
city besieged.

In the midst of all this, Ugo had been trying with limited
success to cheer and court the tragic Inge; but she was her
mother's child, not her father's. She was nearly inconsolable,
and not even the promise that she must now play hostess to the
Queen herself could brighten the stormy clouds of her gloom.
Truth to tell, Ugo was relieved to be called away by Tom, glad
for a while at least to be dealing with physical realities rather
than emotional turmoils.

Yes, he recognized Shaddow's pistol; a fine weapon, deadly
accurate. Indeed he had sold it – who else? – but he had not
made it. And as to the purchaser . . . He shrugged. Business was
brisk, his thoughts elsewhere. He had no clear recollection
without his records.

But when they rode into Blackfriars and climbed the familiar
stairs to Tom's fencing school and rooms, Ugo's records were
the last things on their minds. Even with three of them setting
out on the adventure, against such an opponent they would go
armed as though hunting bears in the *Schwarzwald*, the great
Black Forest in the heart of High Germany.

Because they were likely going into tight places with no room
even to draw a blade, Tom for once left his beloved rapiers
behind; but he took the pair of Solingen-bladed daggers that

199

matched them, each one more than two feet of razor steel. For the same reason, the long flintlocks and even the terrifying *dunderbusses* in Ugo's collection remained locked safely away; but Ugo was a master craftsman with hand weapons of all kinds and he was happy to choose and check for both of his friends a range of dags and pistols. Before the bemused Will, to whom much of this was revelation, Ugo sorted through drawers of deadly merchandise: all reliable, accurate, deadly; many of them illegal; some of them unique; some with as many as three barrels. The last one – his masterpiece – with a revolving chamber allowing six shots, however, he retained for his own use. Powder. Shot. Extra flints, loads, little ram-rods, wadding.

As Ugo sorted out what they would need, Tom had leisure to check his friend's records after all and, never one to let a loose end lie untied for long, he looked the gun up. As he suspected the purchaser's name, it did not take long. Only a fortnight ago Ugo had sold to Master Daniel Petty, haberdasher of London Bridge, a brace of pistols. A brace, but not a matched pair, he noted. For although one of them had a single barrel of some twelve inches with silver chasing etc., the other had short, wide, deadly double barrels.

'We took less than this on to the battlefield at Nijmagen,' observed Tom wryly a moment later as he returned to the workshop.

'At Nijmagen we had an army at our backs,' Ugo reminded him grimly.

'Two armies, in fact,' added Will.

'Why are we taking no other friends?' asked Ugo, growing more nervous suddenly, as they returned the horses to Nonesuch and walked out across the empty, moonlit Bridge.

'I cannot waste more time chasing down Talbot Law and, other than he and you two, there are no other men I can trust. Any one of the men we have encountered since the first head fell at my feet might be the man we seek.'

'But surely, the Master of Logic must see that Perkin would be a priceless ally in this adventure,' suggested Will quietly.

'It is Perkin I fear most of all, old friend.'

The grate opened silently, as Tom had known it would. Van Der Leyden's coachman had been very precise in what he saw and heard. There had been no talk of unearthly shrieks, natural enough though it would have been for shrieks to be ringing out. The noise of pumping blood to be sure; but the evidence had been specific: nothing such as rusty metal might make.

But the implication of that fact was something that gave the Master of Logic pause. For the grate had lain here apparently undisturbed through uncounted centuries. Perkin, the keeper of the Bridge's fabric, was as efficient as it was possible to imagine; but even Perkin was unlikely to tend to the hinges on the grates in the Bridge's roadway. No. The only man likely to do that was the man Tom was seeking – unless, thought Tom, as he had just said to Will, Perkin was that man.

'He's mayhap not so mad, then,' whispered Tom, stepping into the black hole and finding strong iron rungs convenient to his feet and starting his conversation halfway through a thought, as was his way. 'Not so wild-eyed a Tom o' Bedlam as not to have calculated the need for a swift and silent exit from the place where he had done his terrible deed.'

He paused in his climbing so that Ugo could follow him down; but he did not stop his whispering, which echoed strangely in the well, just above the rumbling of the turning tide. 'Not so gibbering maudlin as not to have reasoned that he needed some kind of plan and made preparations accordingly. But he only needed to think ahead if he planned ahead; if he planned to do it again.'

'If he *knew* what he was doing,' echoed Ugo, easing past.

'And *planned* to do it again,' added Will, stepping down off the street above.

Tom watched Ugo lower himself gingerly further into the great black hole, thankful for the moonlight that had brought them this far. But he checked on the flint and dark lantern that he hoped would take them further still, before nodding up to Will, who lowered the grate back into place above them.

Then, prompted by his own growing suspicions as well as the careful emphases of his friends' last observations, he began to think with all the clarity at his command about the creature the three of them were seeking here.

'Could there be a reason for it all?' he whispered. 'Could there be some case which might explain why the man who did these things was knowingly, coldly doing what he was doing?'

Ugo glanced up, his face white and his eyes agleam with the mad moon's fire. The Dutchman spoke feelingly, having just come from a house under the full weight of the horror. 'The acts were so terrible in themselves that madness seems the first and most logical explanation.'

'But could there be some case in the real, sane world of such overpowering pitch and moment that a sane man could be forced to do these atrocities?' countered Tom, and fell silent again as he concentrated on what his hands and feet were doing in the darkness.

But Tom could not stop his mind. The Master of Logic whispered to him like the Devil in the old plays. He had read Foxe's Book of Martyrs published thirty years since and knew well enough what bestial things men will do to each other when they believe their God prompts them. Even had he not, he had been raised in the Borders, son of a murdered mother, scion of a family brutalized by rieving and border warfare, who had seen women and children slaughtered to avenge some spite more than fifty years old. He had lived in Italy, and had been brought to understand the concept of the never-ending *vendetta*, visiting horrors on generation after generation. He had been a soldier and had seen first-hand what is all too often done in the terrible matters of pillage, rapine and slaughter.

To cap it all, he had read the late Nicholas Hazard's account of what the Inquisition had done to him in pursuance of their faith. The description of the terrible boot and how it had crushed his feet until the great toes of each were twisted and all but destroyed, the cropping of his ears and the smashing of his nose, all made the mere taking of a head or two seem simple and everyday-sane by comparison.

Then even his thoughts had to pause. He found himself following Ugo off the ladder, stopping in his downward climb as he felt more than saw an opening gape beside him – a portal of utter blackness in the near-blackness of the well he was plumbing. Within this, like Jonah in the belly of the whale, Ugo was moving almost invisibly. Tom stepped in beside him and unslung the dark-lantern from his belt as Will also crept into the blackness beside them.

'But there's the account given by Beale the Silversmith's lad,' he continued, his thought simply overflowing in the dark and running through the shadows scarcely louder than the restless breeze that seemed to be breathing around them: 'of the great faceless monster who sobbed and sobbed for hours without end over his bloody work; who brought flies without number to feast on the blood he had spilt and came and went through the fabric of the Bridge like a ghost.'

'Except for the fact that ghosts need no passageways,' said Ugo, striking the flint.

'And mad ones were not likely to bother with the greasing of hinges,' added Will, as Tom cupped the tiny spark against the restless gasping of the bridge until the wick within the lantern caught.

'Further,' added Tom at last, 'although the Bridge is a huge and active place, it seems inconceivable that a monster such as the terrified apprentice has described should exist here unnoticed.'

'Unless the creature were truly a ghost, coming up from hell to wreak havoc on earth and then return,' suggested Ugo helpfully – though Tom doubted his solid friend would have entertained the thought so happily had he not been holding the lantern aloft as he spoke.

'Unless he is hot from hell as you say,' added Will.

'You sound more like Kit Marlowe than Will Shakespeare,'

said Tom, using the thought to give them pause and a little breathing space – his eyes as busy as his lips. 'The man who did these things must have been seen. And in the matter of the ghost, then, my friends, we find ourselves forced back to the matter of the greased hinges. Ghosts do not grease hinges.'

'Only men do that,' allowed Ugo.

'And *sane* men at that,' emphasized Will.

'An important point, Will, for the corollary of that thought is that if the man has been seen, then he must indeed seem sane, and act as a sane man acts. For some of the time at least.'

As the light from the lantern flames gathered, they found themselves standing in a good-sized tunnel. Behind them, it opened into a drop that would take them straight down to the river if they missed their hold on the ladder upon their return. Before them, the stone passageway led, like the flight of an arrow, straight into gathering darkness – darkness that folded them into its suffocating breast again as Tom nodded to his companions and Ugo closed the shutter until only a narrow, golden blade of light shone before them along their dangerous way.

'But,' reasoned Tom as he moved forward, with Ugo bearing the lantern at one shoulder and Will with a pistol at the other, 'sane men do not lop off the heads of passing women and put them on poles for display.'

Somewhere deep within his mind he automatically began to count his steps.

'Except for executioners, of course,' said Ugo.

'Another avenue for consideration,' allowed Will.

'Could this man be an executioner commissioned to execute these women?' Tom wondered. 'No. Where was the due process of Master Bacon's law? Where was the trial? The judgement? Not even in the dark and twisted world that Poley inhabits is execution performed like this.'

'Poley executed Marlowe. All the world knows that,' said Will.

'That is true, and Poley did it – but Marlowe's head has never been displayed and the matter has been covered as a tavern brawl. On the other hand, Mary of Scots was beheaded. That too is true and Poley caused it – but there was a process stretching back to Queen Elizabeth's own signature before Mary's head was taken or displayed. And the same is true of Babbington, Titchbourne and the rest, whose heads, for all I know, are still up there on the gateway. This, therefore, is something else.'

'I see where your logic leads you,' whispered Ugo, awed. 'But can such a creature exist? A man through whom the devils of madness move at will? Sometimes seeming sane and sometimes insane?'

Before he answered, Tom held up his hand for silence. Something had been whispering at the edges of his hearing for a moment or two now – something beyond the sighing of the breeze in the passageway or the rumbling of the river in the stones; something beyond the squeaking, whispering scuttle of the rats whose eyes gleamed red in the outwash of Ugo's lantern: a mumbling moaning. It rose and fell monotonously on the outer edge of hearing, and there beside it was a groaning rumble – faintly familiar but disturbingly out of place.

'I saw today a woman seeming cured of the pox,' said Tom, after a while, 'so little marked that even a doctor could not at first tell she was stricken.'

'Then how was her disease revealed?' asked Will at once.

'She passed it to her lover,' said Tom simply. 'It was revealed through him – her disease in his flesh. You saw it. You were there. Panne the Goldsmith.'

'Then she was not cured,' said Ugo.

Will grunted in agreement.

'Ah, but,' whispered Tom, 'you see how it takes us into realms where things are half-so and half-not-so? Neither black nor white, but numberless shades of grey?'

'Such a world would never do for me!' said Ugo with a shiver.

'Nor for me to live in. But I visit, sometimes. It is Robert Poley's world, I think.'

Will, who knew Poley's world, nodded his grim agreement.

'But do not suppose that a world of certainties is always and forever better. It was men of absolute belief, after all, who twisted poor Nick Hazard on the rack and near-crippled him with the boot. It is men who know when white is white who set torches to witches . . .' warned Tom.

'Could this be witchcraft?' demanded Ugo, much struck.

'What! Do you think that some woman sits somewhere in the case with a spell-book and a bodkin, and whenever she casts her spell the axe-man comes?' scoffed Will.

'You make it sound strange; but remember, Panne has been taken and tested for alchemy,' countered Ugo.

'And necromancy too. But by Poley,' interrupted Tom. 'Poley again. Does Poley strike you as a witchfinder, Will?'

'Were I a witch, he's a man I'd fear,' whispered the playwright.

'He seeks Catholics,' mused Tom. 'Spies, plotters against the state. He looks for men who would damage the realm and the crown. And in that pursuit he is ruthless beyond limit. Outside it, I know not . . .'

The three of them paused then, as a warmer draught played across their right cheeks, telling them of another passage there. Ugo swung the blade of light that cut the darkness before them until it revealed, from top to bottom, the centre of a narrow opening. In the silence it was easy to hear that the unvarying moaning rolling rumbling was whispering in from dead ahead.

'No,' said Tom, at his most decisive. 'We go onward.' In his mind, however, he registered one hundred and twenty steps so far.

'Yet, were the witch to threaten the state,' he continued, 'she would have everything to fear from Poley. And as witchcraft must, if it is true, always threaten God's good order . . .' He let his voice drift off.

'At the very least,' said Ugo, product of his times and his beliefs, 'because it upsets the order ordained in the Bible and gives women power over men.'

'And there may be powerful women in the case,' Tom allowed as they got back under way again. 'Mistress Panne. Rich and powerful; fount of the business – almost, one might say, the brain behind it. Like Mistress Van Der Leyden. And Mistress Midmore, come to that. Nor can we doubt from Master Terrill's observations, that Alice Panne is the power behind much of the wickedness in both her father and her lover. Perhaps sometimes it is enough for a man to be weak, that a woman may damn him without the Devil becoming involved at all.'

'You sound like John Knox,' said Will, 'except that he held that women given governance over men were the work of the Devil in their very existence and an abomination in the sight of God in any case.'

'"The First Blast of the Trumpet against the Monstrous Regiment of Women",' said Tom. 'Like the Book of Martyrs, 'tis thirty years old. Why should it return to haunt us now?'

'Has Knox returned to London then? Is that what you're asking?' wondered Ugo. 'Is it John Knox that we seek?'

'John Knox has been dead and buried more than twenty years,' said Tom.

'That is as may be,' countered Will wryly. 'But that would not stop him being a suspect, would it? Given what we have just been discussing.'

But the dark thoughts and the whispered conversation were brought to an abrupt end in any case by the slamming of an iron door, somewhere immediately in front of them. And far too close for comfort.

Ugo's fingers went to close the dark-lantern completely but Tom hissed, 'Wait! The priming!'

Ugo shrugged and nodded, swinging the light towards his companions as they took out their most favoured weapons and made sure they were ready. Even Ugo's pistols were not blessed with perfect mechanisms and a misfire could be fatal. Only the master gunsmith, very much on his honour now, disdained to check his own pistol before he closed the door of the dark-lantern entirely and the three of them became one with the black and timeless heart of the Bridge.

Tom stood. His mouth was open wide, gasping the dank air silently. In his right hand he held one of Ugo's double-barrelled flintlock pistols; in his left, his Solingen dagger. Beside him on his left he could feel Will, also standing stock-still, by the minute variations of the air between them. Then, beyond Will, his adjusting eyes picked out the first of the pattern of golden pinpricks that were the rivets and fastenings on the dark-lantern; and soon these too told him where both his companions stood.

Tom moved forward, counting upward, hoping that the sigh of the restless breeze through the place and the echoing power of the water thundering distantly in the stonework all around them would hide their footfalls, even from devils and ghosts, though, to be truthful, he was less worried about the sound of his boot heels than about the sound his heart was making as it pounded in his chest – particularly now that the moaning and the rumbling that had gathered so weirdly in the darkness ahead had both unaccountably stopped.

They ran into the gateway three hundred and sixteen steps from the opening of the passageway. Tom, in the lead, met the obstruction first, and to begin with he could not understand exactly what it was. For his pistol hand went onward – between two metal bars, in fact. His boot toe, advanced behind the gun, also went part-way through before a formless force seemed to arrest his foot in mid-air; and it was not until the knuckles of his left hand and the breadth of his forehead both met solid resistance sharply and painfully that he realized what was going on.

His first instinct was to jerk the gun back into safety by his side. Then he turned, hissing a warning as Will and Ugo crowded in behind. As he did so, on the very instant that he turned, a great beam of light fell down upon him from above, a huge cascade of brightness so powerful that it seemed to have weight. It was there for a moment while Tom looked back at the faces of his friends, and Will went white as a ghost himself while Ugo actually shouted out with shock.

Then it was dark again and a great echoing *THUD!* of sound followed the first wave of returning darkness down. There was a scrabbling sound of feverish fingers scraping at catches and the hissing of Ugo's breath as he burned himself on the hot metal and blackened glass of the lamp. Then he threw the little doorway in the front of the thing wide and Tom turned to see what his friends had already seen for themselves.

Behind the barred door there stood a little chamber, stone-walled, ancient, running with dampness. In the centre of this stood a table, seemingly as old as the moss-green walls themselves. Against the table, standing level with their own heads, was the head of Frau Van Der Leyden, polled and ready for display, staring at them wide-eyed with shock and outrage. Beside her on the ancient boards lay the axe that had taken it from her shoulders, its blade blackly crusted, its edge gleaming wickedly; and standing beside the table, the source of at least part of that disturbing rumbling: a great old whetstone on a foot-turned treadle.

Hanging on the back of the chair behind this, looking weirdly like the face of a skinned blackamoor, wide-eyed and screaming, was the dead black leather of an executioner's full face mask.

'Up!' shouted Tom, the quickest to recover and understand; and up they went, up a well like the one they had come down out in the street. But this one led to no well-greased grating – only to a closed trapdoor – closed and unyielding. And, most likely, locked.

For, when they came back down, they found the door into the strange room locked and no way to get further at all. So back they traced their steps, Tom counting in reverse, back to the opening above the river beneath the street and the grate. They climbed the ladder and hauled themselves through the greased grating up into the moon-bright roadway atop the bridge. Here Tom turned to the angle of the passageway below, and strode out straight and true across the road.

209

Three hundred steps along his way he came hard up against the door of St Thomas's Chapel. Closed, bolted and barred. Deserted and forbidden since the days of Harry the King.

Soon to be opened after all – and handed over by old Harry's daughter Queen Elizabeth to the rich Dutch aristocrat and recent widower, Julius Van Der Leyden.

CHAPTER TWENTY-EIGHT

Chapel

'Perkin,' said Ugo, pushing his weight against St Thomas's Chapel door until the great lock creaked. 'Perkin has the keys to all the locks upon the Bridge. If anyone has the key to this one, it will be Perkin.'

'Possibly,' said Will. 'But Perkin stands high on the list of suspicion.'

'Could we not call him – then gauge his reactions to what befalls as proof or otherwise of his guilt? Would that not work? Tom?' Ugo asked his thoughtful friend.

'We did not call him for our little adventure down to hell,' persisted Will.

'How else will we get into the chapel? 'Tis where we must go and yet it is barred and bolted against the likes of us. We need a key. And for a key we need Perkin. We must risk what he will learn, what he might do. But we cannot proceed without him. Can we? Tom?'

Tom stood silently with their importunate conversation washing over him. How could he not have seen it? he was asking himself. How could he have been so close – been living next door – and still not have seen it?

The chapel was the heart of the Bridge. And, as such, it was a kind of heart for London itself. The building was ancient – almost as timeless as the fabric of the Bridge, of which it was an integral part. It had been dedicated originally to St Thomas Aquinas, the great Catholic Dominican scholar and mystic, but later to St Thomas of Canterbury as a more English dedication at the start of the pilgrimage road south – while such a road was permitted to exist. Even under Henry it had just managed to survive, becoming first the Chapel of St Thomas the Apostle and then Lady Chapel – the last piece of Catholic ground in London; and that ground standing, like the Lord himself, on water.

Young King Edward had killed it forty-five years ago – ravished it and killed it. So it had stood, defaced, forbidden and barred since then. Even Bloody Mary had failed to breathe much life into the cold stone corpse; but then she was more interested in hot death than cold life, so they said. So there it stood: the kind of place where secrets gathered, like wild birds in open lofts; like teeming flies in hot rooms. But, given what it was and where, secrets such as gathered there could never stand entirely unguarded; never remain utterly unknown.

This was the place that the Earl of Essex had convinced the Queen to hand over to a Dutch interloper, unprotected and in public, in thirty-six hours' time.

'I'm with Will,' said Tom at last. 'If we can do without Perkin, then we should.'

'Aye, but can we?' demanded Ugo, unconvinced.

'I think we can, if the moon and the tide stay with us.'

'What do you mean, Tom?' exploded the exasperated Dutchman. Only to be met with one of Tom's most dazzling, most shallow, smiles.

'Why, Ugo,' he said playfully, 'what is the point of being boarded by pirates in your own fair parlour if you cannot learn a little from the experience?'

Half an hour later, with the moon westering in a clear sky behind them and the full tide sweeping in beneath them, Tom and Ugo held a purloined little ferryboat in place as Will slung his first hook up towards the balcony of St Thomas's Chapel hard by Tom's own shop. The combined expertise of childhoods upon the Avon, Ullswater, Windermere and the Zuyder Zee allowed Tom and Ugo to hold the little vessel still for Will, who was also exercising expertise gained in the setting of stages and scenery – if nowhere else.

As soon as Will's first two hooks were up firmly enough to hold the boat, Tom left Ugo with the oars and lashed the bow as Portia Shaddow had done at the height of the tide last night, to a ring in the nearest starling. 'We're set,' he whispered after a moment, and the three of them were away.

As Tom had observed last night, the height of the tide brought them no great distance below the balconies. A desperate man might have jumped and held the flooring with his hands; but there was no need. The balcony outside the tightclosed chapel was sound enough to take the weight of hooks and men climbing up the ropes beneath them. Soon the three of them were side by side upon it.

The solid wooden construct went round in an L, for the rear of the chapel thrust out along the starling upon which it stood, the rugged brick Chapel House reaching down almost to the water. On this side, and from this close, it was surprising how big the ancient building actually was. On the far side, they had noted as they manoeuvred into place, there were even slipways topped by massive, iron-chained gates.

They had brought the dark-lantern and huddled round it now to light it from Ugo's flint. Then Ugo shone the narrow beam on the boards pegged roughly over the gaping wounds where the stained-glass windows had been.

At first it seemed that the place was as secure on this side as it seemed to be on the other, as it clearly was from the street – almost as impregnable as Tom's house next door, in fact. But no. After some moments of close inspection, Tom found a chink in the ancient building's armour: a loose board which, when moved, loosened another. And so, within the hour following their conversation in the street outside, the three men crawled gingerly in over the ruined altar and stepped down into the wide nave of the place.

Tom at once pulled out his dagger and his double-barrelled pistol, all too well aware of whom or what they had followed into the echoing vastness of the place. He felt Will stirring at his side as his pistols slid into his hands as well; and this time, Ugo put the lantern down to get his own revolving masterpiece out of his belt. All three of them gathered round the dim lamp to look to their priming. Then they were off.

It was almost impossible to move with any hope of silence here. The apparently limitless shadows around them, rising storey after storey towards the invisible roof, multiplied every whisper of cloth on cloth, every breath and every footfall. At the same time, the air was still and dead as though no zephyr had dared invade the place since Edward VI had finally proscribed it and ordered it defaced, without and within. The tide, at the flood, hesitated, so that even the stones were still.

Yet it seemed to Tom that there was something about the place, some bustle just below the obvious, ready to burst into dangerous life; something there, just beneath the still, smooth surface that whispered of terrible danger, had a man the ears to hear it – like the great dark lake north of Glasgow visited during his student days, where the locals said a fearsome monster dwelt. What was the name of the place? Ness. Yes, that was it: Loch Ness.

At least the floor was clear. Tom had entertained visions of them picking their way through splintered pews and the shards of shattered saints. That was some comfort, given the paucity of the thread of light they followed through the echoing cavern of the empty nave, as they searched for their madman and prayed that he possessed only one good axe.

That thought brought a frown to Tom's face too. For had the others not seen the axe below – and the whetstone and the head and all – by the flashing of a great light? A light that had shone down a shaft that led straight down from this place to that strange cell door. From this place – from this very place, if their calculations were right – where there was a most striking lack of light at the moment!

Tom moved forward until he was right by Ugo in the lead with the dark-lantern. 'Look for a small door,' he breathed, 'such as might lead to a side room or chapel.'

Ugo nodded, and turned to his right. There would be great doors at the end of the nave, Tom had calculated, such as were unlikely to open easily or silently; and there was the matter of the humming bustle that seemed to come from all around them – but most especially from below them.

That was interesting to the Master of Logic. For it was the sound that had alerted both the apprentice silversmith and himself to Margery Midmore's chapel and death-room. Both the apprentice's garret and the dead room beside it were hard by the eaves of this place – an inch or two of lath and plaster away from them, like as not; and more than fifty feet above their heads, therefore. Yet this sound now came from below. From the cellarage.

Tom closed on Ugo again and drew breath to tell him to abandon his search for side rooms and to look instead for a stairway; but that breath warned Tom that it was too late to change his instructions now. For Ugo had at last found something: a small side door that promised to lead out of the echoing vastness of the place into something more contained – where some more detailed communication, perhaps, might be risked; if Tom was wrong about what he could smell.

The door was unsecured and swung open easily. Ugo pushed the lantern through before him – while Tom and Will pushed their pistols through on either side of him – and singed his fingertips again as he swung the metal wide to let out more light.

The light fell directly upon a little kind of altar. It was scarcely more than a table, covered with a heavy cloth. There were no crucifixes or plates or ornaments upon it; but there was a picture. The picture, which sat in a gilded frame, was not well executed and clearly of no great worth; and that was fortunate, for it was spattered with blood and crawling with flies.

It was a portrait of a red-haired, green-eyed woman. Even in its current condition and given the lack of expertise in its execution, it was a striking piece of work. It was a picture of the first dead woman – the one with no name, whose head lay in Thomas Walsingham's cellar and whose body was weighted at the bottom of the river, somewhere hard by Captain Shaddow's camp. It was she, even down to the missing earrings that matched the finger-ring Tom had taken from the unconscious Calpurnia Shaddow.

The stench of the place seemed to seep into them – accompanied by the familiar buzzing – so strong that at first Tom thought that this must have been the restlessness that had brought Loch Ness and its monster to his mind; except that he remained convinced that it also came from below his feet.

'How can this be?' choked Ugo, flashing the broad beam round the place. The room was slightly larger than it seemed at first to be. The little chapel was merely a part of it. There were simple, almost nun-like living quarters, piles of simple – spoiled and fly-covered – provisions. Clothing neatly folded. A little truckle bed. But then again, not quite so nun-like. The rotting provisions were ample, necessities enhanced by a range of candied fruits, marchpanes and other sweetmeats. Tom, looking through them, was minded most forcefully of dimpled cheeks and blackened teeth.

'It is the room I have been seeking,' acknowledged Tom. 'It is the first murder room. And I had just realized that it had to be here. But that . . . that cannot be the portrait of the dead woman, surely.'

'How can it not be?' asked Will, clearly badly shaken, for all that he had seen the head itself. 'Who else can the portrait belong to?'

'The dead woman's mother . . . grandmother . . . Look at the costume, Will. Women do not wear anything like that these days, surely. I know that Kate does not, even when rusticating down at Scadbury . . .'

'Well then, who is she? Who are they?' demanded Ugo. 'What was a woman doing here with a chapel given over to the memory of her mother in a defaced church on the Bridge. And how can it be that no one living on the Bridge knew of her? For here she lived, and here she died.'

'Perkin,' said Tom. 'Perkin at the least must have known. For if this place was closed and secured by order of the King and yet a woman came and went, then Perkin must have known. Who else could have permitted such a thing – and yet managed to keep it secret? So secret that no one else upon the bridge can put a name to her. But Perkin must have known. And if he knew but did not say, then . . .'

'Then he also,' said a cold new voice, 'must be working for me.' And suddenly Ugo's little dark-lantern was no longer the only light in the haunted little chamber.

'Poley,' said Tom, without even turning to face the familiar interloper. 'Of course. It had to be. And if Perkin knows who she was, then you know too.'

'Indeed I do.'

'Then who is she?'

'Her name was Mary Barton – the second of that name, I understand – and she lived here by secret permission of the Queen, to keep a little remembrance of her grandmother's sister Elizabeth . . .'

'Elizabeth Barton. The Maid of Kent,' whispered Tom. 'The girl who spoke out against King Henry's marriage to Anne Boleyn.'

'You never cease to astonish me, Tom,' said Poley. 'I scarce need talk at all these days. A syllable or two and off you go, like a coursed hare through the most complex warren, straight to the burrow of truth.'

'Elizabeth Barton was the last woman whose head was put up on the Bridge,' finished Tom. 'But it can't be up there still. They must have taken it down when they pulled down the Drawbridge Gate and replaced it with Nonesuch House.'

Poley took the cloth on the altar and lifted the hem to reveal a black lead box beneath. 'Down, like Thomas More's, and into a good black box,' he said. 'But I fear it will not be buried with its final guardian. Unless I sling it into the river, eh Tom?' Then he sobered down and continued. 'That was all Mistress Mary's care,' he said: 'to keep a little secret chapel here in this vast mausoleum in memory of a poor girl touched with madness. Or by God. Who can tell? Bloody Mary allowed it, and thought of reopening the place I'm told. And the Queen allowed it. In secret. But then, thanks to the Earl of Essex, all that was due to come to an end, of course. Tomorrow, in fact. And so I set Perkin to watch Mistress Mary for me; as he was already doing for the Warden and the Queen . . .'

'Because Elizabeth Barton, and her great-niece Mary here beside, were Catholics – and supported by Catholic gifts. Thus, on the one hand, although she lived upon the Bridge, no one else upon the Bridge would recognize her, for only a very few ever saw her keep her lonely vigil and all of them were silent. But on the other hand, the closing of the chapel might bring more of Mistress Barton's Catholic helpers and sympathizers out into the light,' said Tom. 'So Essex's plan fits in with Poley's profession.'

Poley shrugged coldly, and threw up his hand like a fencer acknowledging a hit.

'Is that why he took her head?' demanded Tom. 'Is that why he took hers first?' And who knows what Robert Poley might have answered had not the rocket gone off then?

Tom for one was not particularly surprised to find of a sudden that there was a Watch officer standing breathless behind his adversary, for he had worked out what the buzzing in the cellarage must be and was beginning to work towards the light as well.

'It's the signal,' said the officer. 'The rocket's gone off, sir.'

Tom's eyes met Poley's then, with scarcely a flicker as his mind leaped nimbly from one branch of the problem to the next.

'The ides are come?' he said.

CHAPTER TWENTY-NINE

The Ides

T he west-facing section of the Chapel House below had
been cleared into a great warehouse almost as big as the
chapel itself above. Here, pulled up behind the chained doors
and the slipway, Poley had assembled a secret armada, which
waited under a great blaze of light for the signal to be launched;
and an army of soldiers and watch officers waited to ride in it,
all of them speaking in subdued tones, their conversation
buzzing like flies. Each man had his assigned place and all
were well rehearsed in attaining it. The only confusion in the
well-practised drill came when Poley took Tom, Will and Ugo
in with him.

Out they went in a flotilla across the height of the tide. In
each boat sat four rowers, pulling powerfully as watchmen
piloted them surely through the Pool of London below the
bridge. Westward and southward they raced through the
anchored shipping of the early hours below the setting moon.
In twenty minutes they had sped across beyond the Beer
Wharf to the first of the slackwater pools where they had
searched for the body of Mary Barton with Watson the water
poet – and found Margery Midmore instead. Across this they
sped on to the sloping lawn of the sheep-filled lower water
meadow where the grounds of Bleeke House undulated down
into the river.

Poley leaped out as soon as they beached and was off at once. Tom went at his shoulder without a second thought, his black boots skidding in the slick grass. Will and Ugo came close behind.

The rest of the army paused, drew itself up into ranks and began to organize itself in due order of battle.

'I left as many well-prepared men in the house as I dared,' yelled Poley with Tom's trick of starting to talk mid-thought. 'More would have tipped the game.'

With Poley, as ever, thought Tom cynically, the game was all.

'I returned a couple more this afternoon – with their dreadful *dunderbusses*,' he added.

'Would I had stayed!' grumbled Ugo.

'Whose work do we do here, protecting Dutch bankers from English apprentices?' demanded Will.

'The Queen's!' spat Poley.

'Not Essex's?' asked the cynical playwright.

'There is more to this than the tobacco monopoly,' said Tom. 'Trust me.'

'Aye, Tom,' said Will. 'I will trust thee – if no one else, in this.'

They topped the rise of the sheep field then and looked across the wide steps of the raised lawns to the back of the house itself, where all was ablaze and a-bustle. Wasting no more breath on conversation, the four of them ran on.

The upper stories of Bleeke House were dark, except where the red light from attackers' torches danced bloodily across it. Downstairs it was different. The lamps and candles in all the lower rooms were lit. The blazing torches carried by the mob surrounding the house expanded the light they gave. Between the two blazes of brightness stood black walls and doors; and windows piled with furniture turned into effective *barricadoes* where the well-armed Hollanders were seeing off the siege.

For the time being at least.

As the four newcomers drew nearer, they saw the simple balance of the situation. The Dutch defenders had enough firepower to keep their attackers back beyond the critical distance over which their torches could be thrown; but once the withering fire of the pistols, dags, muskets and *dunderbusses* began to slacken, the apprentices would get close enough to hurl their flambards inwards and set fire to the house. The balance was beginning to turn against the Dutch, for some of the attackers were armed with more than steel and fire. Even as Tom drew near enough to hear what the men were saying, so a shot rang out close by.

A cheer went up, almost drowning a scream that echoed from the house.

'That's done for one of them!' exulted someone. 'Another couple of Petty's guineas well earned.'

'We'll be in there getting our own gold soon,' said another. 'A guilder's as good as a guinea. It's all as good as gold.'

Tom did not stand and pass the time of day at this. He was watching Poley and Poley was away to the right, flashing in and out of the light like a meteor.

There was no time for Tom to share thoughts or wishes with Will or Ugo. They would have to look to themselves. And each was likely to have plans in this coil that were different from the Master of Logic's, in any case. They would be after money and love. He was after the truth.

Still, he hesitated for an instant for a final word. 'Will! The gatehouse!' he called. Then he went after Poley like the hound that courses the hare.

Outside the ring of fire, beyond the range of the defenders' shot, behind the mob and unobserved, the pair ran round towards the front of the building. Poley ran without variation or hesitation. To a prearranged destination, therefore, reasoned Tom; to an assignation. That was most likely to be with Mark Antony Terrill, who would be waiting to hand over the last of his proof to his spy master: the final details of the identities behind the code-names from the football – Brutus, Cassius and the rest. Ringleaders to be arrested tonight and racked tomorrow, and racked every morrow after that till they met their end on Tyburn Hill, drained of every drop of knowledge they could find or fabricate.

Panne, Petty and Beale, thought Tom. Who else? Any restless apprentices who had tried to profit from this. And any outsider here in the hope of a little fortune who got caught up in the trap. Then, at last, any enemy of Poley's paymasters whose name might credibly be added to the list, until the would-be conspirators were left as flat as the deflated football that had begun all this and sealed their several fates.

Beside the house there was a long herb garden that stood darkly behind a tall hedge. Poley vanished through a gate in this so abruptly that Tom came near to missing it. He turned at the last minute, skidding a little wildly, and hurled himself to one side, lucky not to fall into the bay tree that served as a gatepost. Here, behind the fragrant branches, he froze, for Poley had slowed to a walk.

'Are you there?' called the spy master. And again, a little louder, over the roar of battle: 'Are you there?'

'Here!' came Terrill's familiar voice.

Poley turned and ran towards it, zigzag along the paths between the herb beds. Tom could only make out his progress because he knew roughly where to look – and because Poley was a good deal more vain in the matter of white lace and silver buttons than was safe for a spy at night. Tom was wearing all black, and the only things like to glister in the flickering torchlight or the fading moonshine were his guns. He decided he dare follow, therefore, safely unsuspected in the shadows. Off he set a-tiptoe in Poley's footsteps across the garden.

'Who's there?' demanded Poley, so suddenly that Tom froze again and nearly fell. But Poley wasn't speaking to him. Out of the darkness of the hedge nearest the house stepped three figures. Terrill, Tom recognized at once, in the middle. Two others flanked him. The three were suddenly very near to Poley. And that was bad, Tom realized, because the two strangers were dressed alike in black. Distant light gleamed on boots and spurs; on silver vizard masks and the silvered parts of pistols. One pistol was pointed at Terrill and the other dead at Poley.

'You came here to get information, sirrah,' said a sneering voice in a tone as cold as any Poley used. 'You'll give it instead, if you value your creature here. How soon before the Watch arrives?'

By the time this little speech was over, Tom was flat on his belly on the ground, easing himself closer to the unexpected situation as swiftly and silently as he could.

Poley hesitated, clearly thinking. 'They are serious, master,' called Terrill. 'We are outplayed here – checked and mated. Tell them what they want, I beg of you, without equivocation.'

To emphasize his words the first speaker fired his pistol and the bullet smashed into the ground immediately in front of Poley; blessed inches from Tom's hand.

'A few minutes, no more,' said Poley at once. 'They are marching up through the water meadow as we speak.'

'Excellent,' said the sneering voice. 'Now if you will just describe the guards you have placed – oh, let us say, between here and the Bridge . . .'

Tom was at Poley's boot heel now, an oozing blob of shadow unremarked amongst the black borage and tall rosemary. 'If he asks about London, then they're bound for Dover,' he whispered and Poley jumped like a spring lamb. 'One shot down and no sign of reloading,' he added.

'What's the matter?' snapped the masked interrogator.

'Horsefly bit me,' answered Poley swiftly enough to allay suspicion.

As Tom added further in a ghostly whisper, 'If they ask about the road, they're on the water, as far as Deptford at any rate.'

'Between here and the Bridge there are men taking up positions at the Bleeke House turning into Horsley Down,' persisted Poley, a little too loudly. 'Again at the Beer House turning and at the bridge over Morgan's Ditch . . .'

'Their orders?'

'To stop any man or groups of men on foot, horseback or carriage.'

'Enough!' spat the second figure. 'Go to your master, spy!'

'You know them, Poley?' asked Tom as Terrill staggered forward.

But even before Poley had a chance to answer, a shot rang out and Terrill whirled aside to fall like a chopped oak, pistolled in the back.

Poley hurled himself forward but Tom, who was far ahead of him in mind if not in body, caught his heel and tripped him just at the very instant that the second shot rang out, from the second barrel of the double-barrelled pistol.

The shot whipped through the space that Poley's head had lately occupied, sounding indeed like a massive horsefly come to bite him again, as he crashed to the ground every bit as convincingly as Terrill had done; and lucky not to crush his secret saviour as he landed.

The murderous pair stepped forward to check their handiwork and Tom eased his pistol free, wishing he had had a chance to cock it. But before matters could proceed any further, another figure stepped into the herb garden.

''Urry along you two,' said a disturbingly familiar voice. 'The watch is comin' and there'll be queer-cuffins unnumbered soon. Let them fools cry clubs and go dahn the Newgate Hole. Let's us grab the gelt and get gone dahn the river.'

The pair of masked murderers turned and vanished. The third figure stayed for an instant, surveying the herb garden, masked by shadows if by nothing more.

'Captain sends his compliments,' he said after a heartbeat. 'We'll be seein' you soon, I daresay. Look forward to a little chat then. Goodnight, masters.'

He turned, vanished.

The pair of them were up at once, running over to check on Terrill. There was nothing to be done for him – even in the shadows they could see he was far beyond even Dr Theodore's reach, for much of his head was gone.

They turned to follow the three masked men, but they hesitated, for they knew well enough that the hearty, mildly amused words might be a trap, with more double-barrelled pistols set to spring it upon them.

'He knew we were here,' breathed Poley. 'Why not kill us and end it?'

'Because I let his father live – though I lied to you about it. Also, I haven't yet caught the faceless man,' said Tom.

With the sounds of full battle beginning to rage behind them, and the first stream of deserters beginning to fall back into the arms of the law that waited on Horsely Down, Tom led Poley to the carriages; and, like the master spy seeking his intelligencer, the Master of Logic knew just where to look for them. There, out in the shadows beside the gateposts, three familiar vehicles stood, apparently untended, their horses cropping the grass and whinnying nervously at the gunfire.

'Get Rackmaster Topcliffe up and about,' breathed Tom as they approached. 'The first of his clients lies here. At least I suspect that is what Master Terrill would tell you, if he were here.'

'Can you tell me anything else that Terrill would have imparted?' challenged Poley, his voice tinged with irony.

'Certainly. But let us look to Brutus and Cassius in here first.'

Inside the coaches, trussed like capons fit for the spit, lay Master Petty and Master Panne. 'Brutus and Cassius, as I said,' hissed Tom, easing Panne's gag and letting the man gasp in great gulps of air. 'And I can name if not place most of the others. Now, sir, where is Master Casca? Beale, I mean?'

'He's up at the house,' said Panne at once. Then he persisted, with hardly a pause for breath, 'But you must get *them*! The masked men that robbed us! Get them before they escape . . .' But then he stopped, riven by Tom's icy chuckle.

'You speak of young Metellus and Trebonius, I believe. Are you sure you want them captured, sir?'

'I want the full weight of the law to descend upon them,' wheezed Panne. 'They have attacked Master Petty and myself and made off with our gold. And we are guildsmen, sir. Masters and guildsmen both . . .' Even in his weakened condition, so

226

soon after treatment for the pox, he was capable of considerable energy – but no intuition at all, thought Tom.

Will came puffing up then. 'It's all up with the apprentices,' he gasped. 'The watch has arrived. What's toward out here?'

'Have you seen Master Beale, the silversmith?'

'What's left of him. He was lately hit by a charge from a *dunderbus* out on the front steps. Why?'

'He was the only one of the conspirators obviously unaccounted for.'

'These being?' asked Poley quietly.

'Why, Panne here, and Petty and Beale. Mistress Beale, that ruled the roost in the silversmith's – or thought she did. And poor old Jeremiah in Panne's workroom, just in case. These all confederated together to foment and finance the attack this evening that would clear the Dutch competitor Van Der Leyden off their Bridge and out of their City.'

'But that leaves three!'

'Indeed. They had another game. For their target was never Julius Van Der Leyden. Their target was the gold these fools had brought along to seed the riotous crowd. Did you not hear? Two guineas per Dutchman. And more besides, I'll warrant!'

'But they were part of Terrill's conspiracy, that turned against their confederates! Who would do such a thing?' demanded Will. And even he sounded awed by such bold perfidy.

'The mouths that have already bit the hands that feed them, Will: Alice Panne and Daniel Petty. What better way to add to the riches they had already stolen than by taking what they could get hold of here – for they must both have known of the plan, and been certain how they might best profit from it. It was Alice masterminded it all, I'll be bound. For she has a heart of flint, that girl, and a nerve of steel; Solingen at that. It was she who pistolled both Terrill and you, Poley – and a mercy I checked Ugo's records to find the double-barrel recorded there. Yes. It was she who held all the cards in this and led the others by the nose. Well, except for Decius Brutus, of course. The whole of it turned around him. And, I suspect that it was his name that started things in Mark Antony Terrill's mind rather than his own name; his name or the fact that he called the City by its cant name of Romeville. A joke that might amuse a Cambridge mind, that. A pity there's so little of it left.'

Master Panne exploded into a kind of life again at that, interrupting the Master of Logic's cool summation; and his first words confirmed in Tom's mind that the poor foolish man had half-suspected all along. 'Alice! Alice again! Would that I had never accepted her. Would that I had never married Agnes Barton – aye in spite of the shop and the gold and all. For she never loved me, the icy bitch.'

Petty chimed in. ' 'Tis that witch Alice has led my poor boy astray as easily as you have led me by the nose. A very Eve to tempt him out of the Garden of Eden with all the golden fruits . . .'

'Would that she were dead,' howled Panne. 'Would that she were dead at my feet with my guineas in her fist . . .'

'Enough of this,' snarled Poley, reducing both to sobbing silence. Then he turned to Tom. 'My intelligencers are all dead, so you must lay this plain for me,' he said. 'Who was the last of them? Who was Decius Brutus?'

'Other than being the final conspirator, he is Beale's apprentice boy. Apparently from Gravesend, but actually from closer to home than that. The tenth child of a man wanting a son. Of a man with a taste for classical names. Of a man that needed a spy in the heart of this affair as badly as you did, Poley, and who placed one of his own as even you could not.'

'But who? Who is Beale's apprentice?' cried Poley. 'Who is this last conspirator?'

'Decius Brutus Shaddow,' answered Tom.

CHAPTER THIRTY

Frenzy

A s the frenzy around them spun out of control during the next thirty-six hours, Tom almost began to feel sorry for Robert Poley.

Everywhere Poley turned there was some other force or circumstance demanding to turn back again – or this way or that way – or around and around entirely. And Tom was caught up on the edge of this whirling madness, able to observe it all too closely. Nor was he by any means alone amongst his little band of friends.

Within the next few hours alone there was the matter of the ides to be concluded – rough-hewn if not yet finely shaped. Much against his better nature, therefore, Tom attended Poley in the Bridewell once again, motivated only by the fact that he seemed to know so much of the story Master Terrill had been employed to find out. The interview took place in a different – darker – chamber than the one where they had questioned Portia Shaddow. Here Master Panne, wearing little more than he wore to his pox treatment in the matter of shirt and bandages, was stretched upon the rack while Master Petty, bereft of his pomposity, his clothing and his liberty alike, hung against the wall in chains.

'Tell us what you know, O Master of Logic,' said Poley shortly to Tom, 'and we'll pursue matters further from there.'

'It began with Panne's business,' answered Tom in the same vein, overriding the choking but fading denials from the subject of most of the story. 'Panne was an indifferent student to a gifted master, whose only weakness was that he possessed a daughter. To the daughter, therefore, rather than to his master, Panne paid his attention. Thus he won both her hand and his smithy – and retained both after the old man died. But he knew little of the goldsmith's trade; in his wife lay all the business. They performed their marital duties and so one infant arrived, Mistress Alice. A forward, clever, chilly child. And that was all. The connubial bed became a Frost Fair. If he – or she – sought solace elsewhere, then neither complained.

'But, without Master Barton the father-in-law's genius, Panne's business began to falter. Panne went to wilder and wilder lengths to keep their enterprise afloat; and charges of alchemy were stirred. Later, even, suspicions of necromancy. For he ranged ever wider with his findings and the contacts that supplied them.

'Then came the change. Mistress Panne was lost in the river on St Nicholas' day at the Frost Fair. But then who should come sniffing around but one self-styled Captain Shaddow. He had found a corpse dressed in the robes of a goldsmith's wife. The distraught widower interviewed the scavenger Captain with the support of his clever daughter, grown to young womanhood now and a strong crutch to the weakness of his grief. A bargain was struck that went far beyond the recovery of favoured trinkets from the dear departed. The girl saw that such findings as those recovered from her mother would add to the power of the business beyond calculation, if they could be supplied regularly and in bulk. And so the dark contract was drawn.

'But the daughter of one master loved the son of another and so there came other signatories. Master Petty recovered the haberdashery and Master Beale the silverware. If accusations came that they must be generating their goods through magic, who could be surprised? And were a corpse or two brought up

230

to the Bridge – so convenient for this particular business – then necromancy became another logical fear. So you became involved, Master Poley, if you were not already watching for your own good reasons.

'But the good guildsmen that dealt in this dark business inevitably became fearful. They had been raided. They stood accused. Their places in the guild halls might be barred; their standing in their parish might be diminished. Competitors stood everywhere ready to strip away their power; and most of those competitors were Dutch. So they began to plot against the Dutchmen set to invade their new-found land – especially Van Der Leyden.

'With the help and, perhaps, the prompting of their clever, clever children, they set up the conspiracy to destroy him, using their gold to buy the anger of the apprentices. And when Marley the Dutch-backed goldsmith also appeared in their parish, why they set about ruining him too – and used the tool they had already gathered to hand.

'But the fathers believed they held the reins of this runaway horse. They were wrong. Their children did – or rather Mistress Alice did, wielding power also over Master Daniel. As the fathers gathered their gold and prepared themselves to destroy their rivals, so their children drew their own, darker plans and prepared to escape with riches beyond the dreams of normal folk. They would steal their fathers' business fortunes the day before the planned attack, then arrive at Bleeke House ready to steal again the secret gold so desperately borrowed to ensure the allegiance of the apprentices.

'It was a masterstroke. And I do not use the term mistress-stroke only because Alice for once stood advised by another: Captain Shaddow's son, Decius Brutus, who had already been placed with the unsuspecting Beale to watch matters from the other point of view; Decius, who has led the pair of them down the river, into the clutches of his father the Captain: their only hope of escape; their only chance of help.

'And so we found our two capons trussed and ready for

roasting last night, tricked and gulled and robbed by their gannet-greedy offspring then left for us.

'And that, I believe, concludes the sorry tale – except that you will wish to test my findings against the truth that the racks will wring from these two.'

'She is no daughter of mine! Would that she were hearsed,' said Master Panne as they tightened the ropes on the rack. 'Would that she were hearsed and my guineas in her coffin.' And that was all he said – while Tom was there, at least.

Alice Panne and Daniel Petty clearly needed to be found, however, and their fathers' money restored – restored to the Exchequer, as there would be no claimants surviving to demand it by the time due process of the law had been completed. The money was a tidy sum. And the Exchequer lay in Lord Burghley's grasp.

Then also facts of the matter must be recorded and the due process started, for Tom's submission in the Bridewell had only described the actions of the central knot of conspirators. There were other felons to be tracked and taken: the apprentices and their leaders as apprehended, named and interrogated; any of Shaddow's confederates or clan still at large; any other guildsmen guilty of supplying – knowingly or not – the gold used to seed the riot; even the pox doctors in the stews giving aid and comfort to a known felon. Perhaps even Dr Viner himself, who advised on the comfort in question. All of this needed to be reported by Poley to his master, the man that set him on in the first place. And that impatient man was Robert Cecil. Robert was the son of William and William Cecil was Lord Burghley, who held the Exchequer, already impatiently involved.

Then the grounds at Bleeke House must be tidied up and restored, for tomorrow the Queen herself was due to condescend upon them. Any failure of perfection, any lingering ghost of the fatal unrest would reflect upon the civil order of the capital. Civil order lay in the purview of the Council and the Lord Chamberlain. And Lord Burghley was Secretary to the

Council, while Henry Carey, Lord Hunsdon, was Lord Chamberlain – sometime friend to Tom and temperamental patron to Will Shakespeare – a man to whom Tom's findings must be reported at the earliest convenience, for even though Tom did not hold the Chamberlain's commission, he held his ear and to do less would be derelict. And dangerous, come to that.

Of course the perfection of Bleeke House reflected on even more temperamental – if not more powerful – figures than Lords Burghley and Hunsdon. It reflected upon Julius Van Der Leyden and his daughters – and the memory of his murdered wife. Total perfection, therefore, was not a target but a starting point. Every window, cracked or scorched, was to be reglazed; every hanging, marked or creased, rehung. Every wall or portico, chipped or spattered, was to be repainted; every floor repolished, every flower bed replanted, every path regravelled, every lawn returfed, and every lily regilded. And that blasted corpse they had found in the herb garden despatched with all the others forthwith.

Decius Brutus and his father, Captain Shaddow, deserved a second investigation of their own. The whole Shaddow clan needed to be found – and Master Beale's missing fortune, gone with those of Panne and Petty, though bound in the end for the Moloch of Lord Burghley's Exchequer. Not to mention Portia and Calpurnia and all the rest, no doubt; for their continued liberty was an affront to good order, and a danger to the river. And the river's safety reflected upon My Lord of Essex, through whose county it flowed.

The satisfaction of Essex, Hunsdon, Burghley and young Cecil was suddenly very germane indeed, for they were immediately to hand, each in his London home, demanding time and reassurance. Because the Court was back in White Hall Palace, while the Queen prepared to cross the Bridge tomorrow.

Tom stood in the White Hall office of Henry Carey, Lord Hunsdon and Lord Chamberlain, looking west and frowning. The palaced hump of Lambeth and the thrust of the river's

233

curve hid the Bridge and he was strangely restless out of sight of it at the moment.

'So,' said Lord Henry, looking every bit as fearsome as his supposed father King Henry – or his half-sister the Queen. 'The matter of the apprentices is settled.'

'Bar an arrest or two and some rack-work, My Lord.'

'What else must needs be settled within the day?'

'They are bringing forward Nick Hazard's funeral so that St Magnus' will be clear after evensong. That will be all for the City end. They have laid his body in a chapel of the church rather than in his own home for he has no family to tend it there and they fear the procession from the Curate House to the church will block .the Bridge when work must still proceed. Thus the final dressing of the streets around St Magnus' and the final redecoration of the Bridge will complete things for the Lord Mayor and the guild halls.'

'And you will thither, Tom? To the service at St Magnus'?'

'I must. I remain Apollo Marley until this section of my own slight quest is done. It is Apollo Marley's church – short a brace of wardens and some congregation of a sudden. And the man died saving me from Daniel Petty's spite. But there is much to be completed today before that, My Lord, for I swear the Bridge itself is still not secure . . .'

Before Tom could continue, Lord Henry's secretary opened the plain little door to the long room and showed in two more visitors. They came like a wind from the north and the east, thought Tom – each one colder than the other.

'Master Poley here tells me he fears some Catholic outrage against Her Majesty upon the Bridge,' said Robert Cecil in his quiet, chilly voice. He may have nodded at Tom or that may have been a twitch in his twisted back.

Tom bowed just low enough for courtesy – a little deeper than civility.

Lord Henry watched as though amused. 'Master Musgrave was expressing doubts as you came in,' he said.

234

'Less about Catholic plots and more about a madman loose with an axe,' said Tom roundly.

There was a silence as the two members of Her Majesty's Council took stock of who was clearly mad here.

Then Poley spoke. 'It is the subject of a Crowner's quest already. Danby has deputed Thomas Walsingham in the matter. Three women have been killed on the Bridge within the fortnight. Your secretaries, My Lords, both have copies of all the reports, most recently on Frau Van Der Leyden's death. I suggest you read that first.

'But all of it remains germane to what I am saying. The first victim seems to have been one Mary Barton, whom both of you will recall, but in a different context . . .'

'The Maid of Kent,' said Tom helpfully. 'Also beheaded, if rather more officially.'

'The second victim was Margery Midmore, a Catholic convert who was, apparently, placed to keep Mary Barton secretly supplied, as part of a small Catholic plot to keep their little chapel going. And the third victim you know about . . .'

'Particularly as the marriage between Frau and Meinheer Van Der Leyden seems to have been one of business convenience,' added Tom. 'And because, as I'm sure Master Poley is about to mention, the Hoogewegens, from whose loins the lady sprang, are the last great Catholic family in Holland.'

'Therefore we have less to fear, perhaps, on Her Majesty's behalf,' persisted Poley. '*If* the madman is still alive and at liberty, then he kills Catholics, and that is that.'

'Master Musgrave,' asked Lord Henry. 'You have further worries?'

'Yes, My Lord. I believe the man *is* still alive and at liberty. Only last night I followed him to his lair beneath the Bridge and would be glad of an opportunity to take a guard of armed watchmen back with me thither now. Also I remain unconvinced that he is killing Catholics. There are other things about these women than their religion that might attract the attention of someone seeking to take their heads.'

'Such as?' demanded Cecil.

'They all had red hair. BESIDES – ' he had to raise his voice to cover the snigger his answer brought – 'Besides, My Lords, Master Poley's persuasive case does not really explain why the killer puts their heads up on the Bridge – on poles above the Great Stone Gateway, as though they were traitors too.'

'They were Catholics. Perhaps he thinks that they *were* traitors,' snapped Poley.

'Master Poley brings us exactly to the point!' countered Tom at his most fierce and fearsome. 'The fact that a madman is supposed to *think* at all makes him far too dangerous to leave at liberty.'

'Very well,' decided Lord Henry, overriding even Robert Cecil. 'This must all be referred to the Crowner, whose quest this is. Thomas Walsingham is well known to you both. Therefore refer to him. Poley, you have responsibilities beyond your current concerns about this madman. You had best look to those – but where they involve Master Musgrave, allow him a little liberty for the moment. Master Musgrave, you must refer to the Crowner for the men you need, but as your other responsibilities in the case so far seem to be those of Logic rather than of Law, I believe we should leave with you the responsibility of tracking down this axe-man, mad or not – before the Queen crosses the Bridge tomorrow. For – mark me in this, the both of you – the Queen must be seen to cross the Bridge tomorrow.'

Thomas Walsingham came along himself. He followed at Tom's shoulder as they followed the broad beam of the open lantern, with the rats scurrying away before them, over the three hundred and sixteen steps below the Bridge across to the little chamber. Here the head, the axe, the whetstone and the black executioner's mask had lain the night before; but they were gone now. The room was empty except for the table and the chair.

As well as half a dozen stout watchmen, they had brought

Perkin, unwillingly, away from the task of perfecting the Bridge's decorations for the morrow. Perkin was able to unfasten the iron-barred door for them. Apparently failing to detect the brooding menace of the place – a menace that seemed so plain to all the rest of them – he stepped down into the room. 'I had all but forgotten this chamber,' he informed them. 'I have no idea why it is here and it must be five years since I visited it. If not more. In Armada year, mayhap, seeking for secret Spaniards.' Just as he seemed untouched by the atmosphere of the place, so he seemed unaware of the cloud of suspicion that surrounded him like some kind of plague.

'Well, someone else has been here since,' said Tom, stepping down beside him, eyes busy in the lamplight and gesturing Thomas and his watchmen to wait where they were, outside.

It needed no Master of Logic to tell them someone had been here of late. The mossy stones were marked with recent footprints, disturbingly misshapen by the strange growths into which they had been thrust. The sparks from the whetstone had burned some of the sensitive, dark-adjusted tendrils. But, as opposed to the little murders where these had fallen, there was wholesale slaughter above the torch-brackets in the walls.

'The furniture was here on your last visit?'

'As far as I remember . . .'

It certainly seemed a part of the place, thought Tom, for it was surfaced with tiny hairs, like velvet. Whatever wood it was, it seemed to have been bleached by the darkness as though by sunlight, for it had a pale, drowned look to go with its soft, mossy touch. Yet the softness of the surface had not robbed the wood of its essential character entirely. For as he ran his fingers up the back of the chair, so they discovered a little splinter, a tiny dagger of wood that seemed to have escaped the submarine softness of the rest and retained its bite like the tooth of a decayed wolf. Behind this, Tom discovered a tiny patch of cloth – white, torn, wild-haired with threads – clearly ripped from the clothing of someone who had sat here. And sat here recently;

237

for, unlike almost everything around it, the shred of cloth was dry.

'Who else would have the key?' demanded Tom, wrapping his find in his own kerchief and slipping it into his doublet.

'Well, Master Musgrave, the key's no problem at all. The one key opens most of the locks on the Bridge. The old ones, certainly. They were put here before there was much sophistication needed in the matter of locking and unlocking, if you follow me.'

Perkin held up a great spade of iron that was little more than a lever to turn an interior bolt. 'The old ones were of wood,' he said. 'There's any number of them around.'

The truth of Perkin's words was tested fifty rungs up when Tom shoved the simple key into the simple mechanism of the lock above his head – and opened it.

All too well aware of the death and danger resulting from the last time he had done this – up on the Great Stone Gateway – Tom hurled the trap back and sprang upwards.

Into utter stillness. Absolute blackness. Almost total silence, except for the squeaking scurry of the rats.

As if Tom were not living upon his nerves already, it was an extremely unsettling experience to wait while Thomas climbed upwards with a torch. He stood, shaking with tension, watching the light spread out so strangely from a spot immediately above the trap, flowing across the ceiling and out down the walls, pulling out of blackness into shadow first and then into the light the simple furniture of this utterly deserted little room. Another table – tiny, unremarkable; dry, at least. A truckle bed with straw mattress – rat-chewed but otherwise anonymous. And that was all except for two things: except for the fact that there must have been a dozen sconces and standards in here – a dozen torch-holders, but no door. At first glance it seemed that, apart from the trap, there was no way in or out of here.

That was the first question Tom put to Perkin, who responded with, 'No way out I know of.'

Tom saw at once that this simply could not be so. For when

he had arrived, the room had been full of rats. And when Thomas and Perkin had arrived, there were none to be seen except a half-lame creature caught beneath the open trapdoor. 'Stand back,' he ordered the pair of them, and raised the wooden flap. At once the crippled creature scuttled under the bed. Tom took the thing at once and threw it aside – only to reveal that the rat had vanished. 'This wall,' he said brusquely. 'Thomas. Call your men. There must be a hidden catch!'

It was a simple lever, and Tom himself found it by swift exercise of logic. For how could such a thing be hidden in a plain wall, roughly lime-washed and featureless save for a couple of sconces? In the sconces, of course.

The sconce above the bed's head pulled down to release a panel fitted so that its edges sat in the pattern of the stones, making a small, light doorway apparently massive; and, judged Tom, something relatively recent seem to be of almost incalculable age. 'I wonder,' he said grimly to Thomas, 'who King Edward sent in to deface and destroy the chapel. Perkin? Can you remember?'

'Some men from Kent,' said Perkin openly, without the slightest hint of evasion. 'Same for Bloody Mary. Men sent up to see about reopening it.'

Within the next few hours, Tom, Thomas, Perkin and the nervous watchmen discovered that the chapel was the heart of a web of secret passages and shafts that spread out through the fabric of the nearest buildings – through the timeless masonry of the Bridge itself.

Although both Tom and Thomas were fascinated by what had been done, they soon began to suspect that a thorough exploration of these modern catacombs would likely take weeks longer than they had available and was a waste of time that might be better spent.

When Tom at last proved that there was an opening from the eaves of St Thomas's Chapel directly into the garret of his own house, he drew the line there. 'I see it is of great import,' he said to Thomas, 'to prove how he came into the chapel here and

surprised Mistress Midmore at her devotions. But this is my
bedroom, man. Even in company with Mistress Kate, I am like
never to rise in here again for fear of strangers measuring my
ardour. Or preparing to behead it!'

CHAPTER THIRTY-ONE

Madness

I t was to Nonesuch, therefore, that Tom returned after Nicholas Hazard's funeral. Here he supped with a quietly excited household that proved itself, like Poley, a little torn. Guillem had gone back to Bleeke House to help his father and sisters with the final preparations for the morrow. Kate and Audrey remained, excited at the prospect of seeing the Queen themselves, but too well aware that both Tom and Thomas had a great deal to do – and not a little to resolve – before then. Tom also felt a brooding disquiet that was more than the natural depression of spirit resulting from the funeral. It was the knowledge that, for all of them perhaps, there was deadly danger involved with the discharging of their responsibilities. More than once he found himself glancing across the eel pie that they were mumbling in near silence, to wonder which of them was likely still to be here this time tomorrow.

Tom's feeling was so strong that not even Kate at her most gamesome could tempt him into their private, passion-filled chapters of Roman history and thought when he went up to their room to rest. Rest, therefore, he did, until he heard the Watch at ten, and then he ventured out on to the Bridge himself and spent the rest of the night in silent watch. One word kept returning to his mind all night, however – so deep beneath his thoughts it was more likely to have come from his very spirit:

Guillem's warning: '*Observare*.' At first he supposed the word was there because he was *keeping* watch. Only much later did it occur to him that the word lingered so relentlessly because some part of him knew that he was *being* watched.

However, all remained as quiet as the grave until he crept back to Nonesuch with the dawn like a laggard husband sneaking home to his betrayed wife. Kate grumbled sleepily at the shock of the chilly length of him against her, but her warmth acted like a drug and he was in the arms of Morpheus before he was in the arms of his sleepy lover.

Perkin woke them almost as soon as Tom had fallen asleep, banging on the door and calling for Thomas. In a kind of waking dream, Tom shrugged on a few clothes and followed the pair of them out into the chilly, misty dawn that he had only just vacated. After three steps he knew where they were bound and why he had thought of Guillem's Latin warning all night.

Frau Van Der Leyden looked stonily down from the Great Stone Gateway along the route the Queen would take through the South Wark down to her own mourning household. How she had arrived there, no one had any inkling, for, unlike last time, the murderer had been careful to leave no clues. Perkin had made things a little more difficult for their terrifying foe – but not much. He had set guards to patrol – but they had passed the gateway door only every half-hour. He had discarded the broken padlock – and fallen back upon the ancient door's original fastening. But the key that would open all the others would open this one too. However, as he watched the head being removed to lie with the others below Nonesuch, Tom for one was not inclined to be too hard upon the man. For had he not stood watching all the night in person while the head and the creature that took it had come up here and away again like the ghost of John Knox himself?

Poley arrived at nine to offer him a list of the procession as it would be formed to cross the Bridge, and found him up on the gateway in a vain search for further clues – for any inspiration at all, in fact. The spy master went away again almost immediately, his face like thunder and his brow clenched in worry. Tom followed half an hour later, with still no shred of evidence. Back to Nonesuch he went, lost in a brown study, almost incapable of communication, so deep and dangerous were his thoughts.

Will Shakespeare appeared soon after, with the wig he had promised to have made of Kate's hair when he had chopped it into her apprentice crop. He lingered and it needed no genius of insight to guess he was angling for a place at one of Nonesuch's inner windows to see the procession pass. He remained in any case while she tried the hairpiece on and declared herself well satisfied with it. 'The 'prentice lad is dead,' she announced exuberantly. 'Long live the lady-in-waiting reborn!'

Tom, surfacing from his deliberations, was forced to agree. It was time to change back – to stop thinking, in fact, and prepare for desperate action too. The Apollo Marley disguise had started several foxes – Panne, Petty, Shaddow and the rest; the ides conspiracy, in truth – but it was a trap that had failed to snare the great bear it was laid for. Time to throw it off. He borrowed a horse and rode to Blackfriars, pushing ruthlessly through the excited bustle in the City and back again; and, just as the woman beneath the red wig could hardly have been more different from the apparent boy she replaced, so the swaggering ruffler that returned could hardly have been more different from the Puritan drudge that had left. Tom was still dressed all in black, to be sure – except for his snowy ruff and cuffs. But the boat-bellied doublet was of the finest velvet – paired to perfection with the galligaskins between waist and knee – and bespoke Italian tailoring of the highest order. The boots, like the gloves, were of finest Spanish leather. The buttons and buckles were all of silver, matching the Ferrara hilts of his paired duelling rapiers in the black leather scabbards and swashes. As ever, he disdained a hat, preferring to tie back the Puritan crop of his hair with a plain black-leather bootlace caught up from the shop of his landlord, the haberdasher Robert Aske.

He returned to a Bridge that was different from the one he

had left. It was not only newly garlanded but stoutly guarded now, and he needed to explain himself several times before he was allowed across. Indeed, when at last he gained entrance, Nonesuch too proved subtly different from the one he had left. Thomas was gone. He was, apparently, with the Warden and Perkin, the three of them looking once again – and for the last time – to the security of the Bridge. Should the slightest thing go awry, all of them were likely to pay for it with a lengthy sojourn in the Tower. Kate and Audrey Shelton were gone. Although their names were not on Poley's list, he had apparently come to take them to a place of special importance. So, apart from the servants – and the victims in the cellarage – only Will Shakespeare remained.

Tom ran up the stairs to find him, and discovered him in a chamber he had never visited in Nonesuch – nor indeed in Mistress Midmore's house north of here, even when he owned it as Apollo Marley. It was an inner garret, little better than a mere workroom immediately above the shop. Because of the Bridge's strange construction, it was a small, misshapen chamber with a dull window along one side that looked down upon the street. Similar dull windows stood opposite, bereft of any direct sunlight by the fact that the houses joined immediately above, and the roadway was effectively roofed. The glass had been cunningly fashioned so that it leaned out and Will was curled upon the sill, looking down into the street. The Queen's coach would pass beneath him, and so close by that, were he able to open the window, Will might even be able to touch it.

Tom joined his friend, looking down into the quiet roadway.

' 'Tis a pity I wasn't thinking more swiftly or my fortune would be made,' said Will, only half-joking. 'This is such a fine look-out that the Burbages – aye Alleyn and Henslowe to boot – would have paid a pile of gold to share it. The Queen never crosses the Bridge – and yet here she comes in an hour's time at the most; and under my eye almost alone.'

'Where are the crowds?' enquired Tom. 'I had supposed the Bridge would have been better lined . . .'

'Why, so it is. But only in the squares. You must have seen it as you came across just now. There's scarce room for the royal carriage to pass along these roadways between the buildings. There can be no guards at the doors even, the path is so strait. Were the Queen to open both carriage doors at once they would strike against the house-fronts, like as not.'

'No guards!' What he had seen – and paid such scant attention – as he rode back from Blackfriars struck him now as Will almost magically woke his memory.

'None. All the world knows it and the veriest maudlin could see it looking down from the windows here . . .'

'But dear God, anyone might therefore step aboard, as our man did into Frau Van Der Leyden's carriage, axe and all . . .'

'Fear not. There are commands of guards immediately before and behind. And, while you were at Blackfriars bringing Tom Musgrave back to life, two sets of watchmen have been through every place along the route. We have had the Warden's men, the City Watch, checking and securing every door along the way. And we have then had Poley's men – and Poley was using your friend Talbot Law and his men from South Wark. And what they sealed will stay sealed, believe me!'

'But I got in.'

'You are known, man, to both sets of watchers. And, one house or another, Musgrave or Marley, you live here. However, as I think you will find if you try the door now, once you are in you will stay in.'

So it proved. The street door was locked now and Thomas Walsingham's chamberlain had orders, from several men whose trust he dared not break, that it should now remain so until after Her Majesty had passed. No persuasion from Tom short of direst and violent assault proved like to move him – and violent assault began to occur to Tom as it seemed increasingly clear that he had been trapped here. When the chamberlain finally admitted that the order had been Master Poley's last word upon removing Mistress Audrey and Mistress Kate, Tom at last agreed to let matters rest – to let them rest as far as the chamberlain and the front door were concerned, at any rate.

Thomas's chamberlain had received no orders regarding the cellars, however. In his relief at having overcome his stormy guest, he was happy to allow Tom possession of the old key that secured most of the internal doors in the place. Tom took it up to Will. 'I am going exploring,' he said roundly. 'Care to come?'

'Is it the Americas?' teased Will. 'Or further afield, like Drake?'

'It might as well be,' said Tom grimly, 'round in circles. I would hardly be surprised. But as Montaigne observes, I believe, even the longest journey must start with a single step . . .'

Will hesitated, clearly torn, and Tom began to suspect that Will's involvement – indeed his very presence – was not as innocent or coincidental as it seemed. Will in the past had been every bit as much Poley's man as Kit Marlowe had been. And whose man was he now?

Tom shrugged and turned. Then suddenly Will was at his shoulder.

They ran down to the cellar together and Will lit a lantern while Tom crossed the shadows to the ancient grille in the low back wall. Even as the light began to firm and gather while Will closed from behind, Tom thrust the ancient key into the ancient lock – and it turned as though it had been new-greased yesterday. The gate swung wide silently to reveal a low tunnel, into which Tom plunged, without a second thought and with Will still at his heels.

After yesterday's explorations through the warrened fabric of the Bridge, conversation was unnecessary. Both men knew where this passage was likely to lead and who – what – would likely be awaiting them there. They concentrated, therefore, on speed and silence.

Both of these were difficult to achieve because the tunnel was low and twisting, full of unexpected steps and dips. Their footfalls echoed strangely and their breathing, made more

246

laboured by their twisted posture, seemed louder and stranger than ever. Just as the floor rose and fell unexpectedly, so the roof chopped up and down in a manner that put their crowns at serious risk, while the side walls closed and spread with concomitant damage to elbows and shoulders. And always beneath their feet the wild rats scurried, squeaking and squealing.

Out through the massive old foundations the tunnel led them – foundations built for the brutal Drawbridge Gate on which Thomas More and Elizabeth Barton had left their severed heads; the gate that had seen off Thomas Wyatt and the men of Kent before it was adorned with Sir Thomas Wyatt's head as well; foundations far too ancient and massive for the modern lightness of the Dutch-made Nonesuch. Antwerp-built Nonesuch that matched so well the Dutch-made water wheels that filled the two northernmost spans, pumping water up to a quarter of the houses in the City; English water at a Dutch price. A price soon to be exacted by the soon-to-be Dutch warehouse of St Thomas's Chapel and the Dutch-owned Bleeke House, foundation in turn to the Dutch beer, banking and tobacco industries springing up to the south of the Bridge. As they crept forward into the rumbling thunder of the central spans at the turning of the tide, so Tom's thoughts continued, dulling his senses to the sounds and smells around him: the buzzing beneath the rumbling thunder; the sweet, familiar iron over the rat-dung and fungus.

It was easy enough, thought Tom, to see how Panne and Petty had been influenced by their devious, seemingly Dutch-fearing children into rousing the apprentices against the Dutch apparently threatening their property and livelihoods. And so the conspiracy Terrill code-named 'The Ides' had been born – born and still-born last night.

But what was it that roused the axe-man? Catholic women instead of Dutch men? Catholic women also, seemingly, set to overrun the Bridge?

Or could it be as simple as red hair after all?

Ten houses – ten tall, thin houses – separated Nonesuch from the chapel. Had tall Tom or Will paced it along the roadway, sixty-nine steps would have taken them from one to the other in a little more than a minute's brisk walking. In the tunnels under their foundations, things were different – slower, certainly – and neither of them counted how many hundred times they tiptoed uneasily forward.

Tom's main regret – accepted and then dismissed at once – was that he had been driven by fashion and not circumspection in the matter of arms. His beloved rapiers – one on each hip seemingly trying to take out Will's eyes behind – were a handicap under these conditions and would need careful handling indeed were he to face a madman with an axe. Any one of Ugo's pistols or dags would have been more manageable and much more effective.

It was with this thought in his mind that Tom stepped down the last step of a little, unconsidered series and found his feet skidding out from under him. He stepped sideways, looking around, surprised by the dim brightness if by nothing else – brightness suddenly a-swarm with buzzing flies. Fighting to keep his balance he pushed against a pair of solid walls: one of ancient rock and the other of more modern, solid brick standing on opposite sides of the stinking little chamber. Beams reached out from wall to wall above him, and, between the beams, ill-fitting boards that let in light and liquid.

'Faugh! What is that?' demanded Will, still in the dark behind.

'Blood. I am stepped in so far I am near to wading.'

'What place is this?' demanded the disgusted voice again, immediately behind, with Will hesitating in the maw of the tunnel.

'It is the space beneath the floor of Mistress Midmore's parlour,' answered Tom, and straightened explosively. Immediately above him, the boards between two of the heavy beams reaching out on to the solid little balcony burst and he found his head and shoulders up in the battleground where Shaddow's pirates had met their end. He ducked down again. 'This wall is the ancient outer wall of the Bridge itself.' He gestured to the boulders. 'And this is the strong wall of the strongroom.' He gestured to the brick. 'And this – ' he stamped his foot – 'is where the blood of the slaughtered pirates ran.' Then he raised his hands above his head, gripped, twisted, kicked, and was gone up into Mistress Midmore's parlour.

Will joined Tom at the front door just as he turned, saying tersely, 'Bolted from outside – and chained too, like as not.' For an instant they stood side by side. In the square close by the crowds were bellowing and the clatter of horses' hooves struck close – immediately beyond the unyielding wood.

'What are they calling?' demanded Will, frowning.

Tom glanced up from Poley's list. 'They are calling, "Essex! Essex!",' he said. 'The household guards are next after My Lord of Essex, for he is Master of the Horse. And then the Queen herself.'

'What shall we do?' demanded the playwright, caught up like his friend in the gathering power of the situation, but less used to instant decision and decisive action.

'What would your Romeo do?' demanded Tom with a flash of a grin that came and went like lightning. 'Or mad Mercutio? They would act! Let us run aloft, therefore!'

Up they went to the smaller, more constricted version of that chamber in Nonesuch which looked down on to the roofed roadway. This was brighter, for it stood much nearer the archway out into the square. Only the breadth of the St Thomas's Chapel arch stood between them and the open sky. No windows there, thought Tom as he looked northwards over the heads of the royal guards, who had formed six abreast and stood now in serried ranks as the royal coach itself stopped exactly in the last of the daylight where the square closed in under St Thomas's Chapel.

Tom pressed himself against the glass until the frames groaned, his eyes narrow and frantically busy. All his attention was focused upon the big, broad, gold-coloured vehicle with the high swan's neck of its driver's seat arching low over the tails of the last pair of the four horses pulling it. There was a solid-looking driver resplendent there with another coachman perched beside him – two of Poley's finest, armed with the best guns Ugo could supply, hoped Tom as he looked past them, down at the coach itself, and into the heaving square beyond where he himself had so nearly embraced a terrible death.

When a door in St Thomas's Chapel opened he flinched so massively that he almost tumbled through. Then he remembered that there was to be a brief reception at St Thomas's Chapel to assure the world that it had passed into Van Der Leyden's hands; but instead of a reception, there was only a single figure: Van Der Leyden's representative crossing to Her Majesty's coach holding a great velvet cushion heart-high before him. Then Tom saw beneath the figure's waist – and saw the stiff, formal skirts. He realized then that Van Der Leyden's representative was Inge, taking the place of her murdered mother. At the door of the coach she stopped and curtseyed low. Out through the lowered window, as she straightened, came a regal hand, carrying a golden key to lay with due ceremony upon the cushion. Inge returned. The coach moved forward, silent under the thunder of applause.

As it came under the shadow of the building, equally silently, a panel in the tunnel roof immediately above it fell open – a trapdoor leading down from whatever lay immediately above. Without further thought, Tom hurled himself upwards with such power and vigour that Will cried out.

The bemused playwright, who had not seen the secret trap open above the Queen's coach, no doubt thought his friend had suddenly been gripped by some satanic madness himself. 'Tom!' he cried, reaching forward to grab the Master of Defence by his black velvet shoulder. But the Master of Logic had seen and understood the last of it and Tom Musgrave knew what he was bound to do, no matter what the price. He closed his eyes and put his black-leather hands briefly over his face. Then he smashed the whole of his body through the window and fell, just as the axe-man was falling, down on to the roof of the Queen's coach.

The axe-man landed first, by the merest fraction of time. He stood, crouching on the roof for the instant it took him to swipe the guard and the driver aside with his axe. Then he chopped the blade of it downwards and fell through the roof into the coach itself – just at the very second that Tom tumbled on to the seat vacated by the dead driver and his mate.

Tom had fallen four feet at most and was shaken, not hurt. The glass and splinters still raining around him had not cut him, and would hardly have slowed him if they had. He landed on his hands and knees and hurled himself forward as a part of the same motion to vault over the side of the driver's seat and swing one-handed down on to the road, looking into the carriage with wild, staring eyes.

'We in this our miserable age . . .' bellowed a great voice, seeming to echo from the skies above.

The axe-man seemed huge as he stood beyond the Queen, alone in the carriage with her. He was dressed all in black, his clothes tight, as though straining to contain him. His hands were gloved as dark as Tom's. His face was masked with leather as soft and as black as Tom's Spanish leather boots. Only the wide madness of his eyes stood bare for all the world to see. They looked down at the shocked woman half-sitting, half-kneeling between them.

'. . . are bound to admonish the world and the tyrants thereof . . .'

He reached down with his left hand and took the red-gold ringlets, jerking the royal head forward even as the right hand raised the axe through the ruin of the coach's roof.

'. . . of their sudden destruction . . .'

Tom's toes touched the roadway and he loosed his hold on the coach, tearing the muscles of shoulder and breast as his right hand struck down to the hilt of his left sword.

The red head hit the cushion of the seat, face down, with stunning force. Only the cushions must have saved Her Majesty's decided nose from breakage – or worse. The whole black height of the man seemed to gather and tower impossibly tall. Did he actually rise up on his toes as he put all the power at his command into that terrible downward stroke?

Now it was time for Tom's voice to rise in a stentorian bellow, equalling the axe-man's own.

'PERKIN!' he bellowed. 'You must not do this!' he hissed, his voice at its most commanding.

The mad eyes came up, even as the great axe came down. The axe-man and the logician looked deep into each other's souls as one great blade whispered down and the other one hissed out.

So that neither of them actually saw the red curls in the axe-man's fist tear free of a 'prentice-boy crop as the would-be victim hurled herself back out of the way just as the axe drove deep into the seat opposite.

The whole coach shook with the power of that terrible impact. The blade, as heavy and as keen as death itself, drove through the cushions, the velvet and the horsehair padding and into the good, thick planks beneath, where it wedged – even as Tom thrust, with all his force, over the sill of the window in the solid door. His blade spat straight through the short ribs of the madman who stood looking down at the fainting woman on one hand and the red wig in the other.

He looked up, deeply shocked and pained to his soul by the perfidy that had been exercised upon him. There were actually tears in his eyes; and Tom knew from experience that they were never tears of pain, for the Solingen blade would hardly have started to hurt as yet, no matter what vital organs it had sundered.

'Jezebel,' he hissed.

''Twas the Queen of Scots' trick,' said Tom, almost gently, full of human understanding. With his weight on the hilt in his right hand, he reached across with his left hand for its mate at his right hip.

But the madman whirled – whirled with such unexpected, overwhelming power, that the blade within him snapped short at the hilt. He left his axe with the wig beside it. He stepped up on the seat beside the woman, reached up and leaped. Skewered as he was, he heaved himself up into the ruin of the coach's roof and up again, through his trapdoor and away into the Bridge's catacombs.

'PERKIN!' yelled Tom again, even as the door beside him burst wide and the fainting woman fell back into his arms, using him to steady her aim as she pulled the triggers of Ugo's nastiest little double-barrelled pistol. But nothing happened, save that the trap snapped up and the horses stamped and whinnied.

'Misfired,' he said, in the same understanding tone.

'I should have known it would.'

'They often do, just when you need them most. If you don't look to the priming.'

'Should you have known who it would be with the axe after all?' she asked.

'As well as I should have known it would have been you in the Queen's coach, Kate,' he answered her.

'Is it over?' she asked, stepping out of the coach a little shakily, but every inch a queen, except for the apprentice-boy haircut that had saved her life.

He looked down at the hilt of his broken sword and up at the trap in the roof. 'No,' he said. 'Not quite.'

CHAPTER THIRTY-TWO

Method

W ill Shakespeare dropped out of the shattered window
and on to the driver's seat of the coach then. The horses
jerked forward, spooked by yet another disturbance. The
carriage lurched, throwing the intrepid playwright flat, so that
the shot from Kate's pistol went through the space lately
occupied by his clever brain, close enough to singe his already
thinning hair.

Perkin arrived then, in answer to Tom's great bellow; only to
throw himself backwards at once, fearful that his own dramatic
entrance should beget an equally deadly reply. But Tom's hand
closed over the pan that had seemed empty and useless, trap-
ping the flints with his palm.

'Will,' called Tom, 'reach up and try the trap! Can you reach
it? Perkin, hold the horses.'

The coach steadied; Will reached up. 'Locked tight,' he
called.

'Come down then. Perkin, we need to follow. You are
prepared?'

'Well, Master Musgrave . . .'

'Poley set you to watch things here while he went with the
Queen, did he not? I see he did. Then he must have given you
orders should this very thing occur.'

'Aye, Master. But . . .'

254

'To follow?'

'Aye, Master. But . . .'

'Then follow! And we shall follow thee. But hurry, man! Before Essex's guards arrive!'

'Too late, Master Musgrave!' called Perkin wretchedly, and Tom swung round, like the great actor Alleyn playing Marlowe's Dr Faustus – swung round to find the Devil at his shoulder.

He stood tall, in black-enamelled armour, gold-chased at the joints. He had dismounted and returned in such haste that he still carried his ceremonial staff. He had left his helmet elsewhere and the luxurious ringlets of his hair fell artistically about his long, pale face. His men crowded behind him, waved back by a thoughtless gesture of his black-gauntleted hand.

'Where is the Queen?' demanded Robert Devereux, Earl of Essex, Master of the Horse, captain – for the moment – of the Queen's whim. He made much of failing at first to recognize Tom, the man who had crossed him so direfully less than a month ago. But then, as far as he was concerned, his beloved sovereign had just been attacked by a madman while under his own personal protection. The priorities lay there, thought Tom. There would be a settlement of the other matter, of course, but neither here nor now.

'I would judge that she is gone with her favourite ladies-in-waiting, and perhaps Robert Poley, in a wherry to St Mary Overie Stairs, Your Grace. Not for the first time,' he answered, as civilly as a commoner can talk to a peer of the realm without any form of courtesy at all. 'Mistress Shelton sat in the coach for her, to face down any danger.'

The Earl of Essex hesitated for a moment, and he was a man who never hesitated. 'If Her Majesty is with Poley, then she is likely to be safe enough,' he said. 'So tell me, what is toward here?' Of course he disdained to wait for an answer but looked at once into the coach. What he saw there would have explained things well enough to an intelligence far less than his own. 'Ah,' he said. 'The axe-man that the Crowners have been making so much of. And at your prompting, Master Musgrave, I believe.'

Tom's eyes met Robert Devereux's then, man to man, and rank aside. He remembered what Poley and he had discussed in the Bridewell. Not about the tobacco monopoly or about the Bank of Amsterdam – or even about the danger to the throne – but about the spectre of an axe-man set up by the Council to frighten the Queen; and about how Robert Devereux needed to shackle her heart ever closer to his own. Brown eyes locked on level brown eyes and a kind of understanding, or an ephemera of one, seemed to pass between them; an alliance between bitter enemies briefly joined in the face of a greater foe.

'Perkin,' said Tom, 'we have a fourth joined to our little band of huntsmen.'

'And a fifth,' called Ugo, 'if Mistress Shelton will take Mistress Van Der Leyden into the royal coach and guard her safe from hence.'

Inge Van Der Leyden climbed into the Queen's coach, showing her royal breeding as absolutely as did Kate: two backs stiff and two heads held high. It was Inge's pale hand that fastened on the handle of the buried axe and jerked it free. Wordlessly she handed it to Ugo, who accepted it – and the mission that went with it; and Tom was struck by the fact that it was not just the hot Italians who would stop at nothing in the matter of revenge. The cool Dutch were good at it as well.

So the little confederacy was made – with two more to be added later, towards the end of the matter, making seven in all. And it was Essex who spoke first.

'So, Master Musgrave. Who is our man – and where is he?'

'A short answer and a long story, Your Grace,' answered Tom, turning south to push past Essex into the hesitant throng of his guardsmen.

'Proceed,' said Robert Devereux, his intelligence so piqued that he seemingly overlooked the mortal offence Tom gave by touching his ducal body. For a while he was content to follow, calling questions; and the others were content to follow him, listening to the answers Tom flung over his shoulder like bones to hungry dogs.

'It is Nicholas Hazard, the curate of St Magnus'.'

'The man is dead. Most famously so.'

'As was I, Your Grace. By rumour and fame, at least.'

'True. But no one saw you buried yestereve.'

'Nor no one saw Hazard buried. The corpse I myself saw
hearsed and planted was not Hazard's, for it had toes; and in
the matter of missing members the man was famously bereft of
ears, nose and great toes by the Inquisition, was he not? Also,
the dead man I saw was not bandaged or bound. And he did not
have the pox.'

'But Poley said it was Hazard. It is not like Poley to mistake.'

'True, Your Grace. At first I thought Poley must have pulled
the man living from the river and announced the discovery of
the corpse to cover matters. Hazard was one of Poley's men and
might look to Poley for loyalty and secret tending. But now I
believe things went the other way round, in fact. Poley announced he had found Hazard's corpse while he was still
searching for him, but someone else had already found him
– someone with a network of contacts up and down the river to
rival Poley's own.'

'But who would this wizard be?'

'No wizard, but a witch,' puffed Tom, pushing out into the
square south of Nonesuch and looking up across the heads of
the shouting crowds to the next block of buildings and the
Great Stone Gateway that towered above and beyond them.
'The witch who lies at the Bedlam heart of all of this: Nicholas
Hazard's daughter.'

'Whither are we bound?' demanded Essex at Tom's shoulder,
looking with great distaste at the mob of commoners come to
worship him as he passed.

'The gateway. So much of it has turned round the chapel and
the gateway – the heart and the head of the Bridge itself.'

'Very neat!' said Essex. Then he turned away, catching a
soldierly eye. 'Captain . . .'

'Curate Hazard had no family,' whispered Ugo, almost
fearful to be questioning where Essex himself had not seen
fit to do so. 'How could he have a daughter?'

Ugo, Perkin and Will gathered round as Essex spat orders at the Captain – but remained in earshot of the Master of Logic while he did so. 'Ten years before Armada year, ten years and nine months,' Tom explained as the soldiers began to re-establish a clear pathway through the mob to the next great block of buildings, 'Nicholas Hazard was but recently appointed curate to St Magnus'. He had taken up his post and was yet to start his wanderings.'

'So much is plain from the records on the walls of St Magnus' itself,' said Perkin. 'For the lists of curates and vicars stand posted there, back to the foundation of the church. Some, of course, defaced . . .'

'But the young curate found more than his calling here across the Bridge,' said Tom. 'He found a great love.'

'Who for?' demanded Ugo.

'D'you see it yet, Will? You were ever swift of study, oh Master of Cyphers . . .'

'All I see is a Gordian knot of logic . . .'

'Then let me chop it for you, old friend. Hazard's lady-love was Barton the Goldsmith's fair young daughter.'

'The way is clear,' said Essex then. 'Our legs may proceed while our tongues do so also.'

Onwards they ran, therefore, through a sea of conflicting sound and confusion. At first the crowds recognized their darling and began to cheer and chant – only to see him running with his hand to his sword hilt in company with a ruffian band of variously armed men, at least one of whom carried a blood-boltered headsman's axe.

The cries of *Essex, Essex, Essex* faded into formless shouts and occasional screams, therefore; but through it all Tom's voice rang true. 'Back and forth across the Bridge they stole in secret until their passion was consummated and their dooms were sealed. The curate was poor and Beale the Goldsmith in a good line of business. The man had no son; therefore his business must go with his daughter. Therefore she must marry a goldsmith. And the marriage must be soon, for no sooner was the deed done than the maid was with child. And each went off to his own private hell – Hazard to plague-ridden, Inquisition-held Europe via Poley's school for intelligencers; and his lady to the humiliating Frost Fair of mock-marriage to the hated apprentice Panne.'

'But last night,' puffed Will, 'only last night you said the child was Panne's own daughter!'

'And did you not hear the man deny it? In the coach and on the rack – though you missed the racking I know. "No daughter of mine," the man said. "Would that she were dead at my feet". I did not realize at first, for it is a thing any father might be tempted to say in the circumstances. But then I realized: he meant it – literally. And the last few pieces fell into their places in my mind.'

'You'd best proceed with your story,' snapped Essex then, as they came under the archway of the next set of buildings. 'Or you'll find yourself talking and fighting at the same time. If we ever find this madman.'

'An excellent point, Your Grace. And fear not: I know where we shall find him.'

The black shadow of the tunnel chopped down over them and their steps echoed weirdly in the chill darkness with the tumbling of Tom's dark words and the stirring rumble of the bridge as the tide below them turned. 'A dozen years went past. The marriage grew Arctic in its chill and the child grew clever and chilly in her own way, surrounded by hatred and bitterness. Then Hazard returned to St Magnus'. The wondrous, legend-ary Hazard – an inspiration to the world and a wonder like the Bridge; but a broken and bleeding man. Ten years since, at the outset of his adventures, he had been caught in the great plague of Rheims. And he had survived – but not by a miracle. He had got himself treatment, and the only sovereign remedy guaran-teed to stop the Black Death – as Doctor Viner explained to us. He found a whore that had syphilis and he infected himself, fearing the terrible pox less than the terrible plague. So he survived and escaped from Rheims – only to fall into the Inquisition's hands.'

259

Oddly, unsettlingly, given the terrible subject matter of Tom's story, they burst out into bright sunlight then, into the last great square of the Bridge, immediately inside the Great Stone Gateway. Here the crowd remained well back from the roadway, behind stout ranks of soldiers, for there had been no confusion around the royal coach to call them forward into a mob. All speech became impossible then, for a great roar of sound overwhelmed them as the crowd recognized Essex and began to shout their darling's name as though they wanted the very sky to echo the sound again. Tom for one was glad to catch his breath and order his thoughts a little further. They pounded across the square, Tom and Essex shoulder to shoulder in the lead. As Tom was no longer using his tongue, he was able to use his eyes to excellent effect. Two figures stood in the arch of the Great Stone Gateway, side by side for once: his most trusted friend and his least trusted one – Talbot Law and Robert Poley. Neither man stood there for long, however. The simple fact that the Earl of Essex was running, bareheaded, down the road as though this were some battlefield outside Cadiz was enough to warn them something was seriously amiss.

The seven came together just inside the gateway, therefore, splitting briefly into two small groups as Essex asked after the Queen of Poley, and Talbot quizzed Tom about Kate. Then the two groups became three as Perkin detached himself and shouldered through the guards to the door in the wall behind the open gate itself. Tom, Will and Talbot followed at once, with Ugo bringing up the rear, slowed by the weight of the guards' suspicion as they looked at the bloody axe. Then a great cheer went up from the centre of the Bridge and Tom guessed that Kate had got the Queen's coach under way again. Attention switched away even from the dashing Robert Devereux: Gloriana was coming, the Faery Queene was approaching, and crossing the Bridge for the first time in memory.

They went through the door with Tom immediately behind Perkin and Poley escorting Essex at the rear. Tom's remaining sword was out, as were the sharpest of his wits – and they needed to be, for he was still uncertain where his foe lay at present, or when, or how, he was likely next to appear. As Tom had known he would, Essex called up, 'Come, Master Logic. Your tale is but half-done. The man returned from the Inquisition galleys poxed.'

'You are correct, Your Grace, but I fear you may have overlooked an important point. The man suffered the onset of the pox in the Inquisition's hands. His agonies of infection were likely less than those of their making. And of his agonies of spirit, who can tell? But the important point is that the disease went all untreated – in the dungeons and in the galleys. No mercury and no guaiac wood that so weakened Master Panne as we saw. He suffered and he survived. Theodore explained how the disease has the first and second stages. And a third that's whispered of, for hardly any man has survived to feel it. But after nearly fifteen years, Nicholas Hazard has. What did Theodore call it? General paralysis of the insane.'

'And what is that?' gasped Essex, his voice ringing across the first open chamber that stood, wooden-floored, reaching across the gateway at the turning of the stair, where Tom had found the splinters from Hazard's pole and Alice Panne's kerchief – Alice Hazard's kerchief, to name her by blood, not family.

'Madness, pure and simple. But clearly, Your Grace, a madness that comes and goes at its own whim.'

'Like the Queen's favour,' breathed the Earl of Essex, thoughtlessly, putting all their heads at risk.

'But hold,' said Poley. 'Hazard was never mad. He never drooled or gibbered, or stabbed his arms or such. I have seen enough maudlin girls and Toms o' Bedlam to know the devils of madness in a man.'

'There's the wonder of the thing,' admitted Tom. 'You're right, friend Robert. I never saw him gibber neither. But Decius Brutus Shaddow heard him sob for days on end up in Margery Midmore's secret chapel. And I have seen him stoop like a black falcon out of the sky to take our own Queen's head wearing the black face-mask of the executioner that Decius

Brutus saw, and indeed it looked like no face, for underneath the thing were neither ears nor nose. And as he took the red curls that he craves, he bellowed Knox's words, as clear as death, from "The First Blast of the Trumpet Against the Monstrous Regiment of Women", as though he were John Knox reborn, and talking to the very person of the Queen herself.'

This conversation was enough to bring them up under the trapdoor on to the gallery. Tom took the lead here, curling below the wooden door as he had done on his first visit to the place. It was ironic, he thought, that what he had feared would be up there then he was bound to find up here now. The coincidence was amusing. He would smile at it in time – later, when he was less terrified.

Tom heaved the trap back and leaped up into the light.

And found he was on the gallery alone; except for the heads on the poles. Alone, for five seconds or so, before the others boiled up out of the black well behind him. Then the seven stood below the twenty-four and all thirty-one of them gaped in silence.

'He is here,' said Tom.

'Invisible?' asked Ugo, half-believing still that they were dealing with a ghost.

'Somewhere in the gateway,' answered Tom, frowning with thought.

'How could he get here?' demanded Essex. 'We have come with all speed by the shortest route. How could Hazard have got here before us?'

'If it is Hazard,' added Poley.

'Through the Bridge. Beneath our feet. The structure is riddled with tunnels like a Dutch cheese,' explained Will. 'Your Grace,' he added.

As he did so, Tom clapped his forehead with his broad left palm. 'Fool that I am! Perkin, where do you keep the poles you use for displaying the heads.'

'In a store-room down . . .'

262

'Down in the foundations. An ancient store-room, I'll be bound, and rarely used, save when there's treason about and Poley's work calls out more poles. Lead on, man! Lead on!'

Down they went again, tense and on tiptoe with Tom still in the lead, and Essex still demanding enlightenment. 'Let us say 'twas Hazard, then,' hissed the earl. 'He returned after Armada year, poxed and perhaps insane. Returned to what?'

'To St Magnus', fame and a hero's welcome. He published his adventures and made his fortune but was careful of his reputation. He mentioned no pox – and dared reveal none. Thus the lack of treatment continued. He bandaged his sores as they came and went and never more than that. I have seen Panne's bandaging and in disguising Mistress Kate as an apprentice boy I have bound and bandaged her, using such stuff as I found caught behind a splinter of the chair where the headsman sharpened his axe in that cellar below the foundations of St Thomas's Chapel – where, come to mention it, he left his strange toeless footprints, as he did in the cellar where the bodies lie below Walsingham's dwelling in Nonesuch.

'But he did not return entirely to loneliness. For he had a love he could rekindle if never consummate again and a child to watch over from a distance. Panne had moved his family up out of Southwark and into his new premises here. Hazard watched them from a distance – a little distance enough and one he tried to shrink still further, if in secret. Helped Panne become Warden, with his friend Petty, at St Magnus'. Necessarily became a frequent visitor, though Panne remained cold and suspicious. Watched the two women in his life; for they were all his joy – all his strength, perhaps, beyond the strength of the Lord, that had brought him through hell itself and back on to the Bridge.

'Until the Fair on his saint's day last, where he found himself plunged back into hell; and the madness began, I believe.'

At the foot of the twisting stair, with the doorway into the street standing open behind them, Perkin turned to the side wall of the tiny vestibule. Here he opened another, smaller door and caught up a torch that burned in a sconce at the head of another stair there. Down they went again into the echoing fabric of the Bridge, all astir and a-tremble now with the gathering force of the falling tide turning the Warden's mill wheels in the arches hard beside them.

Conversation was impossible and that was as well. Tom could hardly have brought himself to describe the agonies that Hazard must next have felt without a most inconvenient tear dimming his clear and warlike eye. For on that St Nicholas Day scarce six months since, Hazard had met his beloved alone for perhaps the first time in seventeen years at the Frost Fair on the river – met her, only to see her slip through the breaking ice and have her snatched away from him by the black and hungry Thames. Tom could scarce imagine what the agony of spirit must have done to him – so much that his pain had become for once visible above the surface; obvious to the all-too-clever eyes of his daughter.

Thus as the widower, her hated father, had swiftly sought solace in the arms of his miraculously cured and secretly Catholic mistress, so Alice had probed the truth out of the ruined curate – and discovered that she owed Goldsmith Panne neither love nor loyalty. Owed him nothing, in fact, but yet more hatred and a sound revenge.

There were around Mistress Alice at least three instruments that she could employ in that revenge, to wit: Daniel Petty, Augustus Shaddow and Nicholas Hazard. The greatest, most powerful – and most dangerous – being her increasingly mad father himself.

Tom's thoughts carried all of them down into a tiny antechamber deep in the heart of the arch itself where two walls crowded in on left and right while stairs issued out behind and a great black oak door stood closed before, perhaps six feet from the last step. Perkin crossed first to this and unlocked it, pulling it wide at once. They all surged forward – then froze, riven with shock, horror and simple helplessness.

Behind the open wooden door stood another of iron bars,

also closed and clearly locked. Beyond this was a sizeable chamber that had clearly once served as an armoury as well as a store. There were axes, poleaxes, pikes and halberds, partisans and spears stacked along the walls, as well as the poles standing ready sharpened for the next batch of heads. Ancient armour hung from hooks and, beneath it, half a dozen elderly but still more modern kegs of gunpowder – all still there, Tom guessed, since they had last been used against Wyatt and the men of Kent when Perkin was but a lad.

In the centre of the room, which was well lit by two torches, stood a table, and around this were arranged four stools. On the boards in front of each stool lay piled a few pathetic items: A plain gold ring; a pair of green-and-gold earrings; a red shoe; a crucifix on a silver necklace; a dark-red ruff. Round about the table walked the axe-man – Hazard, if Tom was right – limping in his odd-shaped shoes, formed by the near-toeless clubs of his feet. His torn shirt and stockings displaying swathes of bandage at hip and thigh. His great shape hunched weirdly over the gleaming points of the broken blade still spitting him like a capon ready for the fire, the black-leather executioner's mask sitting flat and featureless against his skull, the lack of ears emphasizing the wild wideness of his mad blue eyes; the lack of nose seeming to add to the working slobber of his huge gaping mouth. As he turned his back to them, seemingly utterly unaware that they were there, so they saw the hump of wadded stuff over the wound in his shoulder where Daniel's spite had almost destroyed Alice's revenge. What a falling-out must have threatened there, thought Tom. Daniel was lucky to have survived that at all. But Shaddow and his men had found the wounded Hazard still alive downstream and brought him back to Alice – that, amongst other things, the brave Captain had confirmed while Tom stopped him bleeding to death and prepared to save him from Poley.

'Locked – and I have no key!' hissed Perkin, breaking into Tom's reverie, even as Essex asked, 'What is he doing?'

Hazard was stooping beside one stool, speaking. His words –

if they were sane enough to make sense – were lost in the rumbling of the water and the wheels. But his body communicated as clearly as any voice could have done – to Will, at least.

'He's deep in conversation,' said the playwright, simply amazed.

'But there's no one there!' spat Poley, outraged that such a thing should be.

'No one we can see,' said Tom grimly. 'But there is someone there. Mistress Beale sits by the earrings and the crucifix, I would judge. The earrings he reclaimed when he called "Eureka!" by the Gully Hole, but had wit enough to swap head for football when Talbot and I pursued him down Tooley Street as he ran to meet his master. That is Mistress Midmore's shoe. In the mad world of that little room, she will sit behind it, and the ruff beside it. It was with her I think that the revenge began. For it was she to whom Master Panne turned for solace and she, ex-whore, believing herself cured of the pox and under Divine protection for this miracle in spite of the secrets she was keeping, was warm-hearted enough to take him in, thus winning the truly deadly enmity of Mistress Alice and her mad old father, ex-lover to the good woman whose memory was slighted there.'

Tom's whispered commentary was cut short as Hazard swung round and screamed aloud. The seven in the tiny ante-room leaped backwards as though they were one. But the mad eyes did not rest on them. Instead Hazard was stumbling backwards, raving, deep in gibbering conversation with a clearly terrifying vacancy – with thin air, shadowed but insubstantial, where clearly he saw some monster of unimaginable horror bearing down upon him. The scream was enough to break at once the black magic of the moment and the flesh around the Solingen blade within him. Blood began to ooze out of each side of him, spreading across the whiteness of his shirt to vanish into the blackness of his breeches and his open coat.

Perkin rattled the iron door again and Poley snatched out his pistol. 'Stand away!' he called and fired. Perkin threw himself backwards so that the bullet missed him; but it sang off the bars like the first bell of Doomsday. Only something as loud as that would have registered over the concussion of the discharge in such a tiny space. Trailing sparks like a meteor, it whirled through the room past Hazard, and smashed into the topmost gunpowder barrel. The smoke from the charge rolled forward, even as Ugo threw himself flat, taking Tom down with him, and Perkin did likewise for the august person of the Earl of Essex, both men fearing the powder was about to explode. By the grace of God, it did not do so.

When the smoke and the confusion were gone, the intrepid little band found itself alone – unless Hazard's ghosts remained, which none of them could tell; or would admit to if they could. At the far side of the room a tunnel mouth gaped behind a half-open doorway and the wounded man had vanished into it.

'Aloft again!' called Tom. 'He will have gone up this time!'

He was furthest in, and therefore last out. As he turned to follow the others he was frowning, and wishing he could remember how many axes had lain against the wall, for he could have sworn at least one of them was missing now.

But he had to push that thought to the back of his mind at once, for in his new, if temporary, position at the rear, he was all too close to the two interrogators Robert Poley and Robert Devereux. 'Why the axe and why the stakes upon the gateway?' demanded the Earl of Essex. 'If we grant him in the grip of madness, why was there even that much method?'

'Poley was in the right of it, I think, Your Grace,' answered Tom at once, 'when he explained to the Lord Chamberlain that he took them and displayed them because they were traitors.'

'Catholics . . .' confirmed Poley.

'No,' corrected Tom. 'Not traitors against the Protestant Commonwealth of England but traitors against the Natural Ordinance of God. Either Alice placed the idea like the worm in the apple of his madness or it was already there and burrowing. But it was the logic of his actions that took him out of her control and made her change her plans within the last few days, for she saw it and understood it – and tried to use it in the end.'

'Moonshine!' spat Poley. 'Madness and moonshine.'

But as they panted past the open doorway for the last time, Essex said, 'Explain yourself.'

'He was beginning to believe he was Knox reborn. He had shared so many adventures with the man: capture by the Catholics, questioning, being condemned to the galleys and escaping . . . The parallels are the backbone of Hazard's pamphlet. And now he found himself confronting Knox's foe: women abusing power; women out of the natural order, who paid no subservience to men, that governed the men in their lives in stead of being governed; the Catholic woman Barton living nun-like in the chapel, whom he had to clear out of his way to gain access to Mistress Midmore. And he needed access to her, for she was the Jezebel that had ruined his daughter's life. But she, too, was her own woman, needing no men in her life – except for the one she took in upon her own terms and destroyed with her infection. And both of them had red hair.'

'You keep coming back to that,' said Poley. 'Why?'

'Because I believe it was then, as he sat and sobbed for days under the ear of the frighted apprentice Decius Brutus Shaddow, that he underwent his sea-change. He had killed twice. He was preparing to put their heads upon the Bridge.'

'And what brought about the change?' demanded Essex and Poley together, their voices echoing across the wide room that stretched from side to side across the gateway immediately below the gallery itself, all outer walls except for the great chimney reaching upwards, Tom realized suddenly. Here the others all waited uncertainly, looking a little sheepishly at him as the double question echoed on the air.

'You did,' said Tom. 'Both of you.'

'How?' spat Essex – the monosyllable could have been a question, an exclamation or a challenge.

Tom turned in the doorway, his foot upon the hollow of the

lowest step and his rapier pointing up into the gloom of the stairwell. 'You, Your Grace, convinced the Queen to cross the Bridge; and you, Master Poley, warned Hazard she was coming, for he was part of your confederacy to protect her when she came. Thus, between you, you gave him the one red-headed woman that most powerfully in all the world stands beyond John Knox's God-ordained providence of men, like her sister and her cousin – both called Mary, against both of whom Knox railed and wrote while still he lived. Who better for a victim, if he was bound to live again in Nicholas Hazard's pox-born madness?'

So saying, for the last time Tom was gone up to the closed trap of the door above. He did not glance behind himself but he knew who would be there. Ugo first, with his axe and his score to settle; then Talbot, pleased to be in at the death. Then Will, busily noting this for some outrageous fantasy Theatre-bound; with Perkin close behind, likely as not, concerned at the very least, for the fabric and reputation of his beloved Bridge. And Poley coming last with Essex – both with much to chew upon and little, if any, of it to their taste.

He hit the door with all his might, grown impatient with the endless running and talking, exploding out into the brightness, his silly head far in advance of his logical mind. But thankfully Ugo was not so preoccupied. The instant the trap slammed back, the Dutchman caught at Tom's heels, tripping him, so that he fell flat – just as the horses had jerked the Queen's carriage and sent Will tumbling under Kate's wild shot.

So it was that the axe sang through vacancy that would otherwise have been filled by Tom's neck. As he fell, Tom twisted to look up the length of the axe-man, who stood wide-footed and swinging. Their eyes met and Tom kicked against the rim of the trap as he twisted out of the way so that the axe spat sparks off the flags where his head had been. Even so, even twisting and writhing wildly as he was, he would never have survived had not Ugo hurled upwards then swung his own axe wildly, with Talbot Law close on his heels. The madman staggered backwards – lucky still to have legs to stagger upon. Tom rolled clear and leaped to his feet – ran back towards Hazard and his friends at the trap.

'Stand clear,' bellowed Poley's voice, and the two friends jumped aside. Another great clap of thunder came and something sounding like a huge horsefly buzzed past Hazard's head. Smoke billowed upwards, thick enough to take a square shape from the trapdoor. Tom continued to hurl himself forward, his rapier high. He knew it had to be a killing stroke, through the eye or ear – or even through the nose, as things stood. To the brain. That was the surest, Capo Ferro had said. Hazard had shown already that a blade through the body was like to do little enough – unless it could be the heart. The heart with one thrust.

Into the smoke went Tom and into the *posta longa*, Capo Ferro's deadly lunge – which came within an ace of dispatching Perkin as he clambered blindly up on to the gallery through the powder fumes. There came at once, even as Tom tore himself aside, a crisp and disturbingly final *crunch!* as the madman's axe hit Perkin's head. But it was the blunt side, not the blade. Still, it was enough to hurl the Warden's man on to Tom and send him tumbling backwards again.

'Your Grace,' he bellowed as he fell, 'stay down!'

The river came to their aid, then, sending a wind to clear the smoke and revealing Hazard standing astride the trapdoor still, an axe in each hand, swinging and howling as he stood. Neither Ugo nor Talbot, armed with sword and axe though they were, could come anywhere near him. Perkin lay beneath him, half in and half out of the door, and Will crouched just below his hanging ankles, blocking the opening further so that Poley dared not risk another shot. There was nothing further anyone could do – other than creep and cower and wait for the madman to tire.

It was then that Tom laid down his beloved blade, and left to one side for a while the method that Capo Ferro had taught him so long ago. It was time for a little madness of his own. For, if none of their civilized weapons could come at the axe-wielding madman, then Tom could find other, more ancient ones that would.

As Hazard swung the axes wildly, tirelessly, Tom looked up at the dead heads above, seeking that one which was wedged upon the sharpest-looking pole. Whose it was he selected he was never to know – nor did he ever enquire. But it was easy enough to lift the sharp pole down and settle it under his arm. Even with the head still in place it balanced well and was limber in his hands. 'HAZARD!' he bellowed at the top of his lungs – and he charged. Three steps brought him to full-tilt and half a dozen took him to his target.

Hazard turned towards him at the call, so that the black ball of the head took him full in the belly at right angles to the lateral thrust of the blade still wedged within him. The head shattered as the spike atop the makeshift spear drove through it and Hazard was simply carried backwards, shallowly impaled, the axes whirling wildly still, a good yard clear of Tom's hunched shoulder, and whispering clear of his out-thrust head. So they went, Tom forward and Hazard careering backwards, until the madman hit the western balustrade. The spear bit shrewdly, then, tearing through shirt, bandages and belly almost as deep as the spine. But Hazard's scream was lost in the happy roars and cheering as, fifty feet and more below, the Queen's carriage came safely through the Great Stone Gateway and down on to the broad South Wark.

The axes fell from Hazard's nerveless fingers then and his head slammed back with stunning force on to the outer edge of the parapet. In unthinking reaction to the stunning pain in his head, Nicholas Hazard jerked his hands up to his face.

Tom watched as, with stricken surprise, the good curate of St Magnus' found that he was wearing something strange across his face. Surprised, he pulled at it with stunned and shaking fingers until it came off in his hand. Aghast, he looked up at Tom, and seemed to recognize his face. 'What . . .' he began to say.

But he never completed whatever words were the last to enter his brain for Ugo fulfilled his mission then and used the axe that had beheaded Mistress Van Der Leyden to do the same to her murderer. Odd the angle and unhandy the motion, but one stroke sufficed; far fewer than for Queens Ann of England and Mary of Scots.

'There was nothing more that he could tell you, then,' said Poley, as the head fell away into the river.

'What more did you want to know?' asked Tom, holding the corpse where it was to save Perkin the work of clearing up when his senses returned to him.

'Frau Van Der Leyden?'

'The perfect rehearsal for today. Red-head and all. How easy was it, then? Step into the coach and out again. And a little water to clear him of the deed.'

'And the girl, Alice,' demanded Essex shortly. 'You say she changed her plans when she learned he meant to attack the Queen? Surely, then, with the madness run so far, she should at least have warned Panne, her seeming father. For it was, after all, the Queen!'

'Consider,' said Tom almost gently. 'It is little more than a day after the attack on Bleeke House. You know who has the money – aye, and the gold all stolen on the night before that. You know who the guilty people are and where they are like to be.' He looked at Essex full on again then, and let his gaze travel to Poley and even to Talbot Law – lawkeepers all and responsible for the river.

'Aye,' said Talbot, seeing suddenly where this was leading.

'And where are the best and bravest of your men? At Shaddow's camp? At Deptford Strand? Searching along the river for a well-laden wherry or two slipping safely away for the Low Countries? No. They are where the danger had made sure they must be. They are all here on the Bridge to guard the safety of the Queen. For against all reason, logic, possibility, there was a madman set to kill her with an axe as she crossed.'

'And he damn near did it, too,' said Talbot Law. 'Had it not been for Tom here, the Queen would be stone dead.'

'Had it not been for *us*,' corrected Robert Devereux, clearly preparing to discuss the adventure with his Queen.

Tom looked up into the shining brown eyes in that long pale, handsome face and knew when the earl's red, curling lips came to repeat the words to Her Majesty in private, they would be bound to say, 'Had it not been for *me* . . .'

Two days later Tom was in a garret room in The Tun tavern on Tooley Street. Terrill's Judith sat uncomfortably on the edge of her bed, weeping silently. 'You must be proud and happy,' lied the Master of Logic gently. 'He is gone about the Queen's business. You must have known he was not like other 'prentice boys. See here, he left you enough money to settle the matter of your leg and return home in confort. Where is it you will go?'

'Home to All Hallows, where I was born, master. 'Tis a little village in Kent, hard by Rochester. You'll never have heard of it, sir, 'less you've heard of the miracle.'

'The miracle?'

'Aye, sir. I came in search of her but I found a small miracle of my own, I believe.'

'What – who – is the miracle?'

'Why Margery Perkins, sir. A branded whore, so they say, begging your pardon, sir. Saw a vision of the Virgin on Christmas Day at All Hallows village church ten years ago that cured her of the pox. True as I'm sitting here. My mother knew her. Said she had gone on to great wealth and power and that I should seek her out in London Town. But I could never find her at all, sir.'

'No,' said Tom, shaking his head a little wearily. 'I doubt you ever will, now.'

Four weeks later it happened that the rains of a sodden August put the Thames into a sudden spate. The restlessness of the water came near to tearing the four wheels out from under London Bridge and stirred up even the muddy bottom of the Pool. That was when Nicholas Hazard's head finally rose up into the current and was swept along the north shore past the Tower and the mudflats downriver on the bank side of Smith Field.

Here, out in the river deeps beyond the quiet slums that had once been scavenger Captain Shaddow's pirate kingdom – to the walls where Her Majesty's rule began – the head settled once again. Like a rock itself, it ground up against a cairn of boulders piled upon the river bed – rocks and boulders in which a pair of stout chains lay secured. In the chains, wrapped in a last and eternally lingering embrace, lay Hazard's daughter Alice and her Daniel. Or all that was left of them after Shaddow played one final trick on them that not even clever Alice had foreseen. Money gone and dreams dead – though revenges perfectly achieved after all. Throats slit and heels weighted, three fathoms down, for as long as the river would run.

Author's Notes

T his book began – as so many do – with my friend Dale
Clarke. On a walkabout through Shakespeare's London,
preparing a course of study for my students (on *Julius Caesar*,
unsurprisingly), we discussed the Old Bridge as we looked at
what is left of its footings. Then we retired to the Museum of
London where I studied more closely the models of the Old
Bridge in the Elizabethan section there and we discussed the
'fun digs' that the Museum runs – and particularly what Dale
and his children found on the mudflats immediately below the
walls of the Tower – discoveries that were to take on a more
sinister aspect in the book itself. This visit led to the purchase of
the MoLAS Monograph *London Bridge: 2000 years of a river
crossing* by Bruce Watson, Trevor Brigham and Tony Dyson,
upon which most of the technical aspects of the Bridge in this
book are based.

But, to be fair, it also had a kind of inception in P. D. James's
Death in Holy Orders. This fine book re-emphasized in my
mind, as Ms James's wonderful work so often does, that the
perfect setting for a murder mystery is a closed society in an
interesting location.

Enter at this point Patricia Pierce's *Old London Bridge*, which
fleshed out the technical aspects of the MoLAS monograph
with vivid history, and my little stage was set. The characters

were all introduced – in name only, I hasten to add. In the search for authenticity, the names of bridge-dwellers except Perkin are taken from Nehemiah Wallington's contemporary list of property-owners disturbed by the fire of 1633. And yes, that list includes Mr Hazard the curate, as well as Petty, Panne and Beale – and Mr Midmore the milliner, all no doubt, perfectly proper and respectable citizens. I had to turn to Thomas Dekker for Shaddow, however; he is named in *Old Fortunatus*, which was played before the Queen at Christmas 1600. His character, like the others, is entirely of my own devising.

Of course, the setting is only the beginning. I still needed a crime, a motive and a 'villain'. A crime, preferably, which could only have been committed in that place at that time. And so to the heads. Most famously, it is the Visscher view (1580), which shows the heads on the Bridge. I blew up a photocopy as big as I could and counted twenty-four – then wondered what might happen should there be twenty-five one fine day . . . So I just needed a man and a motive.

A gleeful lack of taste on my part and a great deal of patient understanding by the staff of the Tunbridge Wells Library discovered a range of books on the history of syphilis, but the one on which I based most of my medical content here was Johannes Fabricius' masterly *Syphilis in Shakespeare's England*. It was the staff of the Tunbridge Wells Library who also found me an (understandably) rare edition of John Knox's fiercely misogynistic 'First Blast of the Trumpet against the Monstrous Regiment of Women'. The introduction to this included details of Knox's adventurous life – as recorded in my own book and passed directly to Nicholas Hazard, the exception being that there was no great outbreak of plague in Rheims in 1580. Catching syphilis, on the other hand, was a highly recommended preventative treatment. It was believed that the two diseases could not co-exist within the same body. And I recommend any reader shocked by the apparent lunacy of such an idea to remember that as late as 1918, patients with syphilis were being injected with malaria, because the two infections do in some cases cancel each other out. This treatment was only superseded by the arrival of penicillin on the medical scene.

The more general background research remains much as it was in *The Point of Death*. Charles Nicholl's amazing *The Reckoning* details the Elizabethan Secret Service and place of Robert Poley within it, though, as with Shakespeare, I have taken some liberties with his historical character while staying as close as possible to accepted historical 'fact'. I also add here Peter Farey's monograph *'The Reckoning' Revisited*, available on the Internet, and Phillips and Keatman's *The Shakespeare Conspiracy*, which fits the Bard neatly into the whole situation and makes my placing of him in the darker outreaches of Elizabethan political underworld slightly less outrageous. It also gave me the code in which Terrill passes the message in a football. The code is real, and needless to say was first published in the early 1600s by Francis Bacon, to whom Will Shakespeare explains it in my book. Will's racy character also owes something to Katherine Duncan Jones's *Ungentle Shakespeare*, which first presented to my mind the theory I later found in Fabricius that Shakespeare himself contracted syphilis in later life. As a balance to *Conspiracy*'s theory and much modern debunking of my dramatic hero, I always keep Ivor Brown's wonderful *How Shakespeare Spent the Day* handy, as well as a huge pile of books on Elizabethan life and times.

It is to the Internet one turns increasingly, however. The HACA's wonderful site gives me all I need on historical arms and techniques. Site after site gives increasingly intimate details of Shakespeare's life, times and theatre; its actors, financiers and patrons. It even took me, room by room, around the Elizabethan hospital of St Thomas's so that I could set the scenes there with maximum authenticity. On the other hand, it was to the Library and to books on the almost timeless arts of gold- and silver-smithing I had to turn to get Panne's workshop right. Stanton Abbey's monograph on both was most useful.

But ultimately I must confess a little failure. Patricia Pearce explained that Elizabeth crossed the Bridge only once in her whole life. *When?* and *Why?* A little mystery for me to try and solve while Tom was working on the fictional conundrum. Perhaps the incident was so famous that Ms Pearce felt she should not describe it in detail. Perhaps (entirely likely) she did so and I have missed it. But I cannot find reference to it anywhere else either. Not in A. C. Black, nor Paul Johnson, Trevelyan, Bindoff, Briggs, not in Nevill Williams, not even in Maria Perry's life of Elizabeth told through contemporary documents can I find it. But it remains accepted fact. Elizabeth crossed the river often, but the Bridge only once. Perhaps it is as well that in this story, also, she decides to give it a miss.

Peter Tonkin, Tunbridge Wells